THE STUDENT SPY:
From Paris to Tehran

By

Brian Tell

979-8-9944793-0-8

Trade Craft Press

Table of Contents

Introduction

For more than twenty-five centuries, the Persian Empire was ruled by a succession of kings known as Shahs. Today, this ancient land is called Iran.

In 1950, Iranians democratically elected Mohammad Mosaddegh, a politician, author, and lawyer, as Prime Minister. He introduced a series of social and political reforms: land redistribution, higher taxes on the wealthy, and strict limits on royal power. But his decisive move to nationalize British and American oil interests, restoring Iran's oil to its people, sealed his fate.

In 1953, alarmed by the threat to Western oil interests and the possibility of increasing Soviet influence, the CIA and Britain's MI6 orchestrated a coup that toppled Mosaddegh and restored Mohammad Reza Pahlavi to the Peacock Throne.

The young Shah ruled with an iron fist. His secret police, the SAVAK, silenced dissent through surveillance, imprisonment, and torture. While the nation's economy faltered and its people suffered and starved, the Shah lived in extravagant luxury, with lunches flown in from Paris, extravagant jewels and couture for his third wife, and multiple palatial residences. Backed by American support, he embarked on an ambitious campaign to modernize Iran and align it with the West, a move that infuriated the country's deeply traditional Shiite majority.

In 1979, what began as a student protest erupted into a full-fledged revolution. The Shah fled into exile, and the cleric Ruhollah Khomeini returned from exile to assume power, establishing an Islamic Republic. The country soon descended into vengeance, death squads, and chaos, a modern echo of the "Reign of Terror" that followed the French Revolution of 1793.

After abdicating in January 1979, the Shah traveled to Egypt and then Morocco before settling briefly in Mexico. Ravaged by advanced lymphoma, he was finally granted asylum for medical treatment in the United States by President Jimmy Carter in October 1979.

The Iranian population was enraged. Days later, on November 4, 1979, a group calling itself the *Muslim Student Followers of the Imam* stormed the U.S. Embassy in Tehran. They seized 66 American hostages, diplomats, civilians, and among them, the CIA officers from the Tehran station, and demanded that the Shah be returned to Iran for trial and hanging.

With no end in sight to this hostage crisis, President Carter authorized a daring rescue mission, *Operation Eagle Claw*, in April of 1980. It ended in catastrophe when a helicopter and a refueling plane collided in the Iranian desert. Eight American servicemen died. The operation was abandoned, its failure humiliating the United States and strengthening the revolution's grip on Iran. The hostages remained for a total of 444 days, being released only after Carter left office.

As with any covert operation, preparation is everything. Assets must be positioned, their movements secured, and contingencies foreseen. This is the story of that advance team, and of a young CIA officer given a perilous task: to slip into hostile territory, assess the possible challenges, and confirm the location and condition of the hostages in a city where every shadow concealed a threat and every step could very well be his last.

But this isn't where the story begins. To understand the decisions he made, we must return to the spring of 1973. To the person that this young man once was. To the choices that shaped a man who would carry a burden across five decades.

ISLAMIC REPUBLIC OF
IRAN
ARMENIA
AZERBAIJAN
TURKEY
TURKMENISTAN
CASPIAN SEA
Ashkabad
Mary
Tejen
Bojnürd
Gorgän
Gonbad-e Qäbüs
Mäku
Sarjamy
Khvoy
Van
Marand
Tabriz
Astärä
Ardabil
Orümiyeh
Maragheh
Mianeh
Rasht
GILAN
Mosul
Mahäbäd
Mändowäb
Zanjän
Röfbär
Sakht Sar
Sari
Ämol
Shähröd
Sabzevär
Mashhad
Arbil
ZANJAN
Qazvin
MAZANDARAN
As Sulaymaniyah
KORDESTAN
TEHRAN
SEMNAN
Käshmar
Turbat-e Heydariyeh
Kirkuk
Sanandaj
HAMADAN
Tehran
Semnän
DESERT TWO
Tayyebät
Herät
Qasr-e Shirin
Hamadän
Säveh
Manzariyeh Airfield
Qom
Gonäbäd
Kermänshäh
KERMANSHAH
Maläyer
MARKAZI
Gonäbäd
KHORASAN
Borüjerd
Aräk
Birjand
AFGHANISTAN
Baghdad
Iläm
LORESTAN
Khorramäbäd
Algudäi
Kashän
ESFAHAN
Karbalä
Al Küt
Al Hillah
Esfahän
DESERT ONE
IRAQ
Dezfül
Shahr-e Kord
Ardakän
Al 'Amärah
Masjed-e Soleymän
Qomsheh
Yazd
Bäfq
KHUZESTAN
YAZD
As Samäwah
An Näsiriyah
Ahväz
Abädeh
Zarand
Zäbol
Bandar-e Mäh Shahr
Zaranj
Al Basrah
Yäsüj
Rafsanjän
Kermän
Zähedän
KUWAIT
Bäländi
Marv Dasht
Shiräz
Boräzjän
Sirjän
KERMAN
Bam
Kuwait
PARS
Bandar-e Büshehr
Firüzäbäd
Jiroft
PAKISTAN
SISTAN VA BALUCHESTAN
National capital
BUSHEHR
Jahrom
Lär
HORMOZGAN
Iränshahr
Provincial capital
SAUDI ARABIA
Bandar-e Abbäs
City, town
Bandar-e Langeh
Minäb
Airport
PERSIAN GULF
Nikshahr
International boundary
Provincial boundary
Main road
Secondary road
Railroad
BAHRAIN
Manama
Ad Dammäm
Ra's al Khaymah
OMAN
Jäsk
Gwädar
QATAR
Doha
Al Hufüf
UNITED ARAB EMIRATES
Abu Dhabi
Dubayy
Bandar Beheshti
Nimitz
GULF OF OMAN
0 100 200 300 km
OMAN
Coral Sea
100 200 mi

Chapter 1

Ann Arbor, Michigan, 1973

David had just completed a morning run. It was early spring; the light snow from the night before had melted, and the trees were beginning to bud. Everything felt quiet and in order, which, had he been superstitious, should have been a sign that things were about to change.

The streets were empty, the town still asleep. David liked the quiet; it gave him space to think as he ran. He lived a few blocks away in a sagging old wood-frame house off Monroe, the sort that tilted slightly with age and held the scent of too many borrowed lives. He shared it with a classmate from Detroit, another aspiring pre-med student, and their girlfriends, all of them tangled in a chaotic arrangement that resembled adulthood but wasn't quite. The run was not too strenuous, perhaps a couple of miles, first down State Street from Monroe, around the Athletic complex, and then back up through the Law School Quad toward University Avenue for his first cup of coffee. The Brown Jug sat on the corner like a relic from another decade. It was the kind of place where bad ideas were born, and better ones were forgotten. It was where the discussion centered on how best to protest the Vietnam War and change the country's direction. The coffee was cheap. The tables scarred with initials and ring stains, and the air smelled faintly of chalk dust, ambition, and last night's cigarettes.

Inside the *Jug*, students hunched over chessboards, eyes feverish. Since Fischer's triumph over Spassky, chess had become an obsession, East versus West in miniature. David watched for a moment, then slid into a corner booth. He rarely spent time at the Jug; he found it too loud, too cluttered, too many opinions floating in the air. He'd gone through a chess phase when he was younger, brief, intense, like most things in adolescence. His father had taught him the game during a long convalescence after his second heart attack.

Chess teaches you how to think ahead and how to analyze before making a move, David. His father had said, pale and still in the family room chair, a wool blanket across his lap. He'd been right, of course. The game was war stripped down to pure logic.

Calculation. Anticipation. Patience.

But David hadn't played seriously in years. There wasn't time. Not with med school looming, the MCATs, the lab work, the constant, gnawing pressure to make something of himself. Life had become a series of tasks to manage, balls to keep in the air. Thinking wasn't the problem. It was having the time to stop and do it properly.

He still had some midterms to study for as he awaited hearing from the medical schools to which he had applied. However, he still had not heard from them, not even a call to come in for an interview! This was somewhat troubling but not entirely unexpected, as most acceptances were late. To be honest, there was a part of him that felt that he was meant for something else, something beyond lecture halls and hospital wards, something that carried more adventure, more edge, than medicine ever would. He often questioned whether he'd have done all the pre-med classes had his father not been a physician.

Since the age of fifteen, it was all he remembered his parents' friends asking.

Will you follow in your father's footsteps? Be a doctor too?

He hadn't given it much thought, not seriously—until Michigan. Until he was forced to. And then there was the arrest. Technically just a misdemeanor, one weekend while visiting his high school buddies in D.C. It was the previous spring. Pulled aside by a cop during an anti-war demonstration. What should have been a lark ended with a day in the D.C. Jail.

It was a cool morning, especially since he started the run so early. David decided that rather than grab the coffee, he would sit down and linger a little longer than usual. He had only his French Literature class at 10, and then nothing until a late meeting with his honors thesis advisor. It was while sitting at that table, in the far corner near the back, that a man approached.

"May I join you?" the man asked. "This place must be popular to be so crowded at this time of day. I'd have thought everyone would be in class. I really hate drinking while standing."

David looked up. "Certainly. Be my guest."

At first glance, the man looked slightly out of place on campus. He had a trace of a Southern drawl and carried himself with a quiet confidence that didn't quite fit. Not old or aloof enough to be a tenured professor, yet too seasoned—too self-assured, to be a graduate student or one of the overworked teaching assistants who drifted through the halls like ghosts. If David had to guess, he'd put him somewhere around forty—maybe a few years younger. But there was something else, something harder to put into words. He scanned the room as if committing each person to memory. In one hand, he carried a thin briefcase; in the other, a copy of *The Washington Post* and the latest edition of *Foreign Affairs*. He appeared both academic and athletic at the same time.

He wore khaki slacks, loafers, and a sweatshirt.

"Do you teach at the university?" David asked.

"No, just in for a meeting and doing a little research."

"What does your research involve?"

He looked around, then back toward David. "Behavioral psychology."

"That's my major, what a coincidence! I just turned in my honors research paper last week." David turned and smiled.

This somewhat out-of-place acquaintance hesitated for a second, then leaned in toward David and asked, "What was the research about?"

"Sensory deprivation. Specifically, how it disorients and ultimately alters one's perception of time."

"Why did you choose that topic for your research?" he asked with a smile.

"To be honest, I was struggling to find a subject that genuinely interested me. And then it hit me—time. I've always been fascinated by it. The more I thought about it, the more I began to wonder if time even exists at all. I mean, it really exists.

We invented it, didn't we? As humans, we needed something to explain the cycle of light and dark, the passing of seasons—something to make sense of the Earth's spin and our orbit around the sun. Our lives are short, so we carved time into hours and years to measure the length of our stay."

The man looked up at the ceiling, then out the window, and said, "Are you sure you're not secretly a philosophy major?"

He let out a soft laugh. "I think your generation would probably call that… *heavy.*"

Pausing, he added with genuine curiosity, "But seriously, it's an interesting idea. What has your thesis advisor said about it?"

"So far, not much. The only feedback has been on my methodology; I really did not go into my theories about time with him. I am meeting with him later this afternoon."

"Are you planning an academic career in Psychology?" he asked inquisitively.

"Well, not actually, I was planning to, up until last summer, but then I changed my mind, and I am applying to medical school. Hence, the last-minute sprint to complete those pre-med classes. It seems to be the popular road these days and would allow me to combine both the scientific discipline and human behavior. And with the war in Vietnam still going on, I wouldn't have to worry about being drafted. Don't get me wrong, I have nothing against fighting for my country. I've given it a lot of thought and just feel that this whole war has gotten out of hand and is inconsistent with American values. In the end, it seems to me to be an unwinnable civil war. If anything, we have backed the wrong side. The Vietnamese people fought against the French, and then we took over. They aren't so much in love with communism; they just want to be free of foreign domination."

"Wow, it sounds like you've given this a lot of thought. I am surprised that you aren't a Political Science major?"

"Well, to tell you the truth, I've always been into history and politics. Back in high school, I read a lot of both. However, once I arrived, my interests began to shift. I ended up getting an earful about everything going on from my freshman roommate, Tuan, from Vietnam, a super bright guy. Speaks four or five languages like it's nothing and unfortunately insists on practicing his damn violin at sunrise every morning."

Great guy, though. He taught me a great deal about Southeast Asia, as well as some aspects of Vietnamese culture. Still, I've got to admit, I was glad when I finally moved out of the dorm and could sleep in occasionally."

"But I have to admit," David continued, "spending that year with Tuan really cemented my interest in world events. It tied in with all the world history I devoured back in high school. The trouble is… I'm having trouble aligning those intellectual interests with a practical career path.

I've always imagined a life helping people, like my father, who's a physician. And I respect that. Deeply. But part of me can't shake the feeling that I'm meant for something broader. Something that affects not just individuals but also systems. Institutions. The world, maybe, in some small way."

He looked up, almost sheepish. "Does that make any sense?"

The man gave a small, approving nod.

"Yes," Donovan said, nodding. "I think it makes very good sense. And I'm glad to see someone in your generation thinking beyond just carving out a comfortable lifestyle."

He leaned back, studying David with a half-smile. "Most don't."

"Oh, and I suppose I should introduce myself. Bill Donovan."

He reached into his jacket, pulled out a slim card case, and slid one across the table.

The business card read:

William Donovan

Vice President -Research

PINACLE PSYCHOMETRICS

1050 DUPONT CIRCLE,

WASHINGTON, D.C.

Bill reached across the small table and, extending his hand, mentioned that he was off to a meeting, wishing David the best of luck and adding,

"If you are ever interested in continuing your work in psychology, please feel free to reach out to me. We may be able to help you perhaps reach both of your goals."

"How is that?" David asked with a slightly confused look.

"We might be able to help you continue to do research in behavior modification and sensory deprivation while maybe even eventually getting a medical degree."

At the time, David had no idea how this Mr. Donovan would alter his life's plan.

Chapter 2

New York, (2 weeks later)

Bill Donovan hated coming up to the city. He had chosen Columbia for its reputation—and at his father's insistence, but never felt he belonged there. His father, a retired 'diplomat', had dragged the family across Asia. After graduation, with his background in Far Eastern studies and proficiency in languages, Donovan was recruited by the CIA. He began his career in New York at the World Trade Center, where he worked in counterespionage, before transitioning to the Far East Desk as an analyst. His dislike for the hustle and bustle of NYC and the long hours spent sitting at his desk reviewing reams and reams of magazines and newspapers was not what he expected. He soon grew antsy and requested a transfer to the Directorate of Operations and case officer training. Following a year of training, he was whisked away to Vietnam to establish a counterintelligence unit in Da Nang.

It was a frustrating 18 months to say the least. He soon realized that the US effort was self-defeating. As innocent Vietnamese were being killed by American soldiers who couldn't tell the difference between the enemy and those they were protecting, and worse, some didn't even care. As the tides turned, more and more Vietnamese became sympathetic to the Viet Cong's propaganda.

He was recalled to Langley and Fort Perry and assigned to a mid-level position in training and recruitment. It was the following April that he was called and told to meet the chief of the Directorate of Operations in New York that Wednesday morning.

"Bill, thanks for coming up," Stewart Blake rose from the desk and greeted Bill at the door to his corner office with a smile and extended hand.

"I'm sure you still know your way around the city?"

With a grim smile, Bill replied, "Like the back of my hand."

"I've been told that you've been doing a great job with recruitment since returning stateside. How has it been going?" Take a seat.

The New York office of the Director of Operations, responsible for all CIA covert and clandestine operations, was surprisingly sparse. As Bill looked around the corner office, he figured that the DO likely came here only rarely. There were a few photographs of him with Nixon, including a slightly faded black-and-white image of him in his Korean-era uniform.

"I flew in from Langley for a meeting at the United Nations and thought we could meet here rather than at headquarters. Thanks for coming up."

Bill raised an eyebrow, puzzled. "United Nations?"

Stewart let out a low chuckle. "Bill, here's a little tidbit you might want to tuck away. Could come in handy as your career moves along."

He leaned back slightly, letting the weight of the moment settle.

"As you know, our charter, the CIA's charter, was established in 1947, after a long and very public fight with J. Edgar Hoover. In the end, Roosevelt pushed it through, but with one immovable caveat: our operations were to remain strictly outside U.S. borders. No domestic activity. Not then, not ever."

He paused, letting it sink in.

"That said," he added with a faint smile, "the United Nations, like every foreign embassy and consulate on American soil, isn't technically *on* American soil. Legally speaking, it's foreign territory, which means, Bill, that certain lines... can be walked and crossed. Very carefully."

Not knowing exactly what direction the meeting was taking, Bill hesitated and then replied that although he certainly missed the excitement in the field, being back in the United States had its benefits.

"Although one does eventually get used to living without modern conveniences, when we return, we realize that there certainly is something to be said for indoor plumbing and a dependable power supply. The adrenaline of being in a war zone was addictive, I'll admit, and it did take a few months to re-acclimate."

"That is exactly why we insist that you meet with our psychologists on a regular basis. I hope you are doing this?"

"Yes, sir, we meet every other week if I can, and I think things are going fine.

"I've been in contact with the Vietnamese professor at Michigan State that you asked me to see. As you're aware, his field of study is the inner workings and politics of the Chinese Communist Party. As such, he is a frequent consultant for the CIA, and he is the one whose son at the University of Michigan keeps an eye out for potential recruits."

"Yes, that is why I've asked you to come in! Please fill me in: what have we got so far?

"His son, Tuan, as you know, left Vietnam with the family seven years ago, when we helped resettle them in East Lansing. Bright kid.

He paused, measuring the next words.

He keeps a watchful eye out for students who might be helpful, either to his father's politics or to our relationship with him. He may have someone in mind. An old roommate, apparently. Could be a prospective recruit."

Bill hesitated briefly.

"When I first heard about him, it must have been over a year ago now—the specifics struck me. Not just the usual undergraduate curiosity. Tuan said the boy had a real interest in psychology, particularly the effects of sensory deprivation. He said he was writing his honors thesis on it. Apparently, he went so far as to pay volunteers, fellow students, mostly, to sit blindfolded for six hours. Foam rubber mittens, noise-cancelling headphones, and white noise fed in non-stop. Boots, too, if you can believe it. The full experience."

He paused, gauging the response.

"My first thought," he continued, voice lower now, "was that he might be of use to the Agency. Not in the field, necessarily. But with the High-Value Detainee Interrogation Group. I know the program has been discussed a bit—publicly disowned, quietly defended —but there are still some who believe it has merit. I'm one of them."

He offered a thin smile, though there was nothing amused about it.

Blake stopped him abruptly and interjected: "You're aware that I am looking for someone for a rather specific Operation in France."

"Yes, and after meeting with him and doing some more digging, I do think that he would fit the part rather well. He paused, folding his hands. This kid seems to check all the boxes that we discussed. He is resourceful, has strong interpersonal skills, and is almost fluent in French. He has even picked up some Vietnamese and has a keen interest in both history and world events while majoring in psychology. Last year, however, he switched course and began applying to medical school. Of course, we won't know until we put him to the test, but as someone who played and succeeded in competitive tennis, it's likely that he can perform under pressure. As I wrote to you, he was picked up during the May Day antiwar demonstration in Washington, but by his own admission, he was not really participating; he was there to photograph the activity. That may work in our favor as you'll see."

"How is he socially? Can he read people? Slip into a closed group without standing out? Charming? at least moderately extroverted? He is straight, I hope not gay?"

"Definitely straight, and I think he could be perfect. Obviously, he'd need to be trained, and we'd not have much time, as I'm told you'd like to have him inserted in Paris in the fall. The normal training at the "farm" is still 18 months, I assume?"

Blake gave a slight grimace: "We could get him into an intensive program and modify some of the training." We could bring him back after the semester to complete the program. Off the record, this might have to be just between you, me, and Paris station, you understand."

Donovan continued, "I contacted his professors and former teachers. I told them I was with the medical school admissions committee from one of the schools to which he was applying. Their opinions were all positive from our perspective, so I flew out to Ann Arbor two weeks ago. I arranged to casually bump into him at one of the town's coffee shops after observing him for a few days. I used his interest in psychology to connect, and I think there is potential."

"What have you been told so far regarding our plan?" Stewart Blake was not entirely sure how much Bill knew about the proposed operation's timing and objectives.

"I was told you were looking for a 'student'—someone to insert quietly into a dormitory setting in Paris. Someone who could pass as a full-time enrollee and remain entirely above suspicion."

He leaned back slightly, tone careful now, almost clinical.

"I believe we can manage his entry into one of the medical faculties. His Michigan degree, coupled with a solid science background and fluency in the language, should get him through the front door without much fuss. Once there, of course, he'll be on his own. As you're likely aware, the French system weeds them out after the first year of medical school. Brutal process. Competitive. And for a non-native speaker, it is nearly impossible. But that's part of the cover, isn't it? If he makes it, he's earned it. If not—well, then he was just another foreign student who didn't."

A pause. Just long enough.

"Needless to say, we cannot involve the French government. Not even in whispers. Placing a NOC inside one of their universities would be… difficult to explain."

Blake continued, "That is exactly right. So far, our best option and working plan is to target one of President Nguyen Van Thieu's daughters. Someone close to the family may be able to get a hint of his long-term thinking. As you know, Thieu is a crafty son of a bitch. Kissinger has been working with him for months to find a path toward ending the war. Nixon is tired of it, and our troops are being slowly withdrawn. The war isn't helping him politically, and he wants out. We need a way to get him to the bargaining table with the North and get this done.

The problem is that he is evasive. We aren't sure whether he is just jerking us off or if he agrees that the South's goals are unattainable, and he just wants to prolong the war. Amazingly, we have no one on the inside of his circle, and even if we did, I am not sure he shares his goals with them. However, he has two daughters and a son, all of whom are now in Paris as students. But he, like all the other bigwigs in Vietnam and Laos, had shuffled his wives and children out of the country years ago as soon as things got hot. I am not sure they are there to stay, but for now the French have been issuing annual student visas and renewing them, regardless of whether students are actively studying. Apparently, the son is supposedly studying to enter law school but is really majoring in the Paris nightlife. Steward walked over to the side table and poured a cup of coffee from the silver pot. "Could I offer you anything?"

"No, sir, I'm fine."

"I think the best bet is the two girls; they are a fixture at the Cité campus, rarely venturing into the center of Paris except for classes. They eat together with friends at the campus restaurant, and when not in class, play tennis almost daily. You mentioned that your potential recruit played on his high school team and did well in the state tournament? If so, that would be an easy entry to make a connection with them."

"Sounds like it could work! During his freshman year at Michigan, he went out for the tennis team but apparently gave it up rather abruptly. I asked around, and apparently, there may have been an incident involving the athletic department doctor, who is required to conduct physical exams on all Michigan athletes. I heard some rumors that he often got too invasive with those exams, if you get my drift." Blake shook his head in disgust.

"If you were able to learn this, how in the world is it that the University hasn't made an investigation?" "Well, it's just rumors," Donovan replied, shrugging. "And you know how these things go, there's a blurry line between what's medically appropriate and what's considered sexual misconduct. So far, no one's been willing to come forward. These kids are young, and most are naïve. Some people don't even realize when the linc has been crossed. And let's be honest, if your scholarship depends on staying on the team, you learn fast that silence is the real team sport."

He glanced down at the folder in front of him.

"Anyway, our boy just walked away from the sport. Quietly. No explanation."

"It sounds like your guy might just work out. So, what's your plan?"

Donovan rose and moved to the window, gazing past the Hudson River toward the Jersey shore. "Well… I may have stepped a little out of bounds, sir."

"How so, Bill?" Stewart pressed.

Donovan's brow furrowed as he turned back. "With a slight frown, he began to explain—"

"I took the liberty to contact the dean of the University and made sure that the professor who summarized David's recommendations for his medical school applications was aware of his past arrest during the May Day anti-war demonstration!"

"I knew full well that he, being a former Marine, would likely not look too positively on such a blemish. With medical school acceptance pending and his senior year ending, I thought it would be a good time to reconnect and update him on our offer to help his country, which would also allow him to obtain his medical degree.

"Wait a minute," Stewart stood up abruptly. "Are you telling me that you basically sabotaged this kid's chances of getting into medical school?"

"Well, yes,"

What in God's name were you thinking? What happens if he isn't interested in working with the Agency and going to medical school in Paris?"

Bill took a deep breath and smiled. "I've got that covered as well! I have a backup plan in place. The head of admissions at Georgetown Medical School is a college friend of mine and a former consultant with the agency. I took the liberty of contacting him and, without going into too much detail, explained that we had an interest in one of the applicants at his school. I assured him that the misdemeanor arrest in DC was unlawful and that he would be doing the Agency a service if he could look positively on this applicant. I told him that the Agency had conducted a thorough background check that he could never have done, and that, in our opinion, this kid would make an excellent physician.

"I hope it doesn't come to this, but he said he'd look into the application and get back to me."

"Well?"

"He called yesterday and said he'd cover our backs. If our boy isn't interested in working with us, he'd receive a call stating that, unexpectedly, a spot has opened up. If he is still interested, a place would be available for the first year at Georgetown."

"Great, so what are your next steps?"

"Well, I am planning on contacting David, that's his name, again by the end of the month. This should give him sufficient time to realize that he may have to rethink his future."

"That certainly sounds like you are teeing him up; now all he has to do is agree that it is something he would be interested in pursuing. He must be excited not only about attending school in Paris, but, more importantly, about taking a small step toward perhaps continuing his career with us. Heaven knows we always need people with language skills and a medical degree, even if he doesn't continue with a full-time career with the Agency."

"We'll get him a room at the Fondation des États-Unis on the Cité Universitaire campus. A perfect fit for the cover—and near the two girls."

As his activity in Paris develops, if he needs additional funds, I'll have them moved through the Paris station."

Stewart Blake stood up and looked skyward out of the south-facing window towards the Statue of Liberty. "O.K., it looks as if this might very well play out." "Let's approach the kid gingerly and explain this opportunity to him in a way that makes it a win-win. He doesn't need to know what our real objectives are at first. We don't need to fill him in until he begins classes in the fall. If he goes for it, we will need to act fast. Let me know as soon as you receive the OK, and I will complete his final background clearance and secure a place for him in the June class at the Farm. The school year in France typically starts in September or October. Therefore, we will have to act quickly and improvise. By my estimation, I figure that he will still need 10 weeks stateside with operational training, most importantly Psy-Ops training."

"We'll only know if the boy has any aptitude once we let him loose," the senior man said. Bill nodded, arms crossed loosely. "We aren't asking him to run agents, just to gather information, at least for now. I get that."

"No," the senior man agreed. "Not yet. But once he's there, we'll push him through the basics—surveillance, counter-surveillance. We'll assign him one of our French speakers, someone discreet. He needs to learn the city, inside and out. Métro lines, alley cut-throughs, taxi habits, blind corners. The works."

He paused, letting the weight of the next thought settle.

"Normally, we'd spend eighteen months—eighteen, just preparing someone for this kind of thing. But this… this is a window. A perfect fit."

"My only concern is Paris Station. Duke Peterson won't like it, none of them will. Dropping an untested resource into their patch without the usual dance? It'll ruffle feathers."

"But operationally, he'll function more like an asset than a case officer, at least at first. He will be there mostly as a full-time student. That should make it easier. He's our man, not theirs. "The boy may not know the rules and politics of the game," he said, almost to himself, "but that's half the point, isn't it? Fresh eyes. No habits. No reflexes honed by bad training or someone else's mistakes. He hasn't learned what's impossible yet—and sometimes that's the only kind of operative who gets results."

He glanced at Bill, eyes narrowed.

"Bill, I'm sending you to Paris. You'll be running the operation from there."

He rose slowly, not out of surprise, but as if testing his own joints. The desk had taken more from him than he cared to admit, instinct, an edge that once came without thinking. Yet beneath the stiffness, there was something else, the excitement of returning to the field, where the world would feel immediate again, stripped of pretense.

"Recruitment's been… comfortable, civilizing," he said at last. "Office hours, polite handshakes, agents with dental plans. I almost started sleeping properly."

He hesitated a moment, then added, "But I must ask—what exactly do you think we're going to get from these girls? What kind of intel could possibly affect the negotiations?"

"Bill, you know how this works. Intelligence is rarely about the secrets or the headlines—it's about context. One meaningless scrap stacked on top of another until the pile starts to look like the truth. A comment about going home early. A shift in tone, a subtle change in who they mention at dinner. All of it matters if you're listening closely enough."

He paused, folding his hands.

"We may hear they're being told to return home ahead of schedule. Or that they're staying put indefinitely. Their father's tone has changed. That their mothers become suddenly withdrawn. None of it matters—until it does."

Bill nodded. He'd played this game long enough to know it was never about the obvious.

"Peterson's been informed," the senior officer added. "He wasn't thrilled—grudging approval, as expected. You'll be working with diplomatic cover at the embassy. Commercial attaché. Paperwork is already in motion. I told them to expect you by September."

"You'll be walking into a mess," he added finally. "But then, you're used to that."

Chapter 3

Ann Arbor

It was a day in early April, a month before graduation, when the phone rang in the house David and his friends were renting. His girlfriend answered and yelled out to David, who was on the porch,

"David, there is a guy on the phone who wants to speak with you."

"Who is it?" he yelled back.

"Won't give his name, says he is a friend of the family and is in town for the day, come on, I am on my way out, come take this."

David, a little annoyed and in no mood to entertain what was likely an old friend of his father's, put down his book and walked back into the living room to grab the phone.

"David, sorry to intrude, this is William Donovan. I hope you remember me. We met a few weeks back over coffee at the Brown Jug. I am back in town and would like to meet with you, as I am in sort of a jam and think that we might be able to help each other out."

The name tickled something vague in the back of his memory. Donovan. Polished, polite. The kind of man who didn't quite belong in a college town—too old to be a teaching assistant, too curious to be a professor. He remembered the coffee: the casual chat that had felt anything but casual. The way Donovan had listened, really listened, like a man filing away details for later use.

Now, a month from graduation, David's life was loosening at the seams. The lease on their house was coming to an end. His girlfriend was heading to New York for grad school. And the future, once rigidly mapped out in pre-med certainty, felt suddenly soft around the edges.

He leaned back in his chair, absently flipping a record—American Beauty. Jerry Garcia's voice crackled to life.

He looked at the phone in his hand for a moment, then let out a breath and thought: *Why not?* What did he have to lose—an afternoon drinking beer, spinning a Grateful Dead album, maybe listening to a story that would go nowhere? He agreed to meet at the Northwest corner of the Law Quad.

It was a beautiful spring day, and David figured he owed the dog a walk anyway. He grabbed the leash, calling out for his girlfriend's adorable mutt, Bozo. As soon as the dog heard the leash jangle, he jumped up, tail wagging, and off they went.

The Law Quadrangle in Ann Arbor was one of David's favorite spots on campus. The quad was a stunning example of Collegiate Gothic architecture, its tall stone spires and arched windows casting long shadows as the sun dipped lower. It reminded David of his visit the previous summer, when he had traveled to England to visit a high school friend, Andrew, who was spending his junior year studying economics at Cambridge.

Just as David stepped into the quadrangle, he heard his name called. He turned, scanning the few law students hurrying to class. Near the tall oak trees, Bill Donovan stood, hand extended in greeting.

"Hey, David," William said, his grin wide and easy, as if they had just picked up where they'd left off months ago. "I am so glad you were able to come."

David smiled back, pushing away the feeling that things hadn't quite felt the same since their last meeting. "Yeah, good to see you," he replied, with a slight quizzical look, shaking Bill Donovan's hand.

Bill looked him over, then raised an eyebrow. "You look like you've been living in the library. "Let's sit over there and chat."

As they sat on the bench near the north side of the quadrangle, David couldn't avoid noticing how Donovan scanned the area instinctively and was careful to begin the discussion when the few law students had moved on, scurrying, perhaps to a late class.

Donovan broke the brief silence,

"So how did your thesis turn out? And what are your plans for medical school next year?"

David, looking somewhat uncomfortable, replied, "Some good news and, unfortunately, some not so good."

"My thesis turned out great, the results were deemed impressive, as was my technique. My advisors loved it, and the jury of three other tenured faculty members was also impressed enough to add to my diploma, 'Bachelor of Science with *Honors in Psychology*.' However, I haven't been able to secure a spot in medical school. It was somewhat strange that I didn't even get called in for an interview anywhere. My college advisors are recommending that I pursue a master's in public health rather than try again next year. They are offering me a spot in the master's program in the School of Public Health, which includes a teaching assistant position and a stipend to cover tuition and other expenses. Even though the University's program is one of the strongest in the country, as you can imagine, I am disappointed."

Bill Donovan let a few seconds pass and then, with a smile, looking directly at David, said,

"Well, maybe I might be able to help. It wouldn't exactly fit into your plans, but if you are looking for an adventure, what I am offering certainly would be one. Let me explain."

"First, I would like to apologize as I may have misrepresented myself the last time we met."

David gave a quizzical look and became intensely interested in what his new acquaintance had to say.

"I am actually with the intelligence community," Donovan said, his voice dropping to a near whisper, his gaze scanning the campus around them to ensure they weren't overheard. "I've been searching for the right person for a very important operation, one that, if successful, could very well help to finally end this war in Asia. As you can imagine, this would save thousands of lives, both American and Vietnamese. My superiors and I feel you may be helpful in that regard."

David, still processing the unexpected shift in conversation, blinked in confusion. "So, you're a spy?"

Donovan's lips twitched upward, but the smile didn't quite reach his eyes. "How could I possibly be of help to you and your 'spy operation'? And how, in the world, would this help me with my hope of entering medical school?"

Donovan seemed to consider this, waiting for a couple walking nearby to pass before he leaned in, his voice a little more urgent now. "First of all, intelligence isn't all about spying. What I do—what we do —is more about analyzing data and information, most of which is public knowledge. But when pieced together, it's far more powerful than you might think."

David's brow furrowed. His mind raced, trying to piece together what Donovan was getting at, but before he could interrupt, Donovan pressed on, his tone smooth, yet insistent.

"What would you say to doing medical school in France? At the University of Paris, specifically. It's rated among the top schools in the world—certainly better than most of the schools you applied to. With your pre-med background and, from what I've been told, at least a moderate comfort in the language, you should have no problem succeeding."

David's pulse quickened as Donovan's words hung in the air, almost too surreal to process. *Medical school in France?* David had fallen in love with Paris the moment he stepped off the train the previous summer. It wasn't just the city—it was everything. The scent of the Métro, the sultry, sexy voice of the FIP radio station disc jockeys, always young women, gliding between Vivaldi and The Doors as if that were the most natural transition in the world. It was eclectic, effortless, endlessly seductive.

Paris wasn't just beautiful. It was *his*—or at least it had felt that way for a brief, enchanted stretch of days, all on five dollars a day. Well, closer to ten, if he was being honest, despite what the guidebook had promised.

It had been enough. Enough for a clean bed, great coffee and a croissant, a student ticket to the Louvre, a carafe of house wine at a place where no one rushed him. Enough to fall in love with a city that didn't care who you were, as long as you looked like you belonged.

And now, impossibly, it was being dangled in front of him again—but under circumstances he hadn't yet begun to understand.

It certainly was a tempting offer—prestigious, unique—but what did it have to do with the war, or espionage, or Donovan's so-called "operation"? And why now?

Donovan leaned back slightly, as if measuring David's reaction. "I'm offering you an opportunity to study at a world-renowned institution," he said, his tone softening just a fraction. "But there's more. Much more. What I need from you is not just your academic ability—it's your mind and your interpersonal skill set. Your ability to think critically, to see things others might miss, and most importantly, your ability to make friends easily and to gain their confidence."

"Think of it this way, David. You'll be stepping into circles and situations where the right connections—friendships—can make all the difference. It's not just about intelligence or training; it's about influence. And from what I have learned about you; charm and influence are something you've always had a natural talent for."

We would have a solid 4 months to perfect your French, learn some basic tradecraft, and get you acclimated."

David paused for a few seconds before asking.

"How do you know that I have been taking advanced French classes, and how do you know which med schools I applied to?"

"To be absolutely frank with you, David, we have had an eye on you for some time now, and that is exactly why my colleagues and I feel that you would be an excellent fit for what we would ask of you."

"Well then, Mr. Donovan, what exactly would you be asking of me?

"Come to Paris," he said, his voice low, even. "Study medicine. Work for us while you're there."

He didn't say the agency's name right away. He never did. But it hovered between them like secondhand smoke.

"You'd be a student first, of course. That's your cover, and it's genuine—you'll be enrolled, you'll attend classes, and you'll walk away with a proper degree. No one's asking you to leap from rooftops or plant bugs in briefcases. Just observe. Keep your ears open. The kind of details that never make it into the newspapers—casual things you know? Like patterns, whispers, tone."

A pause. The kind that lingered just long enough to be intentional.

"Initially, you just need to be a student and get into a routine. It won't be easy, I'll admit; the first year is, I'm told, brutal. Get through the first year, and it will be a breeze. We will only ask you to befriend some people, get close to them, and gather any information you can about them. There is no need to discuss this now. We'll get into specifics down the road."

"Later, when you've found your footing and you are completely comfortable there, we may ask you to do more, and if you're still interested in psychological research, we may even ask you to establish contact with certain researchers—French psychologists involved in sensory deprivation work. Nothing covert. Just proximity. A conversation here, a shared interest there. You'll know when to lean in."

He reached for his cigarettes, "You don't mind, I hope."

"No, not at all."

Bill continued:

"We'll take care of the paperwork. The French bureaucracy is ridiculous and impenetrable, especially if you don't know the right doors to push. Fortunately, we do. Some of my colleagues feel that we should consider having you travel with a Canadian passport and identity. I personally think this is a mistake and not only would it be unnecessary, but it might also jeopardize your cover. Your personal history, as it stands, will certainly withstand scrutiny. Your expenses will be covered. You'll receive a salary on top of that—nothing flashy, just enough to matter deposited into an account in the States. Later, when you're out, you'll have access. It will appear to come from your parents, and from loans, as it should."

"Why in heaven's name do you think that I am the person that you need? What is so special about my background that would be of any interest to the CIA?

"Well, I can't get into the details just yet, but what we need is a student who can get close to our target—someone who can be our eyes and ears when it comes to their family's plans. That's all I can say for now. In six months, your French will be nearly fluent, and you'll be on your way to being a convincing medical student—hell, you *will* be one. We believe your personality makes what we're asking of you entirely doable." What do you say about doing something real that would save thousands of lives?

"Mr. Donovan… when would you need an answer?" His tone stayed measured, though a spark crept in despite himself. "The CIA. Living and studying in Paris. It's more than I ever imagined. How long do I have to think it over?"

O.K., David, here is my number. I'd like an answer by next week. I am heading back to D.C. this afternoon. If you are interested, let the person who answers know who you are and just tell them, "You are interested in what we discussed. I'll contact you to let you know the next steps. If you aren't interested, please call and let her know; that is just as important. And please, if you aren't interested, let's keep this conversation between us, O.K. Either way, I wish you the best."

Chapter 4

Paris

David's first summer in Paris was a complete whirlwind—hectic, disorienting, but exhilarating. It was as if he were reborn. True, he did have to leave a relationship with a very wonderful girl, but he had known for a long time that this was inevitable. With a mix of nerves and blind faith, he'd taken the gamble, accepting Mr. William Donovan's offer to help him enroll at the University of Paris medical school. The terms had been vague, the tone reassuring. No threats, no pressure—just a door, slightly ajar, and an invitation to walk through it. What he didn't know, what no one ever told him, was that a spot at Georgetown had already been secured, quietly, just in case he'd said no.

David knew one thing with absolute certainty: *he had to survive that first year.* He learned quickly that it would not be easy. The *concours,* as it was called, was a merciless series of exams that eliminated more than three-quarters of the first-year students in the class. His classmates looked upon him with mild curiosity, regarding him as a figure just slightly out of place. When he first told his parents about his plan to study in France, they were surprised but encouraging. They were happy that he had made a serious decision about his future. They didn't know, couldn't know—the real reason driving this sudden change.

His attachment to Paris started the year before, when David traveled across Europe between his junior and senior years. Paris struck him immediately, almost viscerally. Even compared to New York, that famously tangled melting pot, the French struck him as more genuinely engaged—more respectful, even enchanted, by how others lived: their customs, their cuisines, their histories. The rhythm of urban life in Paris, its walkability, was seductive.

And then, of course, David, being a healthy, straight 21-year-old male, there were the women.

They were, well, French. It wasn't just their charm—though that was undeniable—it was the effortless elegance, the way they made a scarf look like a whispered secret, or how they never stepped out without a glance in the mirror, as if composing themselves for the world like a painter before a canvas. David sometimes wondered whether his fascination was fueled, at least in part, by the slight language barrier that he still had when he first traveled in Europe.

Was it simply that, unlike with American girls, he couldn't hear the sharp edges of sarcasm or insecurity, couldn't pick up on those verbal tics that might have dulled his interest too soon? In French, their mystery lingered. Silence was seductive. And misunderstanding, he realized, could be its own kind of allure. In Ann Arbor, with the women's lib movement in full swing, the girls never put on makeup, favored baggy jeans and flannel shirts, and clomped across campus in work boots or sandals. In Paris, at least, the women still made an effort—elegance mattered, and femininity hadn't yet been labeled a form of oppression.

The Cité U., as it was called, was like an oasis on the edge of Paris's 14th arrondissement. It comprised 40 individual maisons—each with its own distinct style and cultural identity, nestled within a sprawling 200-acre park. The grounds featured themed gardens, scattered sculptures, and, at the heart of it all, four red-clay tennis courts.

The plan was for him to live in the "Cité," specifically to befriend the President of Vietnam's two daughters, Nguyen Thi Mai (Apricot Blossom) and Nguyen Thi Lan (Orchid). They were 18 months apart; the older one, Mai, was the more serious of the two and was enrolled in the Panthéon-Sorbonne, studying Economics. Her younger sister, Lan, was still learning enough French to enroll in the Ecole de Médecine eventually.

David found his French classmates immature at times—sure, but he couldn't help noticing they were also far better educated than most nineteen-year-olds back in the States. Each of them had a firm grounding in history, geography, and the arts, along with demanding coursework in math and science—especially those bound for careers in medicine or technology. Though David considered his education at Michigan excellent, he was impressed—and at times a little intimidated by how many of his classmates had already mastered two years of calculus and a solid command of physics.

By early September, his French was almost fluent, with a minimal accent that, if anything, suggested perhaps an Italian maternal tongue. He was enrolled in an advanced language program at the Sorbonne as soon as he arrived in Paris in September alongside various business leaders and foreign diplomats. From 9 to noon, and then again from 2 to 6 PM each day, he engages in intensive work, training his ears and perfecting any pronunciation imperfections.

In addition, on Mondays and Wednesdays after class, he would meet a "family friend" at a local café; she was, in fact, a language expert from the embassy and had ties to the CIA. Each day at noon, as his fellow students broke for lunch, David would break away from the crowd and make his way toward the Jardin des Plantes. It was part of the arrangement—street craft, they called it—though to David it still felt like a game. He would drift through the park, blending with the idlers and tourists, emerge at the far gate, and cross toward the busy Jussieu métro stop.

At a café near the entrance, he would take a table by the window, order a café and a sandwich, and wait. His 'tutor' for the day, there were three or four of them, always appearing a few minutes later, all smiles and easy gestures, slipping into the seat across from him as if they were nothing more than acquaintances sharing a quiet lunch.

Then came the questions, delivered lightly but with an unmistakable edge:

"Who was following you?"

"How many did you see"?

"Describe them."

"Where did you lose them?

The conversations were always conducted in French. Jean Pierre, at least that was the name I was to call him, was the most demanding.

Constantly using the term "déformation professionnelle," which by his description implied a transformation of one's outlook on the world, always, always observing the environment, scouting the room looking for that which was just a little unnatural or out of place. Remembering faces and, more importantly, a person's gait. He stressed that how a person walked is as descriptive as their face.

And David, still flushed with the excitement of the chase, would search his memory for the faces, the footsteps, the glances that had seemed out of place —he would answer carefully, methodically, sorting the fragments of his walk into something that resembled a report. Faces, clothes, posture, gait—anything that could be classified and filed away. It took him 2 weeks to identify his first tail, but by early September, he was consistently making a perfect score, often identifying four or five seasoned street artists brought in from out of town. This would continue, week by week, at various locations throughout Paris. His tutors offered no praise—such things were discouraged—but in quiet reports to their superiors, they conceded the point: David was, if not born to it, then perilously close to being a natural.

There were also the hours spent, ostensibly, with a family friend. A middle-aged woman, elegant in that understated Parisian way, who would take David on long walks through the city. To the outside observer, it was nothing more than a genteel cultural tour—a stroll through the Tuilleries, a coffee near the Palais-Royal, a walk along the

Seine at dusk. But beneath the small talk and museum chatter was a curriculum.

The conversations were, in truth, a crash course in recruitment. Because espionage, at its core, isn't about guns or gadgets—it's about people. Information, yes—but always from someone. And to get that someone to talk, to betray, you had to recruit. And then run them.

"Running an asset," she explained, "is delicate work. Intimate. Sometimes romantic. Always personal. It's a relationship." She would pause to let that word land. "They'll give you what you need, but only if they believe you will protect them in return. You need to show real empathy. Their safety becomes your responsibility. That's the deal."

She reinforced what he had learned at the Farm, the acronym— MICE. Four letters that summarized the dark grammar of betrayal.

Money. Ideology. Compromise. Ego.

"Every source you meet," she said, tapping a manicured finger against the café table, "will be driven by one, sometimes two. It's your job to find the crack. Widen it. Gently. You don't push. You don't pull. You present a path and let them walk through it."

She said it all so calmly, as if she were describing the ingredients for a sauce. And maybe that was the point. Make it seem normal. Make it seem easy. But David knew—what she was teaching him was anything but.

After class, David would return to the Cité Universitaire, where he would spend some time with a few other Americans studying art from N.Y.U. for the year. It was only normal that he'd make friends with other expats studying in Paris. They would often either eat together at the student restaurant or splurge and go into Paris to hit the bars and dinner. Classes at the Medical School didn't start until mid-October, Paris was beautiful, the weather sublime, and David realized that he had made the right decision.

By late September, as he stepped off the metro, the crush of bodies nearly knocked him off his feet. Then, through the shifting sea of commuters, he saw him—*Bill Donovan*. His pulse skipped. Yes, it was him. Not in the sharp blazer he remembered, but dressed in worn workman's clothes, a little more rugged, a little disheveled. But unmistakably Bill. It felt like years since that afternoon in Ann Arbor— a different life, really—though in truth, barely five months had passed. They both descended at the next stop, the sound of their footsteps echoing as they made their way toward the street. David followed Bill, keeping his distance, until they reached the corner café. Inside, the place was almost empty. They found a quiet table at the back and sat, the weight of unspoken words hanging between them.

"How is it going, David? I am told that you performed very well during those rushed couple of months at the "Farm" and that you are adapting very nicely here. Your language and streetcraft are also good. At first, David didn't know what to say. After a few seconds, he simply smiled and replied, "This was the best decision that I have ever made."

Bill leaned in, his voice low but steady.

"Well, David, let's not get ahead of ourselves. You've still got a long road ahead—double duty, really. School's starting soon, and I don't have to tell you how important it is that you make it through that first year. If you don't, this whole relationship ends right here."

He paused, letting that sink in, then continued.

"Now, I know I mentioned it before, but it's time to get serious. We need you to befriend a couple of girls. They're living at the Cité— you'll find them on the tennis courts most afternoons or grabbing dinner at the student restaurant. They're staying in the Laotian House, though they're Vietnamese. Nguyen Thi Lan and Nguyen Thi Mai. They go by Lan and Mai—I'm sure you're familiar with Vietnamese naming traditions. You had a Vietnamese roommate, didn't you?"

David gave a short laugh. "Boy, you really *did* do a background check on me."

Bill smiled thinly, then pressed on. From a folder, he pulled out some 8 x 10 photos, including headshots from their visas and others taken from a distance, of them at the tennis courts.

"We think Mai's the better bet," he said, tapping one photo with a knuckle. "Sharper. More open. Friendly enough, you won't have to push too hard. It needs to feel accidental—a meeting that *happens* to happen. Forced, and it's over before it starts."

"Get close. Play some tennis. Be charming. Make it real."

Bill's gaze flicked to the clock on the wall, then back.

"You've got two weeks," he said. "Same place, same time. Next time, bring me something worth listening to."

Chapter 5

Paris

David acted quickly; the following week, he was on the courts with his NYU friend Jeffrey, a theater student. He confessed that he was captivated by one of the "Asian" girls who played tennis and wanted Jeffrey's help in meeting her. "Here's my plan."

"We'll arrange to play on the court next to the two sisters, and you will start complaining of a bad knee and not wanting to run too much. You'll ask the two sisters if they would agree to play doubles with us.

The following day, they headed out to the tennis court before dinner, but there was no luck. They tried again the following day, and voila, there they were.

David had already done his reconnaissance during that week. Only the two sisters were ever seen on the tennis courts, so he figured they must be the ones. From Bill's description, it was obvious which was Mai. In the mornings, he would notice her leaving the dorm and, from a distance, follow as she walked into Paris toward the Sorbonne. She stood about 5'5", slim and small-framed, with sharp, delicate features, high cheekbones, and a small mouth. Her hair, long and straight—fine as silk and jet-black—was most often worn in a low bun or loose ponytail. Although Vietnamese and in Paris for just over a year, she made a clear effort to fit in. Tight-fitting jeans, an oversized sweater, and always a fashionable scarf completed her look.

David scoped out the courts from a distance, noting the rhythm of the games, the casual laughter, the slow churn of players coming and going. The key was patience—not forcing it.

They waited for the court next to the girls to finish and then jumped in. The approach was simple: no awkward introductions. A glance, a nod, maybe a friendly, "Est-ce que vous aimeriez jouer un double?" *Would you like to play doubles?* If the girls were practicing alone, they could offer to rally for a few minutes—easy, no pressure. There might be a shared joke about a missed shot or a quick compliment on a strong backhand.

From there, the rest would unfold naturally: a suggestion to hit again sometime, maybe after dinner. The plan was to keep it light, letting the friendship grow over a few games and a few shared smiles. Nothing rushed. Nothing obvious. Just two students crossing paths at the courts, and deciding, without a second thought, to stick around a little longer. It went exactly as planned. Bill was right, Mai was certainly the friendlier of the two, and although slightly hesitant at first, turned out to be excited and flattered to have met a couple of Americans.

They agreed to play again the following day, late in the afternoon, and then, naturally, all agreed to eat at the University restaurant.

It all felt effortlessly natural—the conversations, the way time seemed to stretch and bend as they spoke. Being a student was like that, he thought. Here, the world felt smaller. Cultural differences blurred in this space, where the only things that mattered were shared experiences, late-night study sessions, and the mutual understanding that both were, in their own ways, far from home.

The fact that he was American and she was Vietnamese came up rarely; it didn't seem relevant. It wasn't that it was forgotten, but rather that it didn't seem to matter that much. The boundaries that might once have seemed so distinct were erased by something far simpler: the connection that formed between two people who understood what it meant to navigate a world about to open up to them.

Bill had been right again. A chance encounter between two students in a foreign land had created an unspoken bond. Their connection was rooted more in what they shared than what set them apart. It didn't feel forced or require effort. It just happened. As they sat together in the student restaurant, the noise and laughter swirling around them, David realized the meeting had drawn him into her orbit. He was now curious, surprised by how comfortable he felt beside her. It wasn't infatuation, not yet, but he noticed a warmth whenever she laughed or looked his way—a mix of intrigue and hope that was new to him. Something genuine sparked his interest. He wanted to know who she really was, what made her tick, and what lay beneath that formal exterior.

And yet, as they departed the restaurant, as he walked her toward the Laotian House, the creeping thought returned: *She wasn't someone he could afford to get close to.*

She was an "asset." That's what they had drilled into him back at Camp Peary, at the "Farm."

His mind flashed back to the rigid training sessions, where everything had been laid out in cold, clear terms. One of the "10 COMMANDMENTS" that had been hammered into him during those strenuous weeks: **Never forget that your relationships are tools, not friendships.**

David felt a slight twinge of discomfort, but he brushed it aside. He was good at compartmentalizing, at separating what he wanted from what was required, though sometimes a faint sense of guilt nagged at the edges of his thoughts. In effect, this is what he had been doing throughout his college days. In the end, she would have to be just a source, an asset, someone to help him get the information that he needed. Nothing more.

But in the back of his mind, a whisper of doubt lingered, just faint enough to make him question the distance between the man he thought he was and the man he was training to become.

The seduction took two weeks. After their second tennis date, David suggested a walk to one of the small restaurants near the Cité. David assured her that the menu was very reasonably priced. Mai, smiling easily, agreed.

They left the student complex and walked down Boulevard Jourdan toward Parc Montsouris. The neighborhood had barely changed in decades. Where there had once been unremarkable cafés with chipped enamel tables and stale croissants, new restaurants, complete with linen napkins and English menus, were now taking over. Past a tabac and a pinball brasserie, a narrow, unmarked doorway appeared—easy to miss unless you knew it already. Inside was a serious little restaurant: quiet, discreet, no need to advertise. It thrived by serving excellent food and loyal locals. The maître d' greeted David like an old friend and led them to a quiet corner with a good view. No frills here—just thick glassware, crisp linen, and the soft hum of real conversation.

Over menus and wine glasses, the talk began—the usual openers:

"What are you studying?"

"How do you like Paris?"

"Can you imagine living in a real Paris apartment—no more dorm rooms?"

The words barely stopped. They slipped into an easy rhythm, laughing, finishing each other's thoughts, as if the whole night had been waiting for them.

As they walked slowly back to the Cité, the conversation slowed, but the connection persisted. Arriving at the entry to the Laotian house, David awkwardly leaned in and gave her a brief kiss on the left cheek, then the right. There was a brief silence as both their eyes were fixed on the other.

"Bon nuit, et j'ai beaucoup aimé notre soirée ensemble. Est-ce que tu veux rejouer encore ce week-end?" *"Good night, I really enjoyed our evening together. Would you want to play again this weekend?"*

"Of course, monsieur, she said jokingly, "J'aimerais beaucoup."

By the following week, they were slipping in and out of each other's rooms, making only a token effort to avoid the knowing smirks of their dorm neighbors. Discretion was the goal, but Mai was happy and carefree.

David was less at ease.

Mai had spoken of past lovers, her voice light, almost careless. But David sensed something beneath it—a kind of distance, an absence that clung to the edges of her words. He didn't pretend it was about being her first, not in the usual sense. But sometimes, when her eyes lingered just a second too long, unsure and strangely tender, he let himself believe he might be the first in a way that really mattered.

This was his first real assignment, the opening act of a life he'd agreed to without illusions. From the beginning, Bill and the others had been clear: a place at a top university, a future in medicine—none of it came free.

Now, he understood the price.

This was the work: earn trust, deceive when needed, mislead, and—if it came to it—betray. Yet he couldn't deny that he was developing feelings for her. And he knew, without being told, that they would have to be set aside.

There was no alternative.

This was the mission. This was what he had agreed to become.

Their relationship slipped into a quiet rhythm as the school year began. David, caught up in the novelty, immersed himself completely. The lectures posed no real challenge. By now, his command of the language bordered on native fluency. A trace of accent lingered, subtle and difficult to place, but rarely enough to draw notice. His years in Michigan gave him a distinct advantage. The first year of medical school in France, he'd found, was a preparatory phase covering material he already knew. Still, he took no chances; this opportunity was too good to squander. In Ann Arbor, David rarely studied before class and reserved study time for the evenings. In Paris, he set his alarm for 6:00 a.m. and put in two hours before starting the day. This was not just school—it was work and his new life!

What struck him most was the classroom itself—more theatre than lecture hall. Many students were repeaters, "redoublés," retaking the year after failing the previous year; others drifted through without conviction. Amid the noise, some stood out: bright, disciplined, quietly determined. David made a point of finding them, knowing he needed allies to survive the gauntlet. Failure wasn't an option.

He would look back at this first month of class as being his toughest. Even if the classwork wasn't too demanding, the dramatic difference in atmosphere at this French University was, in many ways, confusing. In addition, he was being pressured by Bill to obtain real intelligence that might lead to something actionable. David didn't know how to proceed. His relationship with Mai was not the issue; he discovered that her father was rarely in Paris and that they spoke only once a week. His gut impression was that she really did not involve herself in the serious discussions that would seal the fate of her native country.

Ultimately, it was a stroke of luck that moved things forward.

It was one of those crisp, clear fall days in Paris—the kind that made the city feel almost too perfect. Mai had insisted they take a break. Just a few hours, she said. David could study in the morning, and then they'd head to Parc Monceau for a picnic. On the way home, she mentioned they'd need to stop at the Vietnamese Embassy. Some school documents needed notarization. Routine, she said. Nothing urgent.

Parc Monceau wasn't like the parks David was used to. It lacked the rigid geometry of Luxembourg or the Tuileries. Instead, it unfolded slowly, without fanfare—curved paths, scattered statues, lawns that welcomed footsteps instead of forbidding them. It was David's first time there. He took it in silently.

They arrived by metro, found the park easily, and wandered until they came upon a small rise—nothing dramatic, just a quiet hill flanked by azaleas and rhododendrons. Laughter drifted over from a nearby playground. The smell of cut grass and autumn leaves hung in the air.

Mai had packed lunch: a jambon-beurre sandwich on a fresh baguette, a small container of sliced radishes and cherry tomatoes, and a bottle of Orangina. They ate slowly, and Mai insisted on speaking English. David understood how challenging it must be for her to learn English. Vietnamese, being a tonal language with no verb conjugations, was a world apart from English. The complexities of tense, articles, and pronunciation must have felt like a maze to navigate. He tried to be reassuring without correcting every word. Her dream, she said, was to visit the United States someday. She said it lightly, but there was weight behind it.

David listened. For once, he didn't try to analyze it or fix it. He just let her speak.

It was a beautiful afternoon. They packed up their things, and Mai, remembering the stop at the Embassy to get the form notarized, mentioned the address to David:

45, Avenue de Villiers in the 17th.

David pulled out his *Plan de Paris* and quickly scanned the map. It was closer than he expected. They didn't need to get on the Metro after all—a quick 20-minute walk would do.

"That's why I insisted we picnic here," Mai said, her tone light. "I used to come to the embassy often and would walk through this park to get to the Metro. I always dreamed of spending a lazy afternoon lying on the grass."

The walk to the embassy took even less than 20 minutes, and as they approached, Mai gazed quizzically at the black sedan parked in the circular driveway with the Flag of South Vietnam proudly displayed on the hood. She seemed surprised. David asked if anything was wrong.

"No, I don't think so, but that is usually the car that my father is driven around in when he is in Paris. He would have called me to tell me that he was coming?"

At the entrance, security was discreet but thorough. Mai produced her passport without a word, and within moments, they were waved through. A uniformed guard, stone-faced and silent, led them across a tiled lobby and up a flight of stairs. It was there, halfway up, that she saw him—her uncle—speaking with a man David recognized from photos that were shown to him during his training, the Foreign Minister. Their voices were low, their postures stiff. Something in Mai's expression flickered.

"Everything all right?" David asked.

She didn't answer at first. Then: "My uncle. He's speaking with the Foreign Minister—Khiêm. They don't always agree."

That was all.

They were shown into a modest office on the left. A woman behind a desk looked up and nodded politely. Mai switched to Vietnamese and handed over a folder. David caught only fragments, but he gathered she was requesting official confirmation of financial support for her studies. Routine, but evidently necessary.

The secretary offered a small smile, then disappeared down a corridor with the papers. Ten minutes passed. Neither of them spoke. When she returned, the documents were stamped and signed, as promised. The smile remained, though David thought it looked thinner this time.

Back in the corridor, the scene at the far end remained unchanged. Her uncle and the minister now stood closer; the tone was clearly raised, though still carefully controlled. It was immediately apparent that a serious disagreement existed. As they reached the top of the stairs, Mai stepped forward.

Her uncle turned, startled. "Mai? What brings you here?"

She replied in Vietnamese, calmly, showing him the freshly notarized forms. He nodded, then smiled in that formal, restrained way David had come to associate with Vietnamese elders.

"I'll tell your father when I see him this weekend," her uncle said.

He looked at David then and remarked, "I am sure that you are fulfilling your parents' wishes and devoting yourself to your studies?"

With a glance toward David, he continues, "And who is this?"

"A friend," she said. "From Cité Universitaire. He was kind enough to come with me."

Her uncle, with a smile, extended a hand and, assuming David was French, thanked him.

"C'est très gentil de votre part." *"It is very kind of you."*

Mai offered a polite nod. "We'll leave you to your business, Uncle. My love to the family."

They walked back toward the Metro in silence for some time. The autumn air was cooler now. The city felt more guarded somehow.

Then David asked, lightly but not without purpose, "Do you know what they were arguing about?"

She hesitated. "My uncle is loyal to my father. The minister, less so. They often disagree."

"I thought I heard someone mention the Viet Cong." David never mentioned that his roommate, Tuan, taught him some rudimentary Vietnamese.

A pause. "You probably did."

Another step. She didn't look at him when she spoke next.

"The minister is a realist," she said finally. "He sees the world as it is—fractured, unstable, full of compromises no one wants but needs to make. From what I could gather, he was in favor of an immediate ceasefire, halting the US bombing, and even sharing power with the Viet Cong."

She paused, then added softly, "My father... he's not like the others. He believes in principles, in holding the line. My mother told me once, in confidence, that he would never agree to sharing power with the Viet Cong. To him, they're little more than bandits—terrorists dressed up as *patriots*. That is what their argument was about!

Sometimes I wonder if he's still fighting for a country that no longer exists. Or maybe," she allowed herself a faint, bitter smile, "one that never did."

She drew a breath, steadying herself. "In the end, my mother says, even he will have to face the truth: if the war is ever to end, there will have to be a compromise. Whether he can accept that... I don't know."

David gave Mai a sympathetic look, and as they descended the steps to the Metro and onto the Metro platform, the hum of the city above seemed to fade, replaced by the steady rhythm of the train's approach. David's thoughts were already racing ahead, the brief exchange at the embassy, the names, the subtle undercurrents. He couldn't ignore the implications. This is the kind of information that he was trained to look for—unspoken, loaded with potential consequences. If read right, it could shift the balance of things.

He glanced at Mai, and with an uncomfortable feeling, realized that he may have obtained the information that this mission required, and with that, the objectives in this relationship. *Had he developed feelings for this girl?* Clearly, he could not dismiss the fact that some of this was real; yes, he had developed feelings for her. David quickly put this out of his mind *as* the train finally arrived. David's fingers tightened around the strap of his bag. He wasn't sure if she noticed or if it even mattered. He had to process this—later. There was no time for reflection, no space to let the weight of it sink in.

Hours later, David stood in the cramped pay phone booth in the dorm lobby, his thoughts still sharp with the details. He dialed the number he was given. The line clicked twice before it was answered, his voice low and deliberate.

Good afternoon, is this Gibert Jeune, the bookstore? I'm looking for an anatomy atlas by Frank Netter, an American. He asked in French.

A brief pause. A click as if the call was being transferred, then David heard it—the subtle shift in tone, the barely perceptible break in the silence. Bill's response was almost too smooth, too casual.

"I think you have the wrong number, sorry. But I believe that store is in the 5th arrondissement."

David's mind flickered with recognition. The 5th arrondissement. It wasn't just a misdial—it was a signal-code. A simple, understated instruction. Bill was confirming the meeting time. Tomorrow, 5 PM, at the usual café in the Latin Quarter, 5th arrondissement. David replaced the receiver with a click, his thoughts already moving on. He would be there.

The next day, David left class without lingering. He exited the Metro at L'Hotel de Ville and crossed the Seine on foot, letting the press of the crowds cover his route. In the Latin Quarter, he spent twenty careful minutes in the medical section at Gibert Jeune, the acclaimed student bookstore. He selected a thin volume on histology—innocuous, credible—and paid in cash, nodding in thanks to the clerk.

He stepped back into the street and took a longer route to the café. Two blocks stretched to four. He paused at a window display, lingered unnecessarily at a newsstand, and checked the reflections in the glass behind him. Routine, mostly. But his training was already becoming second nature; it was drilled into him that routine was everything.

At 17:00 sharp, he entered the café and climbed to the second floor. It was nearly empty, just as they'd anticipated. He took a seat by the window, placing the book on the table with its spine facing out. A minute passed, then another. Then Bill appeared.

He looked like a technician from the utility company—canvas trousers, dark jacket, a tool belt with insulated pliers and wire cutters. His eyes scanned the room once, quickly, before he crossed to the table.

David didn't stand.

"Got something for you," he said without preamble. His voice was low; the tone stripped of any excitement. Just business. "Wait, Donovan broke in, let's order something."

Bill caught the eye of the waiter, "un tea, et un Orangina si vous plait." Then, from the back of David's memory, he remembered his training, '*a clandestine meeting draws less attention if the participants are eating or drinking.*'

He laid it out the way he'd been taught—chronological, detailed, detached. No speculation unless asked. Facial expressions. Body language. Proximity. Volume. Mai's uncle. The Foreign Minister, Khiêm. The words *Viet Cong*. The disagreement.

Bill asked once for clarification—something about the minister's tone. David gave it. Then he paused.

"There's more here, Bill. Not just talk. This was a real argument."

Bill listened without nodding, without glancing away.

"I'll pass it up the chain," he said finally. "If the group in Paris station agrees it smells interesting, it'll go in a cable to Langley."

He stood. For a moment, his eyes locked on David's—measuring, maybe, or approving. It was hard to say.

"Welcome to the game!" he said quietly. "We'll talk soon."

And then he was gone, just another man in work clothes, folding into the street.

Chapter 6

Paris, Years later

David awoke from a troubled sleep, the kind in which shadows existed instead of distinct memories of his dreams. He stumbled out of bed, dressed quickly, and ran a hand through his now longish brown hair as he peered through the cracked window into the narrow street below. He was told to meet someone from Paris Station—something big was in the works, and he was to be part of it.

As David descended the steps of his apartment and rounded the corner, the comforting aroma of coffee and fresh bread drifted into the cool morning air. He inhaled deeply. Paris always smelled best in the morning—before the exhaust of diesel fuel filled the streets. Despite everything, he loved it here. He loved the anonymity and the vibe.

And up until now, his primary job was still to study hard, keep his ears open, and blend in.

From time to time, they asked him to keep an eye on someone. Nothing dramatic, mind you—just a tail from hotel to café, or a silent presence in the back of a gallery or lecture hall. He was good at not being noticed, and that, as they had told him more than once, was half the job. The agency always needed experienced people on the street and lots of them.

Earlier that spring, they'd arranged for him to replace a Paris chauffeur who had conveniently taken ill. The assignment was simple: collect two visiting diplomats at the brand-new Charles de Gaulle airport and drive them to the George V. His French was natural, of course, and his English deliberately poor. Apologies came easily—a shrug of the shoulders, not the mouth. He played the role of a last-minute provincial hire, polite but incurious, one eye always on the road.

They talked freely in the backseat, as men often do when they believe they are not being heard. Names, times, vague references that would be decoded later. He delivered them, took their bags, nodded at the doorman, and drove off without looking back.

Later that night, in his flat, he wrote his report in longhand. It was neat, methodical, and better than what they'd expected. No embellishment, no theory—just what was said and who said it. Just as he had been trained to do.

Whomever had asked this of him from the basement of the embassy had smiled—just slightly—when he handed it over.

By now, the mechanics of tradecraft had become second nature. He observed without effort. He remembered without trying. And for the first time in a long while, he felt the faint hum of purpose.

Something bigger was coming. He was sure of it.

And he was ready and anxious to take the next step.

*

The meeting, he'd been told, was of the utmost importance, a phrase that, in this world, could mean anything or nothing. As a precaution, he ran a Surveillance Detection Route for a good 30 minutes. Nothing elaborate. Just enough to be able to funnel any tails following him to where they would easily be seen and identified. Down the Rue des Innocents towards the vast construction going on in Les Halles, down the Rue du Pont Neuf, and into the Samaritaine department store. Up a stairway, then down and again out onto the Rue de Rivoli.

For David, such caution was unusual. He was in France under the guise of a medical student, holding a yearly visa, enrolled in coursework, attending lectures, and living quietly. There was no reason for the French—or anyone else—to be particularly interested in him.

But then again, he remembered, there was that episode with 'Elena'—a memory he had trouble folding away, no matter how hard he tried.

It had been a year or two before; it was a Friday afternoon in early spring. David was looking forward to getting home. He'd spent the previous night on call in the Intensive Care Unit—a twelve-hour shift that hadn't been particularly dramatic, but steady and relentless. Ultimately, it's not too demanding. Now, hours later, he was on the Métro, wedged in among the usual crowd, the train rattling its way beneath the city. He stood near the door, eyes half-closed. That was when he saw her—though in hindsight, she was impossible to miss.

She stood by the metro map, a large canvas backpack slung casually over one shoulder. A tangle of blond hair fell across her face, catching the light, while her brow furrowed in concentration. There was a tension in the set of her shoulders, the restless energy of someone unaccustomed to being lost, but it only made her presence sharper, more magnetic. Her eyes—clear, alert—scanned the map with a mixture of determination and uncertainty, and for a moment, David couldn't look away.

He watched for a moment, then spoke—first in French, as polite convention dictated.

"Vous cherchez une direction?"

She turned, surprised, then smiled. "Ah—yes. Sorry. My French is... not so good."

Her English was crisp, tinged with a European accent—perhaps Greek, or from the Eastern Mediterranean. The vowels were softened, the rhythm gently foreign.

"I'm trying to get to Bastille," she said, tapping a line on the map.

"I thought the hostel I found in the guidebook had space, but when I got there..." She shrugged, smiling again. "*Complet*, FULL"

He leaned in to look. "You're going the right way," he said. "Just a few more stops. I can show you where to change."

Her shoulders relaxed a little. "Thank you. It's my first time in Paris. First day, actually. I've already gotten lost three times."

With a slight laugh, he smiled. "You're off to a good start, then."

They stood together in silence as the train jolted forward. Her eyes scanned the tunnels through the window. She smelled faintly of sun and soap and travel—not perfume, but something clean and unfamiliar.

"Are you from here?" she asked after a while.

"No," David said. "American. I'm studying medicine."

"Oh," she said, turning to face him more fully. "You're American. That explains it."

"Explains what?", he replied

It is just that you seem friendlier than the French, and you still have a slight accent.

He raised an eyebrow. "I thought *you* had the accent."

She laughed at that, "Touché."

Their conversation was easy after that—surprisingly so. She told him her name was Elena, that she was a history student on a break before returning to university in Thessaloniki. She'd saved for this trip for over a year, carefully planning her route through southern France and up into Belgium, maybe the Netherlands if her money lasted. She didn't know anyone in Paris, hadn't even been here a full day. Her voice carried an openness that felt unguarded but never naive. Curious, observant. She asked him questions—about Paris, about medicine, about whether American universities were really like the ones in movies.

The train slowed as it approached Bastille.

"This is you," he said.

She glanced at the map, then back at him, uncertain.

"Actually," she said, "would it be strange if I asked you to walk with me? Just until I find this place. It's easier to get lost on foot than on the train."

He hesitated only for a second. "Sure. I've got time."

They walked side by side along Rue de la Roquette, her backpack bouncing softly with each step. She pointed out little things—the smell of fresh bread from a boulangerie, a weathered plaque on a schoolhouse wall. She asked questions, listened carefully to the answers, and laughed easily.

By the time they reached the hostel, it was dark.

David approached the reception. There was a brief conversation in rapid French, followed by a quiet shake of the head. David turned toward "Elena." "Full again, I am sorry to report."

She turned to David, biting her lip.

"Looks like I need another plan."

He hesitated, knowing exactly where this was heading—where it might be going already.

"I live close by," he said. "It's nothing fancy, but you're welcome to crash on the couch if you need a place tonight. No pressure."

She studied his face, her expression unreadable for a moment. Then she smiled—slower this time, with something softer behind it.

"Merci," she said. "That's very kind."

Later, in his apartment, David prepared a simple dinner—omelets, a fresh baguette, salad, and a bottle of wine. The conversation picked up again where it had left off, lighter now, their laughter easier.

She was magnetic without trying. Smart, funny, unafraid to tease him about how he was a true-blooded "American" but could easily pass for a Frenchman, or the way he over-explained French phrases. But beneath the warmth, there were undercurrents—questions threaded with purpose. She wandered through his apartment like someone casing it gently, her fingers trailing across the edge of a bookshelf, eyes scanning the spines of his medical texts without reading them. She noticed a *mezuzah* on the doorpost when he locked up behind them.

"You're Jewish?" she asked. Not accusatory—just curious. Too curious.

He nodded. "Yes. But I wouldn't call myself religious. Agnostic, maybe. As a scientist, I can't honestly say there is—or isn't—a God. No one can. I grew up with the traditions, sure, but I probably couldn't read Hebrew now if you paid me." He glanced toward the door. "And the mezuzah? It was put up by the couple that sublet me the apartment."

"Ah," she said, letting the pause stretch. "That must make things… complicated. Sometimes."

He shrugged, played casual. "Not really."

She smiled at that, but her eyes didn't. Later, over the second glass of wine, she circled back.

"So, tell me again—why Paris? Why medicine? You could study in America, couldn't you?"

"I could," he said. "But medical school at home is very expensive, and in France it is free. Besides, it is certainly more interesting here than if I were at school in New Jersey or Nebraska, and I like it here."

"Do you like the French?"

There was a hint of coyness in the way she said it. Like she already knew the answer.

"Honestly, I've come to realize that no matter where you go, people are essentially the same, and I am in love with Paris."

"And politics?" she asked, leaning back, her voice softening like a thread unwinding. "Do you follow what's happening? Back home. Or here."

He hesitated and gave her a measured look. "Not much time for that. I mostly study. Run. Try to get through medical school and eventually secure a good residency program, most likely in the U.S.

She nodded, pretending to let it go.

But a few minutes later, the question came again—almost in passing, almost like a joke.

"And what about the Middle East? Do you ever think about that mess?"

"Often, but unfortunately, as things are currently, given the craziness of the Palestinian factions, Fatah and the PLO, I don't foresee any easy solution."

There was no reason for his pulse to shift, but it did. Just slightly.

The conversation flowed effortlessly, their laughter blending with the soft music and the clink of wine glasses. At some point, the bottle was empty, though neither of them had noticed until the last pour.

Elena rose slowly and, with a sly smile, asked, "Mind if I slip away for a minute?"

David smiled, already gathering the dishes. "Of course not. The bathroom's just past the kitchen. I'll pretend I'm the kind of guy who cleans and does the dishes right away."

He turned to the sink, stacking plates and letting the warm water run, when he heard the faint click of the bathroom light. The door opened quietly behind him.

He turned—and saw her.

She stood in the hallway wearing one of his old, threadbare Michigan t-shirts, the hem barely skimming the top of her thighs. Her hair was loose, skin glowing from the soft lamplight, and there was something in her expression—mischievous, expectant—that caught his breath.

Without a word, she walked to him and took his hand.

"Come to bed," she said softly.

He started to protest, murmuring something about the couch, blankets, being a gentleman—but she only smiled, silencing him with the gentlest tug.

"There's no need, David," she said, as she gradually led him upstairs to the loft, her fingers intertwined with his. As they reached the top of the stairs, she reached for the belt on David's jeans. She quickly unfastened his belt and jeans, and as they fell onto the bed laughing, David lifted the old, torn T-shirt over her head and tossed it aside. Bending down first, gently caressing and then kissing her neck, breasts, then slowly descending her abdomen, he then continued… but stopped as he looked up at her.

"Elena, I have an idea, maybe you can help me prepare for my next quiz on female anatomy." Giggling, she pulled him up and kissed him hungrily on the lips as she rolled him over on his back and got on top.

The sex wasn't a stolen moment, and it was nothing like a one-night stand. It unfolded slowly and hungrily—his hands exploring her, her breath catching as he pressed deeper—each movement filled with heat and the unmistakable certainty that what they were creating wasn't casual at all. It was desire turning deliberate, something real starting in the way their bodies refused to let go. They found a rhythm that felt less like luck and more like recognition, passion woven through every slow slide of skin against skin. She whispered his name against his ear, he pressed her harder into the mattress, losing the last of his restraint in the growing heat between them. And even as their pleasure peaked, a quiet certainty settled beneath it—an unspoken understanding that this wasn't casual at all. Something had begun here, in the slow collapse of their bodies around each other.

In the morning, David woke to find the bed empty. The sheets on her side were still warm, faintly scented, like she'd just slipped out moments before. On the nightstand, a folded note waited.

Neat handwriting. Brief.

Thanks for the hospitality. Good luck with your studies.

No name. No number. Just that.

David stared at it for a moment longer than he needed to, still half asleep, then set it down gently—like it might mean something if he looked at it long enough. He laughed to himself.

By the afternoon, he was fully awake and alert. Protocol took over, and he remembered the rules. He knew he had to file a report, without going into too many specifics, it had to be truthful and detailed. Within hours, he was summoned to a quiet room in the basement of the U.S. embassy, where, after a detailed description of 'Elena', a junior officer handed him a folder thick with surveillance photographs. It didn't take long. The girl, Elena, was identified.

No longer blond, no longer Greek.

Not lost.

Not Elena! But Rachel Zamir, Israeli intelligence, MOSSAD!

The conclusion, when it came, was professional and detached. The Israelis were conducting soft probes, canvassing the expat community in Paris for anyone who might prove useful down the line, especially Jewish expats. It wasn't personal, they said.

Still, the embassy sent in a sweep team. His apartment was searched, his phone disassembled and examined in detail. Nothing was found. No bugs, no lingering trace of Rachel. Just a reminder—quiet but clear—that even in romantic Paris, even as a student, he was in a high-stakes game of chess, not tic tac toe, and every move had serious consequences. Although still new to this game, he realized that he could not afford to let his training lapse; this was serious business.

Chapter 7

Paris

From the Samaritaine department store, he descended into the Métro at Châtelet, slipping into the crowd without ceremony. Two stops—just enough. At Saint-Paul, he surfaced quickly, his pace measured but unhurried, his eyes alert but not obvious. Then out onto the quai, where the Seine glimmered in the morning light.

Crossing the Pont Marie, onto the Île Saint-Louis, he allowed himself a glance—not long, just enough—toward the second-floor window at 11 quai de Bourbon. The curtains were drawn open. That was the signal. He was told that someone would be watching his back at this important meeting. The watcher was in position. No tails. No opposition. By now, after a few years of doing this, his street craft had become second nature.

He didn't smile, didn't nod. He simply continued.

The Île Saint-Louis had always felt faintly unreal to David—a curated dream of Paris, preserved for postcard seekers and sentimental exiles. Yet its charm was undeniable.

Narrow cobbled streets, tiny bookshops spilling paperbacks onto the sidewalk; antique dealers displayed gilded mirrors and dusty clocks with price tags in looping cursive. Between galleries and artisan shops stood the essentials—boulangerie, boucherie, and fromagerie. Each was run by families who'd lived above them for decades, their standards quietly absolute.

Everyone knew everyone else. And if they didn't, they knew who to ask. Secrets didn't last long.

Every building had its concierge living just off the foyer, curtains drawn, eyes open. They knew every face, every overstayed visitor, every delivery boy who lingered too long. In their way, they were an intelligence service unto themselves.

David had learned early: charm was currency. A box of biscuits or a well-placed compliment in careful French bought access or a discreet name—a whispered timetable of a neighbor's comings and goings. Concierges talked, of course, among themselves at cafés over espresso and cigarettes.

As David walked along the Quai de Bourbon, the pavement still glistened from its morning wash— a ritual that left them shining in the sun. Dogs were everywhere, but unlike in America, few owners bothered with plastic bags.

The bell above the café door gave its usual reluctant chime as David stepped inside. "Bonjour, madame," he said softly. The owner nodded—polite, noncommittal. The French were masters of ambiguous courtesy: just warm enough to be civil, never enough to invite familiarity. When he'd first arrived, fresh from college, he made the mistake of entering shops without a greeting. The grimaces had been instructive. Now he said the greetings like a password—required, precise, expected.

He took a seat at the back—always the back—where he could keep an eye on both the entrance and the quai beyond the window. He ordered a café crème and a croissant, more for appearance than hunger, and began the quiet work of observation.

There were six others in the café.

A well-dressed, bearded man from the neighborhood was buried in his *L'Equipe* and moved only to turn the page. Two women beneath the mirror were deep in a conversation, half-whispered, half-performed. At the bar, three students in last night's clothes jostled with the bravado of those unsure if they were hungover or still drunk.

8:50 am.

He didn't check his watch—one didn't, not in this kind of meeting—but he knew the time. He always did.

The instructions had been simple: 9:00 sharp. No names. The contact would be someone he knew!? That was all they'd told him. And from that contact, he was to receive a full update on an operation that had taken months to design and twice that to argue over. It wasn't training anymore. This was the real deal: his first serious involvement in an op.

Keeping abreast of world events, David had suspicions that it might involve Iran and the insertion of Farsi-speaking case officers. Since the embassy takeover, the agency has been completely shut out, local informers eliminated, and assets kept in hiding. Following the Shah's departure, an initial power vacuum led to mild chaos and uncertainty. Eventually, Ayatollah Ruhollah Khomeini and his extreme conservative movement swiftly moved in to fill the vacuum and consolidate power. It was soon apparent to all Iranians that a new political system based on Islamic principles would be imposed. The news out of Tehran was ever-changing. The streets were filled with a mix of excitement and anxiety. Excitement and relief that the hated Shah and his police were gone, but anxiety that the freedoms that the people had become used to may be threatened by the turn to an ultra-religious Islamic state!

The Ayatollah had been busy during his brief exile in Neauphle-le-Château, just outside Paris. Surprisingly, the US government and the CIA, though monitoring him closely, were unprepared when the weakened Shah—undone by strikes and student uprisings—abandoned the country. Neither State nor the CIA foresaw the widespread support generated by the Ayatollah's taped recordings, or the rapid transition to rule by an elderly religious leader.

The Shah had been in Paris a few years back for a routine checkup and was found to have an enlarged spleen. Coincidentally, in the previous autumn, David was a third-year medical student when the

Shah was at the American Hospital in Paris. The diagnosis was more than routine: chronic lymphocytic leukemia, a degenerative disease with an uncertain but terminal course. The Shah and his French physician kept the diagnosis secret. David had arranged a brief rotation at the same service; it was a mere formality to slip through the cracks and access the Shah's chart. His eyes skimmed the diagnosis. He cautiously brought what he'd seen to his superiors. From that moment, things shifted. Until then, he'd been a junior officer, still on probation—green, unproven, building his cover. However, this was genuine intelligence and demonstrated initiative. Suddenly, they took him seriously.

The café crème arrived first, followed by a croissant—still warm, the edges golden and flaking. The waiter placed them down without a word, just a brief nod. David gave a faint smile in return, his eyes already shifting back toward the door.

The door chimed at precisely 9:00. The newcomer looked American—clean-cut, calculatedly at ease. He paused just inside the threshold, his gaze moving deliberately across the room. No haste just a measured scan. When he spotted David, his steps suggested coincidence, as if fate not intent guided him to this corner of Paris.

The handshake was offered with a smile, the words delivered casually but with just enough edge to carry a second meaning.

"Good to see you again."

At first, David had to think where he knew him from. He was light-complexioned, in his late 20s or early 30s, a young American from the East Coast, with perhaps a Boston accent, dressed in jeans and a leather bomber jacket. Then it came to him! Touch football the year before in the Bois de Boulogne. He was with three or four friends for the usual Sunday pickup game among expats trying to bring a little bit of home to this city, which, in so many ways, was completely foreign. This was serious touch football, and David and his buddies had a hard time keeping the game close. Chatter during the game was kept to a minimum; there was no suspicion on David's part at that time that they were, in fact, there in France, "playing for the same team" as it were. It was certainly suspicious, though, as these guys proclaimed, "Oh, we are here in France working for the US Postal Service." Curious, David thought briefly that it didn't fit.

They were clearly athletic, physically very fit, wearing college sweats from Duke, Yale, and Princeton. Not the usual career choice for the Ivy League graduate. And then there was the fact that their French was natural and completely fluent, with a grasp of the street slang of Paris. Certainly not something one picks up at a college French class.

"Been out to the Blois de Bologne for any good football games lately? David, isn't it?"

"Yes."

He offered his hand, "James Waldon, call me Jim; Oh, and my buddies wanted me to tell you how much fun it was giving you and your guys such a beating."

"Yeah, well, if it hadn't been for that ringer of yours, the one with the big arm, we would have taken you down!"

"Don't tell me he didn't play college ball."

"No comment."

"Let's take a walk. We've got a lot to go over."

David left a 5-franc piece on the table as they walked toward the door, and Jim led him across the street, down the steps to the quai.

Out of the corner of his eye, David registered two of Jim's football pals shadowing them—one fifty meters behind, the other stationed across the river, neither breaking cover. The back of his neck prickled.

Jim pulled out a Gitane and offered David a smoke.

"No thanks, how can you smoke those? They are awful."

"Horrible tasting cigarettes, but I need to get used to them, easier to blend in, as they say, "when in France" …

"I met with the DCOS yesterday at the embassy. How long has he been your case officer?

"Donovan recruited me out of college during my senior year."

"So tell me, David, have our overlords asked you to do anything other than schoolwork since you've been here?" He asked with a slight grin. "What exactly have they got you doing? Any real "field" work?"

"The usual. Camp Peary for 12 weeks, then attending language school in Paris, along with more trade craft. First year was mostly about cover—medical school, blending in, nothing more."

"My first assignment was easy. Live at the Cité Universitaire, stay out of politics, and get close to a few students from Laos and Vietnam. Most weren't serious about school, tennis, cafés, dinners in Vietnamese restaurants. Eventually, being American didn't matter. I made sure they knew I was antiwar. I even told them I'd been arrested protesting."

"Then came the president's daughter—my real target. The Paris Peace Talks were in full swing. Little scraps of insight, not much on their own. But pieced together with other intel, turned out to be somewhat useful."

"Like what?"

"I passed along the details—their families' travel plans, when the parents hoped to be back, family relations, whether there was any optimism left about the war, who was meeting whom. At the time, I didn't think any of it mattered. Routine reporting, background noise, nothing earth-shattering. But then, I got lucky."

Davide continued with the same intensity.

"By pure chance, I found myself witnessing something unexpected: a heated exchange between one of the president's inner circles and the Foreign Minister himself. That, it appeared, turned out to be of interest."

My report made it all the way up the chain. And as it turned out, Langley put this together with other intel and passed it onto Kissinger's people, no less, who found it very useful indeed."

"Yeah, Donovan told me that for a freshman operations trainee, he was mildly impressed with the Intel that you were able to get. After the peace talks concluded, what did they have you do?"

David hesitated only briefly; he well knew that even if he hadn't signed those six "non-disclosure documents," what he had been doing during those six weeks was well above anyone here in France's pay grade.

"The reality was that David was called back to Langley during his first summer break to review boxes and boxes of files from years back that might have been a serious embarrassment to the CIA. With David's background and with the research he did on sensory deprivation, he just assumed that he was chosen as they didn't want any agency psychiatrists not associated with the program learning of it. The fear was that Nixon would launch his henchmen to ransack the CIA's files, and thus he was ordered to go through boxloads of super-classified documents about a program called MKUltra. This super top-secret Black Ops program was created to develop interrogation techniques to use on suspected "double agents."

The problem was that in many cases, psychoactive substances, amphetamines, and especially LSD were given to both willing and unwitting subjects, including CIA personnel, defectors, prisoners, and even civilians. One high-level Russian defector was given LSD after a lengthy period of sensory deprivation. This took place in a specialized facility in Hunts Point, Brooklyn, and within 20 minutes of being given a variant of LSD, when everyone was looking away, he proceeded to jump out of the window.

Unfortunately for everyone involved, especially the jumper, the room was on the 10th floor! The program was personally approved by both Helms and Allen Dulles. It was subsequently confirmed that the defector was completely legit. He would have been a gold mine, a high-level defector. Soon after the summer, Helms got sacked. The powers on the 7th floor, especially the DO, were certain that this information would ruin the agency.

David was ordered to flag anything that might be either an embarrassment or, frankly, illegal. What they did with those files, he had no clue; likely, they were shredded. It was in that moment that David came to understand—clearly, and without the need for further justification—that while his early fascination with psychology and sensory deprivation had been genuine, even earnest, it was not a goal that he could morally continue as either an intellectual pursuit or, more specifically, under the Agency's flag. What had begun as academic curiosity had become something colder, something weaponized. And he wanted no further part in it.

As they walked along the Seine, Jim would casually glance around and check his buddies behind them and across the river.

"Here's the deal, David. The OP is being run by Jonathan Buchanan, Mid East Desk, Langley, through Donovan, who, I'm sure you know, is the new Deputy Chief of Station. He will be meeting with you soon and wants you to report directly to him regarding this project. We will be involving you in an Op that has top priority at Langley. Since the takeover of the embassy in Tehran, as you can imagine, we are effectively blind. The geniuses at State and the Iran Desk never imagined that what happened so quickly and so seamlessly would ever occur. Their opinion was based on flawed and overly optimistic intelligence obtained from the Iranian generals who were close to our military, business elites, and progressive, mostly Western-educated academics in Tehran and, of course, SAVAK. They all gave the impression that most Iranians welcomed the Secular modernization path that the Shah was implementing."

David stopped walking, looking incredulously at Jim.

"What about our reports about the Ayatollah's activity here in Paris. And all those tapes of his sermons that were so easily copied and sent back to Iran. I was briefed on that and was told to keep a watch on any Iranian activism on campus."

"We did pass it along, obviously, but it wasn't taken seriously. The tapes that he made and our estimates that it was part of an underground network of thousands of expats and that this was a real threat spreading his anti-Shah and anti-American rhetoric across Iran."

We had been warning Langley for at least 6 months prior to his return that the mood in Paris among the Iranians here was almost 100% anti-government, anti-American. The State Department's primary objective in all of this was to prevent the Soviets from making inroads into Iran after the Shah's eventual fall. The geniuses at the CIA's Iran Desk's conclusion was that the Iranians themselves, although not at all aligned with the Shah, certainly were not ready for an Islamic theocracy. But that they were at least excited for change, and that wish resulted in those tapes being circulated widely."

As they crossed over the Seine at the Pont de Sully near the tip of the Island, Jim made a hand motion to his followers, now only 30 meters behind.

"How difficult would it be for you to get away from your life as a student for a couple of days?"

"Not a problem, mostly afternoon lectures for which we already have the mimeographed notes, and the responsibilities in the wards during the mornings are so ridiculous as not to be missed." Obviously, weekends would be ideal,

"We'll bring you up to speed on the preliminaries and assess what support we'll need. With luck, you'll meet Donovan before then. Langley already has a plan in motion. They want our assessment in four weeks. We'll be the primary support station. The operation starts here."

"We will meet at the Hôpital St. Louis, at the Musée des moulages of the Hospital, AKA the 'wax museum' of Pathology. Let's say 11:00 Saturday. I am told it is one of the most bizarre, macabre places in all of Paris. There's a small room toward the back; you should be able to find it easily enough. They use it to play tape recordings on the technical side of the work. No one bothers with it, of course. Visitors drift past without a glance, their eyes drawn to the macabre skin lesions common in the 19th century. I'm sure you know more about that than I ever will. As a medical student, it wouldn't be too much of a reach for you to explain yourself. If someone you know sees you, you'll see."

Chapter 8

Paris

It was the middle of the week, and although David was excited, he knew he had to slip back into routine—back into his life as a student.

He woke at 6:30, the old alarm sharp and insistent on the nightstand. Coffee first—strong and swift—then a bracing, chosen cold shower. He slipped out, down narrow stairs to the Metro, borne forward by the press of commuters. By 8:30, sometimes nine, he threaded the hospital's massive stone corridors, air touched with antiseptic and old paper.

The mornings unfolded on the wards. Not structured teaching, not true mentorship—just absorption. Clinical medicine arrived in fragments, filtered through nurses' chatter, the clipped exchanges of interns, the perpetual shuffle of charts and lab results. Since it was a Pathology rotation, the day began when the *chef de clinique* appeared, usually around nine. Together, they began with specimens from the O.R.—the raw substance of medicine. The technicians, mostly young women—cheerful, adept, and, David couldn't help noting, often strikingly attractive—processed slides with quiet precision. Unsurprisingly, the hospital boasted one of the world's premier hematology services, with many staff trained at the nearby Pasteur Institute.

David watched, learned, kept his head down, and paid his dues. A few times each month, if another student on the autopsy rotation failed to show, David gladly offered to fill in and was allowed to assist with the post-mortem exams—a privilege, though no one called it that out loud.

In France, most unexpected deaths were considered for autopsy. By law, the state could claim corneas, skin, and heart valves for transplantation unless the patient or family had filed a formal objection. In cases of brain death, if no prior objections existed and the family didn't object, the heart and kidneys would usually be harvested.

David was also surprised at how many bodies were never claimed! Then again, Paris—like all great cities—was full of shadows. The unhoused slept in the doorways in the Latin Quarter or under the Pont Neuf, their shapes bundled in stained blankets, invisible to the tourists who gazed up at the Louvre or crossed the Seine with shopping bags from the Rue Saint-Honoré.

Near the city's edge, addicts clustered in Métro stations—gaunt and jittery, they traded whispers and glances, slipping syringes or foil packets between wan fingers. Meanwhile, alcoholics haunted the back alleys of the 18th arrondissement: some hunched along the Canal Saint-Martin, others sprawled on the hard benches near Gare du Nord.

He often wondered who these people had been before the streets claimed them, before alcohol dissolved their families or heroin carved the futures from their veins. Perhaps once, they were students in the same lecture halls where he now sat, clerks in elegant shops along Rue de Rivoli, lovers hurrying through the Métro, or parents lifting children onto shoulders for Bastille Day fireworks. There were few other careers, David thought, where you touched the whole of humanity in a day's work.

Chapter 9

Paris

It was a foggy morning, the kind Paris specialized in—grey, cool, and faintly unwelcoming. David woke uneasy, the anticipation of the coming meeting already pressing at his chest. He would be meeting Bill Donovan again, the newly minted Deputy Chief of Station—the man to whom he owed both his presence in Paris and, in no small way, his future. Donovan, now reporting directly to Buchanan at HQ, had been rapidly promoted. Also joining them was Jim Waldon, David's new colleague: weekend touch-football enthusiast, supposed Postal Service employee, Duke man, and, beneath it all, one of Langley's quieter insertions into the city. From what David had heard, Donovan's promotion had not gone unnoticed around Paris Station; it raised eyebrows and touched a nerve, especially with Chief of Station Peterson, who found the arrangement less than satisfactory.

In any small organization, there were always rumors. But inside the CIA, rumors weren't just gossip. They were currency. They traveled along invisible lines, tucked between the official cables and the unofficial ones, passed in offhand remarks over coffee or slipped into the briefest of glances in the corridor.

There was talk—there was always talk—that Donovan's promotion was tied to the success of the peace talks. Officially, credit had gone to Duke Peterson, the Station Chief, who made sure his name appeared on every communique back to Langley. But those who paid attention knew that it was Donovan's operation. There had been another player: David. Still a junior operative, not even three months into his eighteen-month probation, he'd obtained the critical information. Donovan had spotted him, backed him, and signaled upward that there was talent worth cultivating. Of course, it was flattering, David supposed. Yet, he realized this new aspect of life was cloaked not just in secrecy, but in politics as well—a realm he hadn't been trained for. College and now medical school demanded discipline, dedication, and hard work. This was something altogether different: a world where power moved silently, victories belonged to the clever, and the line between ally and rival blurred by design. Late at night, David sometimes wondered what game he was really in. Was he in Paris to achieve his medical education, a pawn in someone else's move, or, in fact, a rising player in this game? Because in the CIA, one thing was certain: you were never as invisible as you thought.

Saturday mornings were unusually still in the neighborhood.

The local prostitutes on rue St. Denis were long gone, as were their clients. The cafes were just opening, and the rest of the neighborhood was still asleep. The meeting was set for 11:00, and he had plenty of time. He showered, got dressed, and descended to the rue de Rivoli, where his favorite cafe was already buzzing with the usual neighborhood crowd.

"Bonjour madame," as he headed toward the end of the 'zinc', where his café creme was already being prepared. As it was finished, his favorite waitress presented him with a tartine, "C'est pour la maison, pour notre docteur préféré.. *"On the house, for our favorite doctor."*

David blushed slightly and thanked Chantale with an air kiss.

He was anxious, yet excited. He was ready for an adventure, and he vividly remembered the rush he had felt when he handed Bill the intel he'd managed to secure from Mai—and from the tense encounter with her uncle. And yet, a knot of conflict tightened inside him. His relationship with Mai had once been personal; he had developed real feelings for her, and it was not merely professional. But he'd had to end it as soon as the mission was completed. *Was it remorse he felt? Or was it guilt?* He wasn't sure—all he knew was that these questions kept him up at night, night after night.

He glanced at yesterday's "Herald Tribune" on the table nearest him. The news regarding Iran was not good.

"President Carter, after sounding out its major European allies, is moving toward a decision whether to seek international economic sanctions against Iran, a high State Department official said today."

The official stressed that the Carter Administration would not press for any collective action until it had fully assessed the impact of such a move on the safety of 52 remaining Americans who have been held hostage in Tehran since Nov. 4.

The official, who spoke to reporters traveling with Secretary of State Cyrus R. Vance on his visits to Britain and France yesterday and Italy and West Germany today, said that President Carter's decision last month to freeze Iranian assets in American banks had succeeded better than anyone expected in curtailing Iranian trade with the industrialized world."

Finishing his café, David left a 5-franc piece on the table and stepped out toward the Metro near Châtelet. He descended into the station, emerged across the street, and continued on to the rue de Rivoli, where he hailed a cab to Bastille. After two Metro stops and a short walk north, he finally reached the hospital.

It was relatively quiet—after all, it was a Saturday—and David had no trouble entering the main hall, flashing his medical student ID at the security point.

"Monsieur, où puis-je trouver le Musée des Moulages?" he asked a passing attendant.

"C'est tout droit, puis vous tournez à gauche au fond du couloir!" *"Straight ahead, then left at the end of the hall."* Came the reply.

David followed the directions, winding through the corridors. He was struck by how hidden the museum was—though, on reflection, it made sense. It was, after all, a place catering to a specialized curiosity.

As Jim predicted, the museum was practically empty, save for one elderly gentleman, possibly a retired physician or just someone taken in by the macabre. As David stepped further into the large, cavernous room, the atmosphere shifted to one of quiet focus. The space was orderly and clean, its rows of glass cases arranged with precision. Inside, wax models displayed a wide array of dermatologic conditions, each labeled carefully with its medical name, the year observed, and annotations.

He moved deliberately from case to case, keeping an eye out for the side room where the meeting was to take place, all the while observing the lifelike representations. The life-size mannequins were remarkably detailed, crafted to accurately depict the appearance of skin diseases, from subtle red scaling to pronounced ulcerations, nodules, plaques, and tumors. Some showed early-stage lesions, while others demonstrated advanced or untreated disease, offering a visual timeline of progression. He had learned of these historic diseases, which were commonplace in Paris during the 19th century, before the advent of antibiotics. The "gummas" of tertiary syphilis were all too common even among the bourgeoisie and upper classes.

The lighting was neutral, and the air carried the faint scent of old wood and disinfectant, the silence punctuated only by the occasional creak of the floor or shuffle of a visitor's steps.

David realized that this was not meant to be a place of spectacle but of study, a resource for the medical professionals of a long-gone era to train their eyes and sharpen their diagnostic ability. He appreciated the historical importance of the collection. Long before color photography, these models had been indispensable, preserving knowledge and helping generations of clinicians learn to recognize and understand the diseases that manifest so vividly on the skin.

Just as David began observing the specimens with clinical interest, David's attention was pulled sharply back. He had stumbled upon a curtained vestibule tucked away near the far end of the gallery. As he approached, the curtain shifted slightly, and he was met by familiar faces: Jim Waldon, Bill Donovan, and two other men he didn't recognize—along with a woman whose presence immediately piqued his curiosity.

Without a word, he was ushered inside. One of the unfamiliar men stepped smoothly outside the curtain, taking up a discreet post just beyond it. David took a closer look at him and noticed that his blazer and slacks matched those of the museum guards, allowing him to blend in as a museum employee.

Bill Donovan began, "We don't have much time, so I'd like to get right down to it."

"Patricia, this is David—the young 'doctor to be' I mentioned. David, meet Patricia Ross. She heads up the Iran desk at Langley. Been here a week, give or take. She's come to brief us on their end—what they're seeing, what they're not, what they need, and how we might be useful."

David, a little surprised, walked slowly as Ms. Lang approached and, with a smile, responded, "Pleased to meet you."

Patricia Ross took a good look at David, and it was obvious that she was assessing him.

"And David, this is Amir." As David went to shake hands with him, Amir smiled and whispered, "GO BLUE." David gave a brief grin. "And you know James."

David paused, waiting to learn who exactly Amir was and what his role would be, but there was no follow-up.

Patricia Ross immediately spoke up:

"We need eyes and ears in Tehran," she said plainly. "As you can imagine, what remained of our networks went dark the moment the demonstrations began. With the fall of the embassy and the collapse of our station, we lost more than access—we lost memory, context, everything. Our assets have vanished. Some are likely in hiding. Some, we suspect, are dead. What remains of our station is held hostage in the embassy!"

She paused, letting the weight of it settle.

"Washington's nervous. The seventh floor is even more so. Everyone wants to know what the future of Iran is going to look like—what happens when the shouting stops, when the revolutionary slogans fade into governance. But we can't forecast anything without real data. And my analysts at Langley, bright as they are, can only argue in circles without it. What we need now is intelligence. Not cables, not theories. Concrete Intelligence."

She leaned forward slightly, lowering her voice just a shade.

"We're asking Paris station to assist with the insertion of six to ten of our operatives into the country. Quietly. Ideally, before the new regime manages to put together a professional security outfit. The staging area will not be here, nor will it be from Europe; more likely, it will be in Egypt or perhaps Turkey. But for now, that is not important; we can leave that for further discussion." They will, for the most part, come with good cover. However, we believe it would be best if they didn't enter the country, pass through customs, and come to the attention of those in charge. Even with an impeccable reputation, foreigners, and even those with Iranian passports who return from abroad, will likely arouse suspicion, a file on them will likely be opened, and their activities will be closely followed. We cannot afford to take chances with them."

She glanced around the room, reading the faces and calculating their capabilities.

"If we succeed, we believe the old networks can be revived—or at least something resembling them. We have other objectives, classified for now, but let me be blunt: without human sources on the ground, none of it is achievable. Not one operation on the books will make it past the planning stage."

With a quizzical look and feeling just a little out of his depth, David, with a glance toward Bill, asked:

"Ms. Lang, as I am sure you've been briefed, my cover here in Paris is that of a full-time medical student. How do I possibly fit into this?" What would my role be?"

Lang smiled and looked toward Bill, who continued.

"Do you know two brothers, Azad and Azimi Behzadi?" Bill asked quietly. "They're in your year at the medical school—Pitié-Salpêtrière Hospital."

David took a moment before replying. "Yes… Now that you mention it. I was paired with Azad in anatomy dissection. He is very intelligent, somewhat standoffish, and not very friendly. His brother, Azimi, was always on the move. The loud one. Likes to joke, a bit of a show-off. Also, Smart—both are. Azad appears to be friends with a couple of Lebanese students. Azimi's the more social one. Girls in the class seem to like him."

Lang nodded, then glanced first at Donovan, then back at David. She took a folder from her briefcase and continued. "Their father is a physician back in Iran. The family belongs to a minority sect—Zoroastrians. I'm not sure if you're familiar?"

David shook his head.

Lang continued, her tone neutral, instructive. "One of the oldest religions in the world. Predates Islam, predates Christianity." And with a slight smile, "Possibly as old as your own ancient Hebrews. They worship Ahura Mazda—a single, uncreated god. The deity of wisdom and light."

He paused. "What matters is this: while the Zoroastrians never had much love for the Shah, they're deeply wary of what's coming. Under the monarchy, they had relative freedom, including legal rights, access to education, and participation in civil life. Secular government, after all. Now, with the new Islamic Republic forming, their position is looking uncertain at best."

Bill quietly interrupted and leaned forward. "We'd like you to get close to them. The brothers. Befriend them. Nothing dramatic. At first, just the usual—conversations, drinks, the occasional night out."

David said nothing.

Bill went on. "You mentioned Azimi likes to have a good time. That's your way in. Unlike Muslims, most Zoroastrians don't abstain from alcohol. And we understand you've had no trouble meeting women. Bring them along. Go out. Keep it light—casual. All we need for now is a connection, a presence."

He paused, eyes steady. "Three weeks from now, we'll meet again. By then, we expect that you will have made some progress in this regard.

David gave a slight nod—just enough to be seen, not enough to fully commit.

As the voices in the curtained room moved on to the next matter, something tighter settled in his chest. He wasn't new to this—not anymore—and that, in some ways, made it worse. The first time they asked him to get close to someone, he told himself it was harmless. Just a conversation. A gesture. Nothing that would leave a mark. But it became more—so much more—and part of him still flinched at what he'd done, what he'd *had* to do. He thought of Mai more often than he wanted to admit. And lately, she had become a person in his dreams.

Azad and Azimi. He remembered them more clearly than he let on. Azad—quiet, sharp-eyed, the type who spoke only when necessary but always knew the answer. Azimi was the opposite: too loud, too eager to be liked, always with a girl on his arm and a joke in his pocket. They were polite and friendly enough, yet beneath the easy manners, David sensed a sharper truth—an aversion to America that Azad made little effort to hide.

The pitch was always the same: the description of it made it sound so easy, just a drink, just a night out, just a bit of trust. But behind every casual evening was a report, a conversation behind closed doors, a file with someone else's name and fate in it. He had done it before. He would do it again. That was the job.

They exited the vestibule, and as they did, Bill nodded to the watcher standing guard; with that, everyone went their own way.

As he was exiting the museum, Donovan bumped into him from behind, casually, and whispered, "Remember, three weeks from today, same time, 'La Terrace des Puces', at the Clignancourt Flea Market."

Chapter 10

Paris

The day was consumed by textbooks, lecture notes, and a kind of mental exhaustion that made the hours blend together. By nightfall, David craved escape; the weight in his chest demanded a shift, a reset.

He arranged to meet Thérèse at a small bar off Rue de Seine, tucked behind a gallery that always smelled faintly of varnish and cigarette smoke. They'd been seeing each other for about a month—nothing serious, nothing defined, just one day at a time.

They'd met at a classmate's party in the Marais—forgettable circumstances. Thérèse wasn't in medicine; she studied Art History at the École des Beaux-Arts, and it showed. Her beauty unfolded gradually: long, honey-blond hair in loose waves, an unhurried smile that was deliberate and considered. Her poise and cultivated detachment set her apart from the harried med students David knew. He was drawn to her control and confidence.

There were no illusions between them. It wasn't love, and neither pretended otherwise. What they shared was clean and elegant—an arrangement without sentiment that brought comfort and a fragile sense of control. Their chemistry was undeniable, their rhythm instinctive. The sex was sensual but restrained, echoing a subtle wariness as if neither could let go completely.

He remembered their conversation at the party,

"My goal isn't to end up as window dressing in some Paris gallery," she blurted out.

He raised an eyebrow. "Then what is it?"

"I want to curate. Seriously. The Louvre, the Musée d'Art Moderne… maybe even the Met in New York. Somewhere that matters."

No promises. No complications. Just a quiet understanding—this was what it was, and nothing more.

They left the bar together without discussion, coats over their arms. The winter air outside felt clean and sharp. It was a relief after the fog of cheap wine and Gauloises in the bar. Streets were still slick from the earlier rain. Café signs and streetlamps swam in the cobblestones.

They walked without hurry, past shuttered boutiques and boulangeries where the smell of tomorrow's bread was just beginning to rise.

"This street?" he asked. "I don't think I've ever been down here."

She smiled. "That's because you don't live here. It's the kind of place Paris keeps for herself."

She led him to her building—a tall, thin Haussmann façade with peeling blue paint around the doorframe.

Her flat was small. Curated. Every object deliberate: a Matisse lithograph above the sofa, a glass vase with a single white lily, the faint scent of sandalwood lingering somewhere unseen. She poured each of them a measure of Chablis. The glasses felt thin and cold in his hand.

"To new discoveries," she said, lifting hers.

He touched his glass lightly to hers. "And to secrets I've been walking past without noticing."

They talked for a while—about a Cézanne exhibition she had just seen at the Musée de l'Art Moderne, about the politics of museum acquisitions, about the absurdities of the hospital bureaucracy.

"At least with art," she said, "the politics are honest. Everyone wants the same thing: prestige."

"Medicine's no different," he replied. "Except no one admits it."

She listened as if she had all the time in the world—eyes steady, smile slight—measuring his words before deciding what to do with them.

When he kissed her, it was with the certainty that she'd been waiting for it. Her lips were soft, cool at first, then warming under his. The sex that followed was slow, deliberate, a dance of restraint and indulgence. Her touch was exploratory but never urgent, his hands tracing the curve of her back as if memorizing the line.

In the morning, she slipped into the kitchen and returned with two espressos in delicate porcelain cups, no sugar.

"Black," she said. "The only proper way."

He drank while standing at the window, looking down at the street where the rain had begun again, fine and persistent.

"Back to the world," he murmured, slipping on his coat.

She lingered in the doorway, gaze fixed on him, her silence as deliberate as the night before. David sensed a brief hesitation—an unspoken wish to hold on—before she let him go. They understood each other. He left just as the streets began to awaken, feeling the subtle ache of departure as he stepped back into the world.

*

By Sunday evening, David began to plan. How was he to get close and befriend Azimi? As it turned out, both were scheduled to start a Parasitology lab that week, which was part of the infectious diseases section they were both taking. Unlike in America, parasitology was a subject that was gone into in detail. In France, there were vastly more parasitic diseases that were seen each day in the clinic. France was just more cosmopolitan. There were patients seen every day in Paris, from the tropics, the Caribbean, and North Africa, to say nothing of those from French Indochina, which included Vietnam, Cambodia, and

Laos, *known as l'Indochine française.* They were from the former colonies and, as such, had been able to travel freely to France for decades.

They got started right away that Monday afternoon. The theoretical material had been covered in lectures a few weeks earlier, so by now they knew what to look for: helminths, protozoa, eggs, cysts. This was the practical side—stool samples, saline mounts, and the quiet satisfaction of making a correct diagnosis, often by little more than shape, movement, or a well-placed stain.

Many of the students would eventually find themselves practicing far from the comforts of a university hospital. You might be the only doctor in a village, miles from a lab, responsible for everything from a cough to kala-azar. You had to know how to spot things yourself. All graduates were immediately trained to become primary care physicians after completing medical school. Perhaps this is why the degree took 7 years.

For some of the males in the class, especially Azimi, the real education was less about parasites and more about the lab assistants— young women, nineteen or twenty at most, each exuding an effortless, quiet Parisian confidence typical of those from the Pasteur Institute. They moved between benches with lazy grace, sometimes leaning in a little too close, offering help that, frankly, wasn't always needed. It was hard to say whether they knew the effect they had, or if that, too, was deliberate. The girls in the class, of course, noticed. Some rolled their eyes at the obvious flirting, sharing looks that ranged from amusement to exasperation. A few leaned closer together, whispering comments— half-laugh, half-eyeroll. "Looks like Monsieur Azimi has found a new parasite," one murmured, smirking.

The afternoons flew by, and by the end of that first week, David, feeling a little bolder, decided to make his move. He spotted one of the lab assistants—the one Azimi had been smiling at all week—and figured it was time to test the waters.

With a casual tilt of his head, David winked at Azimi, then turned to one of the young lab assistants with a grin. "How about a drink after lab work today?" he suggested effortlessly. "Maybe you and your girlfriend could join Azimi and me at that little café on the corner?"

Azimi, who had been watching the exchange with mild curiosity, paused for a beat before flashing a wide, easy smile. With a quick nod, he replied, "A great idea. We could all use a drink."

The two *lab techs* exchanged a glance, a silent conversation passing between them before one of them shrugged with a playful smile. "Pourquoi pas?" she said, her tone light. "Why not?"

The four of them stepped out into the fading light, the last of the sun catching on the upper windows of the lycée across the street. It was that soft Parisian hour when everything felt slightly theatrical. They walked to the corner café without ceremony, slipping into the rhythm of an early evening in the neighborhood, which was kept busy by the massive hospital center.

The girls—Dominique and the quieter one, Claire—answered questions with practiced ease. *What was it like working at the Pasteur Institute? Did they enjoy tutoring the medical students? Had they thought about medicine themselves?* Laughter came easily, but it was measured, the kind of charm handed out in just enough doses to keep everyone a little off balance.

They took seats outside, facing the street, the low noise of traffic and a distant saxophone folding into the moment. The beers arrived, and the girls were drinking wine and a Coke. Cigarettes were lit. Azimi leaned toward Dominique with the soft insistence of a man who knew exactly how he sounded, while David, almost without realizing it, found himself watching, studying Azimi—his gestures, the slight lilt in his voice, the way his eyes lingered too long and too deliberately.

It took a moment to register that while Azimi was doing his best to seduce Dominique, David was, in his own way, trying to seduce

Azimi—an awareness that left him both amused and slightly unsettled by the dynamic he found himself in.

Then the conversation turned, and the girls wanted to know about America. *How did he come to study in Paris?*

"Let's speak in English," Dominique insisted.

Azimi broke in, his accent thick, but his words were clear. "I would love to live in America. In fact, I spent some time in Colorado when I was younger."

David blinked, surprised. "Colorado? You've been to the States?"

Azimi smiled. "Yes. A year there, long ago. Skiing, studying… a little of both." His English, though accented, was perfectly serviceable.

"Well, David," Azimi said, swirling the last of his beer, "when I was in high school, I was certain I'd be a professional skier. Ranked nationally in Iran. At seventeen, I nearly made the Olympic team." He gave a small, almost embarrassed smile. "My father agreed to let me pursue it seriously—sent me to a training program in Vail, Colorado. I was there for three months. I loved every minute of it. America was eye-opening."

David raised an eyebrow. "And yet… here you are studying Medicine in Paris."

Azimi switched back into English, as if the language made the story easier to tell. "We'd been working on slalom drills all day. I was tired. My friend wasn't. He suggested one last run—moguls. Halfway down, I hit something. Went over, headlong. Tore the knee badly. I couldn't stand. They carted me off."

He paused, not for effect, just remembering. "Surgery in the morning. Olympic dream finished by afternoon." There was a flicker of something—disappointment, maybe—but he shrugged it off. "My father's a physician. He was sympathetic about it, but clear. *Skiing would become a hobby. Medicine… the more stable path.*"

He glanced across the table. "I went back to Tehran, finish school, did a science year, and came to Paris. My mother's mother was Lebanese and French-speaking, and we still had some relatives just outside Paris. That helped."

He said it all lightly, as if by now it was all past him, and he was very happy to be here drinking beer and on his way to becoming a doctor.

They finished their drinks slowly, the way people do when they're enjoying the company more than the contents of the glass. David insisted on the tab—charming, offhand—and thanked the girls for coming out. Azimi made sure to get Dominique's number before they all drifted together toward the Métro.

At the station entrance, David kissed each girl on both cheeks, a gesture that was a bit exaggerated but well-meaning. "Adieu," he said, "until next week's lab."

The girls smiled, murmured their goodbyes, and peeled off into the crowd.

David and Azimi continued walking as the crowds started to pick up, with offices letting out and the evening commute commencing. After a moment, David spoke.

"We should keep the momentum going," he said. "Come out Friday night. My neighborhood—Les Halles. There are a few bars where American girls tend to collect. I think you'll enjoy it."

Azimi lit up. "That sounds fantastic," he said, almost too quickly. "And I want to hear everything—your university, the parties, the girls. I imagine it was wild."

David grinned. "It had its moments. And this—tonight—this was good. It's nice to speak English again." Azimi replied. David clapped a hand lightly on Azimi's shoulder. "Friday night, then. I'll be your wingman. You've got my word—we'll find some trouble."

Azimi smiled, the kind of smile that lingers a moment too long and nodded. "Trouble sounds perfect."

They rode the Métro a few more stops in silence, but both smiling—half melancholy, half mechanical. When David stood to make his connection, he touched Azimi's shoulder lightly.

"Friday—don't forget," he said. "Though we'll probably bump into each other before then, in class."

Azimi nodded, and David stepped off the metro at the Metro stop Les Halles. He walked up rue St. Denis as the last of the light slipped behind the rooftops and the construction crews packed away their gear. The neighborhood was a total construction site. The street, once known for its shadows, was changing—glass storefronts where there had once been shuttered bars, where there had once been drifters. Young professionals who were connected snapped up the surrounding apartments, anticipating what the future neighborhood would be like.

He crossed in front of Joe Allen's—an American export wrapped in brick and bourbon, pretending it was really a hotspot on the Upper East Side of Manhattan. Inside, the lighting was dim, and the tables were too close. Red leather booths and signed Broadway playbills gave it the patina of familiarity. It was where half the American expats in Paris seemed to orbit, especially the ones filing columns under fake names for magazines back home.

It was also conveniently where Donovan and his colleagues at the unmarked offices of the US embassy liked to conduct their quieter meetings. No one looked twice at two Americans talking over a burger at 2 a.m.

Outside his building on the rue des Innocents, one of the younger *working girls*—Isabelle—gave him a faint, familiar nod. He knew her name only because one of the older women had called to her in the street weeks before. She was cute, almost girlish, with a smile that suggested something sweeter than the trade allowed. Still, some quiet voice in him knew better. That kind of innocence, out here, didn't last long, if at all.

He returned her smile—no more, no less.

She used a room upstairs, like a few of the others. Business had been slow. Fewer footsteps. Longer pauses between doors opening and closing.

The sort of men who once made quiet detours down this street were being steadily pushed out by wine bars, boutique gyms, and the slow creep of tasteful renovation. The neighborhood had grown self-conscious. What had once been discreet was now exposed under better lighting. As such, it had become the sort of place where you might easily bump into a colleague—or worse, a relative. A place where old indulgences began to look less like secrets and more like liabilities. Harder to explain. Harder still to excuse.

David knew that. He also knew that the girls hadn't changed nearly as much as the street around them had. They still lingered in doorways, scanning faces with quiet calculation. The only difference now was that no one wanted to be seen noticing them. Eyes flicked past too quickly, footsteps sped up near the corners where they stood like living shadows. The world had become slicker, faster, and more critical.

He could sense it in the changing smile from Isabelle—the girl with the small attic room two floors above his. Before he knew exactly what she did, when he first noticed her months before, walking up with an older man in the neighborhood, he thought it was likely her father coming to see the small studio that he was helping to rent. He imagined her father thinking that she was too young to be living alone, too soft for this part of the city. Her face had that untouched quality: smooth, pale skin, wide-set eyes the color of iron wet with stormwater, and a mouth that seemed made for saying something sweet.

But sweetness was a mask, and Isabelle wore it well.

He realized how wrong he'd been one night when she stepped out of the shadows near the alley, lit only by the fractured glow of a flickering streetlamp. She looked older there—or maybe just honest. Red lips slightly parted, one hip cocked, her breath blooming white in the cold air. The worn leather of her jacket stretched tight across her chest, and her skirt was the kind that whispered with every step, deliberate and unhurried.

She tilted her head, her voice low, intimate, edged with something darker.

« Tu veux passer un bon moment, chéri? » *'You want to have a good time?'*

David didn't answer right away. The question hung there, drifting in the space between her breath and his silence. Isabelle didn't move. She knew how to wait. Her stillness was a skill, maybe the most valuable one she had. No twitch, no fidget, no nervous energy. Just those eyes—unreadable, catching the lamplight like polished slate. She leaned slightly into the heel of one boot, her weight shifting just enough to make the hem of her coat open and suggest more than it showed. Everything about her was deliberate. Measured. Economical, even in seduction.

"Isabelle," he said finally, the name tasting strange in the cold air. He hadn't meant to say it out loud.

Her smile curled, slow and sly. "So, you *did* catch my name."

He had. And more than that, the way she tucked her cigarette behind her ear when she climbed the stairs. The small scar at the edge of her jaw, like a whisper of a past life. The habit she had of looking away from people just before they finished speaking, as if she already knew what they were going to say.

"Do you always proposition your neighbors?" David asked, voice half a murmur, half a defense.

David wasn't sure, but something in his eye caught the slightest of blushes, "Only the lonely medical students," she replied, as if it were the most obvious thing in the world.

Then she turned, the heel of her boot clicking once against the damp concrete and vanished into the night—not waiting for an answer. She didn't need one.

And David, who had come out for nothing more than a walk, just stood there. Caught between what he knew and what he wanted to pretend he didn't.

He was shocked. "Boy, am I that naive?"

He felt a flicker of something—pity, maybe. Some of the girls were just scraping by, single mothers or migrants who'd run out of other options. One of them, the one with the low voice and careful lipstick, leopard skin dress, always tried to catch his eye. He never took the bait.

But tonight, as he passed Isabelle, something shifted. An idea—not entirely formed—settled into place. He didn't smile, didn't pause. He just kept walking, slower now, already turning the thought over in his mind like a cigarette he wasn't sure he would light. He told himself he, too, was a professional now, and that professionals do not leave critical events to chance. He would ensure that Azimi had a very good time on Friday night and, accordingly, would be indebted to his new American friend. As he turned the key to his flat, a clear smile spread across his face. He had the beginnings of a plan.

Chapter 11

<u>Secure Briefing Room, sub-level 3, CIA Headquarters</u>

Langley, Virginia, 07:00

The room was cool, if not chilly, the thermostats always set to 67 degrees. Coffee, bagels, and donuts were set out on a side table.

Seated around the oval table were Stewart Blake from the CIA Directorate of Operations (DO); Patricia Ross, Iran Desk, Langley; Jonathan Buchanan, Head of the Mid-East Desk, Langley; Amir Ahmad, Special Operations Group (SOG); Bill Donovan, Deputy Chief of Station, CIA Paris; John Kelly, CIA Station Chief, Cairo; Peter McIntosh, NSA Liaison; Andrew Schneider, Technical Operations Officer; and Joe Anthony, in-house legal counsel. Each took a specific seat reflecting their roles, with operational leads positioned close to the head of the table and support staff distributed evenly among them.

Two large TV monitors were mounted on the wall at the end of the room, and at the other end, a state-of-the-art rear-projection screen. On the side wall are maps of the Middle East, Egypt, and Iran. On the opposite wall was a glass window, behind which a technician, in addition to recording and videotaping the proceedings, ran the projection TV.

Patricia Ross, head of the Iran desk, stood up, arms crossed, eyes scanning the seated officials. Her voice was calm, measured.

"We're calling it Operation BLUEWAVE," she said. "Eight deep-cover operatives. Inserted under non-official cover. Their objective: reconstitute our human intelligence network in-country—starting in Yazd Province."

Stewart Blake, Director of Covert Operations, continued:

"As you are all aware, the situation in Iran has deteriorated beyond our initial projections. With civil unrest escalating and the very real possibility of a prolonged hostage scenario taking shape, our existing network in-country has effectively collapsed. Our assets have gone to ground, and those who haven't are likely doing everything they can to sever ties—changing locations and cutting off all contact. The working assumption, corroborated by signals and human intelligence, is that they're lost to us. Permanently."

"Which leaves us in the position we're in now: starting over, from scratch."

Patricia Ross from the Iran desk and Amir Ahmadi of the Special Operations Group would spearhead the preliminary phase of a high-stakes operation. Backed by the stations in Cairo and Paris, they were piecing together a plan to insert eight seasoned operatives deep into hostile territory. The mission, straightforward in theory, would be anything but in practice: essentially to create believable legends for each operative, embed them seamlessly, and support their efforts to rebuild a shattered network—asset by asset, city by city—from the ashes of what had been lost. It was an ambitious plan. Risky. But given the alternative, there was no choice.

He paused just long enough to let the words settle, then inclined his head toward the man seated to his left.

"As Amir will explain, the newly formed Islamic Revolutionary Guard Corps—what they're calling the IRGC—is rapidly becoming the dominant internal security force in the country. They're young, ideologically driven, and answer directly to Khomeini. This is not SAVAK in a new uniform. These men are true believers."

Amir leaned forward, setting a worn leather folder on the table. His voice, when he spoke, was quiet but assured. Amir had come a long way at the CIA. The son of an Iraqi engineer blacklisted by the government, Amir arrived in the United States at the age of 8 under political asylum. His family settled in working-class Dearborn, where his father found work as a machinist. Amir assimilated—quickly, his mother thought too quickly—losing his accent and abandoning homemade lunches by high school. Yet every slur or cold glance deepened his resolve, never letting him forget who he was.

At the University of Michigan, he joined ROTC and majored in International Relations with a minor in Middle Eastern Studies. Already fluent in Iraqi Arabic, he picked up conversational Farsi and French during his studies. Graduating in the top 5% of his class, he stood out as a calm, intense leader who commanded attention even in silence.

After commissioning, he qualified for Army Ranger School, then passed selection for 1st Special Forces Operational Detachment–Delta (Delta Force). He was one of the youngest to do so at the time. He earned his place not through bravado but through precision, control, and an ability to read terrain—human and physical. He's deeply American in outlook but retains an intuitive grasp of Middle Eastern cultural nuance, making him invaluable in HUMINT operations. From there, he was a perfect fit for the newly formed Special Operations Group (SOG) of the CIA.

Amir continued:

"From what the analysts working with Ms. Ross have learned, they've begun consolidating control over the airports, the border crossings, and the communications infrastructure. Their surveillance net is crude, but it's growing—and effective. Informants are everywhere. Mostly students. Many were recruited from radical Islamic societies on university campuses. They're not in it for money. They want purification. Martyrdom. That makes them dangerous."

A nod to the aid behind the glass window brought a grainy black-and-white image onto the projection screen—three young men standing before the American embassy, fists raised, their faces half-covered by scarves.

"Anyone entering the country under false documentation will be scrutinized. They're watching for accents, for Western mannerisms. They're ruthless in identifying and dismantling threats. And they operate with impunity."

He looked around the table, his gaze briefly lingering on each face.

"It is for this reason that although our operatives will all have reliable cover and legends, as we will outline, we feel that a covert insertion is safest to keep their names off the radar of any Iranian intelligence."

"Our margin for error is nonexistent. One misstep and we're not just dealing with arrests. We're dealing with disappearances. Public ones."

He closed the folder.

As Amir finished, Patricia Ross continued, eyes on her notes.

"We are recruiting sympathetic native-born Iranians, expats living abroad, some here in the USA, most, however, in Europe. We are working to repatriate them before the insertion of our operatives. I would like to emphasize that this is for support purposes only. The expatriates we're recruiting will serve as logistical scaffolding—nothing more. Safehouses, language buffers, access to local networks, perhaps even supply sourcing. But the operatives themselves—the ones we will be sending in—will be ours. Career officers. Highly trained, deeply vetted. A majority are Farci speakers, combat-capable, fully cleared for Tier One insertion."

She tapped the edge of her folder with a manicured fingernail, the gesture sharp, controlled.

"Some of them have spent time embedded in non-official cover roles across the region. Others come from the Special Activities Division. And all of them," she paused, her eyes moving briefly to Blake, "understand the stakes. This isn't reconnaissance. It's a reconstruction. We're rebuilding human intelligence capabilities from the ground up in a country that now considers every American a hostile actor."

Across the table, someone shifted uncomfortably. The truth had a way of doing that in rooms like this.

Amir said nothing, but inside he was already reviewing the names—men and women he knew, some intimately. People he'd trained with, bled with. Some he had personally pulled out of other countries under fire. Now they would be going into Iran. And possibly not all of them would come back.

Ross exhaled slowly. "They won't have diplomatic protection. They won't have fallback cover. If something goes wrong, it will go wrong fast. That's why we build the net first. Not after."

She closed the folder.

"This isn't just a mission. It's a bet. And we only get to place it once."

"We have already narrowed it down to a list of 10-15 possible people."

Stewart Blake, the formidable head of the Directorate of Operations, folded his hands on the table and leaned forward.

"Wouldn't the simplest course of action," he said, tone even but unmistakably pointed, "be to loop in the Israelis? They've been involved in Iran for a decade or more and have had good relations; they have sources and the incentive to do so. They'd leap at this."

The room tensed, ever so slightly.

"Yes," she replied. "There would be advantages—no question. Mossad has assets in-country, and they've offered cooperation before. But for now, the State Department has vetoed that option."

"Why?"

She exhaled lightly through her nose, more weary than dismissive. "The optics, mostly. Langley's involvement is deniable. A joint operation with the Israelis—if exposed—complicates everything. The Secretary of State remains uncertain about the direction this new government in Iran will take the country. If we partner with the Israelis, the narrative writes itself: Zionist interference, Western subversion, the whole package. Tehran would seize on it. And we're trying to build a network, not incite the revolution."

Blake didn't respond, but his silence spoke volumes. He was a realist who knew that the State always played the long game, even when lives were on the line.

Amir's eyes didn't leave the center of the table. He had worked with Mossad before. Efficient. Brutal. Effective. But also, unpredictable. This needed to be clean. Controlled. Entirely under their roof.

Ross looked around the room, her voice quieter now.

"We are the only ones who can do this without turning it into a proxy war. At least for now. We build the network ourselves—or we walk away. And walking away is not an option."

She continued,

"Initial assessments indicate that the safest method of insertion will be via helicopter," Ross said, flipping to a marked page in her briefing binder. "Ideally, we deploy under the cover of darkness, just beyond the perimeter of a modest population center—close enough for eventual transit, but remote enough to avoid early detection."

She adjusted her glasses and looked up.

"Our analysis suggests a location approximately eighty kilometers northwest of Yazd. Sparse settlements. Arid, uneven terrain. There are no major roads in or out, and most crucially, virtually no communication infrastructure to speak of. It's a dead zone. Exactly what we want." Amir nodded thoughtfully. "If we choose the right month, there's little worry about a sudden sandstorm crippling the helicopters. The desert winds shift seasonally, and during spring—March to early May—the skies over Yazd tend to hold steady. Clear nights, calm winds. Perfect conditions for a covert insertion."

Ross added, "That window also gives us a narrow margin for planning and training, but it's critical. A sandstorm in transit isn't just an inconvenience—it's a mission failure. We can't afford to be grounded or forced into a premature landing."

Ross continued. "The area is effectively blind to radar observation, assuming we can neutralize the only functioning electrical substation feeding the district. According to Mr. Schneider, bringing that node offline will be relatively straightforward. Andrew Schneider nodded affirmatively. A power disruption window of ten to twenty-five minutes should give us the corridor we need."

She looked across the table.

Amir glanced at the map again. Yazd was a desert city—ancient, sun-scorched, and now bracing under the tightening grip of the IRGC. The zone she described was perfect in theory. In practice, it would depend on the weather, the rotor noise, and how quickly the Revolutionary Guard responded when the power went out.

Lang closed the folder.

"We'll need to be in and out before they even realize the lights are off."

Amir shifted in his chair, his expression unreadable at first—but the crease between his brows told a different story. He spoke quietly, but with unmistakable weight.

"We're assuming we can vanish into the terrain before they know we're there," he said. "But we also have to assume that the minute the lights come back on, they'll know something's wrong. And they'll respond—fast. And even if our case officers succeed in evading the initial hunt, the whole IRGC apparatus will be obsessed with capturing the intruders."

Lang glanced at him. "You think the response will be immediate?"

Jonathan Buchanan, Head of the Middle East desk, was quiet until now,

"I would certainly think so. The IRGC's internal structure is more agile than we've given them credit for. Decentralized command, direct communications to local units. If a grid goes dark for more than a few minutes, they'll scramble a response—even if they don't know why yet. And once they realize it coincides with a potential incursion, they'll hit the area hard."

He leaned forward, tapping a knuckle against the map.

"This zone around Yazd is quiet now. But once the power comes back online, they'll be watching for heat signatures, tire tracks, anything that doesn't belong. We'll have maybe a two-hour window before they start knocking on doors and ruffling all the feathers."

Blake interjected. "We've planned for rapid dispersal. Once the teams are down, they break into pairs, move in separate directions, and vanish into prepared safe points. Each with a separate objective."

Amir didn't flinch. "That's fine on paper. But what happens when one of those pairs misses a checkpoint? The moment that the blackout ends, every minute becomes a liability."

Ross studied him carefully. "What's your alternative?"

"Staggered insertion," Amir replied. "Smaller units dropped farther apart. Spread the footprint. Make it harder to trace. Maybe even run a diversion—something to draw their attention toward a different province."

Blake's voice was low. "Diversion increases exposure."

Amir met his gaze. "So does a high-profile hunt for foreign infiltrators in the center of the country. Do you want this operation to last longer than twelve hours? We need to think like insurgents. Not tourists."

Ross nodded slowly. In the end, she had to admit that she was an analyst, a planner perhaps, but with minimal, if any, field experience.

"All right. We'll run the alternate scenario. But keep the blackout plan on the board. If we get the green light from the NSA, we may only get one chance at this."

The conversation moved on, but Amir's thoughts stayed rooted in the silence that would follow the blackout— It would be far better if an insertion could be pulled off without raising any suspicions at all.

Patricia Ross continued:

"Assuming the insertion goes as planned," Ross continued, "the immediate priority will be for our case officers to establish contact with the local personnel that we've quietly established inside the country. However, these are not operatives, nor are they seasoned assets— they're native Iranians, complete amateurs without any training. Their only objective will be to assist our assets in establishing residence in the community and a believable cover.

She looked around the room, the gravity in her voice unmistakable.

"Their story is simple but effective. They left Iran mostly to study or for work, but with the fall of the Shah's regime and the old order toppled, they are excited to return and fight for the future they believe in. That narrative gives them plausible cover, rooted in genuine conviction."

Ross's eyes narrowed slightly. "We've been meticulous in our vetting. Every one of them is clean—no political skeletons hidden away, no histories that might raise eyebrows or draw unwanted scrutiny. If they're questioned, their loyalty to the new regime will appear unimpeachable."

She tapped a finger against the folder. "These contacts will be the initial lifeline for our inserted teams—they will arrange for lodging, work, and assist with local knowledge.

Amir leaned back, considering the delicate balance. "We're relying as much on ideology as on training. Their motivations will keep them loyal—at least until the danger rises, and what have we told them about how long they would be staying in Iran, and what measures we'd take to help them return to Europe or the U.S.?"

Ross hesitated briefly, weighing her words carefully. "Yes. We've discussed this extensively. For now, at least, leaving Iran won't be an issue for the Iranian nationals involved in the operation. We've made it clear to them that their help is only temporary." She paused, scanning the room.

"Johathan. Any further questions?" She paused just long enough for silence to feel deliberate. "If not, let's plan to reconvene in a month. With luck, we'll avoid complications. I'll see about arranging a secure video line through the embassies—no need for either of you to make the trip again."

As they rose from their chairs, the atmosphere in the secure room dissipated like cigarette smoke. Blake had begun to gather his folder when Amir touched his sleeve—just a fingertip, barely enough to be noticed by anyone not meant to.

"Stewart," he said, voice quiet, almost apologetic. "A word?"

They stepped aside, two paces into the corridor's gray hush. The walls were lined with acoustic foam; everything spoken here died before it could echo.

Amir kept his eyes fixed on a point just beyond Blake's shoulder. "If this is going to succeed, the insertion needs to be invisible. Not quiet. Not clever. *Invisible.*"

Blake said nothing. He didn't need to. His silence was authorization to continue.

Amir exhaled through his nose. "The Iranians—if they get so much as a whiff that we're in play—they'll go into lockdown. They'll sweep every house, every shack, and double-check every possible defector. You know what they're like when they're nervous."

Blake gave the smallest of nods. A bureaucrat's nod. Not agreement—*acknowledgment.*

"I'm not talking about the usual compartmentalization," Amir added. "I mean total blackout. No briefings outside Langley. No whispers to our friends at DGSE and in the DGS in Cairo. And for God's sake, no analysts trying to run parallel models on an operation they don't understand."

Blake closed the folder, slowly. "Is this a warning, Amir?"

"No." Amir's voice was low, flat. "It's a reminder."

There was a pause—a faint hum from the fluorescent light above.

Then Blake adjusted his cufflink— "I'll see to it. But you understand the risk. If we go that dark, and something goes sideways..."

"Yes, there will be political blowback, but the alternative might be that we lose eight seasoned operatives. And not quietly. If they're taken, it'll be a show. The Iranians will see to that." Blake looked at him for a long moment, then nodded once, this time without ambiguity.

Chapter 12

Les Halles, Paris

David made a date with Thérèse and arranged to meet at Joe Allen's, the American bar just around the corner from his apartment on the Rue Pierre Lescot. He told her that his Persian friend Azimi from medical school would be joining them, along with a 'neighbor' of his, Isabelle, whom he intended to introduce to Azimi. It was billed as a much-needed break from studying, perhaps over a few beers, with a burger and fries. He admitted to Thérèse that although he loved French cuisine, he missed a good burger now and then.

Joe Allen's was "the American Bar" in Paris, a hangout for expats, journalists, actors, and a particular kind of worldly student. It tried to offer a genuine New York-style experience. It was always packed, noisy, and kind of cozy. The waitstaff, mostly cute American girls, were bilingual with a New York attitude, efficient yet sometimes rude. The music from the stereo was a mix of jazz, the Doors, and Carol King. In short, it was like a backstage dressing room where the audience was international, the performance was unspoken, and everyone had a reason to keep their stories just a little bit vague. They arrived a little early and tucked themselves into a booth near the back window. The air was thick with smoke and the hum of a dozen American accents pretending they didn't miss home. At the bar, Jean-Luc, the regular, was pouring bourbons for a pair of NYU students deep in an argument about modern art. David was about to order another beer when he noticed Azimi walk in, dripping wet from the rain.

While in an American bar, Azimi took the opportunity to brush up on his English, which seemed to improve the more he spoke.

"Sorry, David, the Metro was packed and I ended up walking across the river."

"No problem, this is Thérèse, my girlfriend." Thérèse gave David an elbow before kissing Azimi on each cheek.

"My neighbor Isabelle isn't here yet, but she promised she would be here soon."

"Your neighbor??"

"Yeah, on my way home, I bumped into her, and I thought you two would hit it off, so I asked her to join us. I don't think you will be disappointed."

"She is a 'looker' if you get my drift," Therese again gave David an elbow, interjecting, "Les Hommes, vous êtes tous des cochons", *You men are all pigs!*

David signaled for the waitress, and Azimi ordered a Heineken.

David explained that Azimi was Iranian but had spent some time in Colorado skiing, where he had picked up English.

'And how did you like living in America?" Thérèse asked.

"Well, it was great until the accident."

As he was relaying the sad story, David looked up and saw Isabelle enter the bar. He stood up and motioned for her to come to the table.

David gave a two-finger wave, and she spotted them, nodded, and came to the table.

"She's—" Azimi started.

"Yeah," David said. "Told you. Try to be charming."

Isabelle insisted on sliding into the booth next to Azimi, not across. Close enough that her perfume reached him—jasmine, tobacco, something sharper underneath.

At first, David didn't recognize her. The few times he got a good look at her, she was at work on the streets and looked the part; here, she looked completely different. Slightly timid-looking, if not innocent, in a black coat and black boots, with pale skin and very minimal makeup. She could have passed for a sales assistant on Rue St. Honoré, at one of the upscale boutiques.

"This is Azimi," David said. "Azimi, Isabelle."

She offered a cool, dry hand. "Bonsoir."

"Hi," Azimi said. "Enchantée de faire votre connaissance," he responded in French.

David broke in: "Well, since we are in an American establishment and we all speak a little English, I propose we practice our English tonight, OK?" They all laughed and agreed.

Isabelle watched them for a moment, then leaned back, letting them find the rhythm. She ordered champagne without asking what they were drinking.

"You live near David?" Azimi asked.

"Same building. Just above. Thin walls."

David raised his glass. "Tell me something I don't know."

Isabelle gave him a long, knowing look. Then turned her attention back to Azimi.

"I like Americans," she said. "You all act as if you're in a movie."

Therese laughed out loud and agreed.

"Better than thinking we're in a war."

"Are you not?" "No politics, please."

Later, after two more rounds and a few cigarettes, David and Thérèse made their exit. They said something about catching a movie at the cinema. He slapped Azimi's shoulder on the way out and gave Isabelle a look that meant: *He's yours now, remember our agreement!*

She didn't blink. 1500 francs for the night was much better than the usual, and this Azimi seemed nice and was cute to boot.

Isabelle and Azimi left Joe Allen's just after midnight. By then, the rain had stopped, but Paris was still wet and so quiet. Rue Pierre Lescot shimmered under streetlamps, their reflections broken by puddles.

Azimi offered his arm, not quite sure why. Isabelle didn't take it, but she didn't walk away either. They agreed to have another drink at his small studio on the Ile de la Cité.

It wasn't really a studio, really a *chambre de bonne,* maids' quarters on the 7th floor of an old building —top floor walk-up, drafty windows, books stacked where furniture should be. But it was clean, the sheets were fresh, and he'd tried to clean up before leaving for Joe Allen's in case he did *get lucky.*

"Sorry," he said, brushing a jacket off the couch. "Still figuring out how to be a grown-up."

She turned to him, one brow raised, and smiled. "Want a drink?" He asked.

She shook her head. "No. Just come here."

He did.

It was easy between them, but not simple. She kissed like someone who'd been kissed too many times to bother pretending. He responded as if trying not to get it wrong. She let him think he hadn't. Their bodies moved together with quiet precision, a rhythm surprisingly familiar and instinctive. There were no declarations, no promises, only the shared understanding of touch and warmth. Hands traced, lips lingered, and for a brief while, the outside world—the cramped chambre de bonne, the drafty windows, the books stacked like barricades—fell away.

When it ended, they lay side by side, breathing in sync, a faint smile on her lips, his fingers entwined with hers, neither speaking. There was a calm in that intimacy, a fleeting equilibrium where desire was both acknowledged and contained. Nothing more was required, nothing more demanded—just this, and it was enough.

Later, she lay back against his pillow, smoking one of his Marlboros, her bare shoulder visible in the glow of the desk lamp he forgot to turn off. He wanted to ask something—what she thought of him, what she was doing tomorrow, what exactly she did for work—but none of it felt right.

Instead, he said, "I'm glad David introduced us."

She looked at him, expression unreadable. Then she nodded once.

"David always introduces people when he likes them."

Azimi laughed, not sure why that sounded true.

He fell asleep with her next to him. She stayed until dawn. Left quietly, without waking him. A cigarette butt in the ashtray and a faint trace of her perfume on the sheets were the only proof she'd been there.

She didn't leave a note. In the end, this was work.

As she descended the narrow stairs into the soft, quiet early morning, a slow smile crossed her face.

When she bumped into David again, she thought she'd have to tell him one thing:

If medicine didn't work out, she was certain that he had a future as a pimp.

Chapter 13

Paris

The week passed quickly, as they often did, blurred by lectures, late nights, and too much coffee. On Tuesday, in the pathology lab, Azimi spotted David as he entered the room and broke into a wide smile. He crossed the distance in a few strides and gave him an unexpected hug.

"My friend," he said warmly. "I am truly indebted to you."

David grinned. "I told you I'd take care of you, didn't I? So? Was she everything I promised?"

Azimi gazed upward, as if searching for words in the fluorescent lights.

"I can't stop thinking about her. But she left early, without giving me her number. Or even an address."

He looked at David with something close to desperation. "You have to help me find her. I think I'm in love."

David hesitated. Just long enough.

He was going to have to be careful now—very careful. If Azimi happened to wander through Les Halles at the wrong time, he might recognize her on the street. That would unravel everything. The entire charade, the 1500 francs, the carefully staged evening at Joe Allen's—all of it depended on Azimi never knowing the truth. That Isabelle was not just a neighbor but was, in fact, a professional.

David recovered quickly.

"You need to get out more, my friend," he said lightly. "This is Paris. There are women like Isabelle everywhere looking for a bit of fun, no strings attached. You're not in Iran anymore. Here, women don't hide behind burkas."

Azimi didn't smile. He was still thinking about her. David lowered his voice slightly, just enough to sound conspiratorial. "She recently told me she might be moving to Montparnasse, to be closer to her sister. I never had her number either—you know this isn't America, not every apartment has a phone. It was pure chance I ran into her last week."

Azimi nodded, slowly. It was enough—for now.

David exhaled quietly. And made a mental note: keep him away from Les Halles.

David smiled to himself. He was about to suggest they go out again the following weekend—another drink, maybe this time in St. Germain, another "chance" encounter—then thought better of it. He was being paid well after all. A medical education wrapped in a paycheck. Fifteen hundred francs, however, was fifteen hundred francs, after all. He couldn't afford to bankroll Parisian romance every Saturday night. And it was unlikely that the accountants at Paris Station would consider another 1500 francs a reimbursable expense. He smiled again, more to himself this time.

Instead, David offered a diplomatic smile. "I'll see what I can do about finding her," he said, carefully. "But in the meantime, I was thinking… I've never been to a football match in Paris. I thought it might be time."

Azimi raised an eyebrow. "You mean *le vrai* football?"

David grinned. "Don't start. I played in high school and didn't miss a game when I was at Michigan. But please, let's not compare 'soccer' to real American football. They're not even in the same league. Saturday, Paris Saint-Germain will play Olympique de Marseille. And from what I'm told, that's like Michigan vs. Ohio State."

Azimi gave him a playful shove and laughed. "You Americans and your helmets. Try taking a corner kick with a cracked rib and no time-outs."

David chuckled and leaned back. "So, are you in? I'll see if I can score some tickets. It might be good for us—to unwind after a week of dissecting cadavers and staring at tumor cells."

Azimi nodded, already picturing the stadium—the chanting crowd, the floodlights cutting through the soft Paris mist.

"Deal. Just don't wear your college jacket. You'll embarrass me."

David gave a lazy salute. "No promises."

Azimi leaned in, his voice lowered as if sharing a guilty secret.

"Just wondering… You think there'll be single girls at the game? Who knows—we might both hit homeruns."

David smirked. "Wrong sport, *mon ami*. But I like optimism."

They clinked their coffee cups as they returned to arranging the slides on their tables, as the specimens began to arrive. An unofficial seal on the weekend plan.

He had to admit it—by the time the weekend rolled around, David was genuinely excited about the game. He rarely missed a Saturday matchup in Ann Arbor and was curious to see how this European experience would compare.

Azimi, for his part, was just grateful that his new best friend had managed to score such incredible seats.

From the moment the match began, the stadium pulsed with raw, unrelenting energy. It was electric. More intense, even, than the Michigan vs. Ohio State games he'd grown up revering. It felt tribal. Passionate. Like something primal was unfolding. For ninety full minutes, it truly did feel like the most important thing happening in the world.

Paris Saint-Germain edged out a wild 5–4 victory, and as the final whistle blew, the cold Paris air seemed to sharpen everything—the buzz of adrenaline, the crush of people, the thrum of shared experience. It wasn't just a game. It was a moment. And for David and Azimi, it solidified a bond that felt less like friendship and more like fraternity.

They capped the night with one last drink at a quiet brasserie, both of them worn out but wired, before heading their separate ways.

Sunday was for study—grueling hours ahead filled with textbooks, lectures, and the inevitable march of Pathology lab.

But David's mind kept drifting forward. There was next weekend's meeting with Donovan—and the so-called "big wigs" flying in from Washington. Whatever was coming, he knew that it wasn't just about school anymore.

Chapter 14

Paris Flea Market

The flea market at Clignancourt was a labyrinth—a sprawl of alleys, covered stalls, and low-slung arcades that twisted through the northern fringe of Paris like an unspoken agreement between the city and its past. There were serious antique dealers, along with junk collectors, but it was among the junk that the real bargains could be had.

By mid-morning, it was already humming. Vendors smoked Gauloises behind folding tables stacked with old binoculars, vintage records, mismatched porcelain, silverware, military ephemera—objects of uncertain origin and shifting value. One man sold typewriters with the discretion of a fence. Another claimed his stack of film posters came directly from Cinéma du Panthéon before the renovation. No one believed him, but that wasn't the point.

The rain, earlier, had left a sheen on the cobblestones. The light filtered through it all in patches—gray, indirect, never quite committing to brightness. Somewhere, a radio played Serge Gainsbourg & Jane Birkin singing over and over again: "Je t'aime moi non plus", the sound fading in and out like memory.

It was a place of negotiations—spoken and not. Prices, yes, but also truths. You didn't just buy here. You tested your eye, your instincts, your cover story. If you lingered long enough, you'd see it: a discreet handoff between dealers, a glance too quick to be friendly, a man in a long coat who wasn't really looking for antiques at all. It was, after all, a place for shady deals, and David was here for just such a meeting. He made sure to arrive early and took a little tour of the market.

Among the maze of stalls in the Marché aux Puces, in a narrow passageway between a shuttered clock repairer and a stall selling pre-war aviation goggles, a café hid itself in plain sight. Chosen for this very reason, it wasn't marked by signage—just a battered green awning and a door with a brass handle worn to a dull shine.

By now, it was barely 10:00—too early for any lunch crowd. The timing of the meeting had been intentional. They'd arranged to meet well before the midday rush.

As David turned the corner onto rue Paul Bert, he spotted a man across the street, in his mid-thirties, thumbing through a carton of old magazines and records, with a set of Walkman headphones on his head. He looked familiar. Yes—one of Jim Waldon's guys, the same one who had shadowed their meeting on the Quai, back on the Île Saint-Louis. Nearby, his partner sat at an outside table, reading the racing form, also with the same-looking Walkman headphones. And then David saw it—a swell beneath his jacket, just above the waistband. Not big, not obvious, but enough. A pistol holstered low.

Inside the cafe, 'La Terrace des Puces,' it was warm, cramped, and mostly forgotten. Two tables—three, if you counted the one in the back where an overhead bulb flickered without conviction. The espresso machine hissed with a kind of defiance. A television above the bar played muted rugby highlights that no one was watching.

As David stepped in, the man behind the bar gave him a nod and gestured toward the staircase leading to the second floor.

Amir was already seated, a chipped demitasse in front of him and a folded copy of *Le Monde* on the table. He didn't look up when the door opened. Just shifted his eyes slightly, enough to clock the person entering. Bill Donovan was making a call on the bar phone, and Jim Waldon was also present.

Patricia Ross, in from Langley that morning, sat without ceremony, placing a battered canvas satchel on the floor beside her. They didn't exchange pleasantries. A few documents lay on the table.

Stewart Blake, of the CIA's Directorate of Operations, was already seated. Bill Donovan introduced him to David. As they shook hands, David thought to himself that if the DO was here, there would certainly be more security than Walden's two buddies he had recognized downstairs.

"We can't move on this with the DGSE watching," Blake said quietly. "They'll want in, and if they want in, STATE will demand a seat, and then it's a goddamn parade."

Amir didn't raise his voice. He rarely did.

"We have six ready. Three of them have a history in-country, in some cases. Embedded, then pulled. All native speakers, fluent in Belgian-accented French, trained, briefed, and anxious for reinsertion. They've worked closely with us before. Quiet work. Clean work."

He paused, letting the weight of it settle.

"They operated under Belgian cover—executives for an energy consortium in Tehran. Paper trail's still good. They've maintained those industry links, particularly in the oil and gas sector. Our assessment is that, should they resurface, no one would bat an eye. Belgian businessmen looking to rekindle contracts. Simple."

Blake nodded without looking up. He was folding the corner of a dossier, slowly, methodically. He hesitated to mention that he already knew the six agents that were to be inserted. In fact, they had already been selected and vetted by the Directorate of Operations at Langley.

He interviewed them personally. Their briefings, when they were summoned back to Langley, focused on the mission's real objectives. They were told that the true objective—the real mission—was not to be revealed to anyone else within the Paris station.

Amir continued. "Then there's Ali Haddad. Jordanian American. Telecommunications contractor—real one, not the paper kind. Five years across the region. SIGINT specialist. Yemen, Lebanon, Helmand Province."

Speaks Persian with a Mashhadi accent—picked it up near the Turkmen border. That alone buys him breathing room if they pull him over. Knows how to operate when there's no one coming to get him out."

"And the Canadian?"

"Leyla Karimi," Leyla grew up in Montreal but spent her early teens in Isfahan before the family fled. Family left under duress. Cultural chameleon, equally at ease at embassy functions or in a village tea house. She used her academic work as cover to move through Kurdistan and the Caspian corridor, quietly collecting intel on rail hubs and infrastructure. Completed her college education and a year of graduate school in Architecture at Cornell. With her language skills, she was recruited by us just before graduation. She's gone in under academic grants—field research on rural architecture. That's real, too. She's published. Has the natural ability to walk in and out of villages most of us can't even pronounce."

"And the flaw?" Blake said. He always asked.

"She's reactive," Amir said. "When it's personal, she doesn't always stay between the lines. She has contacts among the Lurs and the Kurds. Deep ones. If anything happens to them, she might improvise."

Blake gave a soft, skeptical hum. "What else is new?"

Amir tapped the last file. "Potential fifth. Zarah Shirazi, Mashhad University of Medical Sciences, then Tehran University, now a physician in Paris. She walked in on her own—Beirut consulate. Gave us just enough to get curious."

"She came to us?"

"Asked about studying in the U.S. That was her pretext. But she wanted to be useful. Her father was a pediatrician until the secret police ruined him. That was the crack we needed."

"She trained?"

"Camp Peary, full rotation. Syria, then Iraq. She passed both."

Blake was silent for a moment, then: "Language?"

"Native Persian. Fluent French. Arabic is more than sufficient. Her medical cover gives us insertion flexibility—clinics, hospitals, even universities. Being a woman is an asset here. She gets into places our male officers can't."

"If anyone is suspicious, what's the reason for her return?"

Amir slid the photograph across the table. Grainy. Headscarf askew. Eyes hard, watching something just out of frame.

"She's returning excited to be part of the revolution and secondarily to care for her mother, with advanced diabetes, complications with the legs. A daughter returning to a sick parent. Shouldn't be suspicious. Not yet."

Blake didn't touch the photo. Just stared at it for a moment.

"We'll need to build out that backstory. Medical records. Neighbors."

"It's already in motion," Amir said.

Blake leaned back, the chair creaking. "She's our fifth?"

Amir nodded. "If you'll have her."

The silence that followed wasn't uncertain. It was a calculation.

"We still need at least two more," Ross noted. "As we discussed, we thought we would have three in the Tehran region, two in Mashhad, two in and around Isfahan, and possibly one in or around Karaj."

The room had settled into silence, the kind that suggested the meeting was winding down—until Donovan spoke.

"David, I am sure by now you are a little bewildered. I am sure you've never been to a meeting such as this one."

David, who barely moved throughout the whole meeting, answered:

"Yes, sir, once again, how do I fit in??

Bill continued, voice low and deliberate: "How's your friendship with Azimi shaping up? Close enough to mean something? Close enough that he'd trust you—without hesitation?"

"Well, I think it's going well, we are great pals, if not best friends."

"Here it is. Azimi's family comes from Yazd and still lives there. It is the spiritual center of Iran's Zoroastrian community and lies between the deserts of Kavir and Lut. It is an arid environment. Perfect for a helicopter insertion. That is as long as there isn't a sandstorm! It is here in this region that the fifth floor feels that we should plan our insertion. The heat is dry but can be unforgiving. Our team will need a safe house for at least 48-72 hours, depending on weather conditions. From Yazd, we'll arrange for them to get to their respective objectives. The first 2 days will be the most dangerous. Depending on events, the Revolutionary Guard and what is left of SAVAK will likely be turning over every leaf looking for incursions. The team will need a safe harbor for at least 2-3 days. That is where we think your friends' families can assist us. You'll have to approach this very carefully. Let's not do anything just yet. We can discuss this privately."

Stewart Blake stood up and began to leave. "Amir, let's keep working on those candidates. I don't want to find out at the last minute that there are issues, understood?"

"Yes, sir."

Patricia Ross gathered her papers with practiced precision, her eyes already on Donovan.

"It's nearing that time," she said flatly. "We need to loop in Special Activities and SOC-D. Route, timing, contingencies—not the specifics, generalities. But let's hear all the options.

She paused just long enough to make sure he was listening.

"Egypt's the cleanest option, but Turkey or even the Gulf has its advantages. Fewer eyes, better lift capacity if we need it."

Donovan said nothing. He knew better.

Ross continued, voice even.

"I want insertion windows for both staging sites by the end of the month."

At the door, Blake stopped. He turned back, expression unreadable.

"One last point," he said. "This operation must remain opaque. Completely."

His gaze moved slowly across the room.

"If the Revolutionary Guard detects even the suggestion of an insertion, our assets in Yazd will not survive. They'll be located, isolated, and removed. It will be very public and very permanent."

He didn't wait for acknowledgement. He turned and left.

As David stood, he caught a glimpse through the window—Blake and Patricia Ross moving quickly toward the main street behind the restaurant. The two familiar watchers were already in place, now joined by two more men, broad-shouldered and efficient. Without hesitation, they closed in, forming a loose perimeter around the Langley pair and steering them toward a waiting sedan.

The doors shut. The engine roared. Within seconds, the car was gone.

As David watched on, he felt a tap on his shoulder. He turned to meet Donovan's eyes. "Let's take a walk."

They slowly descended the steps and exited the restaurant onto rue Paul Bert. As they walked deep inside the labyrinth of the market, Bill began.

"We must approach this carefully with Azimi. We cannot afford to spook him. Continue doing what you've been doing and maintain a close friendship for now. Don't let on that we're looking to ask him for anything. Casually, try to get some insight as to his family situation back home? What's the situation like? Is there political activity? Is there anxiety within the community? What do his other family members do, and what businesses are they in? Remember, our goal is to find a safe location for our assets to remain for at most 3 days, so they can be dispersed separately without arousing suspicion. Ideally, we would be looking for a nondescript neighborhood, preferably one where transient population with varied ethnicities is the norm. Any eventual building should have limited visibility from main roads and only a few entry points. One entrance is ideal. Two, if there's a rear alley that can't be seen from the main street. Nothing with direct exposure. Nothing near a mosque, police kiosk, or military post. And absolutely nothing close to the bazaar—the IRGC watches those crowds like hawks."

They crossed under the Peripherique, the main highway that circles Paris, and a black sedan was waiting for Bill Donovan. As he opened the back door, he motioned toward the Metro entrance. David took the hint: "Just keep doing what you're doing for now, I'll contact you in a week or two, and we'll see where we go from there."

David turned toward the entrance of the Métro, a knot tightening in his gut. The feeling had been with him since they stepped out of the meeting, too subtle for him to mention anything, now insistent. He knew better than to ignore it. Those months of training years ago had somehow become second nature. At the corner café, he paused, crouching as if to tie his shoe, eyes flicking to the plate-glass window beside him. The reflection confirmed what he had already suspected: a man, nondescript in every way but one—David had seen him earlier. Once on the boulevard. Again, near the restaurant.

Coincidence? Perhaps. But he'd learned that coincidences were rare and to be suspect.

The man turned away as David hesitated, appearing to drop something into a bin. Too casually, he thought, too clean.

David descended the steps into the Métro, only to double back quickly through the underpass and emerge across the street. He didn't need to look. He knew.

And then he saw him again—same man, now angling toward the Metro station with sudden urgency.

Not a coincidence.

He was being tailed.

David slipped into the café, pulse steady but thoughts moving fast. Training kicked in—reflexive, automatic. He'd been taught to spot a tail, break one, lose one in a crowd. That wasn't the problem.

What unsettled him wasn't the pursuit.

It was the question: who was following him?

The DGSE was the most likely. It was France's home turf; they had the assets and the coordination to operate in the open without drawing attention—especially here, in their city, teeming with tourists and noise. They would've certainly known the DO had flown in on a private jet that morning.

But a darker thought crept in—the Iranians. Had they been tipped off? He dismissed it, then reconsidered. That would be far worse.

He took a table near the back and ordered a beer. Drank half. Left a few coins on the Formica and stepped back into the din of the crowd.

Outside, he paused briefly at the Métro map by the entrance. Just long enough to get his bearings, to decide. Then he crossed to the opposite corner and descended into the underground again, blending with the crowd of teenagers and African immigrants.

He took the metro to Gare de l'Est, got off as the doors were closing, and made the connection. Standard protocol. From there, he made his way toward the Chaussée d'Antin stop—toward the noise, chaos, and anonymity of the Galeries Lafayette department store.

It had always been his preferred method for evading surveillance. Multiple levels. Dozens of exits. Too many variables for a single or even a double tail to control.

He spent twenty careful minutes inside, slipping between perfume counters and crowded escalators, doubling back through men's outerwear and seasonal sales. Watching. Listening. Vanishing.

Finally, confident he was clean, he exited through the rear doors and reentered the Métro.

Home was a quick ten minutes away. But as he emerged from the Chatelet station and climbed to the top of the stairs, she was there blocking the way, smiling.

"David, what a pleasure to see you again."

The voice stopped him cold.

Flawless English. Dark hair, Familiar face.

He hesitated—trying to match the accent to the woman in front of him. Then it hit him.

Elena. The sweet, wide-eyed Greek student backpacking through Europe. Or rather, Rachel Zamir, one of Mossad's most adept field operatives in Paris.

Still smiling, she slipped seamlessly into English, her voice now cool and without any trace of an accent.

"How have you been? And your medical studies—how's that going?"

David, still mildly in shock, remained silent. Ashamed. The tail hadn't been French or Iranian. It had been *Israeli.*

And he hadn't shaken her. Not even close. Rachel was no longer the innocent backpacking student that he remembered. She was stunningly well-dressed, sophisticated, and confident. Flawlessly made up, every detail enhanced her natural beauty without shouting for attention. And so confident, undeniably so—she didn't need to say a word; her presence said everything.

Playing dumb, he managed a wry smile and sarcastically responded:

"Elena? Or is it, Rachel? How nice to see you again."

They began to climb the stairs together. At the top, she leaned in, tone shifting.

"We need to talk."

David gave a slow nod. "OK, let's go up to my apartment."

The streets were unnervingly quiet as they made their way to his apartment. Saturday afternoon in Paris, when the city held its breath— the construction workers gone for the weekend, the shops began to close, drawing down their blinds. It was a silence that felt too complete.

She slipped her arm through his as they crossed Rue de Rivoli, a small but deliberate gesture. Inside, she allowed herself a slow smile.

"It's always good to run into old lovers," she said, the words hanging between them like an unspoken accusation.

David returned the smile, guarded.

"You know your street craft does have some merit," she said, also with a smile.

"You did manage to lose our junior agent back at the flea market," she admitted, "that won't help his advancement, but you overlooked the two other more senior officers trailing you and Monsieur Donovan from the meeting."

She let that settle, then added without preamble, one of our men recognized you from my old report and rang me. "I knew where you lived, of course. Once you slipped back into the Métro, it was only a matter of time before I caught up with you."

As they entered his apartment, Rachel got right to the point.

Her eyes darkened, and the quiet edge in her voice sharpened.

"We want in!"

David blinked, unprepared for the bluntness.

"What are you talking about, Rachel?"

She didn't flinch. "Your CIA Director of Operations and the head of the Iran Desk at Langley flew in this morning for a meeting at the flea market, of all places. And you think that doesn't set off alarms?"

She paused, measuring her words with care.

"Something big is coming. Something tied to Iran. A major incursion, perhaps. A clandestine operation, a rescue attempt, or a covert insertion? My bet is on the latter."

Rachel's gaze didn't waver. "We want in. We have a stake here, at least as important as yours. Our agents in Iran—our resources—are as vulnerable as yours, if not more so. Additionally, I have been informed that, for reasons unclear, your station chief in Tehran once requested a list of our assets in Iraq. We need to know for sure whether that list was destroyed."

Her voice dropped almost to a whisper, a chill that seemed to reach into the room.

"You know what happens to Israeli spies if they're caught. It's not a thing that allows for a peaceful night's sleep."

There was a long silence. David, clearly realizing that not only was his cover blown to the Israelis but that he was also in way over his head, could only manage a stiff reply: he'd pass the request up the chain.

Rachel gave a small, knowing nod.

"It really is good to see you," she said, her voice smooth, sincere. She paused, just long enough to suggest weight behind the words. "What transpired that night in your flat was not all professional, you know, since then I've thought of you often. We should stay in touch. In our line of work, it pays to have... friends. Keeping the lines open has a way of proving mutually beneficial."

She smiled. The irony in it was unmistakable and entirely intentional.

"Pass it on to your superiors… and let's meet again, let's say for dinner next week?"

She let it hang for a beat, then added lightly, "I'll make a reservation at a nice place. I'm sure, as a 'busy medical student,' you don't get out much. How about next Saturday at the Brasserie Île Saint-Louis? Say… 20:00?"

David nodded his agreement, still a little stunned. As Rachel turned to leave, she paused, reached for his hand, and gave it a gentle squeeze. Then, with practiced ease, she kissed him on each cheek.

"À bientôt, mon amour," she said with a dazzling smile, and then walked out into the hallway—composed, radiant, and entirely in control.

Chapter 15

Paris

Sunday morning arrived too quickly. David hadn't slept well—his mind still restless from the previous day's events. By 8 a.m., he was on the phone, ostensibly to request a medical text.

"Bonjour Monsieur, est-ce bien la librairie Gibert Jeune ? Je cherche une tome de Pathology. C'est un peu urgent, car j'ai un examen cette semaine." "Hello sir, is this Gibert Jeune bookstore? I'm looking for a volume on pathology. It's a bit urgent, because I have an exam this week."

Again, there was a brief pause, and David could hear the line being transferred. The voice of Bill Donovan responded:

"Malheureusement, nous sommes en rupture de stock pour ce numéro, mais une nouvelle livraison est prévue pour le premier du mois."

"Merci, monsieur," David responded. He had to stop to remember the code—a phrase used to arrange a rendezvous discreetly. "Premier du mois," First of the month, signified today at 13:00, Cafe de Flore, Boulevard St.Germain.

Yet even after the coded call, David found no peace of mind. Driven by nervous energy, he decided a run might burn off the static in his nerves. He dressed quickly—old trainers, track bottoms, a worn Michigan sweatshirt that marked him as foreign but not vulnerable—and stepped out into the misty cool Paris morning.

The city was just beginning to stir. He cut east toward the river, his breath visible in the cool air, then turned onto rue de Rivoli. The street was quiet, save for the occasional cyclist and the rustle of early commuters. He kept his pace steady, mechanical—his body moving, but his mind miles away.

At the Louvre, he veered into the Tuileries without thinking, as if muscle memory had taken over. He did his usual two-mile loop among the clipped trees and gravel paths, the palace looming behind him like a disapproving parent. The park was sparsely populated—just dog walkers, a scattering of tourists with cameras, and an old woman feeding pigeons like it was a sacred duty.

Still, nothing settled. The run hadn't cleared his head so much as deepened the fog. Rachel's voice lingered. The meeting. The tail. Pieces of something larger, still unfolding.

By the time he returned to the flat, the air was sharper, and the city louder. He climbed the stairs two at a time, showered quickly, dressed with more care than usual, and left again—this time heading toward the Boulevard Saint-Germain to meet Bill Donovan.

David arrived 10 minutes early and took a seat at a quiet table just outside the cafe, a reasonable distance from the sidewalk. A few minutes later, a middle-aged couple took up a place near the entrance. It wasn't more than 5 minutes later that he spotted Donovan turning the corner off Boulevard Saint-Germain. He made no attempt to blend in today; it was a workday for the commercial attaché at the embassy. He played that part just as well, with self-contained American confidence: the tailored navy coat, the polished shoes, the discreet but expensive Dior scarf knotted just so. He didn't shake David's hand. Just nodded once and took the seat opposite him, setting down a pair of leather gloves and glancing once, deliberately, at the sidewalk behind them.

"Busy today," he said flatly, as if the crowd itself was a threat.

"Always is," David replied. "It's Paris." Donovan didn't smile.

"We've got company?" Donovan murmured, barely turning his head. His eyes flicked toward the couple by the heaters—hats, sunglasses, sitting too still.

"Exactly," David replied. "That's why I needed to see you."

Donovan nodded, expression unreadable. "Go on."

"We were followed yesterday, after the meeting, at the flea market."

"Who was?"

"We were!"

"Continue."

"Zamir. Rachel Zamir. You remember?"

Donovan's expression didn't change, but David could see it register. A memory resurfaced, filed and coded, then quietly relabeled as current.

"She was waiting for me," David went on. "Caught me just after I exited the Métro near my flat."

Donovan leaned back slightly. "And?"

"They must have someone at Le Bourget," David said. "They clocked the tail number as soon as the plane touched down. They were at the flea market too. From what Zamir let slip, they suspect we're planning something in Iran. If that's the case, they want in."

Donovan gave a small nod, his expression unreadable. "Of course they do," he said at last. "They certainly are punching above their weight lately. He reached for his cup, though he didn't drink from it. "You really have to hand it to these Israelis," he added. "They've built an intelligence service nearly on par with the best—and they've barely had a country long enough to grow old men."

David spoke up, "For Israel," he said quietly, "with their neighbors dedicated to their total annihilation, espionage isn't strategy, Bill, it's survival."

"She admitted their assets in Tehran are exposed. Possibly more so than ours. Their risk is real—and growing. She also mentioned something about a list of their assets in Iraq that we kept at the Embassy?"

Donovan didn't speak. His gaze wandered toward the traffic.

"I didn't confirm anything," David added quietly. "I denied it. I told her I'd pass along her concerns to my superiors."

"Which you've now done."

David nodded once. "She's playing it carefully. Just... letting us know they're watching. And that they would like, no, deserve a seat at the table."

He paused, drumming his fingers lightly against the tabletop, the only sign of unease. "It complicates matters. But it might—just might—work in our favor. The Israelis have some reach we don't, methods we can't use. If we include them, it just may work to our benefit."

Donovan looked at David now, fully, searching his face as one might examine a compromised document.

"When does she expect a reply?"

"I agreed to see her on Saturday. Dinner. Brasserie Île Saint-Louis."

Donovan raised a brow.

"Romantic."

"She insisted," David replied evenly. "Said no need for cloak and dagger. Just two old friends reconnecting."

Donovan allowed himself the ghost of a smile. "You're becoming quite the ladies' man!"

He leaned forward again, voice low, deliberate.

"Keep it warm. Keep it vague. Don't commit to anything. And if she presses, make it clear you're not authorized to offer anything concrete. Not yet. Obviously, we will have to inform Langley. And I am sure Buchanan will choose to inform the Secretary of State. Well, as you'll learn soon enough, young David, once the politicians get involved, the whole damn operation tends to drift off course."

A silence settled between them—thick with everything unspoken.

Then Donovan reached for his gloves, rising without hurry.

"You'll send me a full write-up by tomorrow," he said, his tone dry, bureaucratic. "I want everything—from the moment we split at the flea market to when she left your apartment. Full sequence, as close to verbatim as memory allows."

David gave a single nod. No questions, just acknowledgement. He was familiar with the protocol for these things.

Donovan adjusted his scarf with the precision of someone who had spent too much time around men who noticed small details; he credited this to his father, the ever-proper Southern gentleman diplomat. He cast one final glance toward the couple near the heaters—not long enough to draw attention, but long enough to register their faces. Then he turned and slipped toward the waiting sedan, shoulders squared, posture relaxed.

Just another American executive overdressed in a good coat on a cold Paris afternoon.

And just like that, David—the medical student and covert CIA operative—was alone again. The clatter of cups and low hum of conversation filled the café, but around him it all felt muted, as if he were sealed off behind glass. The weight of his responsibilities pressed inward, silent and invisible. Yet somewhere in the back of his mind, through the haze of fatigue and unfinished thoughts, he recalled the early lectures at the 'Farm'. They had covered, almost casually, the quiet burden of "liaison duties"—how junior officers were often tasked with bridging the delicate spaces between allied intelligence services, slipping in and out of roles that required fluency not just in cooperation but in relationships.

David stood. He needed to walk. To move was to think, to breathe, to make space for the decision already forming in him. This was a duty he would take on willingly—not just out of obligation, but because he truly felt a real connection to Rachel.

Merging with the early afternoon streets, he headed towards the rue du Bac and then toward the Seine. David crossed the Pont Royal, collar up against the wind that curled off the river. Below him, the river moved like oil, slow and impenetrable, its surface catching the dull orange of the sky.

Normally, David would be enjoying the vista; in the end, he loved everything about Paris, but now his thoughts were elsewhere.

He had a difficult time getting her out of his mind—Rachel: her sudden reappearance, the precision of it; Donovan's unreadable expression earlier at the café. The report weighed on him, a constant pressure at the back of his mind. He felt as though he were walking a narrow line with no clear end, only the sense that one misstep would carry consequences he couldn't afford.

As he stepped off the bridge onto the Right Bank, his building visible a few hundred yards ahead, he began to go over in his mind how he would present the report. He had done such a report a half a dozen times before, but never were any of them as consequential as this one would be. It would certainly be telexed securely to Langley and would likely be read by those occupying the 7th floor.

He began with the essentials, facts only, no explanations or commentary. These reports were not editorials. They would be read by those who could read between the lines, and what was written had significance.

He entered his apartment and immediately sat at his desk and did nothing for a good 10 minutes, then formed an outline and, in the format that he had been trained to use, began:

CONFIDENTIAL

Field Memorandum

From: 'Charcot' (Operative ID #6174P / Paris Station)

To: B. Donovan / S.Blake, Langley Liaison

Date: xxxxxx

Subject: Contact with Agent Zamir, Rachel (AKA Elena) – Post-Marché aux Puces Surveillance Incident

Summary:

This memo documents the sequence of events following the meeting at the Saint-Ouen flea market on [xxxxxxxxx]. Surveillance was noted. Israeli field officer Rachel Zamir initiated subsequent contact. The following is a chronological account of movements, observations, and dialogue to the best of my recollection.

13:20 hrs. – Departed the market on foot with "William Donovan" following the operational briefing at "La Terrace des Puces' Near stall 147, as planned. No immediate tails observed upon departure. We took separate exits according to the prearranged procedure.

13:28 hrs. – I entered the Métro at the Port de Clignancourt station alone, Line 13 southbound. Noted potential surveillance: one male, 6 feet in height, Caucasian, late 30s, dark wool coat, positioned ~25 yards behind. Did not engage.

13:52 hrs. – Exited at Gare de l'Est, transferred to Line 10. Surveillance reappeared at the platform edge. Changed direction unexpectedly. No pursuit.

14:30 hrs.- Exited the Metro and entered Galleries Lafayette. Spent 20 minutes in the store and left unnoticed by any surveillance.

15:10 hrs. – Re-entered the Metro and arrived at my metro stop, Chatelet. Surveillance is no longer evident.

15:26 hrs. – As I was exiting the metro, Rachel Zamir of Israeli Intelligence was there and greeted me. We were acquainted 2 years earlier when she was acting undercover as a lost Greek student traveling through Europe. (This encounter was reported per protocol the next day, and the investigation led to her ID as an active MOSSAD agent.

Verbatim Record of Exchange (as reconstructed from memory):

Zamir: "You lost our junior shadow back at the flea market. Not bad tradecraft. But you missed the other two. Senior men. Good ones. They followed you and Donovan the entire time."

I did not respond. She continued.

Zamir: "One of my men recognized you from my file. I knew where you lived, of course. Once you dropped off the grid in the Métro, it was only a matter of waiting."

She appeared calm, conversational. No visible weapons. No direct threats. Continued speaking without invitation.

Zamir: "We know Patricia Ross and the D.O. flew in together yesterday, if you're wondering how. We're not guessing, David."

Me: "You're reading too much into it. It was a coincidence."

Zamir: "We don't believe in coincidence. Not when it involves Tehran. If you're planning something—and I believe you are—we need to be in the room. Our assets are exposed. Their risk is higher than yours. We can help. We want in."

Me: "If there's something happening, it's above my level. I'm not read in."

Zamir: "You always were a bad liar. Just... pass it along. Tell your people. We're watching. And we want in."

Zamir: "It really is good to see you, David. I've thought of you more than I should admit. No need for cloak and dagger. But let's get an answer; let's say we get together again properly— dinner? Saturday. Brasserie Île Saint-Louis. 20:00."

Before departing, she offered the customary double-cheek kiss. No evidence of surveillance handoff or tail. She exited unaccompanied.

David looked it over again—twice, then a third time. The message was brief, clinical, stripped of emotion, exactly as it should be. He typed it up on the portable Olivetti with a light touch. Satisfied, he slid the carbonless sheet into a standard *pneumatique* envelope and sealed it. It was Sunday. That meant waiting. The following morning, he would drop it off on his way to the hospital—just a modest detour through the 2nd arrondissement to the American Express.

Beneath the boulevards and tourist cafés of Paris, hidden from its curated façades, ran a forgotten circulatory system: the *pneumatique*. A Victorian relic turned Cold War utility, this network of compressed-air tubes had once been the pride of the municipal post. Now it functioned quietly in the shadow of modernity, ignored by most, revered by a few, especially those unfortunate few who were still waiting for their apartments to be fitted with a telephone.

In the dimly lit service alcoves of post offices, uniformed clerks still performed the ritual: insert the capsule, twist the nozzle, and release the pressure valve. *Clunk. Hiss.* A sound like breath through metal lungs. Then silence.

At the American Express Office, behind the famed Opera, and tucked behind the currency counter and travelers' checks, an addressed *pneumatique* capsule marked for P.O. Box 423 would receive special and discreet handling. From there, it would travel not through Paris, but alongside it—by a direct line to the embassy, terminating in the mail chute of the Commercial Attaché: *William Donovan.*

Chapter 16

Paris

David awoke early. His head still reeling from the events of the weekend, the high-level meeting with the DO, the tail from the flea market, seeing Rachel again, and the meeting with Donovan. He was confident that his report would be read and accurately interpreted; he was completely honest and provided a truthful account of the events. After dropping the letter off at the American Express at exactly 8:30 when it opened, he handed it to the clerk, who confirmed twice that it was indeed addressed to PO Box 423.

He rushed to the metro to arrive at the hospital's pathology lab by 9:00, only to remember that they were starting a 2-week rotation in the morgue, where he would learn and assist with post-mortem examinations. He remembered what his professors would say during that second year of med school.

"The post-mortem exam is the jewel of medicine."

At the time, David would laugh and think only a pathologist could think such a thing.

Most of the time, the autopsy merely confirmed what everyone already knew. But in those rare, desperate cases—when the patient slipped away after weeks of unanswered questions, untold antibiotics, and futile procedures—it was the pathologist who stepped in, scalpel in hand, to face the mystery head-on. In the hush of the morgue, long after the machines had gone silent, the final truth waited for him alone to uncover.

There were 4 that month for the rotation in the morgue: David and Azimi, with two girls whom neither of them knew very well.

The professor of pathology walked into the room and, with little fanfare, looked the four students over as if he was about to take a scalpel to each of them.

"Monsieur Behzadi, for the benefit of your good friend next to you, I will conduct this in English. What is required before performing an autopsy in France?"

Azimi blinked. "Uh… the person must be dead."

Laughter erupted from the three other students.

The professor, however, remained perfectly still.

"Idiot," the professor muttered under his breath.

"Anyone else?" the professor said dryly.

David cleared his throat. "Before performing a post-mortem exam, the legal next of kin must explicitly authorize the procedure."

The professor gave a curt nod. "Good. And… are there any exceptions?"

One of the girls, sharp-eyed and composed, raised her hand.

"No consent is needed if a judge, magistrate, or relevant law enforcement official orders the exam as part of a criminal investigation."

"Exactement," the professor said, pleased. "Dans ces cas, aucun consentement n'est nécessaire."

He let the moment breathe, then continued, turning back to the group.

"And what, mes enfants, is the purpose of the post-mortem examination?"

David, continue en français : « *Déterminer les causes exactes de la mort dans les cas de décès suspect, violent ou inexpliqué.* »

"Yes, determine the exact cause of death!"

David, looking puzzled, continued,

"Professeur, what happens if there aren't any next of kin—or if they can't be reached?"

"Good question," the professor replied without looking up. "*Dans ce cas-là, un juge ou un magistrat peut donner son accord pour l'autopsie.*"

"A judge or magistrate could authorize the autopsy."

David, still leaning forward, asked, "And if there are religious objections?"

The professor paused for a beat, as if deciding how far to go.

"Yes, this comes up more and more," he said. "As you may know, in Jewish tradition, burial must take place within 24 hours. *You shall bury him the same day… his body should not remain all night,*" quoting the Torah with quiet precision.

David looked up, surprised—not just at the professor's tone, but at the depth of his knowledge. He was certain the man wasn't Jewish.

"But," the professor continued, almost wearily, "in today's world—even among the devout—that ideal is not always possible. Flights are delayed, paperwork takes time, families argue, and sometimes the body waits."

He folded his hands and looked at the room.

"The law balances the need for truth with respect for tradition. Not always neatly, not always kindly—but it tries."

"The same traditions exist among those of the Muslim faith, but once again, in the modern age, small accommodations are more and more tolerated."

And with that, they began the day's work.

The *chef de service* entered without ceremony, interrupting the professor mid-sentence. He carried a thin file and the tired, automatic authority of a man who'd done this too many times.

"Monsieur, there's a postmortem that needs your signature," he said.

He didn't wait for acknowledgment before continuing, brisk and clinical. "I've already drawn the necessary blood samples. The subject is a male, approximately twenty-five years old. Found in an abandoned warehouse in the 11th, one of the gendarmes knows well—an old squat for heroin addicts. No official documents. Just a faded student ID from six years ago."

The professor said nothing, only nodded.

"The police contacted a family in Brittany. They confirmed the identity but made it clear he was no longer part of their lives. Disowned. Their words. They declined the body."

He paused, tapping the file once with his finger. "There were no signs of violence. Needle still in the arm. No bruises, no defensive wounds. Toxicology shows morphine derivative levels consistent with respiratory failure—a fatal dose."

The professor looked up at last. "So, no autopsy?"

"Not a full one," the *chef de service* replied. "Nothing to indicate foul play, and no one to claim the remains."

He placed the file on the desk, flat and final.

"Unless you say otherwise, we'll mark it as an overdose. Routine."

The four medical students followed the chef de service into the exam room. The body lay beneath the overhead light, pale and waxen, like old marble. Death had settled in, softening the muscles, draining what little youth had remained. He might have been handsome once— sharp cheekbones, jaw angular even in repose—but now he looked more like a cautionary tale than a man.

His arms, extended at his sides, told their own story. A few track marks lined the inner creases, like a failed map of escape routes. Faded tattoos—one of a bird, another a name too blurred to read—peeked from beneath the hospital sheet drawn low across his hips. His fingernails were blackened, and his lips were tinted faintly blue. And in the crook of his left arm, just above the median cubital vein, a single puncture wound still wept a dot of dried blood. The needle had done its work cleanly. It was left in place, taped to his arm as per protocol.

David studied the arm for a moment, noting the single puncture wound in the elbow's crook. The skin was otherwise unblemished— no clusters of scars, no calloused veins, no signs of long-term use. He wondered: was this his first time? A novice chasing relief or escape, unaware this dose would be his last. The mortuary light flickered once, humming with institutional indifference.

David stood at the foot of the slab, hands in the pockets of his white coat. The body was young—far too young—but no one was waiting outside for answers. No grieving parents, no girlfriend clutching a coat that still smelled like him. Just a file, a diagnosis, and a signature waiting to be written before the state functionaries disposed of the body.

As they were walking out of the hospital later that afternoon, Azimi grabbed David and quietly asked, "Have you heard at all from Isabelle?"

David said, "She left a message on my door letting me know she had to leave for Nice to be with her sick grandmother. She didn't know when she'd be back, but asked about you."

Azimi's face lit up. "Let me know as soon as she contacts you again. I want to see her again." At David's request, they stopped at the corner cafe for a drink, where David asked Azimi about his family and the town he grew up in, what it's like now, and how the locals are responding to the political climate. *Where does he see things going?*

Azimi's expression darkened. The brightness vanished, replaced by something harder, more resigned.

"Well, David, to be completely honest, I fear that things in Iran will not be good, certainly not for our community."

David gave a puzzled look, "What do you mean?"

"I'm not sure you know, but my family, we are not Muslims, we belong to an ancient sect known as Zoroastrians, very old and very small now, different from most Iranians who are Muslims. Previously, the climate in Iran and especially in the cities was essentially secular. We could study in the Universities, do business, and intermingle with the general population, just like the Jews did in both Iraq and Iran before the formation of Israel. But now, with the rise of the Ayatollahs… with the clerics gaining power, everything is shifting. There's a new language in the streets. A new kind of fear. My family's nervous. Some of our relatives are already discussing the possibility of leaving. Emigrating before it's too late. Perhaps my father saw this coming, and it was for that reason that he pushed me to come to Paris for my education."

David nodded slowly, keeping his gaze on his drink, but his thoughts were elsewhere. Azimi's words, heavy with anxiety rooted in family and history, made David realize the depth of his classmate's concern. It struck him that this vulnerability presented an opportunity—unexpected leverage he hadn't even known he'd been seeking.

He remembered his training at the Farm. Those words were drummed into him: "Empathy is arguably the most important trait of a successful case officer." Ultimately, the most crucial trait in recruiting an Asset is building a Human Connection. Yes, manipulation is involved. But the most effective kind isn't brute force—it's empathy turned inside out. By knowing what another person feels, the experienced officer can nudge them, gently or decisively, toward betrayal.

Azimi's fear wasn't political—it was existential. A man worried for his people, his parents, his future. That kind of fear made people do things they would never have considered before. It made them cooperate. And while David felt the genuine stirrings of compassion—Azimi was, after all, his friend—there was no denying the calculus forming behind his calm gaze.

He knew better than to press now. Not directly. Not yet. But he'd store this moment, bank it like a valuable wire transfer. When the time came—and it would come—he'd know which string to pull in the end that was his part in this mission.

"That sounds... hard," David said finally, voice even. "I mean, you've never mentioned any of that before."

Azimi gave a faint shrug. "It's not something we advertise. You learn to keep quiet about it."

David raised his glass slightly, the gesture somewhere between a toast and a peace offering. "Well, if things go bad back home, you won't be alone here. Just so you know."

Azimi smiled weakly, and David smiled back—an easy, practiced smile. And suddenly, he was jolted by a 'déjà vu', a similar emotion he had experienced during his courtship with Mai when he realized he had an opening to achieve his objective. It was the quiet thrill of professional accomplishment—precisely the kind of breakthrough he was trained to recognize and exploit. But beneath it stirred something colder, something he didn't care to name. He didn't like the feeling, even as he accepted its necessity.

Chapter 17

Paris

The week passed quickly, with clinical work in the pathology department, a few post-mortem exams, and the afternoon lectures on infectious diseases. David's medical studies provided a useful distraction—an antidote to the unease stirred by his other métier. The rituals of anatomy, the discipline of diagnosis, all helped to dull the sharp edge of anxiety that lingered after typing up the report on his encounter with Rachel Zamir.

He was certain Donovan had already pored over it, annotated the margins, and forwarded it through secure channels to Langley. The nature of the development—Israeli involvement, the implication of another allied service—would require more than routine handling. It would travel, as these matters did, through Agency corridors, perhaps even to the Deputy Secretary of State, if not the Secretary himself.

And so, David waited. No word yet from Donovan. It was unlikely there would be before dinner with Rachel. The silence, as always, was rarely comforting.

*

As David left his apartment and headed toward the Brasserie Île Saint-Louis, he was consumed by a multitude of emotions. On the one hand, this was, in theory, a professional meeting, an exchange of information under the pleasant guise of dinner. But beneath the surface, David couldn't deny the fact that there certainly had been an attraction to the charming and mysterious girl he knew as Elena. Still, a small part of him hoped—against training, against judgment—that the spark might still be there. But what did it mean if it was? Where could it lead, between two professionals who knew better than to trust sentiment, and knew far too well what could happen when they did?

It was Saturday night, and the Île Saint-Louis pulsed with life. Tourists and locals crowded the narrow streets, forming currents of conversation and clinking glasses. Music drifted from open doorways—American rock, jazz, the ever-present Vivaldi's Four Seasons—all blurring together in the air like perfume and smoke. Paris had offered David its usual gifts: exquisite taste in music, art, and culture. The winter weather was mild—deceptively so. He still remembered his first season here: surprised that the cold rarely bit deep, and that snow, when it came at all, never stayed long. How different this was from the brutal Michigan winters he'd endured in college. Tonight, the air was cool but forgiving, just brisk enough to sharpen the senses.

As he crossed the Pont Louis-Philippe, the river reflected the amber glow of the lamps above. Looking south in the distance, the dome of the Panthéon loomed like a silent observer. Ahead, he caught sight of the brasserie—its tables stretching out onto the pavement, packed with couples and clusters of friends. Laughter rang out, sharp and unguarded. Cigarette smoke hung in the crisp winter air. Paris was doing what it did best—behaving as though nothing beyond its arrondissements could possibly matter.

David felt the familiar tension settle in his chest—not unpleasant, not strange. The anticipation before a meeting. Not just any meeting, but with *her*. Rachel—or Elena, depending on the version.

He paused just before the glow of the brasserie lights reached him, adjusted his scarf, and took one last look over his shoulder—not paranoid, just cautious. Then he stepped forward, into the hum of conversation,

He stepped through the brass-handled door into an interior that was classic Parisian brasserie—black-and-white tiled floors, mirrored walls bouncing candlelight, waiters in long white aprons weaving expertly between tables. The scent of garlic, butter, and roasting meat lingered in the air like an embrace. Then David remembered that the restaurant retained its classical roots with Alsatian dishes such as cassoulet. Sausages and sauerkraut, as well as duck and pork, dominated the menu. Cassoulet was his favorite, a slow-cooked stew of white beans, confit of duck, and pork sausage cooked in an earthenware pot called a *cassole*—hence its name.

He paused just inside, letting his eyes adjust. The maître d' glanced up but didn't approach; Rachel was already there, seated at a corner table beneath an ornately framed antique poster of Montmartre, her coat draped neatly beside her, a glass of white wine untouched in front of her. She wore black—with just a trace of silver at her ears.

Their eyes met, briefly. No smile. No waves. Just that look—the one that held a thousand unsaid things.

David made his way to the table, one with a clear view of the entire restaurant, including its entrances and exits. He weaved past diners caught in laughter or low, murmured arguments, past the clatter of cutlery and the faint strains of an old jazz tune drifting in from the kitchen radio.

He approached with a smile, a little surprised, and leaned down to kiss her on each cheek.

"Bonsoir, désolé d'être en retard."

Then, immediately questioning why he was speaking French, he switched gears.

"Oh—sorry. For being late. It was such a nice night, I decided to walk."

He sat down. They looked at each other and smiled.

After a good 15 seconds had passed, Rachel broke the ice. "David, tell me—when did you get involved with those colleagues of yours? Did they recruit you after you started medical school, or was it before you began?"

David didn't know how to respond.

Across from him sat Rachel—Mossad agent, one-time lover, current question mark—did her eyes scan his face out of affection, or for intel?. Or maybe both! That was the trouble, wasn't it? With people like them, the two things were never fully separate.

She began, "Let's be as honest with each other as our professions allow, shall we? You first, being 100% truthful, give me the 5-minute autobiography, then I'll follow."

David proclaimed, "Ladies first", with a smile.

She stirred her drink absently, hesitating.

Rachel's tone was steady, but David could sense that there were strong emotions involved.

"OK, David," she began, taking a sip from her drink. "I was born in Israel, I'm a sabra. On a kibbutz an hour outside Tel Aviv. My mother was Greek, from Salonica—her family and ancestors had lived there for over fifteen hundred years. My mom used to say they arrived with the Romans and stubbornly refused to leave, even when history suggested they should."

Rachel's eyes were fixed in the distance, on something that only she could see.

"In 1942, after the Nazis stormed into Greece, the Jews were rounded up and deported—first to the Bulgarian zone, then to Treblinka, where my mother's entire family was killed. That's where she met my father. He was from Alsace and had already been transferred from a Polish camp. He was an engineer—as such, the Nazis found use for him. She'd also had some training as a nurse.

"Did you know there was an uprising at Treblinka?"

David, with a quizzical look, responded: "No, I've never heard of it."

"There was. A prisoner resistance formed in early 1943. Their goal was to destroy the camp, even if it meant dying. They stole weapons from a German warehouse, but the revolt began prematurely. They couldn't take out the guards or blow up the gas chambers. Hundreds were killed. Nearly 400 escaped. But only 70 survived, hiding in the forest. My parents were among those fortunate few.

Even after the war, suffering persisted. Sickness and hunger followed them. In time, however, they reached what was then Palestine, just before the 1948 UN vote.

She paused. Her gaze fixed on him, without emotion.

"I grew up on a kibbutz, an hour outside Tel Aviv, near an Arab village. I learned Arabic by osmosis. Greek at home. French from my father. English at school. When I turned eighteen, I joined the army like everyone else. And the languages made me useful. Useful enough for Military Intelligence to come knocking."

Another pause. She shrugged lightly, as if brushing off the weight of her own story.

"That's about as much as I'm cleared to share."

David nodded slowly. He wasn't sure whether she had just shared something deeply personal or merely delivered the intelligence community's version of a pickup line. Either way, the effect was the same—he was hooked.

He sat motionless, caught in the undertow of his own double life. He was an officer of the CIA, yes. But also, a medical student. Was the medicine a cover? Or had the cover grown roots and made him forget which role came first? He used his friends, charming them into giving him favors and sharing secrets. And lately, he planned to use Azimi— dear, naive Azimi—as a channel to reach deeper into Iran's future.

Was he a loyal American, advancing his country's interests by whatever means necessary? Or was he Dr. David Rose—dedicated to prolonging life, not subterfuge—struggling through pathology and pharmacology for the simple dream of becoming a physician and helping the sick?

Two lives. Two names, almost. The more he lived in both, the more he began to suspect that he was becoming both of them—two men sharing the same skin, each borrowing the body when it suited their cause. Once, the lines had been clearer: the student with the stethoscope, the operative with the hidden brief. Over time, the roles bled into each other. He no longer knew where one ended and the other began.

What he told her was, for the most part, accurate. He explained that his recruitment during college appeared directly linked to his work on sensory deprivation and its psychological effects. At the time, he concluded that his developing expertise in cognitive manipulation aligned with the Agency's interests. They assured him he could pursue his research concurrently with medical training.

Over the years, however, his involvement shifted. Initially, he thought that he would be useful as a psychological consultant. This rapidly changed, and he was operationally positioned. Though specifics remained classified, he had come to understand that his psychological profile—and his particular skill set—made him uniquely valuable for missions that he was not at liberty to discuss.

He did not tell her everything, of course. There were gaps; he certainly didn't mention his affair with Mai, nor the intel that he obtained from her uncle, like the promises made in fluorescent-lit rooms with people who never gave their last names. But in the quiet clamor of the brasserie, with the wine softening his thoughts and Rachel's eyes steady on his, David let down his guard just enough to feel almost honest.

Of course, he spoke of medicine, of the long nights on the wards, of seeing the final moments of life stripped of poetry. He told her that he still believed, or at least wanted to believe, that his future was with the sick and the suffering and that his relationship with espionage, if he could call it that, was temporary. A means to an end. A favor to his country.

Rachel listened without comment, her expression unreadable, her fingers absently tracing the rim of her glass. When he stopped speaking, she nodded once, almost imperceptibly. Not in agreement. Not in disbelief either. Just acknowledgment—from one fractured life to another.

Still in thought, they were interrupted by the waiter,

"Avez-vous choisi?"

David, a little flustered, looked toward Rachel, who, in her perfect French, replied: "Un salad d'avocat et le cassoulet pour moi."

David, hésitant, "Et pour moi, une salade verte… et votre choucroute garnie maison, s'il vous plaît." Adding, almost as an afterthought, "And a good bottle of Sancerre."

"Bien sûr, monsieur," the waiter replied with the faintest nod, already scribbling on his notepad, the corners of his mouth hinting at approval—either for the wine choice or the manner in which it was ordered. In Paris, it was often hard to tell.

Rachel leaned in and whispered, "Definitely not kosher—but hey, "Sinful, yes—but deliciously worth it."

She grinned. "Not exactly what they're serving in the orthodox sections of Jerusalem."

They both laughed, the tension melting slightly.

Their conversation flowed with a quiet rhythm, as if they were attuned to each other's thoughts—anticipating the words before they left their lips. There was no talk of business, generalities, but through it, they both seemed to get a real sense of who the other was. At last, David leaned back slightly, eyes scanning her face for any hint of tension. "I did pass along your request," he said, voice lowered just enough to remind her who they really were. "But I expect it'll need to go higher—most likely, to State. That means politics, and that means delay. I wouldn't count on a response before the end of the week."

Rachel gave a small, understanding nod, her gaze never leaving his. "That's what I figured," she said, and reached for her glass.

The brief silence was broken with the arrival of the waiter:

"Would you care for a dessert?"

"Pas pour moi, merci."

Smiling David adds: "Non, ça ira, merci, l'addition, s'il vous plaît."

No, thank you, just the check please.

As they neared the restaurant's exit, the hum of conversation and clinking glasses behind them fading into the clamor of the street, David found himself caught in an unexpected stillness. There was a flicker of hesitation somewhere between impulse and uncertainty as he questioned what, exactly, he felt for Rachel, and how he imagined the evening might end. But she spared him the choice. At the street's edge, she turned, thanked him softly for dinner, pressed her lips lightly to each of his cheeks with the practiced rhythm of the French. "We'll talk soon," she said, before disappearing into the golden glow of a streetlamp, as she walked toward the taxi stand. David stood there for a moment, unsure whether it had been a diplomatic exchange over dinner or something that still bore the heat of their old intimacy. No lingering glances, no invitations half-spoken. Whatever had stirred between them over dinner had been neatly folded away, tucked behind the familiar masks they were required to wear. David stood for a moment on the curb, watching the taxi carry her off into the night, wondering if he was witnessing the end of something, or just the beginning.

Chapter 18

CIA Headquarters—Langley, Virginia

7th Floor Conference Room B

Present in the Room:

Jonathan L. Buchanan, Head Mid East Desk, CIA

Patricia Ross, Head Analyst, Iran Desk, CIA

Stewart Blake, Deputy Director for Operations, CIA

Amir Ahmadi, SOG

John Taft, National Security Advisor

Gary Wood, Undersecretary of State

(His assistant, Ms. Wilson, the president's niece, was also present)

Joseph Anthony, in-house Legal Counsel, CIA

The room was austere and silent. A large wall map of the region of Iran dominated the space, its surface littered with red pencil marks and pushpins.

Outside, the snow fell in sharp diagonals. Inside, the atmosphere was colder still.

Jonathan L. Buchanan, Director of Mid-East Operations, stepped to the head of the table. His expression was unreadable. Those who knew him best understood that meant trouble.

"We have a problem," he said.

No one moved.

Mossad's onto us. They know we're planning an infiltration. It's unsettling how easily they've tracked us—especially in Paris. They haven't confirmed the details, but they're close. Very close.

There was a flicker of unease, audible in the soft rustle of fabric and murmured exhalations.

"They followed one of our people. One of our newer operatives, code-named "Charcot," confronted him, subtly but unmistakably. Their message was clear: As allies, they want in. Given their fraught standing with the new Iranian regime, they state that they are entitled."

The murmurs grew louder.

From halfway down the table came a sharp interruption.

Informal Allies, Director. Not treaty-bound. And let's not forget two hundred kilos of enriched uranium vanished from Apollo, Pennsylvania. We all remember that theater.

As the murmurs around the table grew audible, Jonathan Buchanan interrupted, "Yet you will all agree that the United States and Israel have a special relationship. I'll remind you that we signed a memorandum of understanding in 1965, marking the beginning of this strategic alliance. They've given us intelligence no other partner could—on terror networks in Europe, on actors in the Middle East who don't just hate them—but hate us. Call it what you want, but make no mistake: this relationship isn't just transactional."

From the far end of the table, National Security Advisor John Taft's voice cut through the noise. Not an admirer of the Agency, he quipped,

"So, we're sending assets into Tehran? Now? While the city burns?"

Patricia Ross said nothing; she stayed calm. This was all anticipated; involving the politicians, necessary as it was, would only result in a 'cluster-fuck'. Instead, she slid a black-and-white surveillance photo across the table. It showed a man standing at a payphone, half-turned, his features circled in ink.

"One of our few left—Interior Ministry, codename Haddad. He has survived four purges, but he is scared. The Revolutionary Guard makes raids daily. His control is dark, possibly compromised."

Woods shook his head slowly. "You insert now, and we don't just risk a blown op. We risk being seen as co-conspirators with the *Zionists*. We lose plausible deniability, and we lose the Arab street for a generation."

"Or," said Joe Anthony, Langley's legal counsel, crisp in a gray suit and cooler still in tone, "we wait, do nothing, and operate blind. Allow the Soviets to make inroads in the most dangerous, oil-rich, politically volatile nation in the region?"

The conversation went back and forth for a good 40 minutes before Buchanan shook his head, disagreeing,

Mossad wants in. They have assets ready. My proposal: they come with us but don't lead. We'll give them seventy-two hours of cover; after that, they're alone.

"And in return?" someone asked.

"We demand access. Their assets assist with recon, ongoing comms, and protection for our people to the extent that they can provide it, and if the op burns, they support extraction."

A long silence followed. As the meeting finally broke up and they began drifting toward the door, the assistant to the Secretary of State, Linda Wilson, stepped beside Buchanan and, quietly with a smile, asked:

"How do you people come up with these code names, anyway?" "What in the world is a *Charcot?*"

Buchanan was already halfway to the door when he paused, clearly weighing whether to say something or vanish behind it. Nepotism rankled him deeply, and the appointment of the President's niece—Princeton degree or not—was a bitter pill he hadn't yet swallowed. Without turning, he said, "Ever read anything on the history of medicine?"

She snorted. "No. Not exactly my idea of bedtime reading."

He looked back over his shoulder. "Let me enlighten you, then."

He stepped closer, just enough to make it feel like a lecture, but not enough to be unkind.

"Jean-Martin Charcot was a nineteenth-century French neurologist. Mentor to Freud. Godfather of modern psychiatry. He was first to describe and define multiple sclerosis, identified Lou Gehrig's disease, and basically turned hysteria into a science."

She raised an eyebrow.

"He also performed public dissections of the mind," Buchanan added. "Before the French started dissecting their politicians instead."

"And this has what, exactly, to do with an Iranian infiltration op?"

He smiled faintly. "You asked how we choose code names. We choose them carefully. And that is all he had to say. She opened her mouth to reply, but Buchanan was already at the door.

"For the record," Buchanan said at the threshold, "history and the textbooks don't do the man justice."

He turned back slightly, just enough to deliver the parting blow.

"If you're really interested, history gives us insight into how the world works, and a view into the future. Americans these days are too busy or simply uninformed to study it. If they did, they'd learn that most diseases identified in the 18th and early 19th centuries were named after Frenchmen, such as Charcot, Laennec, and Dupuytren. They dominated science, medicine, and culture. Later, in the 19th century, Germans took the lead with a rigid, meticulous, and systematic approach. Most diseases discovered at that time were named after

German scientists. Then, in our century, it was the Americans, many of them immigrants—our century, our labs, our breakthroughs."

He picked up his file and tucked it under one arm.

"But the boys on the fifth floor tell me the future of science, and discovery will belong somewhere else. Twenty-first-century breakthroughs?" He paused. "Won't likely be ours."

A faint smile touched the corner of his mouth.

Ms. Wilson looked perplexed.

"They say it will come from China."

As he turned to leave, Buchanan noticed Amir in the hall, deep in conversation with a former Delta Force colleague. He thought it somewhat strange as Amir had been working in Europe for some time now, and his colleague was primarily assigned to missions in Iraq. He knew that they had worked together in Cambodia and Laos during the war, but not since; as such, he was curious about the nature of the discussion.

And with that, he stepped into the hall, leaving the door to swing closed behind him with a soft, decisive *click*.

Chapter 19

Paris

It was an especially cold afternoon, and David returned from lectures, settling into his small apartment with the plan to spend a couple of hours rereading the chapters and lectures on the budding field of Virology. It was a dull read, as most of the diseases relied on clinical diagnosis, as the practical isolation and identification of specific viruses had not yet been achieved. It wasn't until the mid-1960s that advances in virology and molecular biology revealed that, in fact, viruses are composed of nucleic acid (DNA or RNA) and a protein coat. Interesting science, perhaps, but for a future clinician, he had to admit dull and difficult reading.

After an hour, he decided to take a break. He bundled himself into his only proper winter coat and made his way around the corner to the patisserie he favored. The bell above the door gave its usual soft chime, and Dominique—the pastry chef's daughter, barely sixteen but already sharp as a blade—smiled as he entered. She didn't ask what he wanted. She already knew. A moment later, she handed him a slice of their cream-filled chocolate cake, nestled carefully in a white box tied with twine.

The walk back to his apartment was quiet; the street was damp with the kind of cold that was a Paris fixture this time of year. At his door, he paused. A package rested against the threshold, wrapped in brown paper, the label written in a hand he didn't recognize.

He made tea before opening it.

Inside was a medical text—heavy, well-worn—the title embossed in gold: *Anatomie humaine* by Henri Rouvière. Tucked beneath the front cover was a folded note in French:

"As you requested, Monsieur—Human Anatomy by Henri Rouvière.

"However, the book Neuro-Anatomy by André Delmas is not in stock, but you could try our bookstore in the 4th arrondissement. I believe it's open until 7:00 p.m.

David's pulse quickened. They must have heard from Langley. The message called for a semi-urgent meeting at their 4th arrondissement location, set for 7 PM tomorrow.

He poured himself a cup of tea, the steam curling upward. The brief thrill of operational urgency faded as the mundane ritual began, and his thoughts drifted—pulling away from work and returning, unbidden, to Rachel.

He wondered again if the encounters with Rachel would ever shift from subtle opposition to true collaboration. Sometimes, he allowed himself to fantasize about something romantic. More often than not, they moved like adversaries locked in a delicate waltz. Each guarded their own agenda, careful not to reveal too much.

But lately, he was certain there was something else.

Moments that lingered. That night in his apartment. The quiet dinner at the brasserie on the Ile. A rhythm had begun to form—less rehearsed, more personal.

And though he couldn't quite define what it was becoming, he dared to admit that part of him knew what he wanted it to be. Something real. Something more than the job.

Still, his training whispered caution. Intimacy eroded boundaries. It softened judgment. In their world, blurred lines always ended badly.

But Rachel wasn't an asset. Not one of his "Joes." She wasn't a mark or a source to be turned.

She was something else entirely.

She was an agent of a friendly service, yes. But not a threat. Not a liability. A colleague, perhaps. Possibly a collaborator. He didn't know what this thing between them was becoming, only that he hoped it wasn't just about the work or the mission.

Something else. Something he hadn't felt in a very long time.

David wondered—when Rachel looked at him, did she see the future doctor, or the young CIA operative??

The question hit him harder than he expected—a sudden tightness in his chest. The chill of doubt was working its way under his skin. He broke out in a cold sweat.

And for the first time since he'd agreed to come to France years earlier, David allowed himself to ask the question he'd never dared to consider:

Would he still be doing this after completing his medical studies?

Until now, his Agency involvement had simply filled the space between lectures and rotations. It was something he wore like a second coat: easily shed, easily resumed. But now it felt different. The edges of his two lives were starting to blur.

At the Farm, and later during those midday sessions in the *Jardin des Plantes*, the looks he received from instructors and handlers had changed. They didn't have to say it. He saw it in their eyes—respect, envy, the quiet recognition of one of their own. He might be a natural.

And that scared him more than he cared to admit. The realization hovered uneasily, building on the confidence that preceded it and shifting his mood from pride to fear in a blink.

Not because he wasn't capable. But because he was. Because the instincts came too easily now—the quick assessments, the lies told without a flicker, the ability to disappear in plain sight. It was no longer something he did. It was who he was becoming.

For the first time, he wondered whether the version of himself he had built for the job was still just an act or something more. At first, he thought the growing discomfort came from being recognized. But what unsettled him most was the slow, dawning realization that he had never stopped to ask himself whether he wanted the persona he had crafted to become permanent.

Chapter 20

The Marais, Paris

The meeting place in the 4th Arrondissement was Chez Jo Goldenberg. David knew it well—it was on rue des Rosiers, just a short walk from his apartment, and the only decent Jewish deli in Paris.

There was always a crowd out front, tourists and locals waiting for tables in the back. The front half of the restaurant focused on take-out—efficient and brisk.

The meeting was set for 19:00. David left early, giving himself time to meander through the Marais, doubling back more than once to be sure he wasn't being followed.

David thought it was an unusual spot for a discreet meeting. Chez Jo Goldenberg was always packed. It stood at the corner of a busy intersection—a knot of narrow streets in what had once been the heart of a thriving Jewish neighborhood.

He passed faded storefronts with traces of Hebrew lettering. He felt their presence, like echoes in the stone. He knew his history.

His grandparents, he was always told, left Europe as young children toward the end of the 19th century. He remembered the way they spoke—softly, almost shamefully—of distant cousins who stayed behind and didn't survive.

As the bells from Église Saint-Paul-Saint-Louis marked the hour, David slipped through the door of the restaurant. The usual commotion greeted him—clattering plates, raised voices, the smells of brisket and dill. Near the back, he spotted Jim Waldon, who gave a brief wave and turned without waiting, disappearing down a narrow stone staircase.

David followed, descending into the cool, hushed basement. At the far end, another staircase—older, rougher—led down again, likely to what had once been the wine cellar.

There, to his mild surprise, was a small round table—modestly dressed in white linen, set with plates and proper silver. A waiter stood quietly at the ready. Amir and Donovan were already seated. And across from them, smiling faintly, was Rachel.

Donovan gestured to the room.

"We owe this bit of hospitality to our Israeli friends," he said, with a nod that might have been gratitude or something colder.

Rachel laughed lightly. "We've known the Goldenbergs for a long time. They're always accommodating when we need a discreet corner nearby. Rest assured, the space was thoroughly searched, swept, and scanned for any signs of eavesdropping before our meeting."

Donovan turned to David. "I took the liberty of asking Rachel's superiors to arrange this. He gestured to the middle-aged man seated beside her. The man inclined his head but said nothing. No introduction was offered, and none was expected. Donovan's tone shifted, the warmth draining as business resumed.

"The meeting in Virginia went more or less as expected," Donovan said, his voice low and flat. "The usual dance. Political posturing, policy bickering. But in the end, the wonks signed off. Green light's official. Our friends here get to play—under supervision."

He glanced around the room, letting that sink in before continuing.

"Langley's Directorate of Operations is partnering with Air Force Special Operations Command on this. The Directorate will handle overall operational oversight and team preparation. Air Force Special Operations Command will manage logistics and transportation. Our responsibility is to prep the team, oversee the transfer to the staging site—whichever one they finally settle on—and ensure our readiness to re-establish contact with any remaining assets on the ground. More importantly, we are to arrange for successful insertion and then assist actively in protecting their cover, as best as we are able."

Amir nodded, arms crossed as his gaze shifted to the gentleman next to Rachel.

"There are conditions, naturally," he said. "The head of the Middle East desk put it rather plainly—'You *can ride the bus, but we're driving.' The Middle East desk will maintain primary mission control, with your operational group providing input only where authorized.*"

A few quiet laughs followed, the kind that said no one found it particularly funny.

Rachel offered a knowing smile. Her colleague and another Israeli didn't. He sat stiffly, lips pressed in a straight line, not so much offended as unwilling to play along.

Donovan continued, his voice steely. As the waiter set down a platter of cold cuts, Donovan waited for him to leave, then said quietly, "Planning stays compartmentalized—no exceptions. Until we're set to move, all contact goes through you two," he gestured at Rachel and David. "Listen carefully: you get two seats on the bus. We'll guarantee your people seventy-two hours of safety—no more. After that, they're on their own. The staging site's still up in the air, but it's probably Egypt or Turkey."

"We might solicit your input on some of this, as you likely have assets in both places, after all. Their handlers are expected to handle reconnaissance, maintain ongoing communications, and, if things go sideways, marshal every available resource to assist with extraction."

"We'll want to run through every one of these eventualities before we get started."

Jim Waldon, who had said nothing, was shaking his head. "What is bothering you, Jim?" Amir said softly, "You've been in some similar ops in Laos. What's your concern?"

"We still haven't addressed the problem of discovery. We won't be able to keep any aerial infiltration covert for long. Yes, we may be able to land our people on site, but the Iranians will learn soon enough that their airspace has been breached. They won't catch our guys in the act, but they will make it impossible for them to get out of the region of the landing zone."

David cleared his throat, just a little hesitant to speak up.

"I've been thinking about this," he said. "If we want to pull this off, we'll have to redirect their attention. Convince the Iranians nothing happened. Or better—make them believe we tried and failed."

There was a pause. Then a round of puzzled glances circled the table.

Donovan raised an eyebrow. "So—fake a failure. Spell it out, David."

David leaned forward. "Picture this. A crash site in the desert. Wreckage. Fire. A chopper torn apart. Inside—bodies. Burned, broken. Dressed in recognizable gear. Identifiable papers. Mission briefs. Obvious false IDs. Everything points to a failed American infiltration. Dead CIA agents."

There was a long silence.

Then Rachel. "So, we kill some of our own to sell the lie?"

"No," David said. "We bring the bodies. Already dead. Cadavers. Fresh ones. From the hospital."

Amir looked sharply at him. "You're suggesting we dress corpses in Agency kit and fly them in with the team?"

"Yes."

"Where exactly do you plan to get these bodies?" Rachel asked. "Dig up graves?"

David shook his head. "No need. Every week, in every big city—Paris included—there are unclaimed bodies. Found in alleyways and metro stations. Overdoses. Alcoholics. No family. No paperwork. Most are never autopsied. If the pathologist or a senior resident sign off—natural causes, no suspicion—then they're sent along for burial. Quietly."

Donovan was studying him now, as if seeing him for the first time.

David went on, his tone level remaining steady. "We claim a few of those. The right ones—size, build, ethnicity. Put them on ice. Dress them. Gear them up. We load them on the flight and, when the time comes, we scatter the wreckage and leave just enough for the story to hold."

No one said anything for a moment.

Rachel let out a low whistle. "David, your mind is dark."

Donovan was the first to break the silence.

"All right," he said slowly. "Let's say we do it—pull bodies from the morgue, rig the wreckage. I still need to hear one thing: how do we get the real team out before the bird goes down?"

David had expected the question. He leaned in, voice low, steady.

"The pilot sets down fast. The team offloads with gear—tight, no delay. Then he lifts. Autopilot kicks in, pre-rigged. He jumps."

The others exchanged glances.

"HALO gear," David continued. "Modified. Short drop—a couple of hundred meters max. He clears the bird, lands in scrub or sand. From there, the helicopter climbs a bit, angles down, then crashes on a preset vector."

He let the silence sit.

"We kill the black box, swap transponders, burn it hot. The crash won't look surgical—it won't look like a mission. It'll look like a botched escape."

"We're flying at dawn?"

"Twilight. Just enough light for the op, not enough for locals to catch silhouettes in the air."

A long pause.

"Or even better yet, perhaps we can rig it to reascend—set the bird on autopilot, after the crew and pilot disembark. Give it a timed ascent, then kill the fuel. No one would expect anything other than a crashed landing." He glanced around the table.

Amir folded his arms. "And if someone's watching?"

"Then they'll see exactly what we want them to: smoke, wreckage, and dead Americans. The real team will already be kilometers away, moving on foot or, better yet, by van if we can get assistance from sympathetic locals. There won't be any trace of a second chopper— and no one could possibly survive a crash like that. If there are hostiles, or even just eyes near the site, they'll assume everyone's dead. We will make sure that the manifest documents the number of souls found, no more."

Everyone remained silent for about 30 seconds.

"It's a crazy idea—but it just might work," Donovan said, rubbing a hand over his jaw.

Amir, who was basically silent throughout the discussion, raised an eyebrow, "What becomes of the pilot? OK, he jumps with the crew, but then what? Do we exfiltrate him immediately, or does he just hang out in Iran? And all their gear, they will need to be able to bury it somewhere and quickly."

Rachel broke in:

"I'm not convinced our people can manage a jump," she said. "But one of our candidates is ex-Air Force. Pilot. Certainly, he should be comfortable with your helicopter."

"Well, that would certainly kill two birds with one stone, as it were."

"David looked around the table and smiled. *Who would've thought that a rotation in the morgue could possibly turn out to actually save lives?*"

Donovan broke in, "I'll contact Langley, see if SAC or SEAL Team 6 can war-game the scenario. I'm no pilot, but if the bird can be gently modified, dampened acoustics, and maximized stabilization, I'd bet we could fly a UH-60 remotely for a few kilometers after the drop. We'll need Ms. Zamir to verify her two assets' experience."

"Then, of course, there's the matter of the bodies—where exactly we're meant to find a set of clean-looking cadavers, the right age and build. Not just anyone will do. Ideally, we source them locally—which, I presume, David, is the simplest route, if not the most savory. But that presents its own challenges: how do we preserve them, dress them to spec, and move them quietly to the staging point? Somewhere suitably ambiguous—Turkey, Egypt, or somewhere in the Gulf, if that's decided. Langley's being tight-lipped for now, but I'll float the concept and see if anything takes root."

As the meeting dispersed, chairs scraping softly against concrete and once again the cellar was quiet, Donovan grabbed David's arm and in a low voice said, "We need to go over some things, let's meet tomorrow 15:30, Jardin du Luxembourg, tables near the tennis courts, and if it's not too cold dress for tennis and bring along a racquet."

As David rose to leave, he gave a polite nod of acknowledgment. Rachel caught his arm gently.

"We should go over logistics," she said, her tone casual but firm. "Call our embassy. Leave a message for the cultural attaché. Tell the secretary you're calling about scheduling a concert pianist performance in Tel Aviv."

She paused just long enough for it to register.

"Mention a day you're free to meet. Just say the attaché knows of you and will understand how to reach you." She offered a faint smile. "Then I'll get back to you,"

David nodded in agreement, and as he was heading up the stairs, Amir caught Donovan's eye. A tilt of the head was all it took. The others climbed the stairs toward the restaurant, leaving the two men alone in the bunker-like cellar, which still smelled faintly of damp paper and spilled wine.

Amir waited a moment before speaking, just long enough to suggest discretion wasn't a habit for him but a necessity.

"Bill, there's something I wanted to ask—off the record, as they say."

Donovan gave a slow nod. The room was quiet enough now to hear the fluorescent lights hum overhead.

"I caught some chatter last week, after the Virginia sit-down," Amir said, his voice low and without insistence. "As I was leaving the room, I bumped into an old buddy I knew back in Laos, just as the war was folding in on itself. We were boys then, following orders that no longer mattered. He's still at Langley, buried somewhere in the structure. We exchanged a few polite lies. But in between them, he let something slip—carefully, casually.

He paused, watching Donovan for a flicker.

"He hinted that there's another operation. Parallel to ours. Another team, different objectives.

He let that hang in the air a moment.

"They seemed to think our task—re-establishing contact with what assets may still be breathing—might be just one part of it. A cover, perhaps. That we're meant to serve as a backdoor for something else."

Donovan said nothing, his face unreadable in the gloom. His hands were in his coat pockets, his stance slack but careful. Amir pressed on.

"His source even mentioned the embassy personnel. No names. Just that things were moving. Quietly, as usual. You haven't heard anything?"

Donovan's brow furrowed—not in suspicion, but in something closer to weariness. He shook his head once, then twice, as if trying to dislodge the thought entirely.

"No," he said flatly. "Nothing."

He paused, then allowed himself the faintest of smiles—dry, almost pitying.

"But that's the game, isn't it? We never see the full board. We get a square or two. A pawn, maybe a knight. We're told to move, and we move."

He looked down for a beat, then backed up.

"I learned that the hard way, Amir. Da Nang. First tour. It was part of a counter-intelligence op. We thought we were securing a village for a road. Turns out the village didn't exist, and the road was a ruse. Half my team got chewed up before someone finally admitted we were a diversion."

Amir didn't respond at once. He studied Donovan's face for signs of deception but saw only a man who had long since resigned himself to being left out of the loop.

"So, we proceed blindly?"

Donovan gave the faintest shrug. "No! We proceed *aware* that we are blind."

A long pause followed, both men lingering in the cellar as if to delay the return to the world upstairs, where certainty about what was real was a luxury that, in their line of work, luxuries were just that.

Chapter 21

Paris

It was a mild late autumn afternoon. David had finished early at the hospital and, rather than return to the flat, he let instinct guide him to the Luxembourg Gardens—a favorite sanctuary since his first days in Paris. He took the metro to Odéon and walked uphill past the Théâtre de l'Odéon, moving without hurry, though he was due to meet Donovan within the hour. The forecast was for rain most of the day, so David left his tennis racquet at home that morning but brought an umbrella. The sky was foreboding, but there was no rain yet.

Luxembourg was the first green space he'd encountered on his summer tour through Europe, a lifetime ago. Even then, it had struck him as impossibly serene—chess players under the chestnut trees, children launching boats across the Grand Bassin, and students lounging on benches, tangled in sun-drenched flirtation. He had returned to the garden again and again over the years, always alone, always in search of solitude.

Like most things he admired, David had thoroughly researched it.

It was the kind of place where lovers might rendezvous for the quintessential *'cinq à sept'* or 5-7. It was a phrase David had picked up not long after arriving in Paris. It referred to the quiet hours between the end of the workday and the return home for dinner. On the surface, it was simply a time of day. But beneath it lingered the unmistakable subtext: a couple of hours reserved for discreet affairs, played out in tucked-away hotels or borrowed apartments. For David, it was also the perfect hour he learned to keep secrets and trade.

As he made his way down the gravel path toward the old tennis courts, a familiar pang settled in his chest—regret, mostly. He hadn't picked up a tennis racquet since those early fall days playing with Mai at the Cité courts. Although he tried not to think of her, she returned often in his dreams. Dreams that weren't pleasant. Guilt-ridden, and involving a person that David didn't want to think was himself. He could see it in her face that he had hurt her, a wound that likely would last a long time. It had been early still, in this new life of his—before the lines had entirely blurred. And yet, even then, he struggled with the man he was becoming. Struggled more with the possibility that the transformation was already complete.

As he came into view of the clay courts, he could see Donovan approaching from the west corner of the gardens, racquet in one hand, umbrella and thin leather briefcase in the other. He motioned for them to take a seat at one of the metal tables along the path. As usual, Donovan was all business.

"So how is it going with your buddy Azimi?"

"Fine, I saw him today in lectures, he seems anxious but also very much interested in a girl I fixed him up with a few weeks back, keeps asking if I have heard from her. I had to tell him that she left for Nice to attend to a sick mother."

Donovan didn't miss a beat. "Who was the girl?"

"One of the neighborhood's pros. Discreet arrangement. He hasn't a clue. Fifteen hundred francs. Worth every centime."

David laughed. "Think I can file that under professional expenses and get reimbursed?"

Laughing, Donovan finally looked up, one brow slightly raised, amusement curling at the corner of his mouth.

"You're taking to this rather well," he said. "Just be sure he doesn't run into her working the curb outside Rue Saint-Denis. That would make for an awkward reunion."

"Well, it's about that time. We have to start reeling him in."

"How does he fit in? He is here in Paris studying, I don't get it."

Donovan hesitated just slightly. "He has family in Iran, in the region of Yazd. This is in central Iran, approximately a few hours' drive from Tehran.

"It's an arid place—salt plains, scattered towns. Not much out there but wind and silence. Which, for our purposes, makes it ideal. It is the perfect site for our helicopter insertion. That means we'll need help on the ground—someone to keep our people out of sight just for a few days. Away from prying eyes. And well away from any of those fanatic student sympathizers of the budding Revolutionary Guard."

He paused, pulling out a map of the region from his briefcase and studying the map a moment longer, then looked up.

"We'll need his family involved. Discreetly. I'll handle the pitch. But I need you to bring him in for a meeting."

"What's the cover?" David asked. "What am I telling him—about you, about us, about our relationship?"

"Very simply, I'm someone you met at the embassy when you needed to obtain some papers for your student visa. Just say that we got talking about other foreign students in your school, and you mentioned that you knew an Iranian. Say I brought up how things are changing—and not for the better—for non-Muslims."

"You said it yourself—he's anxious. And why wouldn't he be? His entire family is still there. Everything he knows. And now the country's slipping into a revolution—religious, no less. Imagine that kind of uncertainty. Now imagine it as a minority, a non-Muslim, watching clerics rewrite the rules of society in real time. Take the anxiety you're picturing and multiply it by ten. That's what we're working with. That's our leverage."

He reached for the folder—thick, worn at the corners, heavy with photographs and redacted statements.

"All I have to do is show him what the Ayatollah and his inner circle are planning. Let him see, in their own words, what their plans are for the future of Iran. Then I'll ask a simple question: does he honestly believe there's a place in that vision for his community, his family, and someone like him?"

He paused, almost as if the next part were an afterthought.

"And if this goes well—if they help out —who knows. Perhaps there's a way we can help his family get out. A visa, a quiet entry, and a new life in the States. A promise of eventual citizenship. It's not guaranteed, but it's the kind of thing a man thinks about when the world is shifting beneath his feet."

David shifted in his chair. "Seems reasonable. I'll speak to him tomorrow. I should see him at the hospital on morning rounds. I'll keep it casual. I'll just say that you helped me sort out a visa issue, and the conversation drifted. You mentioned Iran, what's coming, and I said I knew someone who might want to hear it firsthand. I think he'll bite."

"Good," Donovan said. "Let's try to get something on the calendar soon—there'll be a lot to cover."

He began folding his papers into the worn leather briefcase, then paused and looked up.

"And David—start thinking about how we're going to secure those cadavers. Quietly. I've a feeling it won't be quite as straightforward as you made it sound."

And with that, he stood, gave a slight nod, turned up his coat collar against the wind, and, with a slight smile, reminded David not to forget his umbrella as he made his way toward the taxi stand outside the West Gate.

Chapter 22

The following morning, as David rumbled through Paris on the Métro, he remembered that they had switched his lectures to the morning because they weren't expected to go to the wards. It was the week that both the operating rooms and the Pathology labs were deep-cleaned and exposed to UV radiation. A new technology borrowed once again from the Americans.

David's thoughts were not on the morning's lectures; his thoughts were elsewhere, focused on how to steer Azimi gently, almost imperceptibly, toward a meeting with Donovan.

He hadn't spoken to Azimi about Iran in any meaningful way. The subject, like so much among expats, mostly floated between them, unspoken. But David had no doubt the young man was worried. Azimi received letters regularly from his parents and his two younger sisters, filled with snippets of news from their neighborhood and the city. Already, his teenage sisters had written that some of their friends were excited to start wearing a scarf over their hair, and some were even curious about the hijab. His parents, officially, remained cautiously optimistic, writing that the fire and fury of the clerics would fade with the Shah's departure, that a new government—moderate, secular, perhaps even democratic—would eventually take its place.

But David was certain that, deep down, they didn't really believe it. And more to the point, he was certain that Azimi didn't. Azimi had spent time in America, a brief sojourn in Colorado that had left a mark—less from the snow or the sky than from the weightless feeling of saying what you thought without someone listening for the wrong reason. And now in Paris, where freedom came laced with wit and irony and disdain, where political debate was as common as coffee, Azimi had tasted something else: the idea that a person could live openly and unafraid.

He certainly must have known, as David knew, that such liberties would vanish in the Iran to come. If the Ayatollah took control—truly took it, not just in name but in function—the country would change in ways far deeper than slogans and marches. The clerics were not interested in reform. They wanted obedience. They wanted fear and power. And they would get both at whatever the cost.

That was the pitch, in essence. Not a lie. Not exactly. Just a quiet illumination of things Azimi already suspected. What David needed was a way to bring him into the room, to make the meeting with Donovan seem like a chance encounter, a conversation between concerned friends. No pressure, no pretense. Just a whisper that maybe, just maybe, there was something worth hearing.

He looked up as the train pulled into Gare d'Austerlitz, the doors sliding open with a hiss. Outside, Paris bustled, indifferent. Inside, David sat still for a moment longer, the plan beginning to form in his mind, deliberate and with care.

As he crossed the courtyard toward the lecture halls, David felt a flicker of something rare—perspective, perhaps, or something like gratitude, though he distrusted the word. It was too soft, too American. But the feeling lingered. He had been lucky, staggeringly so. Born in America after World War II, after Korea, spared the draft by little more than the accident of timing. He'd been raised in comfort, the kind that never asks its own price, and allowed to wander Europe in his twenties, backpack slung over one shoulder, pretending to be poor while knowing he wasn't really.

Although David liked to consider himself a student of history, it wasn't until that first summer abroad—after his junior year, when he found himself drinking too much red wine and listening more than he spoke—that he began to absorb the scale of what had come before. Elderly Frenchmen spoke of the 'Great War' in tones that made it feel as near as weather. Whole towns emptied of their sons. Villages that never truly recovered. A generation gone, not to statistics, but to mud, and gas, and silence.

What devastation.

We speak of liberty so easily, he thought. A word flattened by repetition, tossed like confetti into speeches and editorials. But its meaning doesn't sharpen until it's under threat. No—until it's gone. Then, and only then, do you understand what it truly was. A condition. A luxury that had been taken for granted. A birthright that could vanish in the space of a revolution, or, for that matter, the ascension of an autocrat. It was this thought, this feeling, that he knew he had to convey to Azimi. He realized it should not be hard at all, because he now understood what it was and that it was real.

As David pushed open the lecture hall door, the thought still resting just behind his eyes, he glanced down at their usual seats by the aisle and saw Azimi already seated, chatting up Danielle, the attractive girl beside him. This section of lectures was on 'Anat-Path'-pathology, which was completely random but lined up nicely with their morning rotations in the Pathology department at the hospital and in the morgue. David slipped in and took the empty seat next to Danielle as the professor came in and walked to the lectern.

"*Aujourd'hui, la pathologie du foie,*" he announced, voice dry and nasal, tinged with the kind of fatigue that comes not from lack of sleep but from the weight of repetition. The Liver. Again. There was a collective shifting of limbs, the shuffle of pages turning, and a few bored moans.

The lecture moved between theory and anecdote, punctuated by references to cases seen at the Pitié-Salpêtrière or Hôpital Cochin. The professor gestured toward a yellowing diagram of hepatic circulation, pinned askew on the board. It had been there all week. No one had taken it down.

As the lecture drew to a close, David reached for Azimi's arm and said, "Come on. Let's grab a sandwich."

Azimi nodded, flashing a warm smile in Danielle's direction, whispering in her ear, *"Till tomorrow, I hope.* She giggled lightly and turned down the aisle, her steps echoing against the cement floor.

Azimi turned to David, eyebrows raised. "She's cute, *n'est-ce pas?"*

David laughed, half to himself, remembering something Thérèse said. "You give us men a bad reputation," he said, shaking his head. "We're not all *cochons,* you know."

They made their way to the corner café-brasserie, a small, smoky place favored by interns and orderlies. They tended to treat themselves on occasion, eating there rather than the student restaurant. Azimi usually insisted on sitting outside, a strategic position for watching the stream of nurses coming off shifts from the hospital across the boulevard. But this time, David steered him toward a quieter table near the back.

Azimi hesitated, looked once toward the sidewalk tables, then shrugged and followed.

David lowered his voice. "We need to talk about something serious."

Before David could begin, Azimi grabbed the passing waiter and ordered his usual, "Un sandwich au thon et un Coca Cola, and for my friend, he glanced at David, "Un sandwich au jambon et un thé."

David, after a nod of agreement, folded his hands on the table, lowering his voice to just above a whisper.

"I had to go to the embassy the other day," he began, focusing his eyes on his friend, "to get a signature—something bureaucratic about my guaranteed expenses for the year. You've probably had to do the same."

Azimi nodded slowly, but there was a flicker of curiosity behind the polite expression.

"I ran into someone I knew there. An administrative consular officer, or someone who helped me with my visa when I first arrived. We got talking. One thing led to another, and I happened to mention that I had a good friend from Iran."

David paused. He could feel Azimi watching him now, more closely.

"His expression changed. Not hostile, not even surprised—just alert. I asked him about it, and he opened up. Started talking about the situation there. Not the headlines, not the press releases. What they're really seeing."

Azimi's posture shifted slightly. He no longer looked curious—he looked concerned. "Go on," he said.

David nodded. "He talked about the Guard. The Ayatollah. The clerics that he has gathered around him. Men, he said, who weren't just interested in power, but in remaking the state entirely—an Islamic Persian state. Not just in name. In law, Sharia Law, in thought."

He let that settle a moment.

"He knew I was Jewish," David continued. "He said there'd likely be no future for Jews in Iran. Not that there really were many left since Israeli statehood, but even what remained—businesses, families, schools—might not survive what's coming."

Azimi didn't speak, didn't blink.

"And it's not just Jews. He mentioned the Kurds, the Azeris, the Armenians, and your people, the Zoroastrians. Anyone outside the clerics' narrow view of what Iran ought to be. He said minorities would find themselves reduced, bit by bit. Not by laws, necessarily. By slow attrition. Less protection. Fewer rights. A new kind of silence."

David took a sip of the hot tea that the waiter put down, giving Azimi a moment.

"I'm telling you this," he said, finally, "because I think you already suspect as much. And I think it's time you talk to someone who sees the whole picture."

David leaned forward, lowering his voice even further. "This person might be of some help; his name is Bill Donovan, and I trust him. He seems to be connected if you get my drift. He's been following what's happening and gathering information—from people who understand the stakes. I really think you should talk to him. Discreetly."

Azimi looked away for a moment, his eyes tracing the lines of the worn café table. "And what... what would I say?"

"Just that we spoke and that you are worried for your family back home, and wanted to know the facts."

David continued, "He might very well be able to help your family."

Azimi's gaze returned to David, searching. "And why would he do that?"

"Because," David said slowly, "you're in a position like very few of your countrymen. You've lived there, but you've seen freedom here. You understand what might be lost. You can speak for those who can't. And because he likely needs someone who's trusted."

Around them, the café murmured on—cutlery on porcelain, the low drone of conversation, the occasional hiss from the espresso machine. But in their corner, the mood had shifted. The air felt closer now, the space between them more private.

Azimi spoke without looking up. "You really believe it'll go that far? That things will change so drastically?"

David didn't hesitate. "From what he said, it already has."

Azimi exhaled slowly, the words sinking deep. "I'll meet him," he said at last. "But let me think about this a little."

David nodded once and rose, slipping a small card from his coat pocket and placing it between the salt shaker and the mustard. "Call him. Say we're friends, let him know you are a medical student, nothing more. He'll understand."

Azimi picked up the card and turned it in his hand, and tucked it into his coat, but his fingers lingered there, unconsciously protective.

They sat in silence for several minutes, idly picking at what was left of their sandwiches. Azimi had barely touched his. Whatever appetite he'd brought with him had long since slipped away. David glanced out the window just in time to catch a glimpse of Danielle crossing in front of the café, her scarf loose, a book tucked under one arm, returning from the student restaurant. A gust of wind lifted the edge of her coat, and for a fleeting second, the scene felt almost cinematic—young, careless, and very French.

He looked back at Azimi, expecting perhaps a flicker of distraction, some comment, even just the trace of a smile. But there was nothing. His friend sat motionless, eyes fixed in the distance, shoulders drawn in, lost in thought.

She had passed directly in his line of sight. He must have seen her. But whatever Azimi saw now, it wasn't Paris, and it certainly wasn't Danielle. It was something troubling, further away. Something closing in. It was as if he was suddenly transported somewhere else, where he was no longer a carefree student in Paris.

David said nothing. He simply reached for the bill.

Chapter 23

Paris

Later that afternoon, as David started home, he passed a florist on the way to the Metro. He was always amazed that in Paris, flowers seemed to bloom year-round, and apartment terraces were filled with greenery—and even flowering plants—well into December.

He was about to descend into the Métro at Quai de la Gare. Then he hesitated, acted on impulse, and turned back. He stepped into the shop to ask about the flowers.

Inside, he was greeted warmly by a man he assumed was the proprietor.

"Bonjour, monsieur. You have truly beautiful flowers," David said. "Mais j'ai une question: où trouvez-vous ces magnifiques fleurs en hiver?" *But where do you find these magnificent flowers in winter?*

The man smiled, amused. "Ah! I note a slight accent, yes? Are you British, monsieur?"

"Actually, American."

"Ah, then we can speak English," the man said, switching easily. "I spent some time in New York as a young man. And my flowers, as you've noticed, are truly something special. Some come from the Netherlands, of course. But at this time of year, the most unusual ones—those must come from warmer climates. Southern Spain, sometimes even North Africa. They arrive by special air transport. Some of the fancier ladies of the neighborhood insist on such extravagance.

He paused, then added, slipping briefly into French as if reciting from memory:

He caught himself and chuckled. "Oh—I'm sorry. I'll try to say this in English."

Planning is crucial. Calculations must include not only the flight duration, but also connection times, of course, the temperature, cut-off times for each flight, and clearance times… Every detail matters when the product is so delicate. They must be in special containers with very strict temperature controls."

David smiled. The man clearly took pride in his craft.

"Merci," David said, glancing once more at the blooms. "They're beautiful. And clearly in good hands."

"Merci, monsieur. Bonne soirée."

David stepped back into the night, thinking not just of flowers—but of logistics. Of temperature control, precision timing, and the quiet choreography required to keep something delicate intact on its journey.

Only in his case, it wasn't blossoms he was moving. It was cadavers.

The idea had taken root the moment the florist mentioned special air transport. If flowers could survive the trip from southern Spain or North Africa, why not something far less fragile?

Yes. They could be obtained here in Paris—easily. A cooperative mortician could manage their appearance, dress them accordingly, and ensure they looked the part. After that, it was simply a matter of transport. Just like the flowers, they would travel discreetly, carefully packed, labeled as fragile merchandise, to the staging area.

And no one would question a cargo labeled perishable.

He descended into the Métro with the trace of a smile. Sometimes inspiration arrives on the petals of something beautiful.

*

By the following day, the UV sterilizing machine tests in the operating rooms and pathology lab had been completed, and students were expected to resume their hospital rotations. David felt an urgency—not about lectures or rounds, but about the next phase of his plan. He needed bodies. And he needed them soon.

On the far wall, the old chalkboard listed the pending cases in neat, tired script. The backlog was significant. The lab had been shuttered for nearly a week, and autopsies weren't performed on weekends unless absolutely necessary—violent deaths, high-profile victims, or those with political sensitivities.

The rest could wait.

David knew that most deaths were routine: elderly patients, overdoses, sudden cardiac arrests. Cases where the cause of death was obvious—and the paperwork would be signed without so much as a blade lifted. Those were the ones he was counting on. The ones that could vanish from the system with barely a ripple.

Afternoon lectures drifted by without incident. Azimi remained unusually quiet. They still took lunch at the *Resto-U*, as it was known, but neither of them mentioned the conversation from the previous week at the Brasserie.

It wasn't until late Friday, as they walked out of the lecture hall, that Azimi finally spoke.

"I placed the call," he said quietly. "To your contact at the embassy. No response yet."

David nodded. "You'll hear back. And when you do, you can trust him."

By midweek, David had begun to shape a workable plan regarding the cadavers. He'd need help, of course—but he knew that would not be difficult. Someone could be found. Paris Station has a large network of people to choose from. And for the bodies that appeared North African, the Israelis might help, or better yet, put forward someone from their network of Arab informers. A relative, a liaison. Someone who could plausibly claim a body as kin. A grieving cousin or brother requesting the release of the body for a proper burial, guided by the familiar rituals of faith: ceremonial washing, a white cotton shroud, the body placed on its right side to face Mecca. A request made gently but firmly, invoking tradition, dignity, and respect for the dead.

Paris had no shortage of young men—victims of addiction, trauma, or simply abandonment. Their deaths were as unnoticed as their lives, and David knew the morgue had little interest in lingering over them., The morgue administrators—drowning in paperwork and a backlog of cases—would be only too happy to oblige. Another body off the list. One less autopsy to perform. One more quiet disappearance beneath Parisian soil.

Anticipating that he would indeed need Rachel's help, he placed a call to her embassy, requesting to speak with the cultural attaché, and inquired about a concert venue, just as Rachel had explained. So far, no response.

As the sun dipped behind the rooftops on a still early-winter evening, David made his way home. The city felt unusually quiet. He guessed the Parisians were already slipping away—many bound for their ancestral homes in the countryside. It always surprised him how many of his classmates would disappear to visit grandparents in stone villages that had barely changed in a century.

His own grandparents had been immigrants, men and women who had arrived with nothing but names difficult to pronounce. There were no family estates, no centuries-old vineyards or shuttered summer houses waiting in the hills. Many of his French classmates, by contrast, seemed to inherit their land—and their history—with an air of inevitability. And when the time came, that property would pass to another generation, as naturally as the seasons.

Chapter 24

Paris

Even his own neighborhood felt still. The clatter of scooters and café laughter had vanished. Fewer girls lingered on the sidewalks. Most shops had shuttered early. Climbing the steps to his apartment, David noticed something off: his training kicked in. The umbrella he always left leaning outside the door was angled 'wrong.'

He paused at the door. Music drifted softly from inside—his stereo was on.

Carefully, grabbing the umbrella, he turned the key. The latch clicked into place. The hallway was dim and warm, faintly scented with jasmine. And there she was—Rachel!

She stood barefoot on the worn parquet floor, wearing jeans and his old Michigan T-shirt—the same one she'd taken the night they had met.

"Bonsoir, David," she said with a calm grin. "I let myself in. I hope you don't mind. I remembered I had to return your shirt."

He opened his mouth to speak. Nothing came. She crossed the room slowly, barefoot. A hint of amusement played at her lips.

At last, he found his voice. "I was just thinking about you today. And how did you get in?"

She stopped just short of him, eyes dancing.

"Least you forget, David, I am a professional. Not a student."

She leaned in slightly. "And you really ought to replace that pathetic excuse for a lock."

Then she winked—sharp, deliberate—and let the silence do the rest.

"I have a plan too," she went on, sliding her fingers into his. "But mine isn't about work. I've been working too hard. I need something else. Something to take my mind off it all."

She guided his hand behind her, under the soft cotton of her shirt. Warm skin met his fingertips. With her other hand, she pulled him in, kissing him deeply as her finger caressed his ear.

"We need to relax a little, or as the French would say, '*se détendre*', she whispered against his lips. "We can talk later. For now, let's relax. Please. *J'en ai besoin.* I need it."

And for the first time in weeks, David let himself admit it too— he needed this. He needed her. Needed to feel wanted and real and not alone.

He undid his belt as she tore off his shirt with a laugh, and they stumbled toward the bed, wrapped in something that wasn't quite love—but close enough for tonight.

The sex was passionate, yet at the same time desperate. It was shaped not only by mutual desire but by the weight of everything pressing in around them: the isolation, the silences, the fragile lies that made up their days. It was a necessity. They reached out in the only language they could still speak honestly.

For David, it was a rare moment of peace, a brief escape from the relentless grind of medical school and the colder demands of his other education—the one that taught him to deceive, blend, and disappear.

Rachel, too, lived between worlds. Born of two—her mother's East, her father's West—she learned to adapt, become a chameleon. Mossad sharpened what came naturally. But here, she let that drop. No missions, no lies, just shared breath and the hush of a foreign bed.

In the end, though, what passed between them wasn't spoken. It didn't need to be. In the warmth of their closeness, in the quiet gestures and the unguarded moments, they found a truth neither had dared to say aloud: that even those trained to withhold, to resist, to vanish—still needed to be seen and held.

They were stirred from a light slumber by the deep, resonant tolling of Église Saint-Eustache's bells, marking eight o'clock in the evening. Outside, the sky had already surrendered to the early winter darkness. David reached across the bed, kissed Rachel's bare shoulder, and murmured, Tu as faim? "Are you hungry?"

"Yes," she said, stretching like a cat. "Ravished. I haven't eaten all day. Let's go out."

David shook his head and smiled. "We have work to do, remember? I'll run down and grab a baguette. I've got some pasta and chicken leftover from yesterday—it's still good."

Rachel propped herself up on one elbow, the sheets barely clinging to her. "Not only are you very skilled in bed, *mon amour*, but you cook too?" she teased.

"You're going to make some plump American girl very happy one day."

David laughed as he dressed, pulled on his coat, and disappeared out into the street.

He returned twenty minutes later with a round loaf of pain de campagne tucked under one arm and a bottle of Bordeaux in the other. Rachel had already set about making a salad—bright, chopped vegetables tossed the Israeli way with lemon and oil—and was warming the pasta and chicken on the stovetop.

They ate simply at the small table by the window, the Fontaine des Innocents visible beyond the scaffolding and dust of the construction site below. Rachel sipped her wine, then set the glass down with a faint smile.

"It'll be a long time," she said, "before the Israeli vineyards can match even the most forgettable bottle from France."

As they finished, David shared what he'd learned from the morgue's administrator: the forms needed to claim a body, how the wording could be adjusted, and how little scrutiny was given to cases marked routine. Then he told her about his stop at the florist—how, to his surprise, there were commercial couriers who specialized in moving perishables by air. Flowers, food, even human remains—if the paperwork was tidy and the box properly sealed, if the paperwork stated that it was something else, no one asked many questions.

Rachel listened carefully, her eyes sharp even as her hands moved lazily over the wine glass.

"You're not thinking small," she said, finally.

David shrugged. "We can't afford to."

She leaned back in her chair, eyes scanning him with something between admiration and concern. "No," she said quietly. "I guess you're right."

"Although I'm sure we have local assets who can pose as grieving relatives—a long-lost brother or cousin claiming a body—we may need your help with the remains of those of Arab descent. Your people must have the right contacts here, individuals who can step into that role convincingly without raising suspicion."

He paused, weighing his words.

"We'll also have to be very careful in our selection. These bodies will most likely be mangled, burned in the wreckage of the chopper. But we can't risk it—if even one corpse is intact enough to prompt a closer look, we can't afford for someone to realize it isn't what it's supposed to be: a tragically killed American operative, nothing more. Just another casualty of a classified mission gone wrong."

He continued: "I've looked at the numbers from the Morgue's admission log. At our hospital alone, we receive on average 2-3 unclaimed bodies. Most could pass inspection with some cleaning. If we can get access to a few other inner-city hospitals, it shouldn't take too long to obtain the 8 or 10 cadavers that we will need."

Rachel rummaged through her bag and pulled out a pack of Marlboros, tapping one loose with the ease of a longtime habit.

"I didn't know you smoked," David said, raising an eyebrow.

"Only when I'm anxious," she replied with a grin, lighting it. "Or when I'm overthinking."

She exhaled slowly, the smoke curling between them as her expression settled into something more focused.

"So," she said, "what exactly are we going to do with these bodies once we've signed them out of the morgue? We'll need a place with refrigeration. Somewhere quiet. Somewhere they can be cleaned up and dressed."

David nodded. "Agreed. Nothing connected to any hospital or the embassy. Something industrial, out of the way."

"We can task Jim Waldon to start hunting around. Quietly. Maybe an abandoned food depot or a disused funeral facility—someplace with cold storage and privacy."

She took another drag, looked around for an ashtray, then, finding none, flicked the ash into an empty espresso cup.

"I'll confirm with Donovan," David continued, "that we'll need someone flown in from Technical Services. Someone who can turn these doubly dead souls into something believable. Shouldn't be too demanding, appropriate haircuts, grooming, some cosmetics, and dental work if needed. We'll need to get clothes, of course. It doesn't have to be perfect. Just believable enough to pass for an American special forces dead in a fireball crash no one's supposed to look too closely at."

David leaned back in his chair, his mind already cycling through logistics: refrigeration units, transportation time, and a temperature-controlled space. Someone to make the bodies look believable, false documentation, the window between morgue release and helicopter staging.

Rachel spoke again, softer now. "We must get this right, David. If even one of these bodies raises a question, it could compromise the whole op."

He nodded. "We will."

Chapter 25

CIA Headquarters-Langley, Virginia

The aide's black, government-issued Suburban crept along the serpentine access road leading to the headquarters of the Central Intelligence Agency, headlights sweeping over manicured berms and discreet signage. Late afternoon had given way to darkness, and night had fallen quickly. No one just *showed up* at Langley. The passenger's credentials had been pre-cleared, as her background had been checked earlier in the day. Still, the vehicle slowed to a crawl as it approached the gate, where the Agency's own uniformed guards waited in dark jackets, expressions unreadable.

The meeting was scheduled the week before. Marjorie Dorman was told of it just yesterday. As the assistant to the Chief of Staff Jon Satterfield, she was surprised that it was on the schedule at all. All she was told was "be there, say nothing, and report back exactly what was said." The Chief of Staff requested the meeting himself, but at the last minute, a Senate briefing was scheduled, and the President advised him not to postpone it.

She lowered the window, took her credentials—a State Department lanyard, Executive Office of the President clearance, and a second envelope marked with a gold seal—from her bag, and handed them to the guard. The guard took them without speaking. He scanned each item, typed something into a terminal inside the booth, then nodded once and waved her through. The security bollards hissed as they dropped into the pavement.

The Suburban pulled into the reserved visitor bay beside the old main entrance—a gesture of protocol as much as a display of control— No aide, no matter how close to the White House, ever parked near the executive elevators.

She stepped out, heels clicking on the concrete, her winter coat tightly belted against the wind. Her briefcase was slim and nondescript, yet it carried embossed folders bearing the President's seal. She felt a little silly even bringing it, as it contained nothing of significance and certainly nothing about the meeting at hand.

She walked with the casual sharpness of someone accustomed to navigating power—confident in the corridors of Capitol Hill and the West Wing—but not entirely at ease in this particular nest of it. The air inside Langley felt different. Tighter. More serious.

Her steps echoed faintly in the polished corridor as she moved past the lobby. She almost didn't see it at first—a pale wall set back in a quiet alcove, framed in cold lighting—just marble and shadows.

Then her eyes caught the inscription:

"In honor of those members of the Central Intelligence Agency who gave their lives in the service of their country."

She slowed. For a brief moment, she stopped breathing. Below the text were rows of stars, carved clean into stone. No names. Just a stillness that spoke of respect and gratitude.

She hadn't been prepared for that—for the anonymity, for the weight of sacrifice.

"First time here?" came a voice behind her. She turned to see a man in a gray suit, perhaps late forties, his badge clipped at an angle. He didn't offer his name.

"Yes," she said. "I mean, yes—first time at Langley."

He gestured down the hall. "They're waiting for you upstairs."

They rode in silence. The elevator was smooth, silent, without buttons. The floor passed with a faint chime, then opened onto a corridor identical to the one below. But the temperature here was cooler. The lighting is harsher. A faint trace of coffee and toner in the air, along with something antiseptic, unplaceable.

She was led into a secure conference room—glass walls that could frost over at any moment. Inside, the Director, Louis Reagan; Stewart Blake, Director of Operations; Jonathan Buchanan, Head of the Middle East Desk at the CIA; Patricia Ross, Iran desk at Langley; and Joe Anthony, CIA legal, were already seated. They didn't stand when she entered. Stewart Blake, whom she vaguely recognized from a pre-brief in the Situation Room, glanced up with a look that asked, "You're the aide from the Chief's office?" his voice was flat and unhurried.

"Yes, sir," she replied, clearing her throat before continuing. "I'm here to receive the briefing materials and return them directly to the Chief of Staff."

He nodded slowly—the kind of nod that didn't signal agreement so much as acknowledgment. "Then you'll need to listen very carefully."

She sat, carefully smoothing her skirt beneath her as she'd seen senior staffers do in Situation Room briefings. She opened her notepad, knowing she would write very little. She held her pen poised above the paper, then let her hand fall still.

Her hand was already slightly damp with sweat.

This wasn't the kind of room where aides spoke, or clarified, or interrupted. She was not here to offer insight. She was here to absorb—to memorize the names, the timelines, the delicate silences between spoken facts—and to carry it all back without embellishment.

The weight of that became clear with each breath.

And for the first time in her young and polished life—four years removed from Stanford, polished and pushed through a fast-track program that favored poise over experience—she understood just how far out of her depth she truly was.

The men at the table didn't speak right away. They didn't need to. They were weighing something, and it wasn't the operation; it was her.

The Director of Central Intelligence began, his voice steady, formal.

"As per the President's directive, we've assembled a preliminary operational framework for the extraction of the American hostages currently being held inside the U.S. Embassy compound in Tehran. The mission has been assigned the code name "Operation Eagle Claw.""

Barring significant shifts on the ground, the proposed window for the operation is early spring—late April to early May—weather and desert conditions permitting.

An advance team will be inserted into the country two to three months before the operation. Only the operatives themselves are fully read in. Their CIA handlers, from Paris Station—by design—are being kept in the dark. This is a strict need-to-know mission, and their role is limited to insertion logistics. The details of the actual objective are, quite frankly, not their concern.

The Director looked the Chief's aide squarely in the eye. "Once the advance team is inside the country, they have three primary objectives.

"First, they must secure transportation—vehicles and drivers capable of moving the assault team safely to and from the embassy compound without attracting attention.

"Second, they'll conduct a detailed reconnaissance of the compound itself. That means mapping guard rotations, security measures, entry points, everything we can use to minimize surprises.

"And most importantly, they must identify the exact location of the hostages. That piece is critical.

"When the assault begins, time will be tight. There won't be an opportunity for a room-by-room search. We need to know where to strike. The difference between success and failure—between a clean extraction and a bloody disaster—hinges on that intelligence."

He paused, letting the weight of the words settle. "That's what the mission depends on."

The compound is formidable—nearly thirty acres, among the largest U.S. diplomatic installations. We believe the hostages are in one of three sites: the ambassador's residence, the main Chancery, or the intelligence annex, called *the Mushroom*.

Once the breach begins, time will be our enemy. We cannot afford to search blindly. Every minute spent inside the compound increases the risk to both hostages and operators. There will be a very thin window of execution.

"The assault team will be deployed from our forward operating base in Egypt," the Director continued. "They'll be flown by helicopters to a remote landing site in the desert, which will have been chosen by the advance team who will meet them and transport them into Tehran. That team will have secured five trucks and a van through local contacts, using untraceable identities. These vehicles will transport the operators from the desert landing zone to central Tehran. To avoid detection, the plan is for them to arrange for a warehouse on the outskirts of the city, where the vehicles can be concealed until go-time.

The warehouse will serve as both a staging ground and a fallback point. From there, the team will conduct final checks, load equipment, and await the green light. The entire movement—from insertion to city entry—must remain below the threshold of Iranian counterintelligence. No local chatter, no visible Western footprint, no mistakes."

He looked around the table. "It's ambitious, but it's doable. We will admit that it is still in the planning stage. We will certainly keep the President abreast as to our progress."

Looking at Ms. Dorman, he asked, "Are there any questions?"

The room was silent. The aide to the President's Chief of Staff, Marjorie Dorman, was speechless. She never imagined that the information she was entrusted with relaying to the Chief of Staff and then to the President was of such gravity. She kept going over in her head everything she had heard, as protocol dictated that, in a meeting such as the one she had just participated in, no written notes of any kind were permitted.

"No, sir", she replied as she thanked them for the briefing and stood to leave.

As she left the room, the Director looked toward the D.O. and asked if there were any logistical updates.

"Well, sir," the D.O. began, folding his hands with studied calm, "as Ms. Ross can confirm, we've obtained confirmation that the main hospital in Tehran lies directly across the road from the embassy compound."

He paused a beat, letting that fact settle.

"This proximity, of course, presents an opportunity. Dr. Zarah Shirazi—whom you'll recall is Iranian-born and embedded in our advance team—we've decided will not be joining the others during the initial insertion. Instead, she'll enter the country via commercial flight into Mehrabad. We're advised that, at present, customs are being changed over and are thus relatively porous; as such, we've arranged for her to leave ASAP. Obviously, we will reconfirm this before her flight."

He allowed himself the faintest of smiles.

"As an Iranian national, she presents no immediate risk profile. The hope is that she can secure a post at the hospital quietly. She has already contacted her former medical director and explained her desire to return to Iran and help the revolution. We are also building out her legend such that she is also returning to assist her elderly mother. Once there, she will begin making discreet assessments of the perimeter, including guards, schedules, and blind spots. The sort of granular detail we'll need later."

He lowered his voice, just slightly.

"Once she's in position, she may try to reawaken elements of whatever remains of the local network. There's no guarantee anyone will answer. There's also a chance—small, but real—that she can persuade her superiors at the hospital to involve her if any medical issues arise among the hostages. That would be a windfall."

He shifted in his seat and turned to the next file.

"The Belgians," he said flatly. "Engineers by training. They've been under instruction with the Directorate for the better part of two months. Paris Station believes its only goal is to make contact with former Agency assets and begin reestablishing our network. That fiction is holding, for now."

He tapped a finger against the folder.

"They've been tasked with reconnaissance—identifying suitable storage sites for vehicles and equipment, ideally abandoned industrial spaces. Their primary role will be transport. They'll secure trucks, hopefully a van, and a discreet warehouse, and stage the movement of Delta from their landing zone—Desert 2—into Tehran proper and on to the embassy compound."

Another pause.

"Following the extraction, they'll reverse the route, bringing the hostages south, to Manzariyeh Air Base. Approximately sixty miles outside the city. By that point, if all goes to plan, Team Three will have secured the runway."

He glanced up, the weariness in his eyes betraying no sentiment.

"Two C-141 Starlifters will be waiting to bring them home."

Chapter 26

Angelina Tea House, Paris

It was Monday, just before eight, when Azimi, still fogged from sleep and halfway into his coat, heard the knock. A single rap, official but unobtrusive. At the door stood a wiry postal clerk in a navy windbreaker, holding out a buff envelope with a red band—pneumatic post, Paris's dying relic of discretion.

Azimi thanked the clerk, took the envelope, and opened it. A single sheet. Typed.

"If you are interested in talking, meet me at Angelina's, mezzanine level, 226 Rue de Rivoli at 18:00 this evening."

Signed: *A friend of your friend.*

He read it once, perhaps twice. Then, without ceremony, he tore it in half and fed the pieces into the kitchen bin. He checked his watch, took his keys, and walked out.

The hospital carried him through the motions of the day. Rounds. Lectures. A discharge summary he had forgotten he'd agreed to do. But the message worked beneath the surface. It was the signature that troubled him. *A friend of your friend*—ambiguous enough to be plausible, careful enough to be dangerous, who really was this acquaintance of David's.

He had been to Angelina's before: chandeliers, mirrors, tourists queueing for chocolate poured from silver jugs, topped with thick cream. He'd taken girls there, mostly foreign tourists. Its real virtue: always busy, noisy, a place difficult to be overheard.

By five-thirty, he was on his way on the Metro. By quarter to six, he was walking along the southern edge of the Tuileries. Halfway across, he paused.

Were things really this bad? Was it really necessary to meet with this American? Doesn't this put me in some danger?

At five-fifty-nine, he joined the crowd outside. Inside, he lowered his voice for the hostess. "I'm meeting a friend upstairs," he said.

She glanced past him, then smiled. "Mezzanine?"

He nodded.

Most customers refused the mezzanine. Too quiet, too removed, and lacking the grand salon below's performance. That made it perfect.

She gestured politely, and he was shown to the narrow stairs. He ascended without looking back.

At the top of the stairs, the mezzanine was empty except for a man leaving the lavatory and a single man seated at a table with a porcelain teapot and two teacups.

"Azimi, *Befarmāid beneshinid.*" Please have a seat."

Donovan, having long ago studied Farci at Columbia, spoke to him in his own dialect.

"You are David's friend?" Donovan nodded.

"We can speak in English. I have spent some time in Colorado and would feel more comfortable speaking here with you in English."

He poured the tea. "He's told me a little about your family, your concerns about what's happening inside the country."

Azimi didn't respond, watching the man across the table.

Donovan went on. "Before we discuss anything further, I need to tell you this plainly: what David said is true. All of it. Iran is changing. And it will not end well for those who aren't entirely aligned with the new regime."

Donovan paused, letting the words settle between them like dust.

"Dissent will not be tolerated—not by the Ayatollah, not by the men who prop him up."

Azimi leaned forward slightly. "You speak as if it's already decided. But what makes you so certain this so-called Islamic Revolution will succeed?"

Azimi leaned in, trying to convince not just Donovan but himself. "Iran is changing. The universities and the middle class are growing. We are becoming modern. I can't believe people would let clerics drag us backwards. There has to be resistance—doesn't there?"

Donovan didn't argue. He let Azimi say it aloud, let him hear the hope in his own voice.

Then, quietly, "People are angry, Azimi. Angry and humiliated. The Shah sold them a future, but it was built on sand: corruption, inequality, foreign influence."

He sipped his tea. "And when that kind of bitterness reaches a certain pitch, it doesn't matter *what* the alternative is. It just matters that it's *not* their future."

Azimi glanced toward the window. The sky beyond the Rue de Rivoli was void of sunlight; night was falling.

"So, you're saying they'll trade one tyranny for another."

"They already have," Donovan said. "They just don't know it yet."

He set his cup down. "Revolutions don't require logic. Just momentum. The mullahs have it now. The students, merchants, and some of the army—they're aligned for the moment. Later, they'll fracture. But by then it'll be too late."

Azimi was silent. The sounds from the salon below drifted up— low laughter, the murmur of lives untroubled by revolutions.

Donovan studied him. "You still have a choice. But not forever."

Donovan waited for the silence to settle again before speaking.

"What would you say," he asked slowly, "if I told you we could change your family's future? Not in theory. In reality."

Azimi said nothing, but the shift in his posture was enough—just a flicker of alertness behind the stillness.

"I'm talking about your parents. Your siblings. Even your grandparents, if they're willing. We could arrange for them to leave Iran. Legally. Quietly. And be resettled in the United States. Housing. Documents with a path toward citizenship. A proper life. Not a promise—an arrangement."

He let that sit, then added, "It's not as far-fetched as it might sound. But—like all things—there's a condition."

Azimi's jaw tensed. "Of course there is."

Donovan offered a faint smile. "Nothing dramatic. No sabotage. No meetings in dark alleyways. We simply need your family to assist us with a few logistical arrangements."

"Spying," Azimi said, flat and unblinking.

"Observation," Donovan corrected smoothly. "A favor for a favor. As David may have mentioned, I'm attached to the American Embassy. One of my colleagues has a team coming in—four, maybe five individuals. They aren't going to stir anything up. They just need a place to breathe. Somewhere quiet. Somewhere, the authorities aren't watching every window."

Azimi said nothing. His face gave nothing away.

"They'll only need a few days. We'll handle the transport. They'll stay with your family—speak to no one unless necessary. What we need is a roof and a reading of the mood. The real mood, not the version you hear shouted in the streets or broadcast on government radio."

Donovan paused, letting the next part settle into place like a chess piece.

"If anyone asks, they're professional colleagues of your father. Foreign medical experts or engineers, visiting perhaps en route to a regional conference. Nothing unusual. Nothing that would raise suspicion in a town like yours."

He leaned back slightly in his chair, easing the pressure but not the weight of the offer.

"After that, they'll vanish. Quietly, without disruption. And in return, your family's future begins—documents, safe passage, relocation to the U.S. Everything handled. Simple. Clean."

Azimi kept his gaze fixed on the teacup in front of him, watching the last curl of steam disappear into the air.

"And if I say no?"

Donovan shrugged. "Then you drink your tea, walk back down those stairs, and nothing more is said. You stay? They stay. And you all take your chances with the wind that's coming."

A good two minutes passed in complete silence. No sound but the soft clink of porcelain as a waiter moved somewhere below, unseen.

Finally, Azimi rose.

"Thank you, Mr. Donovan, for the tea," he said. "I understand what's at stake. I'll give your proposal serious thought and must discuss it with my parents. We are aware of the danger, but I must be sure we won't be trading one risk for another."

Donovan nodded once. Not pressing, not urgent—just enough to remind Azimi that the clock was already ticking.

"Of course. But try not to wait too long. Things are moving quickly now."

He paused, then added, "David knows how to reach me."

Azimi gave a polite nod, then turned and descended the stairs—slowly, deliberately—his expression unreadable, his hands loose at his sides, but his mind already racing as he left the quiet refuge of the mezzanine and stepped again into the swirl of Parisian evening.

Chapter 27

Paris

It was later that week, as David was entering the lecture hall, that he noticed Azimi walking toward him. As he approached, Azimi pulled him aside to talk quietly.

"Your friend, Mr. Donovan, is he someone that you really trust? Are you certain that what he offers is real? He has asked me to assist him in ways that may be risky and highly dangerous, not only to me but also to my entire family."

He paused again. "I'll admit, he seems trustworthy. But I've made mistakes before. I've learned that appearances can easily deceive."

As David listened to Azimi's quiet plea for reassurance, he understood—perhaps more clearly than ever—that the words forming on his tongue were the price of admission to the life he had chosen. Not a life forced upon him. Not something inherited or accidental. A life he had stepped into willingly, even eagerly.

Azimi had been just another name in a class roster. A quiet, capable student, David might never have spoken to, had the decision been left to him. But the decision wasn't his. It belonged to others— men and women in windowless rooms, their suits well-tailored and their intentions precise. People who would never meet Azimi, and never truly know or care who David was beneath the role he played.

This was the trade. He'd accepted it long ago. Names turned into files. Conversations became intelligence. People became tools. That was the work. That was the bargain.

But Azimi had become something else. Not just a mark. Not just a potential Joe. A friend—perhaps not in the traditional sense. There were still boundaries David hadn't crossed, truths he could never offer.

Yet Azimi was a presence in his life. Someone he shared late-night coffee with after lectures. Someone who had spoken honestly to him, had trusted him, even if he didn't know the whole truth.

David knew the names of Azimi's sisters. He knew how Azimi's voice changed when he spoke about his father. He'd seen the pride Azimi showed when he mentioned his family's town and his hope for a better future. These weren't just report details—they were outlines of a real life.

And now, that life hung in the balance because of a choice David had helped engineer.

Azimi was no longer just another classmate. He was a man David had come to know—and perhaps, in the quieter, more complicated corners of his mind, to care about.

And that made everything harder, twisting David's resolve with regret and anxiety he couldn't quite ignore.

In this role, he wasn't David the aspiring doctor. He wasn't Azimi's friend. That persona—the late-night study partner, the affable American introducing him to girls—was a construct. Useful. Disarming. Necessary.

At this moment, he was David, the case officer. A field operative with deep cover and a quiet assignment. And Azimi—vulnerable, uncertain, perfectly positioned—was no longer just a fellow student.

If he agreed, Azimi wouldn't just belong to Donovan. He'd belong to David too—his responsibility, his risk, his burden. He'd be his 'joe'.

And David, with a practiced calm and a heart grown heavier with each conversation like this one, was here to reel him in.

David stepped closer—and lowered his voice further.

"I've only personally known Donovan peripherally. As I mentioned, he assisted me with my visa issue. But I did ask around. I have a friend who works at the embassy. Donovan is high up on the ladder, as they say. I asked him directly, and he assured me that Donovan was an important person in the diplomatic side of the embassy and certainly a straight shooter. He admitted that he's not a saint. He's not a politician either. He doesn't sell hope. But when he says he can help, he can. I've seen it. People who were boxed in—trapped. Families in impossible situations. He got them out."

"Why?" Azimi asked. "Why would he care about someone like me?"

"He doesn't," David said, pausing. "Not in the way you mean. He cares about what you *represent,* about what's coming. He's trying to prepare. He needs eyes and ears where he can't reach. He wants Iran to become a better place for its people."

Azimi didn't flinch. "So, I'd be a pawn."

"You'd be a partner," David corrected. "If you say yes, it's on your terms—your timing. When it's done—when you've done your part—I can assure you that Donovan will keep his word."

Azimi fixed his gaze on David. "And you? Would you trust him with your own family?"

David hesitated. Just long enough.

"Yes," he said finally. "If it came to that—I would."

It wasn't a lie. Not entirely. But it wasn't the whole truth either.

Azimi nodded faintly. "I'll think about it."

David offered the smallest of smiles. "That's all he's asking for. Just don't think too long."

As Azimi turned and walked away, David stood in place, hands in his pockets, watching him disappear toward the lecture hall.

A week passed in silence. Then, at last, Azimi relented.

David reached out to Donovan through the usual method. They met that afternoon, at the same worn bench near the tennis courts in the Jardin du Luxembourg, where a light snow clung stubbornly to the hedges.

Donovan didn't bother with pleasantries. "So, what did our friend decide?"

"He's in," David said. "He's going home over the Christmas recess. He'll talk to his parents then."

"And?"

"What do you think? He wants details. What exactly will you be asking of them? He says it's a tight-knit community. Strangers—especially ones who speak with an accent—don't go unnoticed."

Donovan gave a small nod. "Nor should they. But relocation for his family to the United States isn't nothing either, is it?"

Then, casually: "You'll go with him."

David blinked. "To Iran?"

"To Yazd," Donovan said. "Technically, the outskirts. His family's village."

"That's insane. How am I supposed to land in Tehran, waltz off to some remote province, and then just fly back to Paris like it's a weekend trip to the Alps? I don't speak a word of Farsi. I've never even been to the Middle East."

"You won't be an American," Donovan said. "We'll build you a French identity. Passport, residency stamps, the works. You'll be exactly what you are—Azimi's French classmate from medical school. No one will question it."

David looked away, watching a child chase a pigeon across the gravel path. "It still doesn't explain what happens once we're there."

"Simple," Donovan said. "You arrive with Azimi. You meet the parents. You're welcome, of course. Their son's friend, traveling home for the holidays."

He paused.

"Our goals remain the same: First, when the team is dropped—roughly thirty minutes by helicopter from the city—they need to be recovered. Taken to safety. Hidden for seventy-two hours. Long enough to sell the crash narrative."

David's voice was tight. "And then?"

Donovan's gaze didn't waver. "By then, the search will have run its course. Our people may need help reaching their targets—quietly, precisely, and without suspicion." A beat of silence passed between them.

Finally, Donovan stood, brushing frost from his coat. "You have two weeks. Learn to enjoy Persian tea. He took a few steps, then turned back with the faintest hint of a smile.

"Hell, Azimi may even take you skiing."

Chapter 28

Paris

The week before Christmas break passed in a blur. Lectures were mostly review, summaries delivered by professors who were already thinking of their own holidays. Exams were set for early January, but no one seemed to care.

David found it hard to focus. He suspected Azimi felt the same, though his friend said little. The tension between them now was not about school or grades—but about home, and the journey that lay ahead.

David met again with Donovan. This time, he was joined by two men he hadn't seen before. They explained the pitch: how to speak to Azimi's family, what would be asked, the phrasing, the caution, the logistics. Every word was tested, pre-cleared, stripped of anything that might spark undue anxiety or suspicion.

He took notes. He nodded. But inside, the anxiety roared.

David certainly had known pressure before. It started early, Junior tennis tournaments as a kid. College exams. Living a quiet double life in Paris—American by birth, medical student by day, operative by assignment.

But this was something else entirely.

His cover in Paris had always been a performance—carefully rehearsed, never truly dangerous. At worst, he might be expelled from school and deported to the U.S. In Iran, it would be different. Hiding who he was there wasn't theater. It was survival. The difference between freedom and a prison cell. Or worse. Americans were being held hostage. He would be flying straight into a country already aflame—with forged documents, a false identity, and a mission with no contingency plan.

He told himself it was reasonable to be nervous. Reasonable to be afraid. Any sane person would be. But what surprised him—what unsettled him, if he was to be honest—was how a part of him was beginning to look forward to it. Not just the mission. The danger.

There was something intoxicating about stepping outside the boundaries of his old life, something sharp-edged and addictive. The deception, the secrecy, the feeling that every glance, every word, might carry weight. It sharpened his senses and made his thoughts clearer. He wasn't just managing the risk anymore. He was beginning to enjoy it.

Chapter 29

Latin Quarter, Paris

The curtains were drawn tight against the winter chill, yet the usual noise of the Latin Quarter still drifted up into the second-floor studio on Rue de la Huchette.

Smoke from cheap cigarettes curled toward the ceiling. On the table sat a battered cassette recorder. It wasn't for music, but for duplication. A tangle of wires and scarred decks fed a hissy, insistent voice into waiting tapes. From the tinny speakers, the Ayatollah's sermons bled through, slow and deliberate, each syllable honed to the edge of a blade.

Azimi's brother Azad sat cross-legged on the floor, a stack of blank tapes beside him, a half-drunk glass of tea cooling at his knee. Across from him, two other Iranian students worked in silence, slipping finished copies into plain paper sleeves, then into burlap sacks lined with laundry.

"This batch leaves with the bookseller," Azad said, not looking up. "He'll take them to Istanbul. From there—"

"Qom," one of the others finished, as if it were obvious.

Azad crouched by the small travel case on the bed, the dim yellow light from the bare bulb catching the edge of the false panel he had spent a week perfecting. He slid the last cassette into place; the Ayatollah's voice sealed away beneath cheap plywood and layers of denim.

"The more… let's say *inflammatory* sermons," he murmured, almost to himself, "I'll give to my brother. He can take them home over Christmas break."

He smiled faintly at the thought. *To him, it's just a suitcase full of flea-market jeans.* That was the story —jeans for friends in Tehran, nothing more. He had told his brother that it was a promise to "old school friends" who adored Western clothes, a sentimental gesture wrapped in casual smuggling.

But the jeans were nothing. It was the false bottom that mattered. Inside, the tapes would travel quietly, crossing borders in plain sight. The Ayatollah's voice would slip into Iran without a single customs officer suspecting a thing.

He closed the case and sat back, lighting a cigarette. He let the smoke curl toward the cracked ceiling. The operation was too perfect to fail. If his American friend David ever asked why he had so much luggage, he'd simply smile that disarming smile and talk about Paris flea markets and bargains too good to pass up.

Azad allowed himself a tight smile. "By Ashura, every mosque will have them. They'll know his words, and they'll come to know that only a strict Islamic state can rule Iran."

A police siren wailed somewhere across the river. No one in the room moved. Azad reached for another tape and slid it into the machine. The voice began again, a low rumble that seemed to fill more than just the room.

In the hush that followed, he spoke almost tenderly, as if to himself. "Paris is just the beginning."

Chapter 30

Tehran, Iran

Azimi had wanted to fly Air France. He said the stewardesses were prettier, the service friendlier, and besides, it felt more civilized. David had other instructions.

After a quiet conversation with Donovan, he insisted they fly Iran Air instead. The logic was simple: passengers arriving on the national carrier were subject to less scrutiny. The assumption was that they had nothing to hide. Azimi hadn't argued. But David could see he didn't like it. The French flight would've felt like a buffer—one last breath of Europe before diving into the unknown.

Around him, the shift was almost imperceptible—but unmistakable. Scarves emerged from handbags and carry-ons, unfolded with quiet precision, and were drawn over hair and foreheads. The chatter that had filled the cabin earlier in the flight gave way to silence. From his window seat, as the Boeing 707 jetliner began its descent, David could see the smog-heavy skyline of Tehran rising into view, its flat rooftops and wide boulevards blurred by the winter haze.

He closed his eyes, took a breath. Tried again to slow his heartbeat.

Across the aisle, Azimi sat with a magazine in his lap. He looked composed, even bored, as though this were any other flight home for the holidays. But David knew better. Azimi had grown quieter the closer they drew to Iran's airspace. He had spoken with ease in the airport lounge, over coffee. But since boarding, he had barely said a word.

David glanced down at the passport in his lap. French, issued in Lyon, with four years of border crossings artfully stamped across its pages. His name was now Jean-Paul Marchand, a medical student at the University of Paris. His photograph had been printed onto the page by the same team that had forged hundreds before it—so well, Donovan had said, that it could pass a French consulate inspection. *"They've done less work for greater causes,"* Donovan had told him with a wry smile.

But none of that reassured him now.

This wasn't Zurich or Prague. This was Iran—on the brink. The country was coming apart thread by thread. Shah supporters, revolutionaries, clerics, secret police. A Frenchman with a vague travel itinerary could vanish just as easily as an Iranian dissident.

The seatbelt light flicked on. The pilot's voice crackled overhead, first in Farci, then in French, announcing their final approach to Mehrabad International. Outside the window, David saw the Alborz Mountains to the north, their snow-covered peaks rising like a wall behind the city. They were beautiful, and he realized why Azimi loved skiing. Azimi finally spoke, his voice low. "You okay?"

David nodded. "Fine."

Azimi studied him for a moment longer, then leaned in. "Remember—if they ask, you're just a friend from school. My roommate. Visiting for the holidays. Keep it casual. Keep it boring."

"Got it."

The wheels touched down with a hard jolt. The plane hissed forward, brakes engaging, engines reversing with a roar. David's body swayed forward with the momentum, and a single loud thought broke the silence in his chest:

If they separate us at customs, I'll be screwed!

The thought returned with every passing minute as the plane taxied across the cracked tarmac of Mehrabad. David glanced out the window. There were soldiers everywhere. Uniformed men with rifles slung over their shoulders, pacing the perimeter, watching with eyes that didn't blink. Banners flapped across a chain-link fence—portraits of the Shah beside bold Persian script he couldn't read. Beyond the runway, the city loomed, gray and restless.

The cabin door opened, and the aisle filled with movement. David followed Azimi into the corridor, passport clutched tight in his coat pocket. Inside the terminal, the heat hit like a wave. Not physical heat—but tension, noise, a pulsing thickness in the air. Customs was a long line of narrow glass booths, each manned by a solemn figure in military green. Men and women were being questioned; some waved through, others were led behind dark curtains.

David's mouth was dry. His palms slick. His accent—*would it hold?* His story—*was it watertight?*

Azimi leaned in as they walked. "Don't speak unless spoken to. Just hand him the passport. Let me do the rest."

David nodded.

There were five booths open. They were funneled into the third. The officer behind the glass was middle-aged, with hard eyes and a mustache trimmed to military precision. He scanned Azimi's documents first.

A moment passed. Then another.

Azimi spoke in rapid Farsi. The man replied curtly. David understood nothing but heard the tension in every syllable.

Then it was David's turn.

He stepped forward and passed the passport through the opening.

The officer examined it in silence. Flipped through the pages, back and forth, then paused on the photo. His eyes flicked from the page to David, and back again. David held his gaze as best he could, resisting the urge to swallow or adjust his footing.

Then the man said something in French.

David blinked. "Pardon?"

Again, the man spoke, this time more slowly. "You are student in Paris?"

David cleared his throat. "Oui, à la Sorbonne. Faculté de médecine."

The man stared at him a second longer, then, with a grunt, stamped the passport and slid it back through the glass.

David exhaled.

Azimi was already moving. "Let's go," he said under his breath.

They didn't speak again until they were outside, standing in the arrivals lot beneath a low gray sky. The air smelled of dust and diesel fuel. The terminal behind them buzzed with chaos—families embracing, taxi drivers shouting, soldiers pacing. Sirens somewhere in the distance.

David turned to Azimi. "Did he say anything strange?"

Azimi shrugged. "He asked if you'd ever been to Beirut."

David frowned. "What did you say?"

"I told him you'd only ever been to Lyon, and that you're too taken with French women to survive anywhere else."

David gave a slight laugh. Azimi hailed a battered white Peugeot from the curb. "Come on. We've got five hours of road between Yazd and us. And likely there will be checkpoints along the way."

"You think they'll stop us?"

Azimi looked at him for a long moment, then said simply, "Yes."

The car pulled up and they got in. As they drove away from the terminal, David glanced back once at the city.

Chapter 31

Yazd, Iran

As they left the airport, Azimi continued to haggle with the driver. After insisting on the equivalent of $200, Azimi adroitly haggled him down to $120; he seemed satisfied. He spoke only French to David and made it clear, from his expression, that no one could be trusted, not even this cab driver.

The first hour of the trip was in complete silence, save for the hum of the road and the occasional crackle of a government radio broadcast which broke through the traditional Persian music. The city faded quickly behind them, giving way to the industrial sprawl on the outskirts of the metropolis, where oil refineries, silos, and rows of rusted shipping containers were stacked like forgotten relics. As they left the city, there were many fewer cars, but in their place were armed checkpoints every 20 miles. Azimi handled them with practiced ease, offering clipped Farsi greetings, flashing his ID with just the right amount of familiarity, never arrogance. David kept silent, eyes down, playing the role of the passive French student with an uncertain grasp of the language.

South of Qom, the landscape opened wide: *dry, vast land stretched in all directions.* The terrain reminded David of America's own deserts—Nevada, parts of southern California—which he had once visited. Occasionally, a low village would appear, clustered around a mosque or water tower. These were the only signs of life in an otherwise parched emptiness. Along the roadside, flocks of goats or sheep wandered, herded by men wrapped in scarves, faces half-hidden from the dust.

By late afternoon, the sun began to dip behind the mountains to the west, casting long shadows over the desert basin. The heat faded, replaced by the sharp bite of desert cold.

Yazd emerged on the horizon like a mirage at first—its ancient skyline rising from the plain, a mixture of mud-brick homes, domed rooftops, and the towering badgirs, or windcatchers, swaying slightly in the evening haze. Minarets reached toward the darkening sky, their blue-tiled mosaics catching the last of the light. As they entered the old city, there were shaded alleys flanked by high adobe walls, designed to shield against the brutal summer heat. Archways framed patches of sky. Occasionally, a figure would pass, cloaked in black or dust-colored robes, vanishing into a courtyard before David could decide if they had truly been there. Passing through the city going west, they finally arrived at their destination. Azimi, excited and anxious to greet his parents, jumped out of the taxi and knocked at the gate as David paid the driver with a very generous tip, which was much appreciated.

The courtyard door creaked open on ancient hinges, and for a moment, no one moved. Then a woman stepped into view—slender, wrapped in a dark chador, her face framed by lines that hinted at worry more than age.

She gasped softly. "*Azimi...*" The name was half-breathed, half-sobbed.

Azimi dropped his bag and embraced her. She held him tightly, murmuring a prayer under her breath in Persian, her hands trembling at his shoulders as if afraid he might vanish again.

Behind her, a man appeared in the shadowed doorway—taller, with the same narrow eyes as Azimi, but harder, wearier. He watched for a moment before stepping forward and offering a nod. Not warm, but not cold either.

"You've come home," he said in Farsi.

Azimi nodded. "*Baleh,* father."

Then the older man's eyes shifted to David.

Azimi turned with an easy smile, gesturing toward David.

"This is my friend from Paris—David. We are classmates." He shrugged lightly. "Unfortunately, Azad had to stay in Paris to finish a research paper he promised our professor."

From under his arm, Azimi produced a small, neatly wrapped perfume box and placed it in his mother's hands. "A gift from him to you."

She took it with a grateful murmur, already smiling at the thought of her eldest son thinking of her from so far away.

"That suitcase," Azimi added, pointing toward the corner, "will be picked up later by his friend Kazem. Azad promised to send him some Western jeans. Apparently, there's quite a market for them."

David's eyes drifted to the case—nondescript, worn at the edges, and the sort that wouldn't turn a single head. Still, he felt a small prickle of curiosity that came unbidden. He forced himself to smile as Azimi moved on to pour tea, telling himself it was nothing.

David offered the greeting Donovan had taught him. *"Salām. Khosh bakhtam."* Hello. Pleased to meet you.

There was a flicker of something in the father's eyes—surprise, perhaps, or calculation. But he gave a small, polite bow.

"Please, you are welcome in our home," he said in heavily accented French. Then, to Azimi, in Farsi, "He should not speak unless necessary. You know this." Azimi murmured something in return, too low for David to catch.

His mother, still clutching her son's hand, turned and offered David a faint, shy smile. In very correct French, she added,

"You must be hungry. Come. Eat. You are both tired."

David felt drained. Not the kind of fatigue that came from jet lag or a long drive through the desert, though there had been both. This was deeper. The kind of fatigue that settled in the bones when the stakes were high and the margin for error nonexistent.

He had landed at Mehrabad under a name that wasn't his, carrying documents that could get him killed if inspected too closely. Customs had been slow. For a moment, he thought the game was up. But the officer had stamped the passport and waved him through, barely looking up.

In Paris, he was David Rose, a real medical student. He had a second life buried beneath the white coat. Technically, he worked for the CIA under non-official cover. But the risks there were minimal. If the French ever grew suspicious, the worst they'd do was send him home.

Here, the price of discovery was far more serious.

He thought back to the Farm—the drills, the doctrine, the endless lectures on cover legends and compartmentalization. Back then, it had all seemed abstract.

Not anymore.

He would have loved to take a shower and lie down for a while, but the aroma of the food was intoxicating.

As they made their way toward the reception room, David caught the scent of something warm and richly spiced. Looking at Azimi, he asked what it was that smelled so good. Azimi turned to him with the grin of a man stepping into familiar shoes. "My mother's favorites," he said. "Gheymeh polo—split peas, rice, and meat. Baghali polo with veal shank. And fesenjoon-walnut stew. She always insists on jasmine rice with that."

The meal unfolded with ceremonial restraint. Silverware tapped against china; pleasantries passed, unthreatening, mostly void of content. David, now sharper, studied Azimi's father across the table.

The man had the tired posture of a surgeon who had been standing all day, and though he said little, his choice of words was precise and thorough.

It couldn't be lost on him—David's presence here. Not the typical guest, not in this country, not at this time. To arrive from Paris of all places, now, with students marching and portraits of the Shah burning in the streets, suggested either profound naïveté or something altogether more deliberate.

David understood this. He'd been taught: first impressions are not simply made—they are shaped, curated, deployed. Trust, especially in volatile situations, wasn't earned through honesty. It was secured through clarity of intention. He was advised to make the ask soon— before questions formed into doubts, before the father's silence curdled into suspicion. As the meal wound down, a final tray arrived: sliced melon and figs, rice cookies dusted with cardamom, baklava glistening with honey. A pot of piping hot black tea followed, poured into small glass cups glowing amber in the low light.

Azimi was the first to rise. He thanked his mother for the dinner and mentioned, with a practiced yawn, that they were both exhausted. She nodded, unsurprised. It was late, and boys who'd flown in from Europe had the right to be tired.

David stood, quietly thanking Azimi's mother in formal French. Consciously aware of Azimi's father's gaze, he followed Azimi out of the room, keeping his movements deliberate and respectful.

He realized that whatever happened in the following days would depend on how well he played the part—and on what, precisely, this family chose to believe.

Chapter 32

Yazd, Iran

David was wrenched from sleep by a voice in a language he didn't understand—amplified, insistent, echoing from loudspeakers just beyond the walls.

Allāhu Akbar… Allāhu Akbar… Allāhu Akbar…

Ashhadu an lā ilāha illā Allāh. I bear witness that there is no God but God.

It wasn't shouting, not exactly. But it carried a force that pierced through dreams and memory alike. He sat up fast, heart racing, the final fragments of sleep clinging like mist.

The dream had come again. The one that had returned to him, repeatedly, with a cruel kind of softness.

He was lying down in a garden, on the lush grass, golden with the light of late autumn. Children ran across the lawn, their laughter weightless. The air was scented with jasmine. And beside him was Mai. Sweet, innocent Mai, her eyes dark with tears.

"Why?" she whispered. "Why did you use me? Was all of this just a charade? Were you only interested in information you could get out of me? Was there nothing that was real?"

Even in the dream, he had no answer.

Now the call continued, its cadence mournful, ancient.

David drew in a breath and let it out slowly. He wasn't in Paris. Not anymore. He was in Iran. And the real performance—the one he had dreaded- was about to begin.

The sound of laughter drew David across the courtyard. He paused in the arched doorway of a side room and took in the scene.

Azimi, his father, and the two teenage girls sat cross-legged on cushions around a low table. Bread, cheese, and herbs were spread across it. A woven sofreh anchored the gathering. Azimi's mother moved with unhurried grace, pouring tea from a tall samovar. The steam curled upward in the slanting morning light.

David stepped in and took his place on the thick, worn rug. The two girls—Laleh and Yasamin—had greeted him the night before with the polite indifference typical of teenage girls anywhere. But for their conservative dress and the quiet Farsi between them, they could have been from Boston or Ohio.

On the table: sangak, torn into rough strips; soft white cheese; bowls of morabba-ye havij—carrot jam that shimmered like orange glass in the sun. The smells were simple, earthy, comforting.

"Bon Jour." David smiled as he sat. "Thank you again for your hospitality. The bed was perfect—I slept well."

Azimi's father looked up briefly and gave a polite nod. Azimi grinned and, as he reached for the bread, said dryly, "Well, that's because you didn't sleep on the roof as I told you to. Next time, no mattress."

There was a flicker of laughter around the table, the kind that smoothed edges. But underneath it, David could still feel the pressure—the thing they had not yet spoken of. The ask that could change everything.

He reached for the tea, careful to keep his hands steady.

After the two girls finished their tea, they rushed off to meet friends who were going shopping. Azimi's mother grabbed her coat and mentioned she would bring a tray of herbed rice to their neighbor, who had just lost her mother to cancer. The sound of the door closing left David and Azimi alone with his father. An uncomfortable silence lasted several minutes, and the tea had gone cold in David's glass by the time Azimi cleared his throat.

He spoke in Farsi at first—low and measured—addressing his father, who had barely looked at David since they sat. The old man's hunched posture, his fingers stained from a lifetime of ink and tobacco, gave Azimi a skeptical glance. As a former surgeon, David knew he chose his words deliberately and directly.

At last, while looking directly at David, he spoke.

Azimi translated. "He wants to know why an American student would travel to Yazd in the middle of a revolution."

David had discussed this in great detail with Azimi. There was no advantage to sugarcoating their ask. He should tell his father the truth, exactly what Donovan, the American working at the US embassy, had stressed to Azimi.

"Father," Azimi began in slow, deliberate Farsi, "David put me in contact with a diplomat at the American embassy in Paris."

He paused. His father, although his surprise showed clearly on his face, said nothing, but his eyes sharpened.

Azimi continued.

"You cannot deny what is happening here. The air has changed. The streets, the slogans, the silences. And according to the Americans, it's moving faster than we think—and not in a direction that bodes well for people like us. For Persians who are not Muslim."

Still no response.

"The Americans are convinced the Ayatollah and his mullahs will take full control. Not just of the revolution, but the entire state. What they envision isn't a republic. It's an Islamic theocracy rooted in Shi'a law. No reforms. No pluralism. Anything resembling the West—democracy, freedom of speech, equality for women—will be labeled corrupt. Un-Islamic, 'haram.'"

He paused, letting that sink in.

"They say the government will reflect the will of the people. That's just rhetoric. It won't last. Khomeini has already made it clear in his writings: Islamic law will supersede everything. The clergy will rule directly and absolutely. They'll call it guardianship. But it's rule Absolute."

His father finally looked at him. Azimi held his gaze.

"This isn't politics, Baba. It's theology with a gun. And once it takes hold, there won't be room for Jews or Armenians, and likely not for us Zoroastrians. Or even Muslims who don't agree."

A long silence settled over the room.

Then Azimi added, quietly, "They'll call it holy. But it will be just another dictatorship."

There was silence.

Finally, looking toward David, his father spoke in reasonably good English.

Do you honestly believe these wide-eyed students will manage to realize their revolutionary fantasies and rebuild the country in their image?"

He didn't wait for an answer. Just poured another glass of tea and went on.

"You must understand something, Mr. Rose, we had no love for the Shah, none. He was corrupt, certainly aloof, oblivious to the people, blind to their struggles. But at least his corruption had rules. It was a known quantity. Everyone knew the rules, and for most of us, educated Iranians, things were manageable. What came after… that wasn't our choice. We weren't given one.

"This band of mad mullahs—they should be sent back to Qom, to the seminaries where they learned all that nonsense. Let them preach to each other in some remote province, far from the rest of us, trying to build something real.

"An Iran that's modern. Independent. Where a citizen's voice actually matters. Where the government leads not with fear or piety, but with integrity—and by example."

"In hindsight, maybe it wasn't impossible. Maybe we were just too used to being told what to do and think, that we were fast asleep when the chance slipped away, and all of this craziness took root."

"Father." Azimi lowered his voice. "David's contact at the embassy has offered us an opportunity. If things unravel the way he believes they will, we may need to leave. All of us."

He paused, measuring his words.

He added, "He can arrange the paperwork—American documents. Green cards. It would put us on a direct path to citizenship."

His father's gaze softened, and he leaned in, seemingly eager to hear more.

"I could finish my medical training in the U.S. and work in an American hospital. You could work too, if you chose. And the girls—Laleh and Yasamin—they'd be placed in proper schools. Schools where they could study what they wanted. Dressed how they liked. No one would stop them at a gate or lecture them for a strand of hair out of place."

He glanced toward David.

"In America, no one tells you what to wear. Or what to think. You're allowed to speak your mind—even if it's against the government. Especially then. It's what I tried to explain when I came back from Colorado. There's order, yes—but it's an order built on freedom, not fear."

He exhaled slowly. "It's not perfect. But it's real."

His father, with a forlorn look, replied,

"I do not think that your mother and I would be able to leave our beloved country. Everything that we've known is here. Yes, it may be true that there are many Persians in America, especially in California, where my cousins live, but it would be very, very difficult, especially for your mother."

His father said nothing for a long time.

Azimi let the silence settle. Then he leaned forward, voice lower now.

"Baba, I know what this country means to you. You taught me its history. You taught me to love its poets and the joy of skiing its mountains. To believe we had something worth defending."

He glanced down at the rug, then back up.

"But look around you. Be honest, look at what's coming. This isn't a fight we can win—we are a minority. Not with words, not with books. These men aren't interested in debate. They want obedience."

Still, his father remained still.

"You once told me that being smart meant knowing when to stay—and when to run. The hard part was always knowing which moment you were in." He waited.

"This is that moment."

Azimi's voice softened again.

"You won't lose your country by leaving, Baba. You'll lose it by staying and watching them destroy everything you spent your life believing in. To stay and see what they make of this country will turn you to tears. I feel it would be best not to see that happen.

Azimi finished quietly. "We can stay and be silent. Or leave and continue to speak freely while we still can."

His father finally looked up, eyes steady.

"So," he said. "You want to leave our home. And you want to drag me into something that could get us all killed."

Azimi didn't flinch. "Not drag. Ask."

David, who had been silent until now, finally spoke.

"We wouldn't be here if there were another way," he said carefully.

"What exactly are you asking then?'

David picked it up from there.

"We only need a safe place for a few people, four or 5 at most, to stay for two or 3 days. They're not soldiers. They're engineers, business people, and an architect. Just until transport can be arranged. They'll stay hidden. Quiet. You won't need to speak to them. No one will even know they're in the house."

His father gave a thin, bitter smile.

"No one will know until they do. And then the mullahs won't bother asking questions. You realize that, yes?"

David nodded. "We do."

The old man looked from one to the other. "And why me?"

Azimi didn't hesitate.

"Because you, as I told David, always taught me to know the difference between right and wrong—even when the lines were blurred. Even when doing the right thing came at a cost. And because if you were in their position, you'd hope—just hope—that someone on the outside still had enough decency left to say yes."

The old man let out a long, tired breath. Then:

"My dear son, you've been away too long. Do you think this country is still reasonable? It's not."

Another silence. Then he said, quieter:

"How many?"

David: "Five, maybe six."

He nodded once, grimly. The room had gone still again. The weight of the agreement hung between them.

Then the old man spoke, his voice low but sharp.

"If I do this," he said, eyes on David, "I want something in return."

David met his gaze. "Of course."

"My son," he said. "Azimi. You said he could continue his studies in the United States. I want a guarantee. Not words. Paper. Names. Signatures. Whatever it takes to make it real."

David nodded slowly. "That's possible. He'll need to finish his studies in Paris, defend his thesis, and pass the usual licensing exams first. None of that should pose a problem."

He glanced briefly at Azimi, then back to the father.

"We'll need his transcripts, identification, and a formal letter from our school, same as I'll need myself. However, with the embassy's support, we can expedite the process. He should have no trouble securing a residency program in the specialty he chooses and in the region he prefers."

"I'll make sure of it."

"Not push," the old man said. "Assure. You bring these people into my home, into my life—I want to know my son gets out. That he has a future."

David glanced at Azimi, then back. "You have my word. And I'll make sure you have more than that."

The old man stood slowly, his joints stiff from years of sitting cross-legged on rugs just like this one. "I've lived long enough to know what words are worth. If your government fails on this, you'd better pray to your God that mine doesn't come looking for you."

There was no anger in his voice—just clarity.

Azimi spoke quietly, like a son still in awe. "Baba—"

His father waved him off. "Go. Make your calls. And don't bring anyone through that door who doesn't know the risks that he is incurring for all of us."

Chapter 33

Yazd

David spent the next few days with Azimi, carefully outlining for his father the specifics Donovan had passed along. They explained that the Americans would make their way to the outskirts of town and wait at a yet-to-be-determined location—one that would be relayed to his father the day before their arrival. David assured him that most of these individuals spoke fluent Farsi, were generally familiar with Iranian customs, and had spent considerable time in the country. His role, while not without risk, was straightforward: prepare a credible explanation for their presence in case things went sideways, provide discreet lodging, and then send them safely on their way a few days later.

"I have to say, Azimi, I'm a little surprised your father seems to be taking all this so matter-of-factly. He's a 'cool cucumber,' as we say—taking this adventure in stride."

Azimi looked up.

"My father is a surgeon, David. That comes with the territory. Throughout his life, he was trained to devise a plan, consider surgical intervention, assess the risks and benefits, and then decide whether the risk of surgery was worth the potential benefits. Emotions were always kept at bay. Cold analysis—that's what determined whether he'd ask a patient to take the risk of having him take a knife to them."

For a couple of days, Azimi showed David around the city. He led him through his favorite spots—the winding alleys of the old town with their warm adobe architecture, mud-brick walls, and graceful arched doorways. They wandered through the UNESCO-registered Persian garden, marveling at the tallest windcatcher in the world—an ancient Persian air conditioning tower—and stopped for a taste of local ice cream, creamy and subtly flavored.

When they reached the Atashkadeh, the Zoroastrian Fire Temple, home to a flame said to have burned continuously since the 5th century, David met Azimi's gaze and asked quietly, "How do you feel, leaving your home behind?"

Azimi's eyes darkened with a mix of sadness and resolve. "It will be difficult," he admitted, "but hopefully, the country will regain its senses. Things will change again—and God willing, for the better."

"I think that it is time that I return to Paris."

Azimi was surprised, though he didn't show it. The objective had been met. David, for his part, seemed reasonably assured that Azimi's father understood what he'd agreed to—and was prepared, despite the risks, to see it through.

"If you could arrange for a driver to take me back to the airport tomorrow," David said, "I'll see if I can change my flight to Paris. Hopefully it won't be too difficult—maybe I can call the airline today to confirm?"

"Of course, David," Azimi said, his voice level. "We'll make the calls once we're back at the house. I'll see to it that one of the trusted drivers takes you—someone who knows when not to ask questions. You shouldn't have any trouble getting to Mehrabad."

He paused, then added almost casually, "But tell me—how is it, exactly, that you managed to get that French passport? David hesitated. The question had been coming for days, he knew. Azimi wasn't the sort to let such details drift off unresolved. And while the whole truth was still out of bounds, he owed his friend enough to offer a version of it—close enough to reality to pass, far enough to protect the core.

"Yes," he said finally, keeping his tone even. "I've known Donovan longer than I let on. He did help with the visa, that's true— but he also smoothed the path into medical school. Helped me sidestep some of the usual bureaucracy. In exchange, he's asked the occasional favor. Nothing dramatic. Just small things. Harmless."

Azimi looked at him with a quizzical expression.

"When I mentioned to him that you and I were friends, he asked questions. He was genuinely concerned—for you, for your family. It was out of that concern that he asked me to speak to you about this. About whether you'd be willing to help."

Azimi was silent for a while and then, as if accepting his friends' explanation, motioned for them to head toward his car and go home.

Dinner that evening passed in near silence. David offered polite explanations—he needed to return to Paris sooner than expected— and thanked Azimi's mother with quiet sincerity for her warmth and hospitality. She nodded, gracious as ever. His father said little, eating slowly, eyes lowered to his plate. Whatever thoughts he harbored, he kept them to himself.

The call to Iran Air had gone smoothly enough. There were seats available; the change was confirmed with minimal friction. Later, before bed, David sat once more with Azimi in the small upstairs room, the fan ticking overhead. They reviewed the operation in full— each step, every timing contingency, the most likely point where the Americans would surface, and how they'd be housed without drawing notice. They mapped the safest routes into Tehran and, if necessary, the fallback path to Manzariyeh. Nothing was left to chance, though they both knew chance would have its say regardless.

David rose early the next morning. The house was still—muted, heavy with sleep and dust. He moved quietly, not wanting to wake anyone, but as he stepped into the hallway, he found Azimi's father waiting for him in the sitting room, already dressed, tea steaming in a glass at his elbow.

"Come," he said simply, gesturing to the chair across from him.

David sat.

The older man took a slow sip before speaking, his eyes fixed not on David but somewhere just past him, as if confirming something silently to himself.

"I will do what I agreed to," he said. "But I'll remind you of the terms. No weapons. No documents. No contact beyond what is strictly necessary. They will be treated as distant relatives—quiet, ill perhaps, in need of rest. If anything changes—if I sense the situation becoming unstable—they will leave. Immediately."

He paused, then turned his gaze to David.

"And in return, you will ensure that my son continues his training—not in France, but in America. At a major teaching hospital. Somewhere with prestige. Somewhere with a future. That was the condition. It remains unchanged."

David nodded. "Yes. As I said, he'll need to complete his degree, but I've been assured there's a place for him at a major American medical center. That part is guaranteed."

"I want you to know that I am not a revolutionary," the older man said, "and I am not a collaborator. I am a physician. My duty is to preserve life—not endanger it. Not theirs. And certainly not my family's."

David nodded again. "Understood."

There was a long moment of stillness between them—respectful, but cool. Then the older man rose without another word. The quiet click of his sandals on the tile faded down the corridor.

David remained seated a moment longer, the tea untouched, cooling in the glass.

*

The return journey to Mehrabad was uneventful. Two checkpoints along the road, but nothing serious—David's French passport, worn at the edges just enough to seem lived-in, passed inspection without a hitch. The guards barely looked at him.

It wasn't until he was standing in line at customs, the dull hum of the airport loudspeakers echoing overhead, that the thought settled uncomfortably in his mind: *Getting in had been the easy part.* As he adjusted the strap on his bag and tried to steady his breathing, the line edged forward.

David exhaled the moment the plane lifted off from Tehran's Mehrabad Airport, the knot in his chest loosening only as the aircraft climbed above the city and out of Iranian airspace.

Leaving a foreign country on a false passport was one thing—authorities were trained to be cautious, yes, but since you were leaving, they rarely saw you as a threat. It would be less likely that an Iranian official could detect a false French passport than a French official at Orly inspecting the same. It was altogether more dangerous, more unnatural, to reenter the same country of your departure, but now with a false passport! A Frenchman returning home with papers that couldn't survive real scrutiny. It would be very difficult to explain.

David rarely drank hard liquor, but when the stewardess passed by, he asked for a double whiskey. Someone once told him *the finest whiskey in the world is the one you sip while flying out of a war zone.* He decided they were right. As the glass warmed in his hand, he found his thoughts drifting back to the conversation with Azimi and his father. He felt confident his father would follow through and would help bring the plan to life.

In retrospect, David realized it had been his sincerity, plain and simple, that made his pitch believable. In the end, the most powerful element in recruiting someone was that they had to believe you meant it. That you cared about them, or their country, or their cause. People could sense the difference. And no matter how polished your pitch, it was hard to hide your true character, your real intentions. People could sense it when you meant what you said. Could feel it when you actually gave a damn. And in the end, no matter the tradecraft or the cover story, it was that sincerity, your empathy— genuine or brilliantly imitated, that made the difference.

To his left, his seatmate—slight, fidgety, with the gaunt look of someone who hadn't slept in weeks—let out a quiet sigh. David caught his eye and offered a neutral smile.

"I'll be glad when we touch down in Paris," he said.

The man turned to him, his voice soft and brittle.

"I haven't slept in a month. I've been in the embassy since the assault."

David studied him more closely. South Asian, mid-forties, maybe older. Indian? Pakistani? Hard to tell at a glance.

"What do you mean?"

"I was the cook," the man said quietly. Been working there for three years. I was in the kitchen when it happened. When they came in." He paused, as if still tasting the moment. "They made me stay. Told me to keep cooking—for the hostages." He shook his head, eyes wide with memory. "Yesterday, without warning, they said I could go. Said since I wasn't American, I was free to leave. I bought the first ticket out."

David said nothing. The story had the ring of truth, but too many things in his new life, he had learned, were never what they seemed. He sipped his drink and nodded, offering nothing in return.

Better to wait. The cabin was too exposed—too many ears, too many eyes. Conversations had a way of traveling on airplanes.

Chances were, an Agency car would be waiting at Orly, a silent escort straight to the embassy, a private room, where a friendly yet detailed interrogation could be conducted.

David turned back to his drink, watching the black sky stretch beyond the glass. He didn't speak again for the rest of the flight.

If even half of what the man said was true, he was a gold mine. Proof that the hostages were alive. Clues to their condition. And maybe most important of all, where inside the compound they were being held.

*

As the seatbelt sign blinked off, David turned to the man beside him. "It would be a shame," he said lightly, "to come all this way and not spend a day in Paris—see the Eiffel Tower, the Louvre."

The cook hesitated. He had been quiet for most of the flight, still carrying the disorientation of recent days. But the offer—an unexpected pause in a city he'd once dreamed of working in, was enough.

David added, "My friends are waiting for me at the terminal. We can take you to a decent hotel, central, nothing fancy. You'll be taken care of."

The cook nodded. No argument.

Arrival at Orly went smoother than David had feared. Customs offered only a cursory glance at the passport. Jean-Paul Marchand, apparently, was welcomed home.

They stepped through the arrivals hall together. Just beyond the glass doors, David spotted a tall man in a dark overcoat, holding a sign: **MARCHAND**. One of Waldon's people, Bruce Dillon, sport coat and tie, discreet, already scanning. His eyes locked on David, then shifted, puzzled, to the man walking beside him. This wasn't the Iranian medical student. Still, there was an ease between them, a familiarity. They were clearly walking together, toward him.

Outside, a black Citroën idled at the curb, its engine barely audible. The driver didn't speak, just opened the rear door. Dillon gave David a subtle nod, then gestured both men into the back seat of the car without a word, curiosity hidden behind a mask of protocol. In seconds, they pulled away from the terminal and merged into Paris traffic—destination clear.

Straight to the American embassy.

In the car, David explained that his new acquaintance was the cook in the embassy. He was surprisingly let free just yesterday and took the first flight out of Tehran. Bruce understood the significance of this and told him how lucky he was.

"I convinced him that he should spend a day or 2 taking in the sights of Paris, after all, as a cook, he should at least see what some of the 3 Star restaurants look like? I promised that we would arrange for his flight to Karachi and that at our embassy we would be able to take care of his ticketing and arrange for a couple of nights' stay in a decent hotel."

Dillon immediately grasped the significance of it—the man wasn't just a cook. He was an opportunity, a rare gift of chance.

The black Citroën glided smoothly down the Champs-Élysées. Outside, the Paris evening was beginning its slow descent into velvet twilight, the sky bruised blue and gray. Streetlamps blinked to life.

Beside him, the cook sat rigid, hands on his knees, saying nothing. The driver hadn't spoken since the airport. These were men who knew how to ferry ghosts through the streets without drawing attention.

As they turned onto Avenue Gabriel, the traffic thinned and the tone of the city changed. Quieter. More official. Government plates, tinted windows, uniformed guards at corners pretending not to notice.

Chapter 34

American Embassy, Paris

The American Embassy sat behind high wrought-iron gates, its discreet grandeur hidden in plain sight. No Stars and Stripes flapping proudly—just a brass plaque near the entry, and men with bored expressions and earpieces standing too still.

The Citroën rolled to a halt at the entrance. A Marine stepped forward. Dillon reached into his coat and offered his credentials. The Marine took one glance, then nodded toward the gatehouse.

The gates parted with a soft, mechanical hum. Inside, they were waved into the underground entrance, the Citroën gliding into shadow beneath the embassy. Fluorescent lights buzzed overhead.

David stepped out first, tired from the stress and ordeal of leaving Iran and the long flight, his coat smelling of cigarette smoke. He turned to the cook.

"My friends in the embassy would like to ask you a few questions about the condition of their colleagues who were taken hostage. It shouldn't take long, then they will get you a good hotel and your ticket back to Karachi. Just tell them everything you know," he said gently.

The cook nodded, face pale but set.

They were met at the inner door by a man David recognized from the flea market meeting—one of Patricia Ross's team. Mid-30s, cheap suit, and carried himself with a rigid military posture.

Behind him, another agent keyed in a code and pushed open a thick, soundproof door.

They entered what they called *the vault*. It was a small conference room with what appeared to be foam-rubber wall coverings. No windows, the door closed on the pressurized room with a "whoosh."

Inside, Donovan was already waiting. He was flanked by men in uniform.

He looked up—surprised first by David's early return, then by the stranger at his side.

David explained in a few tight sentences: the kitchen, the hostage days, the unexpected opportunity.

By the end, the air in the room had changed. Surprise had given way to something sharper. Anticipation.

Donovan stood, nodded once.

"All right, David, let's hear what serendipity has bequeathed to us, then maybe you and I can sit down and have a chat."

Donovan began with a warm smile,

"Let's keep this simple. Just talk. Start from the beginning."

The cook, now clearly nervous, nods and begins slowly, in a low whisper.

"I was in the kitchen. Like always. Prep started at six. We were short on supplies—no saffron, no cumin. The Marines joked about it. Said if it kept up, they'd mutiny over lunch.

Then… the shouting. Doors slammed. Footsteps—dozens. I thought maybe a drill until I heard Farsi. Not from the guards. From kids. Teenagers. Screaming *Marg bar Amrika!* Death to America. They took the lobby first. Marines tried to hold them, but they had no orders to shoot. Within minutes, they were swarming the embassy. I didn't see the worst of it—I was in the freezer."

He pauses. His handshakes slightly as he brings a glass of water to his lips.

"After that, when they realized that I was the cook and that they would have to feed the hostages, they must have realized that they needed me. A doctor came once a week. Tall, always wore gloves. Treated the hostages. One of them was sick, with bad kidneys. I stole meds when I could and hid them in the rice. The guards never checked the food.

One of the uniformed officers that David did not know whispered in the station chief, Duke Peterson's ear. He interrupted the questioning,

"Where were the hostages kept?"

"They were moved regularly, but Sunday, I remember them saying that they were going to be put in the chancellery building, where there would be guards on each floor, as well as three or 4 at each of the building exits."

The interrogation went on for nearly two hours. The room had grown warm—an odd thing, considering the state-of-the-art air conditioning. The cook began to rub his eyes with the back of his hand like a child who'd stayed up too late. His answers were drifting, looping back. Names he'd confidently recalled earlier now came out uncertain or reversed.

Donovan called a halt. "We're getting diminishing returns," he said quietly to Peterson.

The cook looked relieved, though he tried not to show it. Pride, even in exhaustion, is a hard thing to shed.

"We're grateful," Donovan said, his voice gentler now. "You've helped more than you know."

The cook nodded, uncertain what to do with his hands.

"We've arranged a hotel nearby," Donovan continued. "You'll be escorted there. Two of our people will stay close, just to be cautious.

Tomorrow, when you've had some rest, we'd like to go over a few final things. Nothing complicated. Just details."

"And after that?" the cook asked.

Donovan smiled thinly. "After that, we thought perhaps a proper lunch. One of those three-star restaurants that you'll perhaps work at one day. You've earned it."

The cook smiled and looked at David.

"Safe?" he asked.

David nodded. "Completely."

They stood, slowly. The cook's knees popped audibly.

"You've done well," Donovan said, and meant it.

They led him out. The two security men, dressed like Parisians on their way to a jazz bar, flanked him quietly. The Citroën was already waiting at the curb, headlights low, engine idling.

David remained in the vault, staring at the chair where the cook had sat. Exhaustion was contagious.

He glanced at Donovan. "You believe him?"

"I do," Donovan said. "I certainly do not get the impression that he was trained; he doesn't know how to lie. And the few things he got wrong were the kind of things no trained liar would fake."

They were silent for a beat. Finally, Peterson spoke, looking directly at Donovan.

"I would still feel better if we put him through a brief polygraph."

There was a brief pause, some nodded in agreement, then David broke in.

"If he passes, he's a witness," David said at last. That information should be helpful if there ever is a rescue attempt.

"Let's take a break, OK", Donovan exclaimed, it's been a long, grueling day, I'm sure. David nodded in agreement with a smile.

"Are you hungry, Donovan asked. "Not really, I nibbled something on the plane, but I am tired.

"OK, but we do need at least an hour or so to go over exactly what transpired in Yazd and your impressions about Azimi's father."

David had barely enough time to take a breath when the questions began.

First came Patricia Ross's second, flown in quietly the night before. He was polite, even disarming at first, but his questions cut with surgical precision. Dates, times, checkpoints, behavior. *How did you get past customs? What was the drive to Yazd like? Roadblocks? What was the name on the sign at the checkpoint? What brand of cigarettes did the Revolutionary Guard smoke?* Nothing was too small.

Station Chief Peterson sat against the wall, arms folded, silent but observing. He would weigh in later, but for now, he let the younger interrogators run the show.

They moved chronologically—David's arrival in Tehran, the transfer to Yazd, the meetings with Azimi's father, and the agreement to shelter the insertion team. His answers were calm, deliberate. He gave them what they needed. There were no dramatics. No performance. That wasn't David's way.

When they reached the part about the insertion—how the agents would be smuggled in through the back roads, concealed as distant family members—there was a pause. One of the officers asked him to repeat the names. Another jotted notes without looking up.

They probed gently at first, then sharper. What was the father's tone? Could he be trusted?

David repeated the conditions without embellishment. "No weapons. No documents. No contact beyond the house. If anything changed, the deal was off."

Then came the part that mattered most to the man—more than ideology, more than allegiance: his son. Azimi's safety and future weren't a request. It was the price.

David made that clear.

A guaranteed position after graduation.

At a reputable American hospital.

Specialist training.

A future, not as a fugitive, but as a physician.

He let the words land, firm and uncompromising.

"That," David said quietly, "was non-negotiable, and I personally gave him my assurances."

Around the room, David noticed that they all nodded but gave no verbal assurances.

It was after the second hour that Patricia Ross's subordinate spoke.

"Do you believe he'll hold the line?"

David met his eyes evenly and quoted the words of Azimi's father, "He's certainly not a revolutionary. He's not a collaborator. He's a physician. His oath still means something."

Donovan nodded slightly, a decision forming behind his eyes. The room was quiet again, just the low hum of the air vent above.

When they finished, they told David to take a few days. Go off-grid. Be a tourist in Paris. You're still on vacation; classes don't start for another week or so. He rose, exhausted but intact, and left the room. Behind him, the officers gathered his statements, cross-referenced the timeline, and sent encrypted cables back to Langley.

The real mission, classified far above David's clearance, remained hidden—even from Donovan. However, this new information would be critical for that mission.

By then, it was almost 6 PM. Carefully making his exit through the back door of the embassy, David walked the few blocks to Place de la Concorde. At the taxi stand, he slipped into the back seat of a waiting car.

"Les Halles, s'il vous plaît. Rue des Innocents."

The words came out low, automatic. He was drained—physically, emotionally, in ways even he couldn't fully trace. The cab weaved its way through traffic, headlights shimmering across wet pavement. Paris moved around him, indifferent.

When he reached his apartment, he didn't bother with lights. He closed the curtains against the early dark, threw down his bag, kicked off his shoes, and collapsed onto the bed. He fell into a deep, troubled sleep.

Chapter 35

Paris

David didn't wake until 10 am—and even then, it felt like surfacing from something murky and unresolved.

The light through the curtains was dim, diffuse. Late December in Paris—gray skies pressed low over the rooftops, the city painted in ash and slate. He sat up slowly, rubbing his eyes, and for a moment, he forgot where he was. Then it came back in a rush—Tehran, Yazd, Azimi's father, the house, the bargain. The promise.

He got out of bed and crossed to the window, drawing the curtain aside. Below, the street had already stirred to life. A delivery truck from the boulangerie idled at the curb. A woman with a scarf tightly around her neck passed by, a baguette under one arm. Everything looked normal. Peaceful.

But it wasn't. Not entirely. Not for him.

Azimi and his family were now, in many ways, his responsibility. The burden had shifted the moment he shook the old man's hand. The moment he said, *yes, I give my word.* He wasn't given clearance for that. There had been no directive. No one back in Langley had asked him to make promises. But he had anyway—because it was the right thing to do. Because it was the only way to make the operation work.

Because he believed in something. Still.

He moved to the tiny kitchen, filled the kettle, and lit the stove. As the water boiled, he leaned on the counter and stared out at the cloud-heavy sky.

This was the job. This was the weight that came with it. Not the tradecraft or the secrets, it is the promises. The people.

Azimi's future, his family's safety. That was now the barometer of success. That was what would keep David up at night.

He poured himself a cup of black coffee and stood in the kitchen, both hands wrapped around the warm porcelain.

"I'll make it happen," he said to no one. "Whatever it takes. Donovan was right; what he needed was a few days to relax, be normal, and forget the stress of the last week. He knew what he needed. He thought of Thérèse, the Art Historian. She was always open to a day with David—offering an expert tour of the Louvre or the Jeu de Paume to admire the Impressionists, or simply spending the afternoon languishing in bed, lazy and content, with no greater purpose than relaxation and pleasure. But quickly admitted to himself that what he really wanted was to spend time with Rachel. Not because it made sense. Not because she offered safety or clarity-she didn't. She was complicated, fierce, and entirely capable of holding her own secrets. But she made him feel alive. And more than that, she made him feel real.

He didn't know where she lived. He didn't have a number. They'd made no promises.

But he remembered what she'd told him, almost in passing, weeks before. Just before disappearing again into whatever diplomatic smoke screen she was required to inhabit.

"Call the Israeli embassy and ask for the cultural attaché. Say you're planning a concert."

He hadn't thought much of it at the time. It felt like part of a game they were both playing. But now it felt like a possibility.

He glanced at the clock. 11:12 AM.

The week between Christmas and New Year's in Paris was a half-holiday—half the city still away in the countryside, the rest recovering from the night before. Still, embassies kept their own calendars, even on weekends. He assumed that the Israeli embassy was likely closed on Saturday, the Jewish Sabbath, but might be open on Sundays.

He walked over to the desk, lifted the receiver, and dialed the embassy operator.

"The number for the Cultural attaché, Israeli Embassy, Paris," he asked in French.

The transfer took longer than expected. Several clicks. A polite hold. A voice in Hebrew that he didn't understand, then another switch—finally, a woman's voice, calm and faintly amused.

"Bureau de l'attaché culturel, bonjour"

"Yes," David said, adjusting his tone to something halfway between casual and official. "I'm planning a chamber concert for mid-January. Small venue, perhaps Tel Aviv. I was told your office might be able to assist with arrangements."

There was a pause.

Then, "Would this be Mr. David?"

He blinked.

"Yes."

"Hold, please."

A minute passed. Maybe less. But it felt like an eternity. Then came the second voice—cool, unmistakable, lightly amused even through the filter of static.

"Well," Rachel said. "You remembered the number."

"I remembered the concert," David said, smiling despite himself. "Do you take requests?"

"Not usually."

"But?"

"But I might make an exception. For a man who survived Tehran."

"You heard."

"I have ears."

He let the silence settle between them.

David hesitated briefly, "I want to see you," he said. "Not Business. Just to be with you."

Another pause. Then, a shift in her voice. I have a meeting at 16:30, let's say we meet at 6 PM tonight?"

"There's a small café-bistro in the 6th. Not far from the Luxembourg Gardens. Rue de Tournon."

"I'll be there."

"Good. And David?"

"Yes?"

"Don't bring flowers. Just bring yourself. The rest we can negotiate."

The line went dead.

He stared at the receiver for a moment, then gently replaced it on the cradle.

Outside, the sky was still gray, but a thin line of gold had begun to push through the cloud cover, casting a faint glow across the opposite buildings.

He went to shower, shaved for the first time in three days, and chose his clothes with the usual disregard. Not too formal. Not too casual. Something between roles. After dressing, he stood by the window for a while, watching the narrow street below—delivery vans double-parked, a woman walking her terrier in a bright red slicker, the corner brasserie beginning to come alive. Paris moved on, unbothered by secrets.

The morning slipped by in silence.

He passed the day outlining the report he would have to write. Not for the Agency's standard case files. This one would be read by the people whose names were never spoken aloud. The ones who ran the gameboard from an ocean away.

He opened a legal pad and began from the moment he landed. The customs line at Mehrabad. The questions that were asked. The taste of the air—metallic, choked with smog and ash. The long drive south, past checkpoints and empty roads.

The detour into Yazd. His father, the pitch, phrases passed between Azimi and his father in Persian, translated only loosely for David. Every flicker of doubt. Every tightening of the old man's jaw. Every condition they negotiated. And most of all— the promise.

That was the anchor.

Of everything he carried back from Iran—his impressions, the conditions and demands for any of the possible safe houses, the cover identities of the men who would soon arrive there—the most important was the agreement struck in the courtyard of an aging adobe home under a cold desert sky.

Azimi's father had asked for one thing: a promise. Not so much for himself, nor for his wife. And not in vague diplomatic terms, but something real. Something lasting. His son's future. A passport and a future at a respected American hospital. A life in medicine, after exile. Something to show that this had all been worth it.

David had looked the man in the eye and given his word.

Now that promise was written in invisible ink, waiting to be deciphered in Langley's secured briefings.

He paused mid-page and underlined a sentence twice:

"This arrangement should be honored at the highest level. Their risk, their cooperation, was conditional on it."

He closed the notebook and set it aside. The real test, he knew, wasn't having convinced the father.

It was getting someone behind a desk in Virginia to care.

By 17:30, he was walking. Down Rue Saint-Honoré, across Pont Neuf, cutting through the polished calm of the Left Bank. Paris in mid-winter had less of the charm of late spring or fall; the trees were bare, but still a few were strung with twinkling holiday lights. And in almost every neighborhood, the air had the distinct smell of a wood-burning fireplace.

He reached Rue de Tournon just before six. The Bistro was tucked between a rare bookshop and a shuttered antiques dealer. No name on the window. Just the rich scent of simple French cuisine and old wood.

She was already there, seated at a table by the window, a scarf looped around her neck, a book open in front of her, a glass of white wine that she was slowly nursing. The early evening light slanted through the window, falling across the pages of her book. David paused in the doorway. For a second, she didn't look up. Then, as if sensing him, some fine-tuned instinct honed by the life they both led—she turned.

And smiled.

It was the kind of smile that didn't ask questions, just spoke of warmth and happiness.

He crossed the room slowly, weaving between tables. He caught the eye of a passing waiter and lifted a hand. "Un verre de rouge, s'il vous plaît— Maison." His voice was quiet, but he spoke with authority.

Reaching her, he bent low, kissing both cheeks, though it lingered. Then, for a beat, he stopped, eyes locked on hers. And softly, deliberately, he kissed her lips.

There was no hesitation.

It wasn't a kiss of lust or apology. It was one of recognition. Of return.

When he pulled back, she looked at him without speaking for a long moment, then closed her book and set it aside.

"I'm glad to see that you made it back," she said.

"I wasn't going to miss this."

She tilted her head, studying him. "You look like someone who's been sleeping with one eye open."

"I have," he admitted. "And even that feels generous."

The waiter returned with his wine, set it down, nodded, and disappeared.

He slid into the seat across from her, the table small enough that their knees nearly touched. For a while, neither said much. He watched the way her fingers traced the stem of her wine glass. She noted the cut on his knuckle, the pallor just under his eyes.

"I got the outlines of your return from Iran," she finally said.

"From our station chief."

"I figured you would."

"Would you say it was a successful trip?"

He didn't answer right away. Took a sip of the wine. It was young, slightly tannic, but good enough.

"I think so," he said. "But as we say in America, the proof is in the pudding."

"Interesting saying, but I guess that is always the case, you'll agree?"

They ordered quickly—Chicken Breast for her, steak for him. She laughed when the waiter looked at them curiously for ordering dinner this early. David shrugged. "We're not French," he said. "We like our sins early."

Over the next hour, the conversation drifted. Paris during the holiday season, how nice it feels without the mobs of tourists. Occasionally, something darker would press through—names, cities, implications—but Rachel would steer them gently back, never letting the evening sink into debriefing.

At some point, she reached across and brushed a crumb from his collar. The gesture was small, but it stayed with him longer than it could have.

"Come home with me tonight," he said, simply. "It's been a long, stressful week, and let's not forget that we are in this together. I'd like to get your impressions before we convene for a formal debriefing between our two agencies. I could use your input and experience.

She looked at him for a long moment, a slight hesitation, then, "Yes, David", but with one condition.

"There will be no discussion of work until tomorrow morning, agreed?"

With a smile, David agreed.

Outside, Paris was slipping toward evening. The rain had stopped. The streets glistened, lit by headlights and café signs. Inside the restaurant, they stayed a little longer, the space between them closing with each passing moment. Not hurried. Just two people in need of human comfort.

They walked across the river arms entwined, mostly in silence, huddling together from the wind and light snow. Arriving at his apartment, they barely made it through the front door before his mouth was on hers again, hungry, a little desperate. She laughed softly, feeling out of breath, and she found herself being more surprised than him. His keys clattered onto the counter. The door swung shut on the city behind them.

Shoes came off somewhere in the hallway. Her coat slipped from her shoulders like water. He reached for the light but missed; the room stayed dim, washed in the golden spill of a distant streetlamp.

They found the bed by memory—bumping into a chair, knocking over the stack of papers he had just written that afternoon. It no longer had the importance that he had given it 6 hours before. Her hands were on his shirt, his fingers on the zipper of her dress, and still, they couldn't stop kissing. It felt necessary like air.

The sheets were cool, the room faintly stale from being gone too long, but none of it mattered. Her skin was warm beneath his palms; her breath caught in his ear. She pulled him down, and the city, the job, the studying, the mission—they all receded.

For now, it was just her. Her body against his. He hadn't realized how much he'd missed wanting something, needing someone—until now, until Rachel.

For the first time in longer than he could remember, he had slept deeply and without nightmares, without interruption. Rachel's head rested on his shoulder, her breath warm and steady against his skin. As the church bell struck eight and the first light of day slipped through the window, he eased out of bed, dressed quickly, and slipped down to the street.

He walked several blocks to gather what he needed: milk, fresh coffee beans, a handful of vegetables, and eggs. The only place open was the *épicerie de quartier*, a cramped little shop run by a friendly middle-aged Algerian couple who always seemed to be open when no one else was.

All that remained was to find a boulangerie open on a Sunday morning—just two croissants and a warm baguette to complete their breakfast.

Heading up the stairs to his flat, he met Isabelle on the landing. Her makeup was smudged, her hair a tangle, last night's dress still clinging to her. She managed a small, rueful smile.

"Bonjour, voisin."

"Long night?" David asked.

She shrugged, lit a cigarette, and didn't answer. He didn't press.

Back inside, he undressed quietly and slid back under the covers. The bed was still warm. Rachel stirred, blinking up at him, her hair a tousled halo on the pillow.

"What time is it?" she murmured, voice thick with sleep.

David smiled. "Almost time for a real American breakfast."

His hand found the curve of her waist, fingers trailing lightly across her abdomen.

"But first," he said, leaning in, his voice low, "we have some unfinished business."

Chapter 36

Paris

The conversation over coffee, eggs, and croissants felt almost like a debriefing. The Israelis were accepted as 'passengers'—if not partners—in the operation, and, as Donovan instructed, David was to serve as the go-between—the official liaison officer. At the Farm, during training, he'd been given very few rules about the dos and don'ts of liaison relationships. Instead, he was told he'd learn on the job.

David remembered what Jim Waldon had said, with that practiced calm of a man who'd been in his current position, too long: that he, David, was chosen to liaise with Rachel not just because of their prior… 'familiarity', but because anyone else—anyone under official embassy cover—would be far too visible. An American officer, or for that matter, an embassy employee meeting with an Israeli, even one wearing the veil of diplomatic protocol, would light up on every third-rate surveillance log from Prague to Damascus. David, on the other hand, had clean operational cover. He was, as far as anyone knew, just a medical student. If a foreign service spotted the two of them together—even knowing she was Mossad—it would, at most, suggest an affair. Not a covert collaboration between intelligence services.

But the unspoken directive was clear: beyond immediate cooperation, the real goal was to gather as much intelligence as possible on foreign services—and, if the opportunity presented itself, to recruit sources from within their ranks.

His relationship with Rachel was different—at least to David. *Still, the question lingered at the edges of his thoughts: did she feel the same way? Or was her real objective to recruit him, to extract intelligence that extended well beyond the mission they supposedly shared?*

He went over in great detail the lengthy conversation that both he and Azimi had with his father. The former physician was extremely knowledgeable and understood exactly what was being asked of him. He understood the risk, yet he agreed to assist them and harbor their 'agents'. He did it out of fear that the future of Iran would not be kind to his Zoroastrian community. He was a patriot and yearned for a democratic Iran free of the Shah and his abuses, but also free from the religious fundamentalism that the Ayatollah represented. But above all, he wanted to secure his son's future. An intelligent and honest young man with a mind for medicine, Azimi deserved a life shaped by healing—not ideology. And that life, his father believed, would begin with training in America. As David wrapped up the long recap of his days at Azimi's home, his voice softened, shaded now with something closer to sorrow.

"I gave his father my word that we would keep our promise."

Rachel said nothing. But the look she gave him was steady, solemn. No smile, no argument, just the quiet recognition of the burden he had taken on.

Almost as an afterthought, David mentioned that, by chance, he'd been seated on the flight home next to the cook from the embassy. He gave a summary of the conversation during the debrief, watching Rachel's face as he spoke.

Her expression shifted—surprise flashing before her training took hold.

"That's the equivalent of hitting the jackpot twice in a row, as you Americans like to say," she said crisply. "Or it means Iranian intelligence—what's left of it—is playing games with you. SAVAK were no amateurs, David. They had, and may still have, a very capable counterintelligence service."

"I'm sure the station will do what it can to back up his statements. As we speak, he's undergoing a polygraph, which should catch it if he's lying. If so, then he certainly fooled me. And I like to think I'm a pretty good judge of character."

"At any rate, the information in my debrief and this new development with the cook will need to be cabled off to Langley. Likely, we won't get a response at all until the end of the week."

Rachel stood, leaned down, and kissed him—lightly, but not without feeling.

"I'm glad you called," she said. "But I have to get to the embassy. It's a workday, after all. And with what you've just told me, I'll need to update my superiors."

David almost asked when he'd see her again—but caught himself. That old question was surfacing once more: *where did the personal end and the professional begin?*

Would their next meeting be business? Or was there still something more between them—something real?

Was this an affair?

That was what unsettled him most—not knowing which game they were playing, or if they were playing the same one at all.

Chapter 37

Louvre Museum, Paris

By week's end, the station chief in Paris had received coded cable from Langley. They had gone over the debrief and the intel obtained and cross-referenced it with other sources. They were satisfied that the Pakistani cook was legit. His story held together and, with other information, was deemed truthful. With this, the instructions were to move the insertion operation up. The OP was a "GO." Langley wanted Paris Station to initiate Phase One immediately—prepare the operatives, secure transport, and begin movement of materiel, including the decoy cadavers, to Cairo within two weeks. There was no margin for delay.

David was contacted by Donovan and told to meet at the Louvre the following evening. The Louvre would be open late until 9 PM. They were to meet in the Rubens Room, the Marie de' Medici Gallery, located on the first floor in the Denon Wing at 19:45 sharp.

David was certain Paris Station had received word from Langley. The anticipation coursing through him was tempered only by the familiar undercurrent of anxiety.

All day, he'd turned over the same question: Had their intelligence aligned with the story the cook had given?

By six o'clock, he was already on edge. He had not eaten all day, yet he had little appetite. He decided to get there early, hoping that a slow walk through the museum might calm his nerves. It didn't.

By 19:30, he began to walk towards the Denon Wing and the Rubens Room, hoping to arrive a few minutes early. Playing the part of the tourist, he found, was not hard, given the overwhelming, almost transportive effect of the huge painting on display.

Rubens's paintings, all commissioned between 1622 and 1625, dramatized the life of Queen Marie de' Medici—the Italian-born widow of Henri IV, exiled by her own son, memorialized here in oil and allegory. The paintings, some over thirteen feet tall, hung in gilded frames that seemed to hover from the walls, as if even the Louvre understood their need for reverence.

For a moment, David lost himself in thought. He knew a little bit about the paintings from his Freshman Art History class at Michigan, but seeing the pictures in a textbook or even in the professor's slideshow did not do them justice. Entranced, he was jolted by footsteps and a gentle tap on his shoulder. Donovan motioned him to the corner where Amir was standing.

"Impressive, aren't they?" Donovan said, his voice echoing just slightly in the vaulted gallery. He didn't wait for an answer. "Tell me, David—how's your history these days? If memory serves, you were something of a student of the world before medicine claimed you."

David said nothing, waiting.

Donovan's smile barely stirred. "Queen Marie de' Medici. The Shah. Funny—their stories aren't so far apart."

He gestured lazily toward the Rubens canvas, then tucked his hands into the pockets of his coat, voice lowering into something close to reflection.

"Her own son exiled Marie. The king she once governed for. A reversal of fortunes, wouldn't you say? The Shah, meanwhile, was chased out by his own people, a revolution of his own making. And like Marie, he's drifting now. One court to the next. Politically radioactive, no real refuge. No one wants a fallen monarch these days—not even the monarchists."

David tilted his head, still listening.

"They both made the same mistake," Donovan went on. "Trusted the wrong men. Marie had Concini, then Richelieu, who proved far more ambitious than loyal. The Shah had SAVAK. Repression in a tailored suit. The people hated it. Hated him for it. And then, of course…" He let the thought trail off, gave David a knowing glance. "Then he had us."

A long silence stretched between them.

"You see, David—history, it seems, most certainly does have a habit of repeating itself."

Donovan motioned to the corner of the room where Amir was waiting.

"Well, David," Donovan said, lowering his voice, "Langley's convinced your cook is the real thing. They've run it through the Mukhabarat in Baghdad and the ISI in Islamabad. Nothing suggests a false flag."

He paused, letting it land.

"ISI confirmed his exit dates and flagged no suspicious financials. No anomalies. All of it suggests that he is clean."

David said nothing but felt the shift.

"That's when it clicked," Donovan continued. "We know where the hostages are, at least for now. And with that, the call came down. Langley and Special Activities want us to move. Target date: January 20th."

"Given the timeline, we'll need to move fast. Cairo's West Air Base has been offered—we'll use it as our forward staging area. The team flies in there, along with the cadavers from the morgue. There is also a chance the main hospital in Cairo can provide a couple of extra bodies if needed. We won't know for sure until forty-eight hours out. Either way, we'll have a day or two on the ground to prepare—dress them properly, finalize insertion protocol."

He paused, then added, "Langley believes that if we can keep our people hidden inside Yazd for three, maybe four days, the situation should begin to settle. By then, their exfiltration, quiet and piece by piece, shouldn't raise alarms."

David took this all in.

"One more thing," Donovan said, pausing long enough to make it matter. He looked directly at David.

"They want Azimi in Yazd when the team arrives—to make sure his father doesn't lose his nerve." He hesitated again, just long enough for the weight to settle.

"And Langley's made it clear. You're to go in with the team."

David stared at him. For a moment, he couldn't even find his voice.

"Donovan… what the fuck are you talking about?" It came out harsher than he intended. "You want *me* to go back into Iran? Into Yazd? For what? Tell me exactly what I'm supposed to do once we're on the ground."

He shook his head, half laughing, half choking on disbelief.

"Sure—I can help in Cairo with the cadavers. Fine. But once that helicopter takes off and lands in Yazd, what possible use am I? I'm not trained for this. I'm not operational. I've had *zero* preparation for being dropped into a hostile environment!"

His voice rose, edged with panic. "And how do you propose I return, after our operatives set out to their respective cities? Call for a helicopter?"

Amir spoke for the first time.

"David, listen. Your presence is critical. Azimi's father trusts *you*— he made the deal with *you*. If you're not there, he might think we're backing out. And in my experience, that's all it takes for a man in his position to change his mind."

He let the thought settle. Then Donovan picked up where he left off.

"Azimi will reenter Iran the same way he did before—no issue there. Once the operation is completed and the team leaves Yazd, you and Azimi will return to Tehran and fly out. Amir will be with you the whole way. He still has a passport and papers provided by SAVAK from a joint mission two years ago."

David raised an eyebrow. "With my French passport? What about the missing re-entry stamps? How do I explain that I returned to Paris, then came back to Iran without an entry stamp in my passport? Oh, maybe I can tell them I came back on an American military helicopter??"

Donovan allowed a rare smile.

"We anticipated that. Your passport—under the name Jean-Paul Marchand—was prepped with a thin, clear film on the page where they placed your exit stamp. We peel it off, and voilà… It's as if you never left Iran in the first place. We are also working on having our people, through back channels, convince one of their French colleagues to get you an authentic French passport, along with all the entry stamps. But that will take some time.

You will be there just to smooth things out; Amir will be in command of the team, and your responsibility will be only to reassure Azimi's father and anyone near the family. Once the team determines it's safe to move, they'll exfil from the safe house outside Yazd. You and Azimi will return to Tehran, then on to Paris from Mehrabad. Just like before. Simple enough."

David stood motionless, his gaze shifting from Amir to Donovan. The silence stretched, the words refusing to come. Part of him was already calculating the risk—measuring the layers of exposure, the odds. The other part—the more troubling part—was caught in something far simpler, more basic: obligation.

It hadn't been the U.S. government that made the promise. It wasn't Langley speaking through him. It was David—just David. That distinction was now perilously thin, yet it was there. He owed it to the old man and to Azimi to be there. At the very least, that. To stand with them when the *strangers* arrived, to serve as a familiar face amidst the unknown, to ease the passage of men whose lives would hang in the balance of trust.

He knew what Donovan wanted. He understood what Amir was saying. But what pressed against him now wasn't strategy—it was conscience. And somewhere beneath that, something more primal: the belief that promises, real ones—still counted for something, even in their world.

"We have a lot to go over before this takes off, Donovan remarked.

"You need to start sniffing around the morgue at the hospital, and at the central morgue on the Ile de la Cité, which is located adjacent to the Hospital Hotel Dieu. We did some inquiries, and bodies that are processed there are, as you said, often unclaimed migrants, homeless, or people without next of kin. Do it quietly. We can only use cadavers that we can pass off as American special forces. We've got about two weeks to find the right bodies—right build, right age, right ethnic markers. Even though the chopper's going down in flames, anyone who examines what's left has to believe those were our men. No doubts, no second guesses. We are, after all, assuming that the helicopter crash will result in a significant fireball and that everything, including the bodies left behind, will be unrecognizable, but what if? The illusion must hold, even under scrutiny."

Donovan added, "Let's have Rachel and her team tap their contacts—find Arabic speakers who can claim any John Does of North African or Middle Eastern origin that fit the profile. Age, build, and facial structure. Remember, small details will matter. We've secured a small warehouse near Rungis. There's a walk-in, temperature-controlled unit inside, plus a prep space for the morticians and disguise crew to work. They'll make the bodies look the part—uniforms, wounds, dog tags. The whole show."

Just then, they heard footsteps approaching; until then, they had been alone in the gallery. A uniformed attendant of the museum approached:

"Messieurs, le musée va fermer. Vous devriez commencer à vous diriger vers les sorties.", *"Gentlemen, the museum is closing; you should make your way to the exit."*

As they started to exit, Donovan reached into his coat pocket and pulled out an envelope.

"There are 5,000 francs here. That should easily cover Azimi's round-trip flight back to Iran, and with the remaining, you may need it to grease a few palms. Use it with discretion at the morgue—but David, account for every centime in your report. And whatever you do, don't raise any eyebrows."

And with that, they exited the museum—Donovan and Amir slipping into a waiting sedan without a word. David turned the other way, collar up against the wind, and walked toward Les Halles and the quiet anonymity of his apartment.

Chapter 38

Paris

The meeting with Azimi was the priority. There could be no doubt that Azimi needed to believe it was essential for both of them to return to Iran to assist his father in securing a safe harbor for the Americans.

Circumstances provided an opportunity: a meeting with the dean and thesis advisors that afternoon, during which faculty would outline proposal requirements, the paper's structure, and the lengthy process leading to the defense.

As David stepped into the lecture hall, his eyes swept the room and found Azimi near the back, locked in a low, tense exchange with his brother, Azad. Azimi's jaw was clenched, while Azad's gestures were clipped, almost hostile, his eyes flashing with irritation.

When David approached, Azad broke off mid-sentence, shot him a cold, unreadable look with narrowed eyes, and strode to a seat on the far side of the hall, shoulders stiff.

"What was that about?" David asked.

"Nothing. Just Azad being Azad," Azimi said, his voice flat.

David frowned. "I've never asked before, but what's his problem with me?"

Azimi hesitated, then said quietly, "Azad isn't really my blood brother."

David blinked. "What do you mean?"

"In 1974, we had a border clash with Iraq. Just a skirmish along the Shatt al-Arab waterway—territorial disputes, Iran backing the Iraqi Kurds. My father and Azad's father were childhood friends. His mother died giving birth to him, so Azad was raised by his father alone.

His father was a devout Muslim. When his father was killed in that war, my family took him in. We were raised as brothers."

"That must have caused some tension," David said.

"Not back then. My parents let him keep his Islamic customs, the faith of his father. It was never an issue… until recently."

David studied him. "Recently?"

Azimi's eyes darkened, lips pressing into a thin line. "Since this new wave of Islamic fundamentalism. And Azad's… newfound interest in politics."

Thirty minutes later, the dean's presentation ended amid sharp questions. David caught Azimi by the arm.

"Let's take a walk. We need to talk."

They stepped onto the Boulevard de l'Hôpital. Once clear of the crowd, David spoke.

"I've heard from Donovan."

Azimi's expression shifted instantly. He stopped, waiting.

"They've moved up the plan. The Americans will be arriving in Yazd in two, maybe three weeks. And they want me to be at your family's home when they arrive—smooth the landing, reassure your father."

Azimi froze mid-step, his gaze fixed on David.

"And you," David added quietly. "They insist you be there too."

Azimi blinked, as if the words had taken a moment to land.

"Two to three weeks?" Azimi said, Tight. "Why so soon? Why do I need to be there?"

David kept walking. "Because it's your family's home, you know the town. They'll trust you, and your father may need some help. And they want this as close-knit as possible, the fewer people outside of us, the better."

Azimi fell in. "And if I'm not?"

David stopped. "That's not an option."

David reached into his pocket and handed Azimi an envelope.

"Two thousand francs. Book a flight back to Tehran for January eighteenth. Keep the return open—tell them the dates may change at the last minute. That should cover it."

Azimi studied the envelope for a moment before sliding it into his pocket.

"You understand, David—I've placed a great deal of faith in you and your Mr. Donovan. And now my family is part of this. I trust you know what it would mean if that faith were misplaced."

David felt the words like a weight settling in his chest. He hesitated, searching Azimi's face—the guarded eyes, the tight set of his jaw.

"What we've discussed, every part of it, is true," David said quietly. "You have my word—not just as a friend, but as someone who owes you more than you know—that we will protect you and your family. And we will honor our part of the deal, whatever it costs."

Chapter 39

Paris

A light snow began early in the morning and turned to rain as the day went on. The rain made the cobblestones on Île de la Cité glisten and gave the Seine a tarnished-steel color. Paris in the rain always carried the same scent. No matter the season—spring, fall, or winter— the city had a constant undercurrent: diesel exhaust from buses, the damp breath of limestone walls, and beneath it all, the faint metallic tang of the river.

David crossed the Quai de l'Archevêché with his collar turned up, head low. The morgue squatted at the end of the street like a fortress of stone, its façade unsoftened by time or weather. No one lingered outside. The living had no reason to tarry where the dead were kept.

Inside, the light was a fluorescent yellow, the kind that turned skin sallow and shadows long. A man in a navy coverall sat behind the reception desk, cigarette burning to a crooked stub in the ashtray beside his ledger. He didn't bother with a greeting.

"Oui?"

"I'm here to see Monsieur Agnostini," David said in careful French.

The man buzzed him through with a nod. "Deuxième porte à gauche." *second door on the left.*

The corridor was narrow, the light flat and jaundiced. David felt comfortable in the morgue, having spent many days during his pathology rotation. They all smelled the same. Death seeped into tile, paint, and steel. Once it got in, it stayed.

Agnostini was in a small office, sleeves rolled, eyes sharp behind a permanent squint. He looked like a man who had learned to keep his questions to himself.

"You said it was important," Agnostini began, his words carrying a heavy accent—close enough to one of the barmen in his neighborhood café. Corsican, he thought. The north coast, probably Bastia.

"And delicate." He added.

"It is," David said. "I need information about any unclaimed bodies that have come through here in the last two weeks, which are still here. Male, ages 25-40. No identification."

"That is not public information."

"I know."

"You are not the police."

"No."

"That makes it harder."

David reached inside his coat, pulled out the envelope Donovan had given him, and dropped it on the desk. The sound it made was soft but deliberate.

"Two thousand francs," he said. "I'd like to see the list. Descriptions, if you have them. Cause of death. Where they were found. Details that don't make it into the official reports. And of course, view the remains!"

Agnostini's gaze flicked to the envelope and back. A pause, then: "If such records exist, they would be in the archives. It is not an easy place to access without a clear reason for doing so."

David let the silence hang for a beat, watching Agnostini's eyes. Then he reached into his coat pocket and drew out a folded wad of hundreds. Without looking down, he peeled off another five notes—five crisp hundreds—and set them on the counter.

"I'll wait."

The man studied him for a beat longer, then stood. "Come."

They passed through a set of swinging double doors into a cooler corridor lined with heavy steel doors. Behind each one was a drawer, and behind each drawer, a body. The low hum of the refrigeration units was constant, almost soothing in its monotony.

David kept his eyes forward, but his mind was already running the operational calculus. The bodies had to be right—close enough in age, build, and general features to pass for the American team. In the chaos of a burned-out chopper, resemblance didn't have to be perfect, only plausible. The wreck would take care of most of the disguising—shattered bones, ruptured flesh, and the blackened mask of fire. What mattered most was what a scalpel might find later. Any trace of heavy drinking, needle tracks, or the chemical ghosts of street drugs would give the game away. No active-duty operators would show that kind of history. The deception wasn't meant to fool Langley—they'd know the truth. It was meant to pass muster with Iranian security, and perhaps more perilously, with the forensic pathologists in Tehran.

The archives were in a narrow room lined with metal cabinets. Agnostini began pulling files—recent, male, unclaimed. Each manila folder was thin: a typed sheet, a Polaroid stapled in the corner, and sometimes a personal effect in an evidence bag.

He spread them on a steel table. David stepped forward, his trained eye moving quickly but with care. Four in particular caught his attention.

First body—Caucasian male, mid-thirties. Brown hair cropped close, a week's stubble on his jaw. Broad shoulders, solid build. Cause of death: massive head trauma, likely from a fall or collision. Found in the 19th arrondissement near an abandoned construction site.

David studied the Polaroid. The face was battered but not unrecognizable, under the swelling and bruises. If they dressed him in the right clothes, this one could pass. A few minor facial adjustments—cosmetic post-mortem—would help seal the illusion.

Second body—Light-skinned male, late twenties. Sandy blond hair, clean-shaven, lean but athletic build. Cause of death: drowning, likely in the Seine. Found near Pont de Bercy. The skin was edematous but not yet bloated, the lips pale, but the facial proportions were good.

David's mind clicked through the requirements; this one might do as well.

Third body—North African male, early thirties. Olive complexion, black hair, high cheekbones. The build was compact, muscular. Cause of death: single gunshot wound to the upper chest, small caliber, close range. Found in Belleville.

Not an obvious fit for the Americans—but David thought about the team's cover legends. The Iranians would expect at least one of the "Americans" to look the part. This one, with the right clothing and documents, could be perfect. The bullet wound could be carefully sutured as if it were from a prior mission.

Fourth body —Caucasian male, mid-thirties. Dark brown hair, heavy brows, nose slightly crooked, broken more than once. Tall and strong, a shade over six feet. Cause of death: undetermined; body recovered from an alley near Gare Saint-Lazare.

David lingered over the form and the sheet-covered shape beneath it. The build was right—military right. The cause of death being "undetermined" was even better. If the pathologist in Paris couldn't pinpoint it, then after a crash and fire, no Iranian examiner would look for anything beyond the obvious trauma. This one, he thought, could disappear neatly into the wreckage.

Agnostini led him to three other unclaimed bodies.

Two had been pulled from the Seine—days, maybe weeks after going in. The river had done its work. Skin bleached and waxy, stretched taut over swollen flesh; faces blurred into something between human and grotesque. The stench clung to the cold air, heavy with rot and river mud. Even with burns and wreckage to mask them, these wouldn't pass muster. Anyone with half a medical eye would see they'd been waterlogged too long.

The third had the unmistakable geometry of violence—a long, deliberate slash low across the belly, another jagged one high near the throat. A knife fight, messy and personal. Not the sort of wound pattern you could disguise as crash trauma without question.

The last lay on his back, bare chest pocked with dark, dried circles—multiple bullet wounds, close grouping, large caliber. The entry points were too clean, too obvious. In Tehran, the first autopsy knife would read them like a confession.

Only the first four had real promise. The others, David thought grimly, would be telling a different story.

As he studied each file, David's mind raced through the possibilities. The raw material was here—bodies close enough in age, build, and appearance to pass. What they still needed was just a little more: details to fill out the story, enough so that when grieving relatives came looking, they would know what description to give and the illusion would hold. Then came the logistics—secure transport, cold storage, precise timing. Every piece had to fall perfectly into place to make the exchange seamless.

He glanced at Agnostini. "Do you have anything else on these four?"

The man crouched, retrieved a battered gray box from a lower shelf. Inside were loose ends—photocopies of IDs, metro tickets, matchbooks from bars, even a fragment of a letter in Arabic.

"May I?"

Agnostini shrugged. "Take what you need. Not the originals."

David pulled a small camera from his coat and photographed the letter, the passport copy, and the matchbook. Each click felt like a lock sliding into place.

When he was done, he closed the files and looked at Agnostini. "You've been helpful."

"And you've been generous," Agnostini said, tapping the envelope. "But you were never here. And if anyone else comes looking—"

"If anyone does come," David said evenly, "it will be a grieving family member finally stumbling upon a long-lost relative and hoping to give them a peaceful resting place. Nothing more."

"And if they do come to collect the remains, Monsieur," David said, his smile slow and knowing, "I have no doubt they'll be as generous as I have been."

For a moment, they held each other's gaze, then Agnostini smiled as if to say that he knew exactly what game they were playing.

The walk back to the entrance was longer. He passed the steel doors again, thinking of the four bodies behind them—silent, unknowing, about to take on lives and deaths they'd never have imagined.

Outside, the rain had thinned to mist. He slipped his hands into his pockets, feeling the camera. The photographs would go to Donovan. The plan would move forward.

The margin for error was razor-thin. They would have to arrange for the bodies to be claimed by estranged "family members." Each would need to be dressed and touched up by Langley's team. If the bodies passed inspection in Yazd, the operation would hold. If not, the entire mission could unravel.

And now, David thought, that responsibility sat squarely in his hands.

*

David handed the camera to Donovan the next morning, along with everything he'd gathered on the dead. Within forty-eight hours, "family members" began appearing at the central morgue, paperwork in hand, to claim long-lost sons and brothers.

The bodies didn't go home. They were quietly diverted to a warehouse north of the city, not far from the airport, where a team of morticians and makeup artists—flown in from the States—was already waiting.

When David finally saw their work, he was stunned. The corpses bore almost no resemblance to the broken, lifeless forms he'd catalogued days earlier. Skin tones restored, wounds concealed, the faces looked… almost peaceful. Almost alive.

Returned to the refrigerated vault, they waited in silence for the next step—a discreet late-night flight to the staging site in Egypt.

Chapter 40

West of Cairo, Egypt – 01:10 hours

David was on the flight with the "cargo." On arrival in Cairo, he arranged for the bodies to be quietly transferred to a waiting refrigerated truck. No questions were asked. The cadavers had already been dressed and made up, ready to be transferred directly into the chopper.

The refrigeration unit hissed as the truck's rear doors creaked open. A puff of artificial frost escaped into the dry desert night. Inside, six cadavers lay wrapped in plastic and covered by a traditional shroud. Each was tagged with falsified morgue identifiers. No names, only numbers. The Cairo Hospital had reported them as foreign expats whose families requested burial in a Muslim land.

David stepped closer. The sharp scent of antiseptic and decay mingled in his nostrils. He pulled on a pair of latex gloves, already sweaty from the desert heat. Two additional bodies came from a Cairo morgue. The mortician, on loan from the embassy—a Palestinian with surgical precision and no questions—stood beside him with a clipboard. He wore a faint look of detachment.

"These were the cleanest I could find," he said in French. "No signs of trauma. Ages and builds match your profiles."

David nodded and motioned toward the loadmaster, who had just emerged from the belly of the HH-3E with a hydraulic gurney and two canvas body bags. The chopper had been carefully modified, adding additional fold-down seats for the insertion team. The pilot, Noam, part of the Israeli team, glanced back from the cockpit window, gave a thumbs-up, then returned to his preflight checklist.

One by one, the bodies were eased onto the gurney and wheeled toward the waiting helicopter. Just the mechanical rhythm of grim necessity. Each cadaver wore scorched fragments of a uniform—falsified tags, fabricated insignia, strategic burns at expected points of impact. Just enough to sell the story when the wreckage was found. Strapping them into the seats was awkward and slow, dead weight never being cooperative. From the shadows of a nearby hangar, Amir watched in silence.

"Hell of a way to fake death," he muttered.

David didn't respond. He simply stared at the last body as it was rolled aboard and seated.

It was grim work, but necessary. The illusion had to be perfect. When the crash site was discovered—and it would be—these bodies would be the only trace. Charred, unrecognizable, but unmistakably human. Evidence of a mission gone catastrophically wrong.

That was the story David would sell. The real team, meanwhile, would be on their way to Yazd before the first of the Iranian military units arrived at the wreckage, having been offloaded an hour before the staged crash.

By 0200, the HH-3E was loaded, buttoned up, and ready for departure. David peeled off the gloves and walked across the darkened tarmac toward the ramp.

Behind him, the refrigerated truck reversed slowly, disappearing into the desert blackness like it had never been there.

The rotor blades turned slowly at first, churning up sand in long, lazy spirals. The air was dry, thick with the scent of aviation fuel. There were no lights and no insignia. Only the silent promise of deniability, painted matte-black across the belly of a borrowed Sikorsky HH-3E.

David watched from the edge of the tarmac. He held a helmet under one arm and clutched a topographical map in the other. The map was smudged with grease-pencil notes—fuel arcs, terrain altitudes, alternate LZs no wider than parking lots. He wasn't running point; Amir was the lead. But this insertion, in the end, was David's baby. If things went south, his name would be the one people remembered.

The men boarding were not a unit. That would imply cohesion. This was a mosaic of usefulness: the pilot, Noam, and co-pilot Etan were Israeli, Sayeret Matkal, chosen by Rachel's team. The "Belgian energy executives" would be the most vulnerable. Their Farci was good, but accented, and they would have a difficult time explaining what they were doing in Yazd. Their mission, as explained to David, was to reestablish the network in Tehran. Ali Haddad, Jordanian American and telecommunications expert with good knowledge of the culture and language. He, too, would be moving to Tehran. Leyla Karimi, a veteran CIA operative with excellent cover as an architectural historian and fluent in Arabic and Farsi, was to meet up with Zarah Shirazi. Zarah, a returning Iranian-born physician and veteran CIA officer, was cleared to reenter Iran on a commercial flight. Her assignment was straightforward: from the hospital across the street, she would gather intelligence on the security surrounding the U.S. Embassy compound.

Alongside them were three special operations veterans, handpicked by Langley, fluent in both Farsi and Arabic. They didn't speak and moved with the quiet confidence of men who could kill you with a butter knife—and use it later to butter their toast. And leading them all was Amir, SOG, former Delta Force-callsign 'the Wolverine'.

They boarded in silence. Each checked webbing and secured gear: silenced sidearms, smuggled currency. David stepped in last. Noam, the pilot, nodded once. By 02:33, they were airborne. The desert swallowed their noise. The night took care of the rest.

The Saudi frontier slid beneath them like an ancient scroll—unfolding in crags, ravines, dry riverbeds. No light. No radar signature. Just rotors synchronized with the pulse of danger.

They flew low to avoid radar detection. At 200 feet, a man could smell diesel from a passing truck. Etan navigated like a phantom. He followed flight lines programmed weeks earlier by a team in Langley who never left their air-conditioned war rooms.

David checked vitals over comms.

"All green," Etan replied in his thick Hebrew accent. "Winds light. Fuel's where it should be."

They'd timed it to the minute. Intelligence had mapped local radar sweeps down to the guards' cigarette breaks. The unofficial gaps were the real routes. Here, goat herders and smugglers moved freely, unseen by both governments.

Ahead lay Yazd. A city untouched by time, carved from dust and memory. Its skyline, with its ancient wind towers and clay domes, was ideal for disappearing.

05:30: They breached the border at 150 feet. No alarms. Clear sailing. But no illusions either. Iran was awake beneath them.

David could feel it in the way the others moved—tighter now. Jaws clenched. Fingers on triggers. The illusion of calm was gone.

Amir met his eyes. A nod. They were committed.

The city glowed faintly in the distance. Not light—just an ambient smudge on the horizon. They swung east, avoiding oil roads and checkpoints.

"Two minutes,"

The team came alive. Gear checked. Radios secured.

Desert Edge, 15 km from Yazd – 0550 Hours

The descent was surgical. The rotors barely disturbed the desert. No flare. No light. Just the sound of possibility narrowing.

They landed on a hard stretch of nothing, hemmed by ruined irrigation canals and the skeleton of an old caravanserai.

Amir jumped out first, then David. Eyes scanning. Air still. No movement.

Then a shape emerged. One man. Long coat. Moving slowly.

David approached, one hand raised.

"You are early," the man, his face covered in dust, said in accented English.

David smiled. Finally, David could make out the face of Azimi's father. "You are alone?"

Azimi's father nodded. "For now. A close friend will assist. Azimi is with him just behind me.

Amir signaled, and the others slipped from the chopper with the fluid precision of a well-rehearsed ballet. One of the special ops veterans, chosen last minute by Langley, looked back to ensure all the equipment was offloaded and the bodies were strapped in. At the same moment, Amir signaled the pilot and copilot to disembark. He opened two jerry cans of highly flammable fuel and carefully positioned them in the belly of the chopper. With the engines still humming, the two Israelis exited. They clutched the remote that would send the helicopter 1,500 meters northeast, only for it to automatically cut the fuel line.

"Clear to move?" David asked.

Azimi's father took a breath. "For now. But always keep in mind that this city has ears."

David nodded. "We'll be phantoms."

"Then remember," the man said. "Phantoms leave no footprints. Not even on sand."

The helicopter with the strapped-in bodies lifted, leaving no trace of its arrival behind. Just like that, the team dissolved into the dust. Twelve minutes later, a huge explosion and fireball erupted in the distance: the chopper with its ghosts.

Chapter 41

Yazd, Iran

"Fifteen minutes," Azimi whispered, voice tight against the muffled early morning air. "We stay on the irrigation paths—no main road until the outskirts."

They moved single file, cloaks and satchels loaded with gear and a few trade goods to complete the cover: traveling merchants from Kerman. No one spoke. Even the crunch of gravel sounded like betrayal in the brittle cold.

They had scarcely taken three steps when Azimi closed in on David and drew him aside.

"My brother, Azad," he said, low and hurried. "He's here in town. He must have seen my tickets and wondered why I was coming back. He turned up at the house last night, with some of his old crowd."

David stopped. A deliberate pause.

"Why would he do that?" His voice carried no more than necessary, though the weight in it was plain.

Azimi shook his head. "I can't be certain. But he's been spending a lot of time in Paris with the exiles. The ones praying for Khomeini's government. The fall of the Shah."

"Has he said anything? Indicated he knows the reason we're here?"

"No, not yet. But we should assume he suspects something.

The path wound between low mud-brick walls and abandoned orchards, the silhouettes of pomegranate trees clawing at the moonlight. Somewhere far off, a dog barked, then another, then silence again.

By the time the first minarets appeared—thin spires etched black against the paling horizon—their breath fogged in the morning chill. The domes of Yazd shimmered faintly ahead, turquoise tiles catching the first hints of sun.

Azimi's father whispered, "Checkpoint ahead."

David saw them—two Basij militiamen in mismatched uniforms, rifles slung carelessly but eyes sharp. The men leaned against the rusting hood of a Paykan truck, watching the road that ran toward the old city gates.

Azimi's father glanced over his shoulder. "Stay behind me. Speak only if spoken to."

They stepped forward, hearts steadying into the rhythm of the role they would play. Those fluent in Farsi were at the head of the line.

One of the Basij straightened, blocking their path with the lazy confidence of a man who knew he could summon trouble with a single shout. He eyed Azimi's father first, then spat into the dirt.

"You see anyone suspicious on the road?" he asked. His voice was rough, provincial. "We were told to watch for outsiders—strangers moving about at night."

Azimi's father didn't blink. "Only merchants, like ourselves," he said evenly. "And no one travels after dark here. You know this."

The militiaman studied him a beat too long, then grunted and waved them through. His partner didn't bother to lift his rifle.

The two Basij at the gate barely looked up again when Azimi moved past, his father beside him, their wool coats and his father's thick beard giving them the air of respectable tradesmen. A few words in the local dialect, a nod toward the satchels of "merchandise," and the militiamen let them vanish into the old city without another word.

Inside the gates, Yazd unfolded in narrow, twisting alleys lined with centuries-old adobe walls. The dawn was gathering strength now, light spilling over wind towers and across the pale roofs. Somewhere nearby, a muezzin's voice called the faithful to prayer.

Azimi leaned close. "We split here. Too many of us together will draw eyes."

His father took six of the men—the two Belgian oil executives, Ali Haddad, the Jordanian American telecommunications expert fluent in Farsi and steeped in the culture, Noam and Etan, the Israelis, and one of Langley's special operations veterans. The last two were the only ones carrying weapons. Without a word, he led them away from the main route, veering right into a passage so narrow their shoulders brushed the mud-brick walls on either side.

Azimi led Amir, David, and the remaining team members through a different route—a zigzag of covered walkways, hidden courtyards, and arches that seemed older than memory.

They passed a bakery, the smell of fresh flatbread cutting through the dust and damp clay. Shopkeepers lifted shutters. Women in black chadors moved silently, their eyes flicking over the strangers but revealing nothing.

Finally, Azimi stopped before a nondescript door in a wall the color of sunbaked earth. He knocked twice, paused, then once more— a rhythm. A latch clicked, and a boy no older than twelve let them in without a word.

Inside was the small courtyard that David recognized, a trickle of water running in the central pool. Pigeons scattered from the rafters.

"Our home," Azimi said quietly. "You will stay here until nightfall. The others will be in the outbuilding two streets over—my father will see them hidden before the bazaars are busy."

He glanced up at the rooftop, then back to David.

"You'll be safe here," he said. "But don't forget—every wall in this city has ears. And some of those ears belong to the clerics."

David set his pack on the cool tiles, listening as Yazd woke outside the high walls. His team vanished into the city's ancient veins, waiting for night to move again.

Two streets over, Azimi's father pushed open the warped wooden door of the outbuilding. He gestured for the men to enter. From the outside, it looked like nothing—just another mud-brick storage shed on a forgotten lane. Inside, the air was cooler. It was heavy with the smell of dried figs, wool, and dust.

"Stay quiet. No lights after dusk," the old man said, his voice rough. He pointed toward a pile of rolled carpets in the corner. "If anyone comes, you hide beneath them. It will not be comfortable, but it will keep you alive. I will have food brought to you later today."

He left without another word, the door closing behind him with a muted thud.

The four agents stood still for a moment, listening to the faint sound of footsteps fading into the alley.

"Think we can trust him?" one muttered in English.

"He's Azimi's father," one of them said, though the words rang hollow. "Maybe that still counts for something here. But even with Donovan and David vouching, I'm not sure I want to stake my life on it."

They began setting up quietly—packs lined against the wall, water skins topped from the clay jar in the corner. Every creak of the building made them pause.

One of the men leaned toward a narrow slit in the wall, his eye catching the street outside. A figure in a gray coat lingered a moment too long before finally drifting away.

"Eyes on us already," he muttered.

"Could just be a neighbor," another offered, though without conviction.

"Or a neighbor working for the Komiteh—the revolutionary committees," a third said, his tone edged with suspicion.

The room went still. Every noise outside seemed magnified: the bleating of a goat, the slam of a distant door. Each one felt sharp enough to be a warning.

They had been on Iranian soil less than two hours, but already Yazd's ancient walls felt as though they were pressing in, tightening around them.

*

The rest of the day passed uneventfully. At Azimi's home, the visitors were introduced to his mother as French businessmen, an architect, and a telecommunications consultant. His mother welcomed them without fanfare.

Later that evening, the house had fallen into that strained silence that precedes a storm. Azimi had just set his satchel by the door when the knock came—three deliberate raps. Not the neighbor.

And then, Azad walked in without so much as a greeting, no raised voice. Just presence. The kind that tilted a room without effort.

Azimi looked up. "What are you doing here in Iran, Azad? Why aren't you back in Paris?"

"I might ask you and your American friend here the same question, Azimi."

Azad looked around, slowly scanning the room. Four men and a woman he didn't know stood in his father's sitting room, their coats still powdered from travel, eyes that missed nothing. He studied them like a customs officer with too much time on his hands. His gaze came to rest on his brother.

"Who are these people?"

Azimi moved as if to speak, but Azad was already circling, his attention locking on David. He lingered there, taking the measure of the foreigner who didn't look away.

"You bring strangers here. At a time when the city bleeds informants. Why? Unless you've already chosen your side." He leaned in, his tone lower now, colder. "If you've chosen wrong, I'll have no choice but to tell them."

The air seemed to compress. Azimi tensed, his father's hand gripped the arm of his chair, but David remained perfectly still, his expression unreadable.

When he finally spoke, in French, his tone was calm, and his pronunciation crisp. "If we were soldiers, Azad, you'd be on the floor already. That's not a threat—it's a fact. And you know it."

Azad's eyes narrowed. "Is that what you are? Soldiers?"

David shrugged. "Travelers. Merchants. Pick whichever story helps you sleep." He let the silence stretch, then added, softer: "But you've already guessed that, haven't you? Otherwise, you wouldn't be standing here trying to decide whether to shout."

For the first time, Azad hesitated—not visibly, not to anyone but a professional like David, who caught the flicker of doubt behind the man's eyes. Azad quickly covered it up with a sharp laugh.

"Merchants who move like soldiers. Who drinks tea but watches every door and window. You don't fool me."

David leaned forward slightly, lowering his voice until only Azad could hear.

"I don't need to fool you. I only need you to decide which version of this story you want to tell. Choose wrong, and you put your adopted family, who took you in and raised you, in the same fire as us. Think carefully about whether that serves you."

Azad froze, his eyes darting to the old man in the chair. The calculation was visible now—the tug of family against conviction, loyalty against ideology.

He straightened, the mask sliding back into place. "Be careful, Azimi," he said finally, his eyes never leaving David. "Be careful who you invite under this roof."

He turned and walked out, the door closing hard behind him.

The silence returned, thicker this time.

David reached for the teacup, his hand steady. "Your brother," he said quietly, "isn't finished with us. He'll circle again. We probably should move up our departure."

They agreed it would be safer to leave Yazd a day early. Azimi's father would drive north with the two Special Ops veterans and the Israelis, Noam and Etan, bound for Tehran. David, Azimi, and Amir would escort the Belgian oilmen and Leyla Karimi to the city center bus terminal. From there, the group would split, scattering onto separate buses bound for different destinations—each route chosen to blur their trail and buy them time. Azimi's cousin agreed to drive Azimi, David, and Amir into Tehran later that day.

David's jaw tightened as he thought of Azad. Somewhere, the younger brother of his friend Azimi had learned too much, and worse, had chosen sides, or more likely had always been on the side of the Ayatollah. Each unexpected checkpoint, each suspicious patrol, each near miss pressed the weight of betrayal onto David's shoulders.

By the heat of the following afternoon, Amir decided it was time for the Belgians—and for Leyla Karimi—to move on. David didn't argue. They drove into the city center, to the central bus terminal, and saw each of them to their respective buses. As they returned, the Israelis and the two Special Ops veterans were packing up and heading out with Azimi's father, headed for Tehran.

*

With all the operatives on their way, David, Azimi, and Amir returned, entered the family home, thanked their mother, and decided to walk into town to meet the cousin who agreed to drive them into Tehran that night.

The sun was still high, although it was beginning its descent. They walked slowly and deliberately, still dressed as merchants, toward the cousins' home at the edge of town. As they approached a main road, they spotted two young soldiers with rifles, stopping pedestrians.

Azimi stopped. "Let's go through this alley, it will take us to the next road, which is just a few meters from my cousin's home."

They were halfway into the alley when they saw him—Azad!

He stood in the now shade of the narrow alley, shoulder pressed lazily against a sandstone wall as if he owned the ground beneath his boots. Two older men flanked him, their beards thick, their eyes colder still. Each held an AK-47.

Amir's eyes flicked past Azad and locked on the two bearded men at his side. It registered immediately—the way they carried the rifles told the whole story. These were not student conscripts, not street-corner zealots. These were men who had lived with the weight of an AK pressed into their palms for years. Their stances were loose and balanced. Trigger fingers rested along the safety, disciplined. The magazines were fully loaded. Their eyes didn't dart or wander; they watched. Clearly, these were professionals.

Amir felt the old calculus stir in the back of his head—distance, angles, cover, odds. The numbers weren't good. Not in broad daylight. Not here in this alley.

Azad's gaze moved quickly between his brother and David, but lingered on the stranger—Amir. A half-smile touched his lips, sly and deliberate. This narrow alley had become his stage now, and the rest of them merely actors in whatever drama he intended to unfold.

David stopped dead, heat pounding in his temples, heart hammering in his chest. Beside him, Amir muttered something low, almost a prayer. The alley was deathly quiet, still, leaving only the six men and the potential of violence hanging in the air.

"Azad," he called, voice low but firm. "Step away from the wall. Now."

Azad's smile widened. "David. Just like an American, always in a hurry." His tone was light, but his eyes gleamed with menace. "You know my colleagues here; I could tell them who you really are, but I doubt they would be very welcoming." David stepped forward, muscles tensed, but Amir, standing just behind him, shook his head subtly. His expression was calm, resigned. He knew the rules of engagement better than any of them.

"You don't have to do this," Azimi said, each word measured, trying to reach the brother he once thought he knew. "Walk away. You don't have to start an incident."

Azad laughed softly, with a careless sound that cut sharper than any blade. "It's too late for that. You know that it was you and your American friend who brought me here."

Before David could even draw a breath, the two bearded men moved, assault rifles snapping upward. They must have recognized the word 'American'. The taller one swung his rifle around, and David heard the spray. He ducked to the ground, but as he fell, he saw Azimi fall as well. He was hit. Instantly, Amir was already moving—steady, deliberate, every movement measured. The 9mm FN-Browning HP-35 rose silently in his hands, a shadowed extension of his will.

The shots came, whisper-quiet from the attached suppressor, unnervingly fast. Two rounds into each man's chest, two men down—precision so clean it felt unreal. The alley held its breath, caught between disbelief and finality.

Azad froze; shock carved into his face. He looked down at his brother, seeing the blood squirting from his neck. He immediately bent down for the rifle beside the fallen man.

"Azad—leave it!" David shouted.

Too late.

Azad spun, raising the rifle toward him. David barely had time to recognize the look in the young man's eyes before a fifth shot tore through the air—then another. Azad jerked, folded, and fell in a heavy, final heap.

For a moment, the world and David's entire existence seemed to end.

David lunged forward and dropped to his knees beside Azimi. His hands pressed desperately over the wound in his friend's neck, slick with blood that pulsed hot between his fingers. He pushed harder, harder still, as if force alone could reverse what he'd set in motion.

But the blood kept coming, and Azimi's eyes were already fading. And then, David felt the life drain out of him.

It was over, and David knew that he was ultimately responsible for his friend's death. His legs gave way, and he sagged forward, trembling, the truth slamming into him with brutal clarity. There were no words. No excuses. No way to pretend this was anything other than what it was.

This was his doing.

The street around them fell unnaturally silent. David's breath came in shallow, ragged bursts, each one thick with shame. He had pulled Azimi into this world—had nudged, steered, and persuaded him into dangers he barely understood. He had believed he could control the variables, the risks, the people. He had thought his plan was clever enough, careful enough.

Instead, he had delivered his friend to an execution.

Azimi and his brother lay dead at his feet—because of him.

Amir crouched beside the bodies, face composed, movements precise. There was no judgment there, no triumph, no visible grief— only the steady resolve of someone who understood necessity and accepted its cost. He folded a jacket over the brothers with a practiced solemnity. But David felt none of that certainty.

As Amir rose, the stillness of the street closed in around them, and David knew this moment would follow him for the rest of his life. A quiet verdict passed in blood: he had made the choices, and now he would carry their ghosts.

And in that instant, David understood, with cold certainty, that the price of survival was far steeper than he had ever let himself imagine. Azimi was dead because he had brought him here. Success, if it came at all, would come with the memory of this night—of what it had cost, and it would follow him long after the mission ended.

*

The gunshots echoed down the narrow alley, sharp enough to carry across the quiet streets. Azimi's cousin, who had been pacing anxiously at home. Stiffened at the sound. Something was wrong. He ran toward the noise, heart pounding, and skidded to a halt when he reached the alleyway.

He said nothing.

His eyes fell on the bodies of his two cousins, and a silent grief settled over his features—a grief too deep, too sudden for words. He looked once at David, then at Amir, understanding far more than either of them could explain.

Without a question or accusation, he motioned for them to follow. He led them quickly to his truck, climbing behind the wheel with a grim resolve. Moments later, they were tearing out of Yazd, the city shrinking behind them as the weight of what had happened pressed in on all three of them.

Chapter 42

Tehran, Iran

The road back to Tehran offered no surprises, only repetition. Checkpoints reappeared: the same young soldiers, pretending not to be afraid. With ease, Azimi's cousin managed them—the local accent, the papers, David's student card from Paris—each enough to send them on their way. They were waved through with barely a glance. Just south of Qom, another checkpoint appeared: a crude barricade of sandbags and twisted rebar. This time, Azimi's cousin, at the wheel, recognized one sentry from school. He spoke with him, a smile exchanged, and they were waved on with the lazy indifference of men who were paid poorly and eager to leave for home.

They drove the rest of the way in silence, the city lights drawing closer through the haze. David stared out at the road as it unspooled before them, unable to feel anything but the dull, suffocating weight pressing down on his chest. The thought clung to him like a shadow, whispering that no matter how far they drove, no matter where he went, he would never outrun it. David watched the road unwind and tried not to dwell on another question that wouldn't leave him. Why was he told that a new 'cleaner' passport had been given to Dr. Shirazi—and not Amir—he still didn't understand.

"It was complicated, David," Amir had said as they were taking off from Cairo. "It was feared that your old passport wouldn't have held up. Technical Services got nervous—nervous enough to call in a favor from their French friends. They arranged for a genuine French passport, issued in the name of Jean-Paul Marchand, complete with your photograph and the entry stamps and exit papers. But things like that take time. It wasn't ready when we left for Cairo."

What he did not say, and what Donovan never told David, was that his role was far from over. Langley had decided that he would need to assist Dr. Shirazi. Part of her mission, in addition to gathering as much on-the-ground intel as possible, was to convince her professor that she could help with the medical needs of the hostages in the embassy. Langley wanted eyes inside the embassy. Although her English was good, Stewart Blake had his doubts. Given her Iranian background and her 'sudden enthusiasm' for the revolutionary cause, it was unlikely that any of the hostages would trust her with anything that mattered, despite whatever she would say.

That was where David would come in. If he could go in with her, reach them, speak their language, connect with the Agency personnel held hostage, reassure them they hadn't been forgotten—then perhaps the line between captivity and rescue might begin to blur. In addition, the specifics of the guard situation, their weaknesses, and their daily routines would need to be relayed accurately back to HQ. David, on his return to Paris, would be able to relay this information.

As they neared Tehran, where the Qom Road narrowed into the old suburb of Rey, David felt his unease return. Every corner held a sentry—thin, nervous boys barely teenagers, their rifles too large for their shoulders. Their youth didn't make them less dangerous. If anything, it made them unpredictable.

"So, what is the plan, Amir? Does this Dr. Shirazi expect me? Where are we supposed to meet her?" David's voice was anxious as they entered the late-afternoon traffic jam in Tehran. "How are we supposed to find her?"

Amir continued, "You don't have to worry about her, David. She is a 'Veteran Agency'—served in Syria, then Iraq. Don't be fooled, I'm told she is smart and tough as nails.

"She's a native Persian who trained in the Paris hospitals, same as you— that's the link. You'll be received as a visiting colleague, curious about how medicine is practiced in Iran."

He paused, watching the traffic inch forward. "Your classmate, Azimi, has family here. If anyone asks why you came in the middle of all this, it's because he needed to see his elderly parents. However, he had to stay with them in Isfahan. Nothing more. And remember, above all, do not mention Yazd; you were never there.

As they turned onto the main boulevard, the hospital loomed in the distance. Ambulances screamed past, racing to dump the wounded from clashes with the Shah's security forces. Protesters, their clothes streaked with blood, were carried on stretchers toward the doors.

Banners of Khomeini hung from windows or were hoisted by shouting students: *"Down with the Shah! Death to America, Allahu Akbar!"* The streets were littered with faded flyers calling for strikes, denouncing the government, and honoring the martyrs. Dust swirled around blood and debris.

It was chaos, raw and unrelenting, and David could only say to himself—How *the fuck did I ever agree to this?*

As the traffic slowed to a crawl near the hospital entrance, Amir gave David final instructions. "Remember, first impressions are everything." Looking straight at David, he continued,

"We'll pull up to the entrance, exit, and walk up to whoever seems to be in charge and demand to be brought to 'Dr. Shirazi, the French physician. Speak with authority; remember, these guards are no more than schoolchildren, not seasoned security personnel. You are a visiting physician invited to the hospital to observe and learn about the advances in Iranian medicine. Unfortunately, your Iranian classmate had to stay behind to care for his aging father."

"Do not take no for an answer. You must connect with her before too many eyes are on you. She knows you will be coming and has planned and informed her superiors that students from Paris will be observing. If they give you trouble, insist on speaking with their equivalent of the "chef de Clinique." I need to meet with someone and will connect with you before you leave." David nodded in agreement, and as the cousin pulled the curb, they exited the vehicle and were immediately hit by the air that carried the acrid tang of burned rubber and diesel. David walked toward the hospital entrance, Amir in the other direction.

Posters of Khomeini hung from every wall and light pole—his eyes watching from beneath a black turban, the paper edges curling in the cold wind. The broad avenues were choked with traffic and people: students in rumpled coats, nurses in white headscarves, angry pedestrians chanting slogans. *Pasdaren*, the revolutionary militia in green fatigues, curiously resembling the old Cuban revolutionaries, manned improvised barricades of oil drums and sandbags. Loudspeakers tied to lampposts crackled with sermons as they moved quickly toward the hospital's main entrance, their heads down, the crowd parting just enough to let them pass.

"Stop."

The command came sharp as a rifle crack. Two young guards blocked the doorway, rifles slung low, fingers resting near the triggers. David froze. The air smelled of disinfectant and smoke.

David turned and stopped. His voice was firm, and in precise, professional French, he continued, "I am a physician from Paris, here to see Dr. Shirazi—she is expecting me."

He produced his student ID, holding it out with deliberate calm. The younger guard squinted at the documents, lips moving silently over the French words he clearly couldn't read.

He hesitated, then called out, "Hossein!"

An older sentry appeared from behind the desk, eyes dull with fatigue but sharper than the boy's. He studied the papers, then David. A long moment passed. Finally, he gave a small, reluctant nod and motioned them down the corridor.

In broken French, he replied, "She should be in triage—if she's still working today," he muttered.

David inclined his head in thanks. He stepped past him, walking slowly now, every instinct alert. Behind them, the chanting roared again, a tide that felt closer each time it rose.

Inside, the noise dulled but never vanished. The corridors were a blur of white coats, shouts, and the metallic rattle of gurneys. Dried blood trailed across the tile floor in long, rust-colored streaks. Somewhere down the hall, a man was screaming.

David continued toward the triage ward, nodding at a nurse who glanced up just long enough to take in his Paris ID card. She looked away quickly when the man's screams continued.

He turned a corner and saw her standing there.

Dr. Zarah Shirazi stood beside a treatment bay, her sleeves rolled to the elbow, a mask hanging loose around her neck. She was younger than David expected, mid-thirties perhaps, but her eyes carried the look of exhaustion. Her hands were still gloved, smeared with iodine and blood, wearing a long skirt, scarf barely covering her lengthy hair, she looked up.

"Monsieur Marchand?" she asked quietly, her Iranian accent threaded through the French. "Vous l'avez fait" *You made it.*

"Barely," he answered.

She motioned for him to follow. "This way. We shouldn't talk here."

They passed through a side door into a narrow office that smelled of coffee and disinfectant. The windows were blacked out with newspaper; the light came from a single desk lamp. She shut the door behind them and exhaled.

"The city's turning inside out," she said. "Half the staff's disappeared, and the new ones report to someone I don't know. Although my old professor has allowed me to attend to the embassy personnel, we cannot take too many chances; you'll have to move carefully. I was told that you came with an Iranian friend, also in medical school in Paris. Where is he?"

Silence hung between them. When David finally spoke, his voice was low, unsteady. He told her about the alley in Yazd—the brother and two militiamen, the flash of gunfire, and how it ended with his friend Azimi and his brother, Azad, both dead in the alley.

For a moment, no one spoke. Outside, a siren wailed, then faded into the distance.

"I'm sorry about your friend," she said softly. "It won't make things any easier. Once word of the shooting spreads, security will tighten—certainly making everything more difficult."

Dr. Shirazi looked at David. "You understand what's expected?"

He gave her a quizzical look! "What do you mean? I was told that you were given a passport for me and that I was to get it and then be on my way to Mehrabad airport and back to Paris!"

There was a long silence as David looked stone-faced at Dr Shirazi.

"My orders were clear," she said quietly. "You're to go into the embassy with me. With much difficulty, I was able to convince my former professor that I might be useful—he's agreed to let me attend to those Americans in need of medical care. Three are diabetic and without insulin, one of the Marines has a broken leg, a few others have minor injuries, and two others, one listed as a diplomat, have trouble breathing."

She glanced toward the window, where the sound of distant chanting drifted in. The students holding the compound requested medical help from the hospital. It won't raise suspicion if I go. And if I press the right people, I should be able to bring you inside with me."

"You're coming in with me," she said. "We'll assess their medical condition, map the security, evaluate their potential weaknesses, watch the shift changes, and note where the hostages are held. Take whatever information the hostages can relay. That information is critical to any attempted rescue."

David's laugh was a short, humorless grunt as if to say, *are you kidding?* "Rescue?"

"Whatever your mission has been up to now, David, it was only in service of the real one," she said, her voice flat as a scalpel. "The primary objective is, and has always been, the eventual rescue of the hostages. Planning's been underway for months and is entering its final stages. The intelligence you bring back to Paris—and then on to Langley—may well determine whether it succeeds or fails."

He stared at her; the room suddenly felt too small, as if all the oxygen had been sucked away.

Chapter 43

Tehran

Following through with the deception, Shirazi led David through the Triage ward, where they ran into her old professor. Introductions were made in French, and David respectfully thanked him for allowing him to observe and learn from their experience. Late in the evening, as they took a break for a simple meal in the doctor's cafeteria, Shirazi obtained a room in the interns' wing where they could sleep. Throughout the night, however, David's thoughts were elsewhere. As she laid it out, going in as visiting French physicians, he convinced himself that if all went as planned, the risk should be minimal. Go in, assist Dr. Shirazi with the sick and wounded, keep his eyes and ears open, try to connect with the agency personnel, get whatever intel they could provide, and return to the hospital. Thank the professor and off to the airport. He could do this.

David slept fitfully. By morning, his restlessness had hardened into purpose; he was eager to get into the embassy, watch, and listen. Scout out the security and assess the condition and location of the embassy personnel. With luck, he hoped, he would be able to identify one of the four 'Agency' men known to be among the hostages.

There would likely be little that they could do medically, dole out some antibiotics, attend to some wounds, and most importantly, make sure that the fractured leg of the marine was adequately splinted and that the others were holding up. That would be the biggest concern. During a rescue attempt, the Marine would need assistance ambulating. The rescue team would need to know exactly how severe his disability was.

Of course, David knew his primary task: identify the hostages' locations, understand the security and weak spots, and, if possible, connect with the undercover CIA operatives. They were under deep cover, aware that the Iranians hunted them as relentlessly as he did.

Dr. Shirazi knocked on his door and entered, carrying her backpack and a case of medical supplies, including insulin, bandages, and antibiotics. Really not much more than that. "Ready to go?"

David nodded, leaving his small backpack on the bed.

"You'll need this," she said, handing David the authentic French-issued passport.

He flipped it open: *Jean-Paul Marchand.* His photograph. Legitimate entry stamps. Everything perfect. A yellow immigration slip was tucked inside. He folded it carefully and slid it into his boot, leaving only his student ID in his pocket.

"Make sure you destroy your other passport," she added.

David nodded. He asked for a lighter, sparked the flame, and watched his bogus passport curl, blacken, and collapse into ash. He gathered the remnants and flushed them down the toilet.

As they stepped out of the hospital, the day staff were just arriving for their shifts. Shirazi nodded to a few new friends she had made. Exiting, they were met by the cool morning air, a shock after the stale corridors. Only then did the city begin to come alive, shops' metal grates clattered open, and the smell of bread and diesel mingled in the half-light. Even at that hour, Taleghani Avenue teemed with Revolutionary Guards and the odd cluster of students, already laughing and chanting slogans.

Street vendors laid out their trays of tea, bread, and cigarettes. Around them, oil drums cluttered the street like relics of some forgotten barricade. Meanwhile, young Basij in mismatched clothes drifted in, yawning and reporting for their shifts, rifles casually slung over their shoulders.

Across the way, the embassy compound stretched out—twenty-seven acres. The twelve-foot wall, once plain, was now a mural of fury: Anti-American slogans, *Death to the CIA*, portraits of Khomeini, painted fists raised in perpetual defiance.

The Embassy entrance was just across the avenue, but between them lay a frontier—barricades, sandbags, and a tangle of students and militiamen pressed against the wall, guarding the revolution's prize.

As they set off toward the embassy, David and Shirazi were joined by one of the professor's young assistants—a thin, nervous man clutching a notebook. Shirazi doubted he'd be of much help. Still, she knew he was there to watch over them and to record every detail of the hostage's condition, the treatments administered, and, later, to report directly to a representative of the newly formed Revolutionary Guard, a man named Mohsen Rezaee.

They were chaperoned by two *pasdaran*, revolutionary militia from the group that had seized the embassy as they approached the entry. These students stayed close, watchful, their manner courteous, yet their suspicions were plain enough as was their mistrust.

They walked slowly, finally arriving at the main gate, where three guards looked suspiciously at the five of them. An older man approached and nodded. He explained their presence was expected. A few words passed, and they were let through the gate. Once inside, the scene was jarring. The great seal of the United States hung defaced over the entrance. Spraypainted slogans were everywhere: *"Death to America, Death to the Shah, Down with Imperialism." Their* chaperones led them toward the building on the right, the Chancery. Formerly the embassy's administrative heart, home to its communications and CIA offices, it now served as a control center for the student revolutionaries and home to the hostages.

They were led through a hidden door cut into a large mural. As they entered, their guide, smiling, told them that this was the office of the local CIA station. There were file cabinets turned over, documents and papers scattered everywhere. David recognized shredding machines and, against the wall, electromechanical ciphers. Immediately, they saw men and women huddled on the floor, hands bound, faces drawn with exhaustion and fear.

He heard a child's voice. Then a few others. As they moved past the doorway, he instinctively glanced inside. Young children were sitting on the floor piecing together bits of shredded documents as if they were assembling a jigsaw puzzle! One of the young Iranian students chaperoning them smiled and, in halting French, explained.

"We've put our young revolutionaries to good use, as you can see, they are carefully piecing together the shredded documents —evidence of the CIA's efforts to overthrow and destabilize our new regime."

Across the hall, they were led into a room where two men lay on cots; their labored breathing was audible.

Shirazi rushed to them and, grabbing her stethoscope, listened to their chest. "Asthma," she called out.

Grabbing her bag, she pulled out two inhalers and pressed them gently to the man's lips. As they inhaled, the tension in their faces began to ease, slowly falling away.

"You will need to get these two medications and inhalers. It is clear enough that they have asthma and are suffering from all the dust and stress being here.

"Why didn't anyone see that? Are we the first doctors these men have seen?" she demanded, anger rising in her voice.

While Shirazi was attending to these men, one of the student revolutionaries motioned for David to follow. He was led down the hall to a room where the marine was alone. He was moaning in pain. David tried to speak to him in French, but he didn't seem to understand. He had to be careful not to let on that he was a native English speaker, as one of the two Pasdaran was right behind him. It struck him that he'd rarely tried speaking English with a French accent—and now his life might depend on it. *Speak as little as possible, use very proper English, and try to use inflections as if you were French,* he kept telling himself.

Gently, David undid the bandages on his leg. There was no break in the skin, a simple mid-femoral fracture. Two plywood splints, taped on either side, with minimal deformation. David was relieved when he palpated the pulse at his ankle. Blood flow was good. He likely had lost some blood and was in pain, but being young and healthy, he'd recover without complications. But extracting him from here would be more difficult. Langley needed to know this.

In very broken English, David told him that he would be OK, then turned to his watchful chaperone and told him to get pain pills from Dr Shirazi in the next room. As he turned to go, David looked the marine in the eyes and, in sharp English, with his East Coast accent, whispered into his ear.

"Semper Fi"

It was as if the Marine had awakened from a deep slumber. Leaning in close, David got straight to the point.

"Are all the hostages in this building? Any security other than what I am seeing now? How about at night? Hang in there; we're going to get you out of here." Finally, David remembered to ask, "Where is Thomas?" At the mention of Thomas—the CIA station chief in Tehran—the Marine flinched. He knew the Iranians didn't know who Thomas really was. That reaction told David everything he needed to know. The Marine's eyes flicked with recognition—he understood. David could be trusted, likely Agency himself.

The man's voice now changed, as if awakening.

"Yes… Security's thin in the early mornings—half the student soldiers are asleep. Most of us are here in the Chancery now. Woods and another diplomat were beaten, kept in solitary confinement for weeks, but they brought them back. Two from the diplomatic corps are without their asthma medication, but the rest are holding up. Still…"

Before he could finish, a young revolutionary guard entered the room and shouted something in Farsi. In an instant, three men burst in, grabbing David by the shoulders. It was evident that he was speaking into the Marine's ear, and not about his medical condition.

"Take him to the Residence," one barked. "He is not what he seems."

David was yanked to his feet, hit on the back of the head with an IV bottle, and hauled away as the Marine's hope seemed to fade with each step.

Chapter 44

Tehran

"Take him to the basement. We'll notify our compatriots from the old SAVAK. They will certainly know how to deal with this 'so-called Frenchman.'"

Still groggy from the blow, David raised his head as they dragged him inside. Déjà vu swept over him. The building's corridors, echoing footsteps, and institutional smell faintly recalled his old high school. But here, there was no innocence. Only terror.

They dragged him into what had once been the grand salon of the Ambassador's residence. There, the spacious windows were now shuttered, the walls hung with stern portraits of the Ayatollah. Around the room, men hurried back and forth with the pieces of the shredded documents the children had so carefully reconstructed earlier. As he was dragged across the wide room, eyes were turned toward him— hard, suspicious, full of anger. He was hauled down a narrow stairway into the cellar and shoved into a small, airless room. A single table, two chairs, and a bare lightbulb hung overhead.

David forced himself to steady his breathing. *Remember what was drummed into you at the Farm.*

Deny, deny, deny—that had been the rule. Hold to your legend for as long as possible. Really, he thought, what evidence did they have that he was not who he proclaimed to be, Jean-Paul Marchand, a medical student from Paris offering to attend to the sick and injured?

Was he whispering to the injured Marine? So, where is the harm? No real proof of complicity. As he lay there on the floor, still dazed from the blow to his head, he was surprised that his emotions changed from fear to outright anger. He could deal with these ass holes, keep to his story, but something deep inside him feared that with the beatings, he might break into English. That would be lethal!

Just then, David heard arguing outside. Three young *pasdaran* barged in, faces angry, zealous, and vengeful. They questioned him,

"Who are you really?", but they did not wait for an answer. The blows came sharp and fast, first to the gut, doubling David over, then a slap in the face before pushing him to the ground. The three closed in, kicking him again and again. David felt a rib crack. Blood dripped from his lip. They were ready to strike again—when the door to the room swung open. An older bearded man stood there, barking a few harsh words in Farsi, and the three younger men froze. Lowering their heads in shame, they squeamishly exited the room.

The older man regarded David in silence, his expression unreadable as David struggled to lift his head, still dazed and throbbing with pain. When their eyes finally met, the man's gaze held an unsettling calm, the poise of someone who had witnessed this scene many times before. In flawless English, he allowed himself a thin, knowing smile.

"You know," he began, almost conversationally, "some soldiers of the CIA tried to slip into our country a few days ago. They thought they could steal across our borders, probably try to pluck their countrymen from captivity, and vanish quietly into the night."

He clicked his tongue softly.

"But their pilot, poor man… he wasn't prepared for our desert winds. A sandstorm took him and his crew of CIA operatives. The helicopter went down, burned to ash. Every one of them died."

He let the words settle, then added with a thin smile,

"Perhaps now the colonialists will think twice before meddling in our revolution."

"I think we should wait for our colleagues from SAVAK," he said, the words smooth as polished steel. "I'm sure they'll be far more… *professional* than those teenagers."

There was no need to elaborate; the implication hung in the air like a tightening wire—professionals who knew how to ask questions, and how to make sure they were answered.

He turned and stepped out, pulling the door shut with a final, echoing slam.

The pain in his head throbbed with the beat of his heart, and his ribs ached with each shallow breath—yet lying there on the cold floor, sleep crept over him. It wasn't exactly sleep, more like another level of consciousness, but it made him forget his surroundings for a few hours.

*

Still half asleep on the floor, David was jolted by the creaking of the heavy metal door. Still dazed, gazing up at the ceiling light, he made out a figure in silhouette as it entered quietly. Another one of the revolutionary militia! David withdrew from him, expecting to be kicked.

"Get up, now. You need to leave," the voice hissed in urgent, accented English.

David, still groggy, snapped in French, "Parlez plus lentement. Je ne comprends pas. *Speak slowly, I do not understand.* I am a French doctor here to treat wounded and sick hostages. Nothing else."

"Please, you need to get out of here now. I know who you are and what you are doing."

"I am doing only what was asked of me by my colleague."

You can trust me, Dr. Rose. I am a friend of a friend! David stopped. He was puzzled; even Dr. Shirazi only knew him as Jean-Paul Marchand!

"Who is this friend?"

"Let's just say you know her well. She wanted you to hear this—her words, not mine—She said that: '*you'd make some plump American girl very happy one day.*'"

Rachel!!

"Who are you-who are you with?"

"I'm a colleague of your friend. I've been embedded here with the students for over a year now. She contacted me, against all protocol, I might add and told me to watch out for you."

MOSSAD!!

"We're out of time. Exit's at the end of the hall. The guards are switching shifts—they're still at dinner."

"A black Peugeot waits on the next street, ready for us. The driver has a ticket for Jean-Paul Marchand for the plane that leaves in about two hours. He'll get you to the airport. We should go now, before they realize you're missing and shut down every flight from Tehran. You have your passport, right?"

"Yes."

"Then come on, we don't have much time."

Chapter 45

Paris

When David landed in Paris, a car from the embassy was waiting. He was taken straight to the embassy and ushered into a windowless room.

Donovan was already there, flanked by Duke Peterson and Stewart Blake, who had flown in that morning. Blake, the DO, spoke first.

Blake said, "Lay it out for us, David. From the moment the choppers lifted off in Egypt. Don't leave anything out."

David leaned forward, hands clasped. "The insertion was clean. We diverted the helicopter as planned. Landing and offloading went smoothly, no incidents. After the Israelis jumped, the bird was put on remote control. At 1500 meters, we cut the fuel. It came down a few clicks north. We could see the fireball in the distance. From there, Azimi, his father, and a friend met us. We made it to the safehouses without much trouble. There was one incident as we approached the town. We were stopped at an intersection checkpoint by two Basij militiamen. Azimi's father spoke to them, explained that we were merchants, they smiled, and they let us pass."

Peterson asked, "And the days there?"

"Two only," David said. "Long. Quiet—until Azad showed up."

"Azimi's brother?" Blake asked flatly.

David nodded. "We didn't know about his political affiliations." He glanced at Donovan. "We should have, and that's on me. Nor did Azimi. He was hostile. We moved up our departure.

"Amir, Azimi, and I left to meet his cousin. We ran into Azad in an alley; he was there with two armed zealots. One of them lifted his rifle." David hesitated, the memory flickering behind his eyes. "Then everything broke loose. Gunfire at point-blank range. Azimi took a round to the neck. Amir dropped both men, but as Azad reached for a weapon, he too was cut down. Azimi bled out in my hands seconds later."

The silence stretched, heavy.

"I tried to control the bleeding, but it was no use; he was gone."

Blake's pen scratched across his pad. "So, Azad was hostile? Threatened the mission? That's your assessment."

"That's the fact," David said, though without conviction.

"From there, you went into Tehran and met with Dr. Shirazi?"

"Yes."

"No complications?"

"I wouldn't say that." He hesitated. "We went into the embassy the next morning. It was a mess—as you can imagine."

"We'll get into the details later. Did you see the hostages?"

"I did. I examined the Marine—his leg's broken but splinted. He'll recover, though he'll need help moving when the time comes. Oh, it would've been nice to have been queued in on the rescue mission."

"Paris Station only learned of it yesterday," Donovan replied evenly. "That's how these things work, David, you should know that by now. You didn't need to know—until you needed to know."

As I was getting information from him about security, I was overheard and grabbed by two militia members who were following us. Dragged down to the cellar of the Residence, kicked and beaten, hence my appearance. A senior man stopped them. He spoke fluent English. He was waiting for former SAVAK men to interrogate me.

I'd still be there if it weren't for one of Mossad's embedded agents, thanks to Rachel. He got me out with minutes to spare for the last plane out at midnight."

The questions went on—David gave them the critical information: where the hostages were held, the security of the embassy wall, each perimeter, the best routes, locations, and the embassy guards. By evening, he felt hollowed out, every detail wrung from him. By the end, it was clear: he hadn't left Iran unscathed.

"That's it?"

Donovan closed his notebook. "Anything else?"

David shook his head. "No. I only wish I had more time to connect with someone from the Station."

Donovan pushed back his chair. "That's enough. Go back to your apartment. Get some rest."

"You'll hear from us in a week," Peterson added. David rose. "Understood." He left without another word, the door closing softly behind him.

Chapter 46

The following weeks were just as stressful as he tried to put Yazd and his friend Azimi out of his mind. He was still a student, and he knew that he had to buckle down and finish his thesis. He wanted to be done with it, with this life in Paris.

He was accepted into a surgical residency at NYU, which would start in July, and thus, his thesis had to be completed, defended, and judged before that.

A month passed before Donovan reached out. He asked how David was holding up. David gave a vague answer and suggested they meet. They chose the tennis courts, since the weather was mild and the garden would be crowded with tourists and Parisians.

The following week, as David crossed the gravel path toward the courts, he knew exactly what he had to say.

Donovan was already waiting, arms folded, his gaze sharp beneath the brim of his cap.

"You asked for this meeting," Donovan said. "I assume it's not about operational details."

David exhaled slowly. "No. It's about me. About what happened."

Donovan's expression didn't change. "Azimi?"

"Yes," David said. "Azimi, Azad. I watched them die. And I stood there knowing it was because of me."

Donovan leaned forward, elbows in his lap. "Because of you? No. Azad made his choice; he is the one responsible for his brother's death."

David shook his head. "That's the problem. He never would have been there if I hadn't been here. Suppose I hadn't dragged his brother into this. I convinced Azimi to help us. I wrapped it in friendship and loyalty, but it was manipulation all the same. I used him."

"You recruited an asset," Donovan said, his voice calm, almost gentle. "You did your job."

"My job," David said bitterly. "My job, as you promised me back in Ann Arbor, was to get a medical degree. Healing people, not turning them into pawns. I came here thinking I could help, that I could serve some greater good, as you said. Instead, I watched my friend bleed out in an alley. And I told myself it was for freedom, for security. But that's a lie. It was about advancing a plan hatched in Langley, a plan that, for all we know, was about the flow of oil, a plan that cared nothing for the lives it ruined along the way." Donovan's jaw tightened, but he said nothing.

"I can't do it anymore," David continued. "I can't stand in another alley, watching another body drop, wondering if my hands are just as bloody as the man who pulled the trigger. This—" he gestured at the city and the mission, "—this isn't who I am."

"You think walking away will be easy?" Donovan asked quietly. "You think medicine absolves you? You'll carry this with you no matter what path you choose."

"I know," David said. His voice broke, but he steadied it.

"I'll tell you what: when the American people finally wake up—when they choose to take part in the decisions made in their name and insist that our foreign policy reflect the values we claim to hold, rather than the ambitions of the corporations that bankroll it—give me a call.

"I'm not blind to the realities of statecraft. Nations have interests, and economics threads through every one of them. But there comes a moment when those interests begin to eclipse the ideals that have shaped us from the beginning. And that, I suppose, is the moment we ought to ask ourselves who we've really become. Those students in Tehran, Donovan, aren't entirely wrong, you know.

"But until then, at least in New York, in the hospital, I'll be doing something to repair the world instead of tearing it apart. I can live with the weight if I'm working for it. I can't live with it if I'm compounding it."

Silence stretched between them. Donovan studied him, eyes narrowing, as if measuring the resolve behind the words. Finally, he nodded once.

"Then I assume you're finished," he said. "Go home. But understand this, David—men like us don't retire. The work follows. The memories follow. Don't expect peace."

David rose, feeling both lighter—the burden of decision released—and unbearably heavy, sorrow still anchoring him. "I'm not asking for peace," he said quietly, searching Donovan's face for understanding. "Only for the chance to be the man I was meant to be."

And with that, David walked away—no fanfare, no final orders, only silence. As June ended and his thesis was completed, so too ended his seven years in Paris and his long pursuit of the title *Docteur en Médecine.* The decision hadn't come all at once. It crept in slowly, between lies he told and faces he betrayed. Eventually, the weight became unbearable. He would leave Paris the way he had entered: quietly.

A week or two passed. He arranged a final meeting with Donovan. This time, they met in their usual café in Saint-Germain-des-Prés, a very public spot. David shared news of his thesis and his professor's good wishes. Donovan knew there was little point in discussing David's future with the agency. As David was about to stand, Donovan reached into his briefcase.

"Just a few formalities, David."

Donovan reached into his briefcase and pulled out a slim folder—four or five documents inside.

"Nondisclosure forms. Nothing dramatic. Just need your signature."

David didn't ask questions. He took the pen, signed quickly, and handed them back without a word.

Then he turned, walked toward the Metro, and stepped into another life—this time, for real.

His presentation was well-received, and all his professors congratulated him on an excellent paper. They wished him well in his upcoming surgical residency and hoped that he would return often to Paris and keep in touch with his French colleagues.

EPILOGUE

New York City

Surgical residency at NYU was brutal. He'd traded one kind of exhaustion for another, but this felt honest. When a patient was dying on the table—from a gunshot or car crash—there was no subtext or agenda. Just a patient, opened, waiting to be saved.

It was an afternoon in early September, a year later, when David found himself with a rare window between cases, and he slipped out for lunch to his usual spot, a corner deli on Second Avenue. He ordered coffee and a sandwich and sat at his preferred booth near the window. Steam curled from his cup. Outside, the city moved with its usual indifference.

And then—

There she was!

Rachel.

Walking briskly, alone, a folder clenched under one arm and heading uptown, toward the UN or perhaps the Israeli consulate. Her face angled slightly away, but he recognized that purposeful stride. He knew the way she tucked her chin against the wind, how she clutched paper as if it might betray her. Yet, today, her brow knotted, and she glanced nervously over her shoulder, hands tightening around the folder as if it might slip away. She radiated anxiety.

As she passed, she glanced sideways.

Their eyes met instantly.

A beat. Maybe two. As if she knew somehow that he would be seated right there.

She slowed and stopped. He didn't smile. Neither did she. But something passed between them—recognition, memory, concern—an echo of what was left behind. Her expression seemed to say, "follow me."

Then she turned very slowly, as if to give him time to think, and then kept walking.

David sat still for a moment longer. Then he stood, threw ten dollars onto the table, and stepped out into the sharp air of Second Avenue, unsure whether he was chasing a woman, a memory, or the last unfinished thread of a life he thought he'd left behind.

He didn't call her name.

Something shifted. Nothing dramatic—just a flutter at the edge of vision, the kind of detail most would overlook. But not him. Not anymore.

A sixth sense, dull in ordinary life but razor-sharp beneath the surface, flickered awake.

The signs were subtle. Her pace quickened, but not dramatically. She glanced over her shoulder at traffic. She lingered too long at a shop window reflection. Her spine stiffened, bracing for something unspoken.

It was the language of the watched and the watcher. And he understood it fluently.

She was being followed!

He scanned the crowd across the avenue, a well-dressed woman—middle-aged, carrying a closed umbrella despite the clear sky—matched Rachel's pace exactly. Just ahead of him on the same sidewalk was a younger man, solid build, Middle Eastern, who moved with quiet intent. His jacket hung too loosely, as if it were concealing something.

David dropped back instinctively, keeping a hundred yards between them, then cut across traffic, jaywalking through a lull in the cars. Rachel, he figured, was heading to the small park near 35th Street. Predictable. Crowded and perfect for a meet.

He looped around the block and got there first.

Midday in the park was chaos—children shrieking by the jungle gym, nurses on break, a man with a saxophone playing something that might've been Coltrane. He blended into it all, taking position by the wrought iron gate. From there, he could see her as she entered— tension riding her shoulders, her eyes scanning just enough to reveal she wasn't sure who was on her tail, only that someone was.

As she passed him, their arms brushed.

He felt it immediately. A whisper of movement. Her left hand slid something into the deep pocket of his white lab coat.

A 5-inch floppy disk.

"Bring this to my consulate," she whispered, not breaking stride.

And then she was gone.

The woman with the umbrella veered off. The younger man paused at the park's edge, looking both ways, unsure.

David stayed where he was, heart pounding in his chest—not from fear, but from something older, colder—the feeling of stepping back into the current after trying so hard to swim free.

He didn't look at the disk. Not yet.

He didn't head back to the hospital, either.

Instead, he walked aimlessly down Third Avenue, hand in his pocket, fingers wrapped around the plastic square. His white coat collar up. Eyes on the reflections in shop windows. He thought of Donovan. Of that folder of documents. Of promises that were never truly meant to be kept.

Maybe this was nothing. Maybe Rachel was in trouble. Perhaps it was all a test.

Or maybe—he realized—it didn't matter.

The line he tried to cross wasn't a line at all. It was a loop—a Möbius strip of service and sacrifice, a mask he wore so long it fused to him.

He thought of Rachel's face. The moment their eyes met. The weight of it.

Then, at the corner, he saw a black sedan idling. Diplomatic plates. A man inside, pretending to read a newspaper. The way he turned the page was wrong, reading it back to front.

David didn't break stride.

He headed east toward the river. Not running, not hiding. Just… deciding. The disk was still in his coat pocket. Its weight growing heavier by the block.

Behind him, the street resumed its rhythm, as if he'd never been there. Paris had done the same. But somewhere—somehow—someone was waiting for that disk.

And someone else was waiting for him to bring it.

He kept walking.

Not toward safety.

Not even toward Rachel.

But toward whatever came next.

END

Author's Note:

While I have endeavored to capture the atmosphere of the Iranian Revolution—the unrest in the streets, the uncertainty that gripped the nation, and the desperation surrounding both the hostage crisis and the attempted rescue—*The Student Spy: From Paris to Tehran* remains, ultimately, a work of fiction. My years in Paris during the 1970s, when I attended medical school, inform the descriptions of Les Halles, the Île Saint-Louis, and the rhythms of French medical training. Those elements are drawn from memory and experience; the espionage, however, is entirely a product of imagination.

Much of the technical detail surrounding the planning and execution of the rescue mission is drawn from an excellent *Newsweek* article published on July 12, 1982, "The Iran Rescue Mission: The Untold Story," by Pentagon correspondent David C. Martin.

His thorough reporting on the key figures—most notably Richard Meadows and Charlie Beckwith—provided invaluable insight. Even the anecdote of the embassy cook who, by extraordinary luck, found himself seated next to a CIA officer as he fled Tehran—described memorably as "hitting the jackpot twice in a row"—is drawn directly from that account.

Tim Weiner's comprehensive history of the CIA, *Legacy of Ashes*, proved equally indispensable. Through his meticulous reporting, I first learned of **MK-Ultra**, the Agency's clandestine program devoted to researching the use of LSD, amphetamines, and electroshock as tools of interrogation. Its relevance to my protagonist's interest in psychology and sensory deprivation made its inclusion both natural and necessary.

Some readers will observe that Bill Donovan—David's recruiter and "controller"—shares his name with William Joseph "Wild Bill"

Donovan, the legendary head of the Office of Strategic Services, the predecessor to the CIA during the Second World War. When I began writing this novel, I used memorable placeholder names to help keep my characters distinct, fully intending to revise them later. Yet as the character evolved, the name fit him so naturally that it became impossible to imagine him as anyone else.

Acknowledgments

People say acknowledgments can drag on like movie credits; nobody stays to watch. Maybe so—but I can't resist thanking my wife, *Linda*, who deserves billing above the title. She put up with my late nights of research and typing, cold dinners, and habitual "five more minutes" that made us late more often than I'd ever admit. She encouraged a husband who never took a writing class in college and had no business attempting a novel—except she made me believe I could.

My heartfelt thanks go to *Steve Kasdin*, my editor, whose insight and steady guidance helped shape this story into the novel I hoped it could be. His sharp eye, careful hand, and gentle honesty elevated every chapter. He offered candid critique, urged me to cut what wasn't working, and encouraged me to strengthen what was. For his dedication, honesty, and craft, I will always be grateful. This book would never have been completed without the help, patience, and encouragement of friends who took the time to read early chapters, offer candid criticism, and push me to make the story stronger. Thank you.

Regarding the events that led to the failed rescue mission—Operation Eagle Claw—I am especially grateful to *Dr. Colonel Carl Savory*, who, as the lead physician for the 1st Special Forces Operational Detachment-DELTA, generously shared many details of the actual mission with me.

As this book is based on that attempted rescue, it is only fitting that it be dedicated to the servicemen who gave their lives in that courageous mission—*Maj. Richard Bakke, Maj. Harold Lewis Jr., Tech. Sgt. Joel C. Mayo, Maj. Lyn McIntosh, Capt. Charles McMillan II, Marine Staff Sgt. Dewey Johnson, Sgt. John Harvey, and Cpl. George Holmes Jr.*

May their memory be a blessing, and may their sacrifice in the service of their fellow Americans never be forgotten.